Code Name: Baby

***Also by Christina Skye
in Large Print:***

Going Overboard
Code Name: Nanny
Code Name: Princess
Hot Pursuit

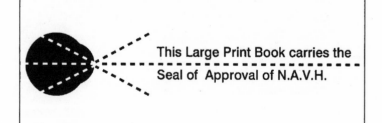

Code Name: Baby

Christina Skye

Published in 2006 by arrangement with Harlequin Books S.A.

Wheeler Large Print Romance.

The text of this Large Print edition is unabridged.
Other aspects of the book may vary from the original edition.

Set in 16 pt. Plantin by Ramona Watson.

Printed in the United States on permanent paper.

Library of Congress Cataloging-in-Publication Data

Skye, Christina.
    Code name — Baby / by Christina Skye.
      p. cm. — (Wheeler Publishing large print romance)
    ISBN 1-59722-215-1 (lg. print : hc : alk. paper)
    1. United States. Navy. SEALs — Fiction. 2. Dog trainers — Fiction. 3. Large type books. I. Title.
II. Series: Wheeler large print romance series.
PS3569.K94C626 2006
  813′.54—dc22   2005036649

ACKNOWLEDGMENTS

I raise my glass to Abby Zidle,
For too many insightful comments
to count.
With patience, humor and wit
you smoothed the writer's path.

Many thanks . . .

PROLOGUE

The dogs were howling.

Their noise echoed through the underground lab from cage to cage while monkeys clung to their metal bars and mice raced in blind circles. The dogs dumped their water dishes and slammed against metal walls insulated to cover both threats and screams.

The only man in the room watched with eyes like ice.

Gabriel Enrique Cruz savored the disorder, arrogant even now. With the bearing of a born leader, he measured the activity around him, calculating his next tactical move.

Once — before the drugs and the lapses — he had been called a hero. Now Cruz was simply another lab animal, entirely expendable, valued only for research data in a secret government report.

One glance told him that both surveillance cameras were running. A security team would be here within four minutes. Whenever something went wrong, they always came looking for him.

This time he would be ready.

He tossed his shredded blanket over the nearest camera. While the monkeys howled and four Rottweilers banged against their metal cages, he checked the clock on the opposite wall. Ninety seconds until the armed response team hit the double doors to the lab.

Locked inside a six-by-three-foot cage, Cruz ignored the restless animals, the boxes of experimental medicine and the rows of top-secret equipment.

Sixty seconds.

He shaped his thoughts to stillness and power, becoming the deadly weapon he was trained to be.

An owl flew from its perch near the door and slammed full force into the camera above his head, cracking the glass. The other animals froze.

Watching Cruz. Waiting for his next command.

Forty-five seconds.

As he stared at the Rottweilers, the dogs began to tremble. Working together, they nosed the heavy steel bar off its hook at the front of their cage. Under the force of Cruz's mental commands, their muscles jerked and strained while the bar climbed slowly — then crashed to the floor.

Thirty seconds.

One silent command brought the dogs hard against their doors. The biggest Rottweiler raced to a crowded desk and nudged an electronic key card from a pile of papers. With the card between his teeth, the dog raced back, and Cruz grabbed the plastic from his jaws.

He waved it at the scanning unit on the wall. A green light flashed.

His cage door slid open.

Freedom.

The animals were silent now, twisting with excitement. Ruthlessly, Cruz crushed all feelings of pleasure. He couldn't afford emotion until he was miles away from the underground military base that appeared on no map.

As he stepped out of the prison that had held him for months, the Rottweilers raced through the lab, lifting the bars, cage by cage, to free the other animals. Two black howler monkeys leaped on to the keys of the big mainframe computer on the far wall. Cruz scattered them with a silent command and brought the databases online. When the computer screen queried him for a password, he smiled, prepared for this, too.

His fingers raced through a carefully

memorized string of numbers and a file opened. Quickly he scanned the highlighted data, noting birth, military training and current residence of the Navy SEAL he sought. Then he pulled up another password-protected file and scanned its contents.

A bullet cracked behind him, ricocheting off metal cabinets. Snapping silent orders to the Rottweilers, Cruz closed the file and hit the escape key. The computer screen went dark just as a uniformed figure staggered through the doorway.

Instantly, the two dogs lunged at his throat. Blood sprayed as the soldier fell, jerked once, and lay still in a crimson pool.

The big dogs turned. Their ears pricked forward as they stepped delicately over the body on the tile. Awaiting Cruz's next command.

The din grew, every cage open and every animal freed. A gorilla shuffled past, his eyes sullen and watchful. Cruz's silent command was sent and received. The animal lurched forward, unaware that he was about to face a wall of bullets. The second he cleared the double doors, shouts exploded in the hallway, drowned out by gunfire.

More animals poured out after the gorilla.

Quickly, Cruz flipped off the lights and crawled inside a red bin with a warning logo stenciled on the lid. The underground facility's medical waste was collected like clockwork. For once the well-oiled procedures would work in Cruz's favor.

The worker in charge of transporting medical waste had negotiated hard: thirty thousand dollars for the initial transfer — with ten times more to come as soon as his hidden passenger was safely delivered outside the grounds.

The irony didn't escape Cruz. In the government's eyes, he was no more than medical waste, the end product of an expensive and highly experimental program using human genetics to shape superior tactical capabilities.

But Cruz had gone rogue.

And though his captors didn't yet realize it, their experiment had been a stunning success.

CHAPTER ONE

Wolfe didn't mind the tarantulas. Even the rattlesnakes left him with only minor discomfort.

It was the naked women, with their bloodred lips and leather masks, who really annoyed him. They studied him like tigers facing raw meat, then scraped their long nails across his chest.

He didn't move, wouldn't give them the pleasure of a response.

Which only made them dig harder. Tattooed skin brushed his arms. When their breasts teased his mouth, Wolfe Houston decided enough was enough.

He drove everything out of his mind — tarantulas, rattlesnakes and tattoos. With stronger focus, he picked up the slap of liquid against metal walls, the only sound in his darkened containment area. Here in the bowels of the building, there was no time and no light. In these insulated compartments, collectively called the pit, fiberglass walls sealed out noise, smell and external vibration.

A high-tech digital tomb.

After one day inside, most men lost their bearings. After three days, most men lost their minds. Only a few had the ability to endure the silent death of the containment unit.

Wolfe Houston was one of them.

He was well into the fifth day now, and his hallucinations were intense. Sensory deprivation amped up all his senses until he could have heard a fly walk across the ceiling near his head — if a fly could have breached the security of the pit. At the same time Wolfe was acutely aware of the other men floating in nearby units. Men from different backgrounds, each with different training and skills, over time had come to form one finely honed tactical team.

If the public knew their skills, they would have been called supermen — or monsters. Each of them had the power to read energy or transfer images into apparent reality with the sheer force of the mind. Most of them had never suspected their unusual skills before the government identified them through arduous testing. After long months of sweating and swearing and fighting together, they had become a silent, deadly team called out when everyone else — from Rangers to SEALs — had failed. They were tougher than tough, trained to deploy when the government's highest security was threatened, and so far they had never failed on a mission.

Wolfe wondered how long their record would remain unbroken.

He closed his eyes, rocking gently on the cool gel inside the hermetically sealed unit while ghostly tattoos writhed above him. As the images grew sharper, he slid into level-three hallucinations, feeling his psi ability shoot beyond all his previous limits.

The naked blonde trailed crimson nails toward his groin. Distantly, he felt his body respond and wondered if she was a hologram projection or whether she'd been pulled from the deeper recesses of his mind, stirred to life by the extended sensory deprivation.

Wolfe, are you there?

The silent question swam into his thoughts, sent by his second-in-command. Trace O'Halloran had guarded Wolfe's back more times than either man could count, and Wolfe had always repaid the favor.

Right next to you, O'Halloran.

One question. You got the same woman

in there as the one that's crawling all over me? Platinum blond, probably five-seven?

What's she wearing?

Nothing but oil and tattoos, looking damned fine.

Wolfe felt the brush of naked thighs. So the blonde wasn't his own private fantasy. That meant she was one of the new training constructs, designed by Lloyd Ryker, the facility's civilian chief, to test mental focus and physical response. No doubt Ryker's sensors were picking up every detail of his team's heart rates and body temperatures right now. The man had made surveillance a high art form.

Sounds like you've got her pegged, Trace.

I'd like to do more than peg her, boss.

Not allowed.

Wolfe felt the energy of Trace's laughter. *Hell, I've never seen tattoos on a woman's nipples before. Wouldn't that hurt? I mean, think about getting tattoos on your —*

You know the drill, Trace. Put all the details in your report — nipples and everything else. Don't leave anything out or they'll ram it down your throat in the follow-up evaluations.

I always thought sex was supposed to be private.

Wolfe grinned into the darkness. *Welcome to Foxfire, Lieutenant. In here your thoughts are noisy and sex is as public as it gets. Don't tell me you're complaining about having a knockout babe with her hands wrapped around your joystick while she test-drives your cruise control.*

Complaining? Who, me?

Wolfe felt his thoughts blur. When his own illusory companion licked her way expertly toward his belt, desire sucker punched him hard. He knew there were no rules, no fouls, no time-outs when Ryker set up the game. Dark and twisted training scenarios were his specialty. Some people said they reflected Ryker's own fantasies.

Wolfe didn't have an opinion one way or the other.

Hell, boss, this one is too hot to handle. That mouth of hers is doing real damage.

Red lips closed with unerring skill. Wolfe felt his brain oozing out his ears. Closing his eyes, he slipped deeper into theta, blanking out the construct of the blonde with the velvet mouth.

You feel that, boss?

Wolfe picked up a faint vibration from outside the pit. The blond vision faded pixel by pixel as he shaped his concentration into a tight line and slammed it toward the distant intrusion.

I make it Sector Three, Trace.

That's just what I'm reading.

Alarms on Levels Four through Seven. Ryker's on his way down here right now.

Any idea why, Chief?

Not a clue.

Drifting in the darkness, Wolfe considered the images he'd just picked up. Training sessions down in the pit were never interrupted — not for any reason. To Wolfe's knowledge, three men had cracked during their training because of too-abrupt transition. If Ryker was headed downstairs to interrupt a psi immersion, all hell must have broken loose.

Since hell happened to be Foxfire's specialty, the team would be the first called out.

Wolfe assessed possible options and explanations. If the country was under attack, Foxfire would go active immediately — whether the team was in the pit or not. Ryker's movement indicated that was a real possibility.

In war you fought with whatever ammunition was at hand. Some ops called for ICBMs; some used remote surveillance drones. Foxfire used human energy as a tactical weapon in highly controlled scenarios, and the success rate of the secret seven-man team was unmatched anywhere in special operations.

Wolfe intended to keep it that way. *Trace, do you read me?*

Loud and clear.

I need more data. Set up a level-two energy net while I follow Ryker.

Can do.

The silence rippled and grew heavier.

Done, Wolfe.

Ryker's almost here. Do we have a threat situation upstairs or is this an exterior attack, something large-scale?

I'm picking up fear — lots of it. There's something else, Chief. Hell if you're going to believe it.

Hit me.

It's Cruz.

Wolfe felt his hands clench. *Impossible.*

It's Cruz, all right. I scanned up, down and sideways, and his energy signature is leaking everywhere I look.

Wolfe knew that Trace didn't make mistakes when he spread a focused energy net. Each member of Foxfire had a different specialty, and Trace's skill was to set energy nets and carry out controlled psi sweeps, with his mind rather than with his eyes.

Both men knew that Gabriel Cruz, the Navy SEAL who had paved the way for Foxfire, had snapped under pressure. But he couldn't be anywhere near the secret New Mexico facility. He had died over two years ago, killed when his cargo plane crashed somewhere north of Juneau.

Trace and Wolfe had stood point together at Cruz's military funeral. They had walked cold vigil as part of the honor guard that long night, and they had seen the casket lowered into the ground.

Negative, Trace. You were there beside me. Cruz is gone, so you must be reading something else up there.

The vibrations grew louder. Wolfe picked up the faint hammer of feet, along with the tense energy of shouted commands. Ryker was steaming about something, that was certain.

I'm dead right about this. Whatever's going on upstairs has Cruz's energy wrapped all over it.

Wolfe forced his body to relax, forced the anger and stabbing uncertainty from his mind. *Be sure, Trace. That's an order. Do you copy?*

After a brief pause Wolfe felt an affirmative response. Then he sensed Trace's thought flow change. It drew up hard, like a wire snapped tight. *What?*

Ryker's right outside. You don't think he'd be stupid enough to override the codes and burst in here, do you? Without time for psi terminus and transition, we'll be fried. The last poor SOB they did that to. . . .

O'Halloran didn't finish. Both men had seen the mass of nerves and self-inflicted wounds carried screaming out of the pit after an immersion was cut short without warning.

No way. Wolfe managed to project total confidence. *Ryker knows the rules. He wrote most of them. It's too damned risky.*

He had barely finished the thought when boots hammered above his head. Automatic weapon fire punched through the silence, and Wolfe realized that he'd been dangerously wrong.

Brace for containment breach, Trace. Open a net and send the order down the line immediately. Wolfe snapped out the command, determined to protect his unit. Ryker was going to get his ass chewed royally once this incident was over.

The containment unit shook, tilting sharply.

Trace, are you psi shielded? Do it now, because they're coming in!

Metal grated on metal.

Light cut through the darkness. Instantly, Wolfe was slammed headfirst into an angry wall of pain.

CHAPTER TWO

Lost Mesa
Northeast of Taos, New Mexico
One week later

Kit O'Halloran stared at the canine teeth inches from her throat. A low, throaty growl shocked her out of a lazy sunset swim in the warm waters off Belize.

Blast it.

Just *once* she'd like to finish a fantasy. . . .

The growl stretched into rising notes and ended with a bark loud enough to snap the deepest concentration.

Kit pushed up onto one elbow and stared at the sixty-pound black Labrador puppy pressed against the sofa. "Drop, Baby."

The next growl ended in a whine. The Lab dropped and went completely motionless.

So much for Kit's nap. The dogs weren't used to her taking a rest after the predawn chores were finished, and Baby, her smallest Lab, was especially relentless when it was time to play. And it was playtime *right now.*

Because they were smart and very determined, her puppies usually had the last word.

"Good girl. Good, sweet girl." Kit reached to the floor for her treat bag and held out a pea-size liver snack, Baby's favorite. "What's all the fuss? Are you ready to practice?"

Baby downed the treat and turned her head toward the door, too well trained to rise from her down position until Kit gave the freeing command.

"Outside?" Kit fought a yawn. "You want to go outside and work?"

Baby's keen chocolate eyes narrowed intently. As she had before, Kit had the singular sense of being probed, measured, almost trained.

Which was beyond funny, considering that she had eleven years of experience training service dogs for law-enforcement and military units. Never before had she felt one of the hundreds of dogs try to train *her.*

Fighting another yawn, she ran a hand down the Lab's lustrous coat, pleased to feel its thickness. The feed mix she had developed seemed to be a success.

Kit wondered what new kind of chaos awaited her downstairs. With four puppies currently in training as military service dogs, upheaval was the norm, not that she minded. In her experience, dogs gave far more than they took.

"Up," she said firmly. Instantly, Baby shot from the bed, twisted at the doorway in a blur of fur and skidding feet, then looked back. Kit could have sworn there was a silent command in those clever brown eyes.

Hurry up.

Of all the dogs she had trained, these were definitely the smartest and strongest. The breeder who had placed the litter with Kit had told her their parents were extraordinary, and from the very beginning, Baby and her littermates had run harder, jumped higher, learned faster. They were also larger than the average Lab puppy.

Kit ran a hand through her tangled hair. The dogs would run her ragged if she let them. Labs were notoriously exuberant and playful, just as they were focused and intelligent. Already Baby had the energy of a fully-grown dog. It was no wonder Kit usually felt exhausted at the end of the day.

She knew she invested too much of herself in each training group. She also knew that letting go was a necessary fact of life in her work.

On a good day, she could accept that.

Still seated near the door, Baby looked back, her voice rising from snarl to soft whine, like conversation in some unrecognized language.

"Okay, okay. Just don't expect me to make sense until I grab my sweater and tank up on coffee."

Baby nosed under the big chest and appeared with Kit's oldest blue sweater dangling from her head. Laughing, Kit tugged the hooded cardigan over a white cotton T-shirt that had seen better days.

Not that her underwear mattered.

She lived forty miles from the nearest town. Since her closest neighbor was eighty-two and lived on the far side of a six thousand foot mountain, she didn't receive many spontaneous visitors. Whatever she wore made no difference to anyone but her — and that was exactly the way Kit liked it.

Stretching her arms over her head, she watched sunlight flood through the big bay windows. Judging by the sky, it was a little after six. She had brought the dogs in from their kennel and checked some medical references on her computer while they ate. Her nap had lasted all of twenty minutes, and now it was time for training.

"Stay," Kit said firmly. Baby didn't move, her big velvet eyes shimmering with intelligence.

Since the stay command was one of the hardest things for a puppy to master, Kit was delighted. "Good dog. Good Baby." She pulled an old leather glove from the pocket of her sweater, making a low hiss, and Baby's ears rose sharply at this cue to pay attention.

"Come," Kit ordered, holding out the glove.

In three excited strides Baby crossed the room, sniffing the leather with a back-and-forth motion of her head.

"Find," Kit ordered.

Like a shot, the puppy put her nose to the floor and raced down the stairs, skidded at the front door and started sniffing.

Kit checked her wristwatch.

Four seconds later she heard Baby bark once from the back of the laundry room, where Kit had buried the glove's mate under a wicker basket and a pile of dirty laundry.

Find complete.

"Good dog." Jotting a note in her spiral

pad, Kit headed downstairs, where Baby was waiting. Baby's head pointed straight to the spot in the laundry basket where Kit had hidden the matching glove.

The puppy had just shaved three seconds off her most recent record.

"Good, good girl." Another pea-sized treat appeared from Kit's bag. Baby nuzzled the reward delicately off Kit's wrist and swallowed it.

Abruptly the dog's ears pricked forward. Looking up at Kit, she gave a low series of snarls.

"What? What's wrong, Baby?"

The dog shot around in a blur, out the dog door and across the courtyard. Kit made a stop at the locked gun cabinet in the hall, then raced after her. Near the side door, she heard low male voices drifting across the outer wall of the compound.

This time there were two of them.

Baby hadn't barked, so the intruders wouldn't yet realize they'd been discovered. When Kit cracked the patio door silently, she could make out low whispers.

"I told you this whole idea sucked, Emmett. If she had the box, she wouldn't leave it all the way out here. Hell, she probably sleeps with the thing under her bed. She's crazy like the rest of her family."

Kit inched up beside Baby. "Stay," she whispered. "Stay, Baby."

The dog's position didn't waver, though her eyes glinted with wary energy.

Kit swung open the gate and leveled her father's old Smith & Wesson revolver at two men in dusty jeans peering down the well beneath a huge mesquite tree.

Fear prickled at the back of Kit's neck. The speaker was a big, sullen man she'd seen hauling feed at the local tack store or drinking from a brown paper bag outside several different bars.

"You're trespassing here, gentlemen."

The smaller man spun around with a surprised curse. "You said she was in town, Emmett. Why'd you lie to me?"

"Because you're too damned stupid to know better." The man named Emmett stood up slowly, his gaze locked on Kit. "Tell us where it's hidden. We'll just keep coming back until you do."

There was no point in asking what they meant. This man was just like the others, hoping to find the famous treasure supposedly hidden somewhere on the ranch.

Except there *was* no treasure.

Kit's hands tightened on the grip of the revolver. It had been her father's gun, and he'd taught her how to handle it safely and well. "There's no treasure here, fellas. You think I'd be driving a ten-year old Jeep with no air and bad brakes if I was sitting on a fortune? With that kind of cash, I'd be living the high life down in Santa Fe."

Emmett appeared to think this over for a long time before spitting on the ground beside the well. "I figure that's exactly what lie you'd tell us, but we both know there's Apache treasure hid somewhere in this damned well. Bones Whittaker saw it with his own eyes. That old Injun gave it to your father."

Kit kept her expression calm despite the anger burning in her throat. "Bones was seventy years old and a drunk to boot. Why believe him?"

"Because he saw it," Emmett said tightly. "So did his best friend and they was sober when they told my uncle. No way they'd lie about that gold your father got out on the mesa."

"Bones Whittaker was drunk and sick," Kit said flatly. "He wanted to be important so he made up the whole thing, right down to the story of the box he supposedly saw my father lower into the well. He even admitted it to my mother when he came up here a week before he died."

"Your ma told you that, did she?"

Emmett's eyes narrowed. "Well, I guess she would. Best way to quiet things down and keep your nice nest egg hid. But that's mesa gold, and it belongs to anyone that finds it. That's exactly what I'm fixing to do."

Kit took an angry breath. The rumors of buried treasure had begun when she was a girl, fed by the tales of an old, lonely man desperate to feel important before he died. When her parents had come into extra money after the death of Kit's maiden aunt, they'd bought a badly needed truck and built an addition to the kennels, adding fuel to the flames of local suspicion. Unfortunately, more than a few people still believed Bones Whittaker's crazy story.

When Kit's brother was at home, no one came sniffing around, but Trace had been gone for over a year now, and this was the second set of trespassers in the last month.

Kit felt a sharp tension at her neck. She glanced up and saw something move up on the ridge. A coyote?

Emmett continued to watch her, frowning when Baby barked inside the courtyard. "That your dog?"

"Yes, it is. And she —"

A callused hand shot around her shoulders from behind. "Got her, Emmett. What do we do now?"

A third man. She should have realized Emmett had an ace in the hole.

Kit dropped her revolver into the pocket of her baggy sweatpants, out of sight. Unable to break free, she pivoted and drove her boot heel down against her captor's instep.

She fought to stay calm, to wait for her moment.

A second arm locked at her waist.

She caught the smell of aftershave and old sweat as she tried to jam her elbow into his solar plexus, but he was fast, constantly twisting out of range.

"Get her gun." Emmett's voice was strained. "Damn it, Harry, do I have to do everything?"

Her captor slammed her forward and pinned her against the courtyard wall, driving her cheek into the rough stucco.

She blinked back tears, refusing to show weakness or pain to these lowlifes. "My brother will kill you for this."

"But your brother's not here, is he? Maybe he won't be coming back."

Kit kicked viciously, felt her boot strike bone.

"Ben, where's her gun? You see her drop it?"

"I don't see no gun here, Emmett."

Low growling drifted over the wall. "It's those dogs of hers again." Ben sounded frightened. "You said they wouldn't be here, Emmett."

A mass of dark fur and angry feet shot over the courtyard wall. Missiling down, Baby struck Emmett's shoulders. Moments later two other furry shapes crossed the wall. One rammed the back of Ben's legs, knocking him to the ground, and the third landed in front of Kit, teeth bared and menacing.

Then she was free, her revolver trained on the intruders who were circled by her snarling seventy-pound puppies. The dogs had waited for their moment to strike, working together.

"Get moving, you three. And spread the word that the next man who comes up here will be dodging my bullets." She sighted down the length of her revolver, glaring at Emmett, who was clearly the instigator of this harebrained operation. "But first take off your shoes. Do it now. All of you."

Three sets of eyes measured Kit, then cut back to the snarling dogs.

"Do what she says, Emmett. Never knew a woman could handle a gun worth shit.

She'll kill all of us in a second." Ben pulled off his boots and tossed them to the ground. "Can I go now?"

Kit waved her hand and the man immediately took off over the dirt. "What are you waiting for?" she snapped at the other two.

"Dogs don't scare me." Emmett crossed his beefy arms. "Especially puppies."

Baby bared her teeth while Butch and Sundance, Kit's other dogs, moved into a tight line next to Baby, the three ranged together as one unit.

Kit stared coldly at Emmett. "They could break your arm in a few seconds. Probably chew up your face pretty bad, too."

"Don't think you frighten me none, O'Halloran. Don't think it's over yet, either."

"Come on, Harry," Ben called from down the hill. "Let's get the hell out of here."

"Fine by me. I've had enough." The other man pulled off his boots, tossed them beneath the mesquite tree and headed down the slope after Ben.

Two down. One more to go.

"You too," Kit snapped at Emmett. "Don't forget your shoes."

Color surged into the man's heavy cheeks. After some angry fumbling, he freed his battered sneakers and threw them hard through the air.

Kit was surprised to see Baby jump up and catch them in her teeth.

"One day you won't be so lucky. Those dogs of yours might not be around."

Kit kept her expression cold. "Get going, and remember what I said. Next time I'll shoot first and consider the legalities later."

Dust drifted over the hillside. Kit didn't move until all three men had made their way past a row of cottonwood trees far down the hill, where an old pickup was hidden. After they shot out of sight, her knees began to shake, her stomach twisting in knots.

There was no reason to feel sick. Emmett and his friends were gone. She was safe now.

Saying it didn't help.

She leaned forward against the mesquite tree and threw up. When the spasms stopped, she set her revolver carefully on the ground and sat down on the wall above the well where mesquite leaves shivered in the wind like whispered promises.

But Kit didn't believe in promises any-more. Every promise that ever mattered to her had been broken. Even her brother had left, tossing all the responsibilities of the ranch onto her shoulders.

She took a deep breath, sagging against the old tree. Her father had planted it the same day he married her mother. Together they had watered it, staked it and tended it. Now the thick, gnarled trunk was twisted into three knots, towering over the well like a rich, dark rope beneath a canopy of green.

Small leaves blew free, raining down on Kit's face. She sank to the ground. How much longer before Emmett and his friends came back?

How much more could she take?

The three dogs pushed closer, licking her face with small whimpers as if offering exuberant comfort while their tails churned up little circles of dust beside the well.

She frowned, wondering where Diesel was. The most curious of the lot, he was probably back in the courtyard, tracking a squirrel or some other small animal.

But before she could go look, she leaned forward, throwing up all over again.

Some days definitely sucked.

He watched her because it was his job to watch her. His orders had come down from the very top: no involvement, no explanations, no contact of any sort. Surveillance and covert protection, nothing else.

But that was before Wolfe had seen Kit ambushed by three men right in her front yard. He'd watched, held back from intervening only by Ryker's explicit orders. But all that was about to change.

He punched a code into his secure cell phone, all the time studying Kit's house. "Ryker, it's Houston. Yes, I'm in place. But I'm requesting permission to break cover."

"Permission denied. Cruz is almost certainly headed your way, and I don't want anything to scare him off."

Wolfe watched clouds shadow the nearby ridge. "Sir, she was attacked a few minutes ago. Three men." His voice was cold and hard.

"Did they hurt her or threaten the dogs?"

"Negative. She managed to frighten the men off. The dogs helped."

Ryker's breath checked. "In that case, there's nothing to worry about. Do your job and stay under the radar."

The line went dead.

Wolfe gripped the phone, then shoved it back into his pocket. Orders unchanged.

He couldn't reveal his presence, and the situation was spiking his bullshit meter big time. There were things that Ryker hadn't briefed him about, foremost among them the fact that Cruz's death in Alaska had been faked. Everyone had seen how Cruz experienced mood changes during his last months on active service. There'd even been mental and physical side effects brought about by the program medications, but nothing that had been obvious, and Ryker had never briefed the Foxfire team about potential problems. All he had said in response to Wolfe's questions was that Cruz had become unstable. And that he had been taken into protective custody for the good of the program — and the country.

Wolfe was certain there was more to the story, but no one could pry anything out of Ryker until he was ready to talk. He had also ignored Wolfe's questions about why Cruz would be interested in Kit and her service dogs. That silence added to Wolfe's uneasiness.

He had to keep Kit and her special dogs safe, without breaking cover to do it. He shook his head, remembering the shy girl with pigtails who had blushed and stammered whenever he was in the room. Now she could scare off three garden-variety thugs without any help but her half-grown Labradors and a well worn revolver.

Times change.

Kit was grown up now, a woman with killer legs and a mouth that called for long, slow exploration. Not that she would remember him after all this time. To say that Wolfe had changed would be an understatement. But she was still his best friend's baby sister, off-limits for a man who could never put down roots.

It had been years since he'd been back, years since he'd stood on Lost Mesa. Her family's ranch was as rugged and majestic as ever, offering forty-mile views of sage, mesquite and piñon in every direction. Coyotes still called from the high ridges, reminding him of long, lazy summer afternoons.

Ancient history.

Cutting off bittersweet memories, he scanned the hill, hidden behind a line of sage in full bloom. As coyote song echoed from a nearby wash, Kit vanished and returned with a pair of binoculars. Silhouetted in the sunlight, strong and tall, she sought the loping pack.

Wolfe remembered the summer when she was twelve and he was a know-it-all high school kid on fire to save the world. Things had been black and white then, good versus evil. But the world didn't get saved and life had taught him that softness was a trap, trust only a crutch. He'd learned how to live without either.

Watching Kit focus her binoculars, he could sense her fierce determination to protect her ranch, and the dogs lined up beside her seemed almost an extension of that drive. He wondered if so much un-spoken communication between dogs and trainer was normal. He also wondered if they had sensed his presence yet. It was only a matter of time before they did.

As the coyotes howled and snarled their way across a neighboring slope, she fol-lowed their progress through her binocu-lars.

She would never see him unless he al-lowed it. Thanks to his skills she could stand a foot away, yet swear she was alone. He'd implanted focused images on missions in Indonesia, Sri Lanka, and the Middle East, distorting the theta patterns of his targets until all they felt was a tem-porary dizziness. But in that moment of extreme suggestibility, Wolfe could shape and recreate reality — or what appeared to be reality.

He smiled grimly. Once he'd made a trigger-happy potentate in Afghanistan see dinosaurs charging out of a cave. The man had fled, screaming orders at his men, allowing Wolfe and his team to stroll into the fortified insurgent camp, locate a pair of stolen Stinger missiles, and pack them out before anyone was the wiser.

With time his skill had grown to be second nature. Sometimes he had to work at remembering where reality stopped and his own creations began.

He spread his focus, noting wind direction, weather scenarios, and optimum surveillance points. Though he remained hidden, he missed nothing. As the current leader of the Foxfire team, he demanded two hundred percent from himself in training and in the field, and failure was not a word in his vocabulary.

Unconsciously, his fingers rose, tracing the piece of metal buried in the skin above his collarbone. This chip was one of his first implants, allowing satellite tracking with precise accuracy. Other chips had enhanced his endurance and allowed him to monitor his own brain waves.

Wolfe knew his skills came at a price few people would be willing to pay. For the team members in Foxfire, pain was a given and isolation was constant. Once you entered the program, you left your past behind forever.

If not, you were summarily booted out of the program.

He sensed the force of Kit's restless gaze. Abruptly she bent double, painfully sick, and he felt a twinge of sympathy. One-on-one combat was a bitch, no mistake about it. The adrenaline rush afterward was almost as bad as the attack itself.

He felt something strike his boot. When he looked down, he saw pieces of an old toy truck sticking out of the dirt beneath him. Blurred memories shot through his mind. Wolfe remembered the day he had dropped it. The beating he had gotten for losing it.

But he didn't want to remember.

The mesa was silent now. The coyotes had drifted on without registering his intrusion on these rocks.

Down the hill, Kit vanished, followed closely by two of her dogs. Behind them the smallest Lab hesitated, ears raised. For long seconds the puppy didn't move, staring up the hill at the spot where Wolfe sat motionless.

The power of the dog's fierce intelligence felt like a physical touch.

★ ★ ★

Lloyd Ryker had finished searching the lab for the third time, and once again he'd come up with nothing.

Staring at the blank gray walls, he considered his options. The facility had been on full alert since Cruz's escape. Two hundred personnel — military and civilian — were being checked for possible involvement. With enough pressure and scrutiny, one of them would eventually crack.

In the meantime Cruz was off the leash, and there was no way to calculate the damage he would cause if Ryker didn't find him soon.

The veteran of three presidential administrations frowned at the monitors above his desk. He had never felt completely comfortable with the full implementation of Foxfire. The program's concept was brilliant, but its personnel were far more dangerous than conventional weapons, which could be tracked and quantified as needed — or stripped and scrapped completely.

It wasn't so neat with people.

His eyes narrowed as he replayed the footage from the hidden lab camera — at least the rogue operative hadn't disabled *all* their security. He watched Cruz move to the mainframe computer and type quick lines of code. Why had the man accessed Wolfe Houston's service files, pulling up his training records and current duty assignment? Was there a covert connection between the two men?

He couldn't believe it. Foxfire's current leader was a straight arrow, his loyalty tested and confirmed.

Frowning, Ryker watched Cruz change screens, pulling up local topo maps and facility blueprints. After that he'd slipped past a million-dollar security system with three levels of password clearance and located complete medical data on all the dogs currently in the program. Now Cruz knew every animal's location and unique potential. To the right bidder, that information would be worth a fortune.

Coupled with the right trainer, of course.

It was a security nightmare.

Ryker shut off the surveillance tape and closed his eyes. He didn't have to replay the final footage to remember how Cruz had smiled coldly before hitting the lights, plunging the room into darkness. There was still no clue as to what he'd done next or how he'd escaped. By the time the response team hit the lab, the room was empty.

Ryker opened his eyes and sat forward slowly.

Or *was* it?

CHAPTER THREE

Somewhere on the horizon Kit heard a clap of thunder.

Restless for no reason she could name, she studied the gunmetal sky. The dogs were jumpy, too, interrupting their usual play to shoot wary looks at the high ridges around the ranch. Right now Baby was standing motionless, her nose pointed into the wind.

"Do you smell something up there, honey?"

The puppy whined faintly, but didn't move.

One by one dark clouds began to billow over the mountains, blotting out the sun. Butch and Sundance sat nearby, panting. Only Diesel moved, his pure black coat streaked with dust as he sniffed furiously at a retreating gecko.

Gravel skipped over the rocks, carried in eddies by the restless wind. After a last glance at the sky, Kit opened her backpack and took out Baby's red collar. Strapping on the work collar always signaled a transition to focused commands, invaluable re-inforcement for service dog training.

Warmed up from a good run across the mesa, the dogs were ready to focus on training. Baby's dark eyes probed Kit's face, and the dog quivered with excitement, awaiting the first command. No one could say that these animals didn't love to learn.

Kit began by reinforcing simple stay commands, then followed up with a variety of heel and halt repetitions, alternating ten minutes of training with five minutes of play and copious amounts of praise. After Baby ran through her moves, Kit slipped collars on Butch and the other dogs in turn. Accustomed to working serially, the dogs seemed to compete for fast command acquisition. Sometimes they even seemed to think as a team.

A family of quail shot out of the brush, making the dogs start. Even then, none moved, still on down command. "Stay," Kit repeated quietly.

Baby whimpered, bumping against Kit's leg. Lightning cracked over the ridge, followed by the roll of thunder.

Baby's ears flattened.

From a cluster of rocks up the slope Kit heard a shrill, rising wail. On a punch of fear, she recognized the cry of a mature cougar. Despite the wild pounding of her heart, she suppressed a primal urge to run.

"Stay," she ordered, one hand on Baby's head. If the dogs bolted, the hunting cat would be on them in a second, drawn by their motion.

Across the clearing Kit saw her rifle in its sling next to her backpack, and she cursed herself for not keeping the weapon within reach. Over the last months she had seen a rare cougar track on the higher slopes, but none of the animals had ever come close to the ranch.

Brown fur flashed up the ridge. Kit felt the skin tighten along her neck. She gripped her big oak walking stick, the only weapon at hand against a predator with ten times her strength.

Wind sighed through the cottonwood trees.

Kit heard the big cat cry again, the high wail like a physical assault. Beside her leg, Baby gave a powerful twitch.

"Stay, all of you." Kit's voice shook.

She knew she would have to take on the big cat armed with only her stick. Her father had done it once, and he'd told the story in electrifying detail for years afterward.

Staying calm was crucial. Sudden movement would trigger an immediate attack. In the face of a cougar, she also had to stand tall, raising her stick so that the cat would recognize her as an intimidating predator prepared to fight back. Her father had also warned her never to stare into a cougar's eyes, since this was considered a dominance challenge from one predator to another.

With one hand still on Baby's neck, Kit raised her big oak stick. "Heel." She spoke loudly to the Labs as she moved backward. As the wind shook the trees, she took another cautious step, the dogs ranged close beside her.

The low, stubby branches of a mesquite tree shook furiously. Brown fur brushed against shivering leaves, and a mature male cougar stepped onto a boulder, mouth open in a snarl.

Too close.

There was no way Kit could possibly reach the rifle now.

Swinging her heavy stick, she took three running steps forward, answering the cougar's cry with her own loud shout. Despite her terror, she reached deep and found her strength, shaping it to match the predator's cry. Cougars ranged by territory, killed by territory, and were famously unpredictable, especially if they were defending their young or a previous kill.

This would be Kit's only chance to save the dogs and herself.

The cougar stared at her, all hunger and rippling muscles. Her dusty sneakers slipped in a patch of gravel, and she fell to one knee, then lurched up instantly, her hands raised while she shouted hoarse warnings in a voice that sounded like a stranger's. At the top of the ridge, the narrow path twisted past a huge boulder streaked white with quartz, and there the cougar waited, smudged by sunlight, muscles taut, ready to jump.

Ready to kill Kit and carry away her dogs.

Warm sunlight slanted down. A hawk called far down the slope. Kit felt every detail cut deep into her mind as the dogs tensed beside her, barking wildly.

The big cat took a step closer. Grimly, Kit prepared for the attack she sensed was seconds away. The big predator swung sharply to one side, then circled the boulder, snarling in a mix of anger and pain while its powerful shoulders flexed, almost as if it were wounded.

Then the brown body jumped high and

cut through the streaming sunlight past Kit, past the dogs, landing less than four feet away. In an instant, the big cat was gone, swallowed up in the shadows cast by junipers and sage.

The glade fell silent. Even the dogs were still.

Kit spun around, guarding the route where the cougar had vanished. When there was no more sign of movement, she raced back to grab her rifle, racked in a shell and leveled the barrel.

With her rifle on one arm and her walking stick in the other, she issued sharp commands to the dogs, herding them up-hill away from the trees where the cougar had left the trail. It was a longer route back to the ranch, but no overhanging rocks would conceal a stalking predator.

Kit wasn't about to be cornered again.

Her hands shook, wind brushing her face. Dimly she realized her cheeks were wet with tears.

Wolfe couldn't breathe.

His fingers dug into the dirt as he watched Kit's shaky progress up the steep slope. He still couldn't believe she'd gone after the cougar armed with no more than a stick.

Fearless — or just crazy. Maybe both.

He'd been on his way up the ridge even before she'd seen the animal stalking her, but she'd done all the right things to make the cougar back down. Her quick, smart response had prevented him from breaking his orders to remain undercover.

She would never know how he had seen the big cat when it was poised to attack. She would never suspect that the animal's growl of anger and fear had come from Wolfe's silent intrusion. He couldn't control the animal, but he could enhance Kit's appearance to make her resemble a fearsome predator.

Despite the jagged emotions Kit must be feeling right now, she was doing fine, keeping the dogs close as she set a good pace across the mesa. If he had his way, he'd be up there beside her, close enough for protection should the need arise.

But orders were orders. Right now Ryker wanted only deep cover surveillance on Kit and the dogs. Protection if needed, but no exposure.

Crouched near a juniper tree, he watched her. She was quick and confident, with spare elegance in every long stride. Short and spiky, her hair glinted with hints of copper in the shifting sunlight. When she moved into the shade, the color changed, dark as French wine he'd tasted once in Burgundy. The short, uneven chunks hugging her face made him want to slip his hands deep and feel her warmth. He stifled the unfamiliar longing and forced his thoughts back to his mission.

Thanks to his training, he was adept at burying his emotions and forgetting them. The sight of a woman's uneven hair wasn't going to make him backslide.

In Wolfe's line of work, feelings got a man killed faster than bullets.

He kept that thought in mind as he followed Kit back to the ranch, careful to stay out of sight.

Kit watched shadows pool across the empty courtyard, feeling unbearably tired.

She was still shaken by her encounter with the cougar. Shivering, she stared at the ridge above the ranch and realized how lucky she was to be alive. She wanted to believe that her quick response with voice and motion cues had scared the predator away, but she couldn't. The animal had looked wounded. Perhaps something else had frightened it and sent it running away into the brush.

Too keyed up to sleep, she paced the

living room, unable to forget the cougar's shrill cry. Silent and smart, the animal could be outside the wall right now, searching for a tree branch with access into the nearby courtyard.

Enough.

Disgusted, Kit grabbed her old sweater from the arm of the couch and strode down the hall. If she couldn't sleep, she might as well tackle the pile of bills that had accumulated over the last week. Food, equipment and medical care for the dogs were just the beginning, yet she refused to stint on materials or food for her animals, even if it meant that she wore threadbare jeans and sneakers with holes in the bottom.

The ranch was a steady drain on the small legacy that had come to Kit at her parents' death. With forty acres of high desert stretching between two mountain ranges, the land was unsuited for ranching, and the cost of adding modern irrigation would have been prohibitive. Thanks to Kit's growing reputation training service dogs, her bank account had finally crept out of the red, but it might be five years before she could actually take a vacation.

Five years. . . .

Frowning, she sank into the old chair behind her wooden desk. It was the same place where her mother had handled the ranch's account books and budgets. The pitted wood was cool beneath her fingers, smooth from years of use. Closing her eyes, she could imagine her mother lining up pens and stacking bills in neat piles as she calculated new ways to stretch a dollar.

Kit did the stretching now.

A local dog food company was pestering her to endorse a new product. The money would help her buy new tires for her Jeep and install an alarm system at the ranch.

As she reached for her checkbook, she saw the red message button flashing on her telephone and quickly scanned the calls. She would be devastated to miss a call from her brother, who was impossible to reach and always phoned at unpredictable times. If she'd missed Trace today, it might be months before she heard from him again.

Triggering her replay button, she fumed through two mortgage offers. The third message was from her oldest friend.

"Kit, it's Miki. I just got back from a new project in Santa Fe. You are not going to believe the assignment I landed this time. Let's go drink double shots of tequila while I tell you about it, okay? I need some advice. Stop spoiling those gorgeous canines and give me a call."

Kit smiled, wondering what kind of bizarre situation her old friend had gotten into now. A year ago it was making a tour documentary for a punk band that performed with defanged rattlesnakes, and her most recent job had been shooting trailers for indie horror movies. Whatever her new assignment, it was bound to be strange. Miki attracted *bizarre* like honey attracted flies.

The next message was the crisp, professional voice of Kit's vet, calling to make an appointment for a vaccination titer, a procedure required to check the immunization status of the four puppies. Liz Merrigold had been the O'Halloran family vet for nearly a decade, as well as the local contact for the breeder who had supplied Kit's current litter of training dogs. Liz always kept a sharp eye on the animals placed for training under her supervision, gladly providing medical advice and moral support, day or night.

Kit jotted a note on her calendar to call and confirm a time for the visit. While she wrote, she triggered the last message.

"This is Doctor Rivera's office, Ms. O'Halloran. Doctor Rivera asks that you call the office at your earliest convenience. He'd like to speak with you."

Kit looked down at her hands. All the energy seemed to bleed out of her body. She sank lower in the chair, staring at the breeding awards that lined the walls of the study. Presidents, generals and movie stars smiled down from mismatched frames, mute records of her family's contribution to humane and practical training techniques for service and working dogs. In twenty-five years her parents had personally trained over two thousand dogs, and Kit was determined to expand on their legacy.

But her body might have different plans.

After a long day of exercise, she could no longer ignore the deep throb in her right hip. Wincing, she pulled a heavy medical textbook from a nearby shelf. She didn't expect to find anything new because she had read every relevant page at least fifty times. All of them pointed to the same conclusion: joint deterioration, pure and simple.

Kit wished that Trace would come home. She missed his outrageously bad jokes and his off-key Rolling Stones renditions.

But she never knew when her brother would appear, and she tried not to think about the possibility that he might never come back. Although the details were secret, Kit knew he was part of a highly trained covert operations team, and right now they could be deployed anywhere.

Almost certainly, it would be someplace dangerous. More than once she remembered Trace calmly telling her that hell was their specialty.

Baby gently nudged her leg. Kit sensed that the dog had come to offer reassurance with the warmth of her body and the soft thump of her tail. It was uncanny how pets developed a skill at reading their owners' moods.

Kit took a deep breath, stretching her legs slowly. Her joints felt stiff, but they were no worse than any other day, and that was something to be thankful for. Leaning down, she slid her hand through Baby's soft fur. She had cried herself dry months ago, cursing her body, her genes and nameless bad luck. Neither the tears nor the curses had made her feel better.

As she stared at the medical book filled with grim facts and sad pictures, something shook free inside Kit. Slowly it uncurled against her chest, blowing away restless fears and dreary expectations. She wouldn't plan her future based on old medical files. She was strong. She would make her *own* future.

She closed the textbook with a snap. No more obsessing about medicine and new discoveries. If you gave in to fear, you'd lost already.

Outside the moon drifted above the mesa. Kit ran a hand through her hair and stretched. "I'm in the mood for a hero tonight. What do you guys say? Gary Cooper or John Wayne?"

Diesel stared at her, cocking his head in the half-listening, half-baffled pose that always made her smile.

Baby turned in a slow circle, stretching out on the floor.

"Bogie it is, then." Shaking her head, Kit went out to find *Casablanca.*

Twenty minutes later the Germans were storming Paris, Bogie was fighting a broken heart, and Kit couldn't have been happier.

Curled up on the couch, she watched black-and-white images play across the wide-screen TV that had been her father's single vice. She smiled as the story wrapped around her, pulling her in and making her forget her own troubles. Ilsa and Rick would always have Paris, and she would always have *Casablanca.*

Claude Rains leered at her. Kit fought a yawn as the day finally took its toll. She fell into dreams of black and white and a world filled with weary heroes.

Moonlight shimmered across the floor. Baby stretched out at Kit's feet, gnawing on a rubber chew toy.

As Kit slept, the four dogs moved closer. At a look from Baby, Diesel vanished to patrol the courtyard while Butch and Sundance moved to check the backyard and rear doors.

In silence, Baby lifted her paws to the windows that overlooked the mesa. There in the moonlight the dog's ears pricked forward.

A family of quail scurried for cover, routed from sleep by the shadow of a passing hawk. Wind hissed through the juniper branches that tossed in the moonlight.

Baby absorbed all of these movements, assessing them as unimportant. But something else moved in the darkness, and it was a thing the dog had never sensed before.

The other three dogs appeared from the shadows, drawn by the force of Baby's uneasiness. As one, they sank down before the window, alert to the night.

While the moon rose higher and war waged across North Africa, Kit slept on, caught in restless dreams. Ranged around her, the dogs kept a wary vigil, sensing new predators afoot beneath the desert moon.

CHAPTER FOUR

Silent and controlled, the highly trained covert operative jumped the courtyard wall and scanned the outside of Kit's house. At the edge of the shadows, certain he was alone, he triggered his cell phone.

Ryker answered on the second ring, sounding irritated. "0200 hours. This had better be important, Houston."

"Permission to break cover, sir."

"You're persistent, I'll say that."

Wolfe didn't answer. The night was silent, the air rich with the pungent bite of piñon and burning mesquite logs.

"Any new threats, Commander?"

"A cougar in the area. She drove the thing off with a stick. Added to that is the possibility that the men from this morning may return. I can't keep her safe if I'm hidden at the top of the hill, sir. It's simple physics."

"There's nothing simple about physics," Ryker muttered. "Foxfire proves that every day." He cleared his throat. "Permission granted. But keep things airtight. I'm holding you personally responsible, is that understood?"

"Affirmative, sir."

"Then good night," Ryker said sourly. "*Some* of us need to sleep."

When Ryker disconnected, Wolfe reconnoitered. He knew the layout of the ranch from his mission documents, but even without the plans, he would still have remembered his way.

With quick movements he jimmied the side door lock and broke into the house. Once inside, he listened for Kit's voice or the sound of footsteps, but all was quiet. Only as he turned down the front hall did he hear low voices — male and female.

Instantly his hand flashed to the Sig at the small of his back. How had someone gotten past him? He'd been watching every road, window and door for a week. During his brief naps, his scattered motion sensors took over, so the property was always monitored.

Light flickered from the far end of the hall. Muffled voices rose in anger.

Neither of them was Kit's.

When he glanced around the corner into the living room, he saw Kit asleep on the couch, legs curled up, her hand flung over the back of a pillow. Ranged around her were the four dogs Ryker had briefed him about. Smart, fast, and highly motivated, they were products of the same genetic technology that made Wolfe one of the government's most valuable military assets. Kit mumbled in her sleep, one hand in Baby's fur, and the big puppy moved closer, almost protectively, as Wolfe surveyed the room. Currently Kit had no idea about the nature of the dogs she was raising. Though her supervision of the dogs' training remained hotly contested by the Foxfire scientists, the bottom line was results: as long as Kit's dogs showed superior skill acquisition, they would stay right where they were.

For long seconds none of them moved, Wolfe by the door and the dogs keenly alert near Kit. Baby's head rose. She sniffed the air softly, and Diesel came to stand beside her, their intensity was nearly palpable.

Muted voices continued to come from the flickering television on the far wall as Wolfe monitored the room, staying far back in the shadows.

Then Baby turned in a circle, sneezed and sat down beside Kit with no further wariness or hostility. Wolfe felt some of his tension ebb. The dogs appeared to have accepted him as friendly. Ryker had assured him that their shared chips would make this likely.

Better than getting an ankle savaged, Wolfe thought wryly.

He made a mental note to drop this observation into his next report, along with a description of the dogs' quick threat response when they'd shot over the courtyard wall to protect Kit.

Spirit and courage. Both were key traits for a military service dog, and these animals would be amazing assets when their training was complete. Healthy and clearly curious, they shot forward to sniff at his legs and circle him excitedly.

But Wolfe was watching Kit and the way light from the television played over her face, outlining her cheekbones and full lips. The surveillance photos in his file didn't show the gold in her short hair or the dark curve of her eyelashes. Nor did they capture her restless energy, even in sleep.

As he came closer, Wolfe noticed the ugly welt on her arm where she'd fallen on the trail this morning. Near the welt was a bruise from Sundance, who had kicked her accidentally while running through an improvised obstacle course on the mesa.

She's changed, Wolfe thought. Grown up with a vengeance.

There was no mistaking the smooth curve of her breasts or the line of her thigh beneath the nightshirt she wore.

Bad news, pal.

Frowning, he looked away, studying this airy room with views over three mountains and forty miles of sagebrush. He'd spent some good hours here, playing pool with Trace, arguing about cars and politics. He'd felt safe here once.

Memories rushed over him, good mixed with bitter, drawn from his few hours of normal boyhood. In this house he had glimpsed all the things his life might have been in a different family.

One with a father who didn't enjoy casual cruelty.

Wolfe hadn't thought about his father for years. His past was a closed book, the wistful boy buried deep. Before joining the Navy, he had changed his name and dropped the bitter memories like a stone hurled far and long into deep water. Only seventeen, he'd already been a man when he left Lost Mesa. He'd worked in the fields, backbreaking labor that had carried him from county to county and harvest to harvest. Two days after his eighteenth birthday he'd seen a recruiter's office and felt a light go on.

Two days later he was on a bus bound for the closest training facility. The Navy had made him whole again and he'd met every challenge thrown his way, proud to become a SEAL. When he'd been selected to join the ultra-secret Foxfire unit, his new life had seemed complete.

All these thoughts flashed by in seconds as Wolfe stood in the blue-gray light of a movie he didn't recognize. The four dogs didn't move, faces alert beside the couch where Kit slept, and Wolfe knew beyond a doubt that they were measuring him, analyzing every action. He avoided any swift movements that could be mistaken for aggression, and when the dogs continued to show no sign of hostility, he crouched beside the smallest one, a black Lab with melted chocolate eyes.

So this was Baby.

The runt of the litter, she was also the smartest and most gifted, if Ryker's files were right — and they almost always were. Wolfe raised his hand, checking the dog's response.

The big dark eyes focused intently. She sniffed his open palm and nudged his hand, her tail bumping on the rug.

The SEAL felt a little surge of satisfaction when Baby rolled over calmly in a gesture of trust, raising her head to meet his hand. The animals were well nourished and superbly groomed. Their coats were thick and smooth, their eyes clear. According to Ryker, none of the government's in-house labs had produced dogs with anything close to Kit's record of health and growth rate. Wolfe made a mental note to check the ingredients of the new food mix she had developed. He had already sent back photographs with a 12X zoom and detailed notes about her training methods. Clearly she deserved her excellent reputation.

Ryker wanted to know how a civilian working alone in an isolated and meagerly equipped location could outperform highly paid scientists in state-of-the-art facilities. Some people were convinced that Kit's parents had stumbled across a food additive to enhance the dogs' training speed. Others had called it blind luck. For his part, standing face to face with Kit's dogs, Wolfe suspected a different process was at work.

Kit didn't hesitate to crawl through the dirt on her stomach to show a six-month old puppy how to be silent in the brush.

She didn't hold back a laugh of pure glee when she jumped from a ladder into a mound of straw with two wriggling dogs in her arms. She offered unquestioning loyalty and her animals responded in kind.

Wolfe wasn't a scientist, but he sensed that Kit herself was the secret ingredient.

He looked up to the scrutiny of chocolate-colored eyes. Baby continued to study him for what felt like a lifetime, sniffing his hand. Damn if Wolfe didn't feel as if he'd been scanned, analyzed and dissected from forehead to big toe.

When Baby nudged his leg, Wolfe winced. She was a little too close to the jagged cut he'd received during his insertion jump from a military chopper north of Taos. But he didn't pull away, sensing the dog's concentration.

Seconds later Baby was nudged aside first by Diesel, then by Butch and Sundance. Each dog sniffed the area on his thigh where he had been wounded. When they were finally done investigating, they drew back into a motionless line.

The seconds stretched out. Wolfe felt the dogs' concentration grow.

What in the hell was going on? Why did he feel as if he was being ruthlessly analyzed all over again? Suddenly Wolfe realized it was his wound that fascinated the dogs, possibly because they sensed something unusual — or familiar — about his blood chemistry. Another observation to go into his report to Ryker.

Across the room, Kit twisted suddenly. Still asleep, she kicked free of her cover, her hand hitting the remote on the side table.

The images on the screen multiplied, twelve small boxes of the same street scene.

Curious, Wolfe moved closer. He'd never seen a complicated TV screen like this one. Back at the lab, facilities were tight and schedules strict. Training constantly, the team members had little time for entertainment, since they had to be able to deploy at a moment's notice, day or night.

It was fair to say that he had missed a few things, given his lifestyle. With Baby by his leg, he followed images of tanks rumbling through the streets of Paris. Against the haunting chords of a piano, he saw Humphrey Bogart's ashen face when he was left alone for a second time.

War was hell, all right. Wolfe could identify with that.

Kit twisted again. Her other hand hit the

remote, changing the display to one small box in the bottom corner of the screen.

Fascinated by the technology, Wolfe picked up the remote and sat down in the far chair while he studied the unfamiliar control. He could rig complicated trigger units for every kind of explosive device, so he figured this equipment wouldn't be much of a problem.

He touched one of the buttons.

The action froze on the big screen.

He touched another button. In seconds he'd worked out how to resume action, mute the audio and fast-forward. After making sure that Kit was still out cold, he started the movie again. Diesel moved closer while Baby nuzzled his shoulder. With the dogs ranged around him, he felt oddly safe and protected.

But safety was an illusion with Cruz on the loose. Jumpy, he rose and circled the room, checking windows and doors. After each pass, he was drawn back to his seat beside Baby and the images that flickered over the screen.

Without a sound Sundance moved to the big window overlooking the front porch. Diesel and Butch slipped away into the shadows. Baby didn't budge, her head resting on Wolfe's shoulder. For one strange moment the SEAL felt an unshakable sense of belonging.

But he didn't belong. Not as a ragtag boy, and definitely not as a man. Because of Foxfire, he would always be different, and he had accepted that difference, both gift and curse, the day that the government had implanted his first chip.

And he had work to do. Now that he had ascertained Kit's safety, there was no reason for him to sit watching a sixty-year-old movie and enjoying the sight of Kit's hair aglow in the lamplight.

As Wolfe stood up, Baby slanted her head and met his eyes.

He wasn't sure if he imagined what happened next. Across the room the sound climbed, voices murmuring. Wolfe tapped a button on the remote, wondering if he had accidentally hit something without noticing. But a second later the volume climbed again.

A defective television?

He frowned at the wall of high-tech equipment and lowered the audio again. Behind him the dogs were lined up in a row. Panting, they stared at him expectantly.

As a test, he muted the sound. Instantly, it shot back to its prior level.

Wolfe dropped the volume, sorting through possible explanations. A wiring malfunction? Battery failure?

Flipping the remote, he removed the batteries. He was about to pry off the inside cover and check the inner circuitry when the TV muted on its own.

The batteries were in his hand. The dogs were ranged on the floor in front of the television, unmoving. Baby's tail thumped once.

The dogs?

He didn't buy it. This kind of skill had never been part of their genetic package. The source had to be an equipment malfunction.

Tensely, he pocketed the batteries and moved to the far wall. Leaning down, he scanned the controls and manually triggered the volume.

Nothing happened.

Wolfe thought it over. Then he thought it over again. His gaze returned to the dogs.

Baby sat down in the middle of the rug. *Casablanca* stopped, and the television switched over to regular programming, where a man with a sequined cowboy hat waved his arms and pitched used trucks.

"Hell if I believe this," Wolfe muttered, muting the volume.

Kit stirred restlessly, and he dragged a hand through his hair, then switched off the television and waited — not sure what he was waiting for.

The silence stretched out, deep as the New Mexico night. He stared at the dogs, and they stared right back at him. A branch scraped the window. Baby draped her head across Diesel's neck, looked at the television and wagged her tail. Coincidence?

Wolfe shook his head, returning the batteries to the remote and placing it next to Kit so she'd assume that she had turned off the movie in her sleep. Baby yawned. The previous phenomena with the television appeared to have stopped. Though Wolfe waited, nothing else happened.

Time to go.

But at the door he paused, unable to resist one last look at Kit. She was striking even in her sleep. In a dozen ways she reminded him of her mother, who'd still turned heads at sixty. Wolfe remembered the night Amanda O'Halloran had found him sleeping in the old barn, desperate and exhausted, still bleeding from his father's drunken beating.

She had cleaned him up without a word, fed him without a word, then opened her heart as well as her house to him. When his father had come looking for him, she'd run him off with a shotgun.

He hadn't thought of that night for years. It was this unnerving house, the dogs on the old Mexican rug and the fire that crackled happily.

He rubbed his thigh as he walked down the shadowed hallway. The wound had torn open again and was throbbing — a minor discomfort after the abuse Wolfe's body had suffered over the years. He had a full supply of medicine in his field pack to deal with exactly this problem.

Something moved at the end of the corridor. Quickly Wolfe slid against the wall, listening to a shuffling noise in the hall.

The sounds came closer and then Baby appeared a few feet in front of him. Her ears perked up as she stared at the spot where Wolfe was standing, hidden in the shadows. Moments later Butch and Sundance moved to face the kitchen entrance, while Diesel prowled the house, going from window to window, alert and wary.

Baby let out a low growl and trotted to the kitchen door, staring at the window. She was soon joined by the other two dogs. When Diesel finished his circuit, he joined them in front of the kitchen doorway.

A noise brought Wolfe around, low and fast. Kit stood in the shadows, looking sleepy and mussed. The rifle she held was dead level. Then Diesel began to bark, and the other dogs joined in.

"Baby? Diesel? What's wrong?"

She hadn't seen him yet, Wolfe realized. She must have heard the dogs prowling around earlier.

But something else was moving in the darkness. Wolfe heard the faint crunch of feet on gravel outside.

Grabbing Kit, he pulled her out of sight, his hand clamped over her mouth. Seconds later the kitchen window shattered in a noisy explosion, glass flying over the tile floor.

She fought his grip as he pinned her against the wall with his body, feeling her panic in the wild rise and fall of her chest. She tried to kick him, but he nudged her leg aside and blocked her clawing fingers.

He brushed her breast, soft and warm beneath thin cotton, and the contact made him jerk as if he'd been burned; his hand locked over her mouth when she tried to protest.

Glass crunched.

Across the kitchen a man climbed in over the windowsill, his knife glinting in the cold moonlight.

CHAPTER FIVE

What *else* could go wrong?

He pushed Kit down the hall, fighting her every step of the way. When she tried to scream, Wolfe cut her off with fast, focused images of herself floating in bubbling hot springs until he felt her body relax and slump against his chest, arms askew.

Grimly, he called up the floor plan of her house, memorized during mission prep.

Four steps left. One step right and then around the corner. She was still slumped as he carried her inside a closet and left her sitting against the wall, snoring faintly.

One problem solved.

Quickly Wolfe closed the door and wedged a chair under the knob.

There was a bang in the kitchen, followed by a muffled curse.

Silently, he crossed the room and waited beside the door as Kit's intruder inched through the darkness. Moonlight touched the blade of a saw-edged hunting knife.

Wolfe's lips twitched. *Bad move, pal. You just used up all your chances.*

With one sharp movement, he captured the man's wrists and smiled coldly as he felt the bones begin to snap. Within two seconds the man was on his knees, begging to be released.

"Who sent you?"

"Nobody."

"Try again, peanut brain." Wolfe increased the pressure on his wrists.

"No more. It was just me and the boys, looking for — for that Apache gold that's hid up here."

He was whimpering now, and Wolfe was inclined to believe him. The man didn't look like a professional who could lie in the face of pain. As he pulled the man around into the muted light from the window, Wolfe recognized the troublemaker who had assaulted Kit that morning. Apparently he'd decided to return by night and complete the job.

"Give me a name," Wolfe repeated as he twisted the man's hands, grinding bone against bone.

"Nobody — I already told you. That's the truth, damn it!"

Wolfe considered the quickest way to tie up loose ends. He could kill the man without leaving any marks, then dump him off a ridge. After the body had dropped sixty feet and rolled down a wash, there would be no doubt in anyone's mind that it was a simple hiking accident. For a second, the urge for murder pounded through his veins.

He pulled himself back from the edge, and in one quick movement of his foot sent the man flying to the floor. Ignoring Kit's muffled curses from the closet, Wolfe pulled up an image of the toughest, most frightening Apache warrior he could remember from his reading as a boy. Then he sharpened the image, adding streaks of color at face and chest along with a honed hunting knife.

This was the exact image that the man on the floor saw bearing down on him. No amount of thought or argument would change the force of that vision later.

"If you come back here, ever again, we will find you." Wolfe figured that the words should fit the image, and he chose them carefully. "There are four of us here. Together we guard the ranch and this family. If you come back, we will find you. Then we will kill you. But first we will skin you slowly while you scream."

The man's body trembled at Wolfe's feet. He was crying openly now, consumed by Wolfe's terrible vision. "I won't. I swear it. Lemme *go*."

Growling, Baby and the other three dogs lined up around the intruder. Kit's cursing from the closet was turning shrill.

Time to dispense with Einstein here.

"Go back to your town. Tell your friends what I have told you tonight. Know that if any one of you returns, we will be here waiting."

"We won't come back," the man blurted. "None of us will, I promise."

Wolfe wasn't going to take any chances. He focused the man's fear, shaped it. Then he drove it deep inside his head to fester and grow.

The intruder's face was slack with terror when Wolfe finished. As the man staggered to his feet, something fell out of the front pocket of his shirt.

Wolfe caught the torn piece of paper with one hand.

The faint, irregular lines appeared to be some kind of drawing. He realized the marks were a clumsily drawn map of Kit's ranch.

But there was no time for closer investigation. Wolfe shoved his stumbling captive back toward a broken window in the kitchen. The dogs were still growling when the bulky shadow plunged through the window and dropped out of sight. Footsteps drummed, a car door opened, and then a truck's engine roared to life.

The big dog, Diesel, circled back to the closet where Kit was locked, while Baby jumped up and rested her front paws carefully on the window, looking out into the night. The only sound in the house was the furious sound of Kit's fists as she hammered at the closet door.

Wolfe figured the safest thing to do was engineer exactly what she would remember in the morning. He'd have to clean up outside and then replace the broken window so the dogs wouldn't be hurt. He could easily have blocked Kit's memory entirely, but he would have to make an appearance sometime, and it might as well be now. He couldn't guard her effectively if he stayed hunkered down halfway up a hill outside.

Kit's curses stopped. The sudden silence was broken by the crack of shattering wood. What the hell had the woman done now? But Kit would have to wait until he checked out the house.

Quickly, he scanned the courtyard. There was no sign of the last intruder or any accomplices. Standing motionless, he feathered his senses through the darkness in search of Cruz's energy trail.

Nothing even close. Not here or in any of the other rooms.

At least one worry was dispensed with. When he crossed the first floor hallway, he heard Kit's urgent shouting from the closet. He figured she'd be pretty surprised to see him after all this time, but no matter. Surprise, he could deal with.

Outside the closet, he pulled the chair away from the door, which immediately shot open against his hands. She came out fighting — aimed a savage left hook at his face, rammed something heavy into his stomach, then shot past him toward the door.

Hell.

Wolfe sighed, following her down the dark hallway. A barrage of metal pots caught him at the far side of the kitchen. He ducked and nearly tripped on a bench she'd overturned near the door.

When Wolfe stepped over the bench, the dogs were positioned around his feet. Diesel rammed his leg, forcing him to jump sideways to avoid stepping on Baby and Sundance.

When he again looked up, there was a rifle pointed at his forehead.

"Hands up where I can see them."

Wolfe cursed silently, glaring at the dogs.

He hadn't expected that last stunt by Diesel, which was pretty damned amazing.

In any case, it was time to cool her down before she shot him.

"Lower the Winchester. It's me, Kit. It's Wolfe."

The rifle stayed right where it was. "Someone breaks my window and invades my house, he's going to regret it." The kitchen was dark and Wolfe realized she still hadn't seen his face.

"I had some leave and Trace told me to drop by and look in on you. Sorry I drove up from town without calling first, but I never figured I'd get a rifle in my face for forgetting my manners."

In the darkness, she reached back to run her hand along the wall. "When I count to three, I expect you to be sitting in the chair next to your right hand. Meanwhile, if I see anything I don't like, I'm going to fire. Are we clear on that?"

Wolfe's lips twitched. She had spirit to burn, his little Katharine. Except she wasn't little anymore, and those long legs of hers looked damn good under her nightshirt.

Slowly Wolfe raised his hands in the air, just the way she'd ordered. He wasn't about to give her a reason to shoot him.

"Hell, Kit, don't you recognize me? Your brother was supposed to call and let you know I was coming. It's Wolfe."

She stopped moving. Wolfe thought he heard her breath catch.

She blew out an angry breath. "Shut up and keep your hands in the air."

In the dark he listened to her stalk toward him. "Whatever you say. But all you have to do is turn on the lights and you'll see I'm telling the truth."

"I just tried the lights, and they're out. But you'd know that because you turned off the power before you broke in here."

So Einstein had been smarter than he looked, tackling Kit's electricity. "There's a penlight in my pocket," Wolfe said quietly. "Top right side of my jacket. Pull it out and see for yourself that I'm not lying."

"And let you jump me? No way. You're staying right there, and I'm staying right here with my rifle. I just called the state police on my cell phone. They should be here shortly."

Police were the last thing Wolfe needed. He moved away, slipping around the corner beyond the closet.

"Where are you going?"

Wolfe heard her stumble, her legs striking an overturned chair.

83

He didn't answer, moving silently through the darkness, staying low as he circled the counter. Then he stepped in fast, pivoted and knocked the rifle from her grip.

All in all she had put up a pretty good defense, but Wolfe was still furious. Trace should have installed an adequate security system before he left, damn it. He should also have taught Kit a fallback plan in case of an attack. She was living miles away from neighbors or police and she was pinned against the counter, the rifle behind her on the floor. Anyone else could have done some real damage to her.

Wolfe felt the dogs close in. Baby pressed against his leg, whining, and Diesel nuzzled his thigh.

"What are you doing to my dogs?" Kit said sharply.

Typical, Wolfe thought. Pinned to the counter, she worried about the dogs, not her own safety.

"Nothing. Stop fighting and I'll pull out my light so you can see my face." Wolfe found his penlight and raised it slowly, shining it up at his head.

She winced in the sudden blue-white beam, her eyes tracking to his face. Her breath caught. "Wolfe?"

"I'm sure as hell not the Avon lady."

"You should have said something sooner." Her voice sounded unsteady. "I could have shot you."

"Next time I'll be sure to send a telegram and flowers," he muttered.

Her voice was tense. "Why are you here? It's not Trace, is it? He hasn't been shot or anything . . . ?"

"Trace is just fine."

Her breath hissed out slowly. "Then why —"

"He wanted me to see how things were going here." The lie slid smoothly off Wolfe's lips. "So here I am."

She leaned back, trying to get a better look at his face. "I don't believe you. Trace would have told me if you were coming." She cleared her throat. "Do you mind? You're flattening me against this counter."

Wolfe silently cursed and moved a few inches back. "Reflex. Sorry."

"Why did you lock me in that closet? And who broke my window?"

"We can discuss it later. Let's get your power back on first."

She shoved against him, her body brushing him from knee to chest. When she turned her head, her lips were only inches away.

Concentration deserted Wolfe for a moment. With an effort he managed to focus again. "Where's your fuse box?" he asked gruffly. He sure as hell knew where *his* was.

She didn't answer, her cheeks touched with color as he backed out of reach.

"Well?"

"Beside the kitchen door." Her voice was hoarse. "I'll go outside and check."

"Hold on. Let me take a look first."

She turned slowly, her face pale in the half shadows. "What aren't you telling me?"

Wolfe shrugged. "It never pays to take chances. Trace should have taught you that." Taking her arm, he steered her toward the far side of the kitchen, away from all the broken glass. "I'll go out this way."

"You still remember your way around after all this time?"

"I remember a lot of things." Most of them were bad, but Wolfe didn't mention that. "What's with the body I feel against my leg?" She'd definitely expect him to be curious about her four dogs.

"That's probably Baby. She has to get her nose right in the middle of everything."

"Baby?" Wolfe managed to sound puzzled.

"The four-legged kind. Shine that light

86

down here." Crouching near the door, Kit was instantly surrounded by eager, panting dogs. "Meet my newest pupils."

Wolfe ran his light from dog to dog, pretending to be surprised. "Four of them? You never do anything by half, do you?"

Kit smoothed Diesel's fur. "I'm a sucker for a beautiful pair of eyes."

"I'm a leg man myself." Wolfe cleared his throat as the penlight flashed on her long, slender thighs.

"You still haven't told me what you're doing here."

"I told you, Trace asked me to —"

"You never could lie to me, Wolfe." Kit jerked down her nightshirt as she walked to the side door. "The fuses are out here, by the way."

"I'll take care of it." Wolfe cut in front of her and checked the darkness. "Looks quiet enough." When he glanced down, the dogs were right beside him, their noses pressed against the glass door. "Back, you guys."

"Down," Kit said quietly.

Instantly, all four dogs were on the floor, motionless.

"Stay."

Wolfe raised an eyebrow. "I'm impressed. You and the dogs had better stay inside just the same." As he held up the penlight, his other hand edged to the pistol hidden at the small of his back. "How far to that fuse box?"

"About six feet. It's just above the power meter on your right."

Wolfe opened the door and listened. Nothing moved. He felt no hint of Cruz or any other intruders. Silently, he followed the wall to the fuse box. "Circuits have been reset. Hold on," he called.

A moment later, light flooded from the windows. He closed the box and turned to find Kit staring at him. "Something wrong?"

"You look . . . different."

As a welcome, it could have been worse, Wolfe thought. And it was true, he did look different — bigger, faster and harder. Now there was a coldness in his eyes that made people step out of his way.

Inside the door, he turned to face her, ready for more arguments. But she surprised him again, gripping his chin and turning his head up toward the light.

"You're bleeding, you idiot. I'm going to kill Trace for not telling me you were coming." Kit leaned closer, frowning. "What was that noise from the kitchen?"

"Someone broke in. He was alone, and I

handled it." Wolfe tried to pull free, uncomfortably aware of the heat triggered by contact with her body. "Forget about my face." His cheek was swelling from the one blow Emmett had managed to land. "It's nothing."

But Kit moved closer, pressing him against the refrigerator door. "I'll clean it better than you would." She dodged under his arm, her long legs flashing in a way that left Wolfe's throat dry. "Why didn't you say something about it before?" she called.

"There wasn't a lot of time for conversation. It's just a scratch anyway." Distracted by what felt like blood dripping into his eye, he let her shove him down into a chair beside the sink. "Kit, you don't have to —"

"Shut up, Wolfe."

"Yes, ma'am," he said meekly. He was trying not to notice the warm brush of her fingers, the pressure of her breast against his shoulder. He especially didn't want to watch how her nightshirt rose over her thighs as she reached into cabinets and opened drawers. The sight of her was making his body respond in all the right ways, which happened to be the *wrong* ways.

"What are you staring at?"

Wolfe cleared his throat. "The cabinets.

Ah . . . you painted them blue," he said gruffly.

"I got tired of all that white." Kit looked across the kitchen at the shattered glass. "He did a nice job on my window." Her voice tightened. "Who was it?"

"Big guy, built like a fire hydrant. Ugly as the backside of a bull."

"That's Emmett. He's convinced there's treasure hidden here somewhere. He came back just like he said he would. I wish I could have seen his face when you stopped him." She frowned at Wolfe. "Always being a hero. I see you've gotten your leg hurt as well as your face."

"I'm fine."

But she vanished into the bathroom and returned with a handful of boxes and bottles. "Take off your pants."

"Kit, I don't think —"

"Strip, Wolfe. Otherwise, I'll cut them off you."

"I'll pass."

"You think the sight of your naked butt is going to make me faint dead away?"

Wolfe felt his body tighten as she stared at the blood on his dark pants. "There's no need to get upset."

"Who's upset? I'm just being practical, but you're being the same as you always were. Mr. Tall, Dark and Silent, always in control." He tried turning to look at her, but she held his face still. "That was your nickname in high school, didn't you know?"

Somehow it didn't surprise him. High school had been a blur of anger and confusion. The Russians could have invaded, for all he would have noticed. "Can't say as I did."

Kit finished cleaning the cut at his jaw, and then her gaze cut down to his leg. "Are you going to take your pants off or not?"

"Definitely not."

Her eyes glinted as she went for his belt. They circled one another for a moment and Wolfe realized she wasn't giving up. With a sigh he grabbed alcohol and cotton from the tray beside her on the counter, then removed a blood-soaked pad covering the wound just visible beneath his torn pants. He cleaned the area thoroughly, threaded a surgical needle, and went to work.

She stood watching, her hands locked at her sides.

Wolfe put in two precise stitches. As wounds went, this was only a scratch, so the sewing was no problem. He'd already shot himself up with antibiotics and covered the area with a gauze bandage, but he should have closed the wound sooner.

No time like the present.

With steady fingers he held the torn skin in place and shoved the needle home.

"You should take something for the pain."

"Not necessary." Wolfe put in another neat stitch.

Kit swallowed and looked away. "You've done this before, haven't you?"

"Basic field medicine." He shrugged. "No big deal."

"I can see you don't need me." She pushed away from the counter, her body stiff. "I'll get Trace's bed ready."

"Don't go to any trouble. I can sleep down here on the couch." Not that he'd do much actual sleeping.

"You're sleeping in a bed, understood?" Her voice was tight. "It's the least I can do."

Turning, she collected the leftover bottles and bandages. When her gaze fell on the dogs, who were watching the byplay quietly, she frowned. "Do you hear that?"

"I don't hear anything."

"That's my point. The dogs didn't bark at you. What's going on here?"

Baby's tail thumped on the floor, and Diesel gave a happy little yelp.

Kit glared at both of them. "What kind of guard work is that, you two?"

Baby's tail thumped harder.

"Something's wrong." Kit rounded on Wolfe. "Have you been here before? Is that why my dogs know you? There's no way they would let a stranger in here without a fuss."

Wolfe cut a new piece of gauze and covered the wound loosely. The easiest thing to do now would be to brush away her memories, painting out all the unwanted details that would make her ask difficult questions. But he couldn't make her forget. He needed to stay inside the house. That would be the best way to keep her safe while he took a closer look at her dogs.

"What's going on?" she demanded, standing stubbornly in front of him.

"Just a friendly visit, like I told you. When I came in the dogs growled a little. Then they smelled my hands for a long time, but they didn't seem upset. Maybe they could sense that I'm not hostile."

"Mind reading isn't one of their skills, Wolfe. I don't buy any of this."

"You must be sleepy. I'll finish up down here and take care of the window," he said quietly. "Go on to bed."

Kit shook her head. "Not until you explain."

"We'll talk about it tomorrow."

"You bet we will. If I weren't exhausted, I'd make you talk now." She winced a little, rubbing her hip. "The dogs don't sleep in the house." She yawned. "They need to go outside to the kennel."

"I'll take care of it."

She didn't move.

"Go on. Get some sleep, Kit."

"I always hated it when you gave me orders. I see you're still doing it." She looked away. "You're not going to tell me why you're really here, are you?"

"I already told you. Trace asked me to —"

"Skip it." She took an irritated breath. "You know the bad part? Part of me really wants to believe you. But that's my problem, not yours." Her back stiffened. "The bed will be ready for you upstairs."

Wolfe could see the muscles tighten in her neck. "Thank you."

"Don't thank me yet. Tomorrow you'd better go. It will be easier that way." She turned away, the dogs close behind her.

He felt as if she'd pulled all the warmth from the room when she left.

CHAPTER SIX

He didn't do windows.

He knew how all right, but it wasn't in the job description.

Wolfe glared down at the mess at his feet and shook his head. Apparently there was a time and a place for everything. If he didn't clean up the glass all over the kitchen floor and replace the pane, one of the dogs could get hurt.

He rubbed his neck, remembering that Kit's frugal father always kept panels of uncut glass for repairs. Unless she'd changed things, they would be neatly stacked, separated by particleboard, out in the shed near the kennels.

Ten minutes later, glass crunched beneath his feet. Baby whined, watching him from across the room while he worked.

The dogs sniffed the broken glass, but didn't come closer. Was that normal, Wolfe wondered? He didn't have a clue, so he'd list it in his report, along with everything else.

After he dug the remaining fragments

out of the window frame, Wolfe ran his fingers over the inside pocket of his shirt, where the map was now carefully stowed until he could get it analyzed. Why had Emmett been carrying a diagram of the ranch, especially one that looked new?

The simple answer was that the map stemmed from the old local belief that a treasure was buried somewhere on the O'Halloran ranch. Every few months Kit's father used to catch someone prowling around, digging in the deserted washes near the house.

But why a *new* map?

He stopped as Kit's phone echoed somewhere down the hall. After two rings, her answering machine clicked in, and Wolfe went back to work lining the clean window frame with putty. The dogs watched him, absorbing every move, while the moon's silver eye rose above the mesa.

Carefully he lifted a six-foot pane of glass over the frame and checked the placement. As a teenager he'd worked as a handyman for extra money, and one summer he'd learned the glazier's trade. Now the techniques came back to him, putty moving smoothly under his knife. It felt good to watch something take shape beneath his hands for a change.

Not like running surveillance out of a filthy shack in the jungles of Paraguay while you tried to track a money trail that led to Mexico or Burma or downtown Chicago.

As he laid down the last line of putty, Wolfe saw his reflection, cool and silver against the new glass. There were deep shadows at his cheeks, and his eyes were the color of bitter coffee. He looked tough and aloof, as if he'd seen too much too fast — and he had. Those memories were carved into his face, leaving a distance that could not be crossed.

But Kit had crossed it. He didn't frighten her in the slightest. He thought about how she had nearly decked him, then threatened him with her rifle, and a faint half smile crept over his face. No, she wasn't the kind of woman who ran from hard problems.

He feathered his knife along the frame, sealing the glass with long, deft strokes. When he was finally done, he faced his own reflection once again.

He was a hard man, trained to have the hands and mind of a killer, but there in the moon's cool light, Wolfe was reminded that he could also be surprisingly gentle.

CHAPTER SEVEN

The waitress at the Blue Coyote Truck Stop looked as if her feet hurt and she needed a smoke.

But there was no mistaking the interest in her eyes or the way she bent over the counter to expose the front of her low-cut uniform. "Want anything else with your coffee, honey?" She put one hand on her hip. As if she learned it in the movies, Cruz thought. "Anything at all, you just tell me right out."

"More coffee will be fine, thanks." The soup had been hot and filling, all he really needed. The coffee was an unthinkable luxury.

It was a Wednesday night, almost 2:00 a.m. She'd have cash from tips in her pockets and credit cards, too. But he wouldn't touch the cards. Too dangerous.

"The praline pie is pretty good tonight. Lemon meringue's fair. You look like you could use a couple slices." The waitress topped off his coffee and pushed the worn metal canister of sugar toward him.

"No thanks. I don't eat sugar." He had to keep his body clean. Strength came first. With his strength restored, he could concentrate on revenge.

His eyes flickered through the quiet restaurant. There was no one else around except for a short-order cook bustling somewhere in the kitchen.

When the waitress leaned in closer, he focused and made her forget everything but that she was tired and ready for a smoke. Her eyes went blank and she stood behind the counter, motionless.

He cleaned out both of her pockets and moved around the counter, fishing through the purse she kept pushed to the back of the low shelf.

Ninety-seven dollars. Car keys, too. He'd risk driving for an hour, no more. He knew exactly where his brother would be waiting.

Wind howled across the floodlit courtyard. The rain that had been threatening all night finally broke loose, pelting the windows with small bits of gravel.

Time to go.

The cook yelled. Cruz released the waitress from the images he'd just constructed.

"No dessert." The waitress looked dizzy for a second. Then she turned, frowning, her eyes predatory. "Hell, just what *do* you do for fun, honey?"

Cruz watched a layer of oil gleam on the surface of his coffee. Once he had trained for the sheer joy of being the best. He had laughed at danger.

But three years ago, something had changed. At first it was little details like reflexes off by mere seconds. After that had come the memory blips and subtle mood shifts. His handlers had told him not to worry, that the changes were to be expected. Stress, they said. The result of constant training.

Like a fool he'd swallowed their lies, one after another. He had never questioned what he was told, not even when the mood shifts became severe.

That's when they'd increased his medicine, and the new surgeries had begun. He'd believed every lie they'd told him, despite the continued deterioration of his mind and body.

Cruz drank his coffee slowly, savoring its heat even though he knew it was a poor mix of bad beans and sloppy preparation. After months in captivity, fed from an IV with only enough nourishment to keep his heart and vital systems functioning, even bad coffee was ambrosia.

"Looks like you could use a little fun." The waitress was very close now, her fingers on top of his. Cruz had a clear line of sight down the front of her dress, and there was no bra anywhere. The woman couldn't have made her invitation any plainer.

He couldn't have been any less interested.

"I'll take my bill now." His face held no emotion as he pushed away the empty cup and stood up. He'd taken a chance to come inside only because he'd needed food, cash, and little time to warm up. He'd already dismantled the single surveillance camera at the front door, and he'd handle the waitress in a moment.

"You're leaving already? Honey, there's no bus for another three hours, and I know you don't have a car."

His fingers shot around her wrist. "How do you know that?"

"I saw you walk in from the woods, that's all. Kinda odd, I thought, but hey, it's a free country. You ain't one of those damned tree huggers, are you?"

"What else did you see?"

"You looked around everywhere and you didn't go near any cars, so I figure you walked from one of those parks up north. We get hikers in here now and again. They look thin, the same way you do."

He released her wrist. She'd made a lucky guess, nothing more.

He put a five-dollar bill on the counter — one of hers — and smoothed it with his fingers. He had forgotten what it felt like to have money of his own.

For too many years he'd let other people control him. He'd been an empty-headed killing machine pumped up with the certainty that he was some new, advanced kind of hero.

Now he knew better.

"Keep the change." Cruz picked up the backpack that was never far from his reach, scanning the parking lot outside.

"Hell, honey, why not tell me to go suck exhaust and die? And where are you going at two in the morning anyway? If you ask me, you don't look so good."

"I'm fine."

"Maybe you are, but the nearest town is fifty miles away, and that's a damn long hike."

He could walk twice that distance. He could run it easily, in fact, despite his long confinement. *Good genes,* Cruz thought wryly.

He studied the waitress's face, sifting through the fairly boring mind beneath her straw-colored hair. "I'm catching a ride to El Paso. I've got friends waiting for me there," he said calmly, pleased that all the old training was in place.

Never tell the truth when a lie will do. Never trust anyone outside the team.

She rubbed her wrist slowly as if it hurt. "You one of those G-Men working over at the New Mexico base?"

Nothing changed on Cruz's face. "What makes you ask?"

"Don't know. Your eyes, maybe. You don't say much, but you don't miss much either. And you sure don't like the idea of anyone watching you."

So she wasn't as stupid as he'd first thought. "I'm FBI," he said quietly. "And I've never been here, understand? If I hear you told anyone different, I'll be back and that won't be good for you." As he spoke, he shaped the warning, driving it like a knife into her brain until she nodded, looking disoriented.

"FBI." She rubbed her forehead as if it hurt. "Sure — never seen you," she repeated.

He sensed that she was afraid of him now. Pleased, he tightened his knapsack over one shoulder. After reinforcing his warning and wiping her memory of him, he headed out into the night, but it was hard to focus. His head ached and the coffee left him a little dizzy.

He heard the rumble of distant tires and the blast of a truck horn. He needed to make contact with his brother as soon as possible.

Maybe he'd chance taking the waitress's car and driving to Albuquerque. He had her keys now, and he'd picked up the model and color of her car. Cruz hesitated, considering the idea. He'd made a deep wipe of her mind, but he wasn't sure how long it would last. In recent weeks his skills had become unreliable. Sometimes he could pull the faintest thought from a crowded room. Other times he could barely remember his own name.

And if the waitress reported the theft, the police would be watching for her car.

The truck horn blasted again and he swung open the restaurant's grimy front door, smiling up at the nonfunctioning surveillance camera as he left.

The truck didn't seem to be slowing down, and a second rig was straining up the hill maybe a hundred yards back. Cruz took in the Illinois plates and the muddy windshield. Long-haul trucker with no reason to stop at a crummy little diner three hours from anywhere.

He flipped up the collar of his stolen jacket. He liked the feel of the sheepskin lining and the soft suede body. He couldn't remember the last time he'd worn a coat this nice.

Turning away from the well-lit parking lot, he melted into the trees while an owl called somewhere in the night.

An unmarked white sedan pulled into the parking lot from the other direction. Drawing back into the shadows, Cruz studied the two men who got out.

Hard faces. Concealed carry holsters.

If they hadn't been sent by Ryker, they were sent by someone close enough that it didn't matter.

The restaurant door opened. The waitress walked out, looking confused. She stared at the parking lot as if she didn't know where she was, and the men from the white car started walking toward her — the last thing Cruz needed.

Somewhere the owl cried its two-note dirge and Cruz followed the sound, his eyes cold and focused.

The owl's dark shape cut through the darkness, headed back toward the bright lights and the woman who was turning slowly, studying the parking lot. Like a sleepwalker, she crossed beneath the big mercury lamps, one hand shading her eyes.

"Ma'am, is something wrong?" The two men were walking faster now.

Cruz watched the owl with renewed intensity. He *wasn't* going back into a cage.

Not ever again.

The owl circled, dropped. The second truck was up the hill now, motor racing as it picked up speed. Cruz focused, feeling pain behind his eyes, down his neck. But the pain brought power.

The owl folded its wings and plummeted, talons extended, striking the waitress, who covered her head vainly. Cruz focused on the attack as the owl surged upward and plunged again.

The men from the sedan were shouting now as they ran toward her.

The waitress stumbled and then ran out into the path of the oncoming lights. . . .

And screamed.

Moonlight crept slowly across the old adobe walls. The kennels were quiet. A hawk cried somewhere in the night, and the long wings of a hunting owl hissed over the juniper trees.

Baby awoke suddenly, shooting to her

feet and waking Diesel, who was curled up beside her. She sniffed the air, her body tense.

In the shimmering glow her fur looked like dark water beneath new ice. Only her eyes held the snap of heat and restless energy. Though she didn't move, all the other dogs awoke.

Soon they were standing together, noses to the wind, painted in cold moonlight.

CHAPTER EIGHT

Caught in sleep, one foot in dreams, Kit heard a low, steady *tap-tap* on the roof, a rare sound in the desert.

Yawning, she burrowed back under the covers. During the last storm, Baby and Diesel had raced through the mud like creatures gone mad, scampering in circles, their heads raised to the sheeting rain. Butch and Sundance had simply lain down and rolled until they were completely encased in brown slime.

A dark nose rooted under her quilt, searched right and left, and then a second nose appeared.

"How did you guys get out of the kennel?"

Downstairs, pots clanged. Kit took a deep breath as she smelled the unmistakable aroma of coffee brewing.

Wolfe.

Hit with a sudden dose of memories from the night before, she closed her eyes. She'd heard the sound of breaking glass, armed herself with her father's rifle and moved quietly down the hall. . . .

And then Wolfe had knocked her weapon away, tossed her over his shoulder like a sack of potatoes and dropped her in the closet.

Baby's head appeared from under the quilt. Her tail banged loudly on the edge of the bed, signaling keen excitement. Diesel wiggled out next and laid his head at an angle over Baby's.

"High-handed jerk," Kit muttered. She didn't care if the man was back or how he looked. She didn't care why he'd come back either. She'd had a crush on Wolfe Houston for way too long, but it was over now. He was no good for her, and nothing was ever going to happen between them, so she'd packed up her memories and shipped them off to the same dead letter box that held her belief in Santa Claus and the tooth fairy.

He wasn't swooping into her life again, no way. She was *over* him and that was final. Guaranteed. Definite. The thought made her feel good.

Kit frowned at what Wolfe had told her about Emmett's return and break-in. The man was nuts as well as nasty, and she had called to report him to the local police before she'd gone to sleep. The deputy was the son of her father's best friend, and he'd assured her that Emmett would be taken into custody the following day.

More pots rattled downstairs. Diesel took off at a run, clearly hoping for edible handouts.

What was the freaking man doing down there, cooking for the 75th Infantry Division? Sighing, Kit looked at Baby, who gave two quick barks. "Okay, I'm coming. After a quick shower, everything is bound to look better. But I've made up my mind. I'll eat his food — assuming it's edible — and drink the coffee I smell brewing, and then I'll kick him out on his tight and very attractive butt. I don't need his kind of trouble back in my life. Not for a second."

She'd dreamed about him for ages and planned her future around possibilities that involved him. But somewhere in the last months working with these four special dogs, Kit had grown up and gotten over her fantasies. She had important things to do with her life and she wouldn't go on looking over her shoulder, hoping for an illusion.

Baby's tail thumped.

Pleased with her determination, Kit threw off the covers — and fell back with a groan.

Pain hammered at her back. Her knees felt frozen. She tried again to sit up and grimaced, wishing she could tell herself it was nothing. But she knew what her X-rays looked like. After fifteen months, she'd read enough online medical articles to be nearly as conversant with her illness as her family doctor.

But that was books, and this was real. Books didn't capture how pain *felt.*

She studied the room dizzily. Something had made her worse. Something that she couldn't remember.

She forced down deep breaths, trying to relax. More stress meant more tension.

For the first time Kit considered the possibility of getting weaker. Her doctor had warned her the disease might progress, but Kit had been resolutely optimistic. She didn't want to hear about diminishing capability or limited strength.

She gripped her soft quilt, shivering. If she lost joint mobility, she couldn't adequately care for her dogs, which meant giving them up to another trainer. Without strength, she couldn't handle the constant demands of the ranch and that would have to go, too. She couldn't ask Trace to come home and help. This was her world, not his.

She took a sharp breath. She wasn't giving up. There were always new medicines, new techniques —

Tensely, she stared at the top of her nightstand. Her pills were exactly where she'd left them, each day's dose carefully marked in her own handwriting. Last night's compartment was untouched.

Relief blazed through her. In all the turmoil after the break-in, she'd forgotten to take her pills. She'd been watching *Casablanca* and dozed off, and then Wolfe had shown up. For some reason, that part was still a blur.

But there was no more worrying or wondering about why she felt so much worse.

She grabbed the container and gulped down two pills, confident that she'd be better in fifteen minutes, maybe less. Then she could get back to living her life.

With stiff legs, she stood up and tugged down her nightshirt. First, a shower. Second, coffee.

Third, kick Wolfe out of her house.

As the first hot spray of the shower hit her face, Kit sighed in primal pleasure. After allowing herself several long, indulgent minutes under the pounding water, she forced herself to face her situation honestly. Was she really going to throw Wolfe out?

It wasn't that she didn't find him incredibly sexy, because she did. It wasn't that her gut response to his gorgeously chiseled body had changed, because it hadn't. The man still spiked her awareness meter right up into the red zone.

But Kit refused to waste any more time mooning over a man who'd always be a shadow, slipping in and out of her life when he could fit her in around whatever covert mission he was on at the time.

Which brought her to question two: What *was* he doing here?

Kit glared at the steam covering the glass door. He said Trace had asked him to come by. A perfectly reasonable story, except that it didn't ring true. Trace knew she'd always been vulnerable where Wolfe was concerned, and he would have made a point to tell her that his friend was dropping by, so she'd be prepared.

Wolfe couldn't leave New Mexico fast enough all those years ago. He hadn't been back once since he'd joined the Navy, and it wasn't as if he had anything new pulling him home. So why did he appear now?

Either something was wrong with Trace, or Wolfe was lying. Since Kit didn't think he would lie about Trace being fine, that meant he was lying for another reason.

None of the possibilities looked good.

Frowning, she shut off the water and grabbed a towel. It was time to get a few answers from the man who was currently making free with her kitchen.

Which brought her to question three: why hadn't her dogs shown signs of wariness or hostility, or attempted to warn her when he'd arrived? They'd never met Wolfe and had no reason to consider him a friend, but they'd all taken to him immediately.

The question kept gnawing at Kit as she dried her hair and pulled on her oldest, most threadbare jeans. No way was she going to fuss for the man who'd ruined most of her teenage years and a major part of her adult life.

Just by being gorgeous . . . and unavailable.

She took a quick glance in the mirror. Her hair was uneven from the last time she'd cut it. Her face was sunburned and there were faint lines under her eyes. That was A-okay with her, because she wasn't getting dressed up for Wolfe Houston ever again.

Baby stayed one step ahead as Kit headed for the stairs, drawn by the heavenly smell of coffee. Had the man ground fresh beans? The scent seemed to be from a new bag of Jamaican Blue Mountain she'd stashed in her freezer because she hadn't had time to grind it.

Now *that* was strictly hitting below the belt.

Irritated, she strode down the stairs, where more delicious scents assailed her.

Warm maple syrup.

Blueberries and cinnamon.

Pancakes sizzling in fresh butter.

What kind of sneaky pool was the man playing? He'd cooked her favorite things for breakfast. How had he remembered all that?

Kit stopped just outside the doorway, her senses on full alert as Wolfe moved easily around her kitchen. Today he was wearing some kind of tan camouflage pants and a simple white T-shirt, but his shoulders were rippled and his biceps stood out in perfectly cut lines.

Okay, he looked good. Maybe even fantastic. Mouthwatering, in fact. But it meant zip to her. Zilch. Nada. She wasn't falling victim to him ever again. Pancakes and caffeine be damned.

With that thought firmly in mind, she yanked the last button closed on her flannel shirt and stalked into the kitchen, nearly tripping over Butch, who was lying across the threshold.

They were guard dogs. Alert, highly trained service dogs. Hel-lo?

"Are you still here?" Kit snapped, annoyed to see Sundance following every step Wolfe took, while Diesel perched in the spot where food was most likely to drop.

"Looks that way. The state police called. Someone should be here to take a report before noon. There's a big pileup on the interstate, so that's the best they can do." He slid a stack of pancakes onto a plate and pushed it down the counter toward her. "Sit down and eat. You look like you could use something in your stomach."

When he reached for a clean mug from the cabinet, his muscles flexed and Kit realized she was hungry all right, but not for breakfast.

Irritated by her lapse, she moved around him in search of her own mug. As she did, their bodies bumped together, his taut thighs pressing against her hips.

No drooling.

"Sorry." He stepped back carefully, getting another plate.

"Nice of you to cook," she rasped. "But I'm not hungry."

His eyes narrowed. "You're too thin. You should eat."

"What are you, my doctor?" With a glare, she wrestled down a mug and filled it with coffee. The smell of freshly brewed beans made her close her eyes in a wave of abandoned hedonism. "You ground my new stuff." She managed to make it sound like an accusation.

"I couldn't find anything else." He slid silverware across the island. "You want butter on your pancakes?"

Kit stared at him over the rim of her mug. "I told you I'm not hungry." She had barely finished when her empty stomach rumbled loudly.

Wolfe's mouth twitched as he set a small bowl of warmed maple syrup down next to the steaming pancakes. "Whatever you say."

Okay, that was definitely hitting below the belt. She *loved* warm maple syrup. It ranked right up there next to no-holds-barred sex. Not that she was thinking about sex right now.

"Don't you have somewhere to go? Missing plutonium to find or a terrorist cell to infiltrate?"

He flipped a dishtowel over one shoulder, smiling faintly. "The world's at peace for a few hours, it appears."

Kit sat down, nursing her coffee. "They teach you to cook in the New Army?"

"Navy, not Army. And I can cook pancakes fine. Your mom taught me how. Said it was part of a liberal education." Wolfe looked out at the rain coating the windows. "One hell of a lady, your mom." He cleared his throat. "How's the coffee?"

Excellent, and he knew it.

"Okay," Kit said coolly, trying to ignore the seduction of a slab of butter melting over a hot, golden stack of blueberry cinnamon pancakes.

Chill, O'Halloran.

She took a gulp of coffee to keep from reaching for the syrup. "So the world's at peace, is it? That's a relief. Now maybe you'll tell me how you got inside last night without my dogs going berserk."

"Probably because of Trace."

Kit sat up so fast that coffee sloshed over the counter. "He's here?"

"No, not here. Sorry if I said that wrong. I meant because of this." Wolfe pulled a sweatshirt off the chair behind him. "This belongs to Trace. I took it by mistake when I was packing my gear."

Kit frowned at the dark cotton sweatshirt. She didn't recognize it, but it was the

118

kind of thing her brother would wear.

Wolfe held the sweatshirt out to Baby, who sniffed it thoroughly, then tugged it out of Wolfe's hand and carried it across the room.

"Hey, I need that, honey."

Baby barked once, her tail waving in the air.

"She thinks you're playing fetch."

"You mean she expects me to go after her?"

"Not exactly. She's trying to see what you'll do — or what she can get you to do."

Wolfe's mouth curved. He lunged for a dark cotton sleeve, only to grab air.

Baby skidded under a nearby chair.

"How'd she do that?"

"She's very fast. And limber. All of them are."

When Wolfe wasn't looking, Kit snagged a piece of pancake and popped it into her mouth. The syrup and butter melted together on her tongue, so delicious she nearly moaned.

"Did you say something?"

"Not me." Kit took another furtive bite and gave up the fight. Pride had its place, but not where blueberry cinnamon pancakes were involved.

Wolfe made another grab for the sweatshirt. This time Diesel shot under his legs, and the two went down in a sprawl on the floor.

Kit jumped to her feet. "Are you okay? Did you hurt Diesel?"

"We're both fine. Only our pride was hurt. Right, boy?" Wolfe rolled to one elbow, petting Diesel, who licked his face. In a flash, Baby nudged her way into the tangle, followed closely by Butch and Sundance.

"How about some help over here?" Wolfe said, buried beneath four excited, furry bodies.

Kit laughed and finished a wedge of pancakes, the pleasure bordering on a religious experience. "You're the super Navy SEAL guy. You can handle a couple of puppies."

She was surprised when Diesel trotted across the room and dropped something in her lap. The item looked like a white T-shirt, but it was made out of a stretchy fiber Kit hadn't seen before. She examined it slowly. "Is this yours?"

Wolfe stood up and stepped around the clustered dogs. "It's mine, but how did you get it? I left that shirt in my bag."

"Diesel must have found it." Kit fingered the fabric curiously. "What is this stuff? It feels thick like denim, but it's stretchy as yarn, and it's incredibly soft."

"It's something I'm testing for the Navy, a prototype for possible uniform material." He crossed the room, his expression unreadable. "I'd better put it back."

Kit sensed that the fabric was a lot more valuable than Wolfe was letting on. "Another secret?" She tossed him the shirt and watched him fold it and then refold it until the fabric was the size of a dollar bill. "Wow," she murmured.

"Forget you saw that. It's not for public release yet."

"My lips are sealed." She couldn't resist a smile as she watched him reach over a chair and tug Trace's sweatshirt away from Sundance. Outside the rain was easing up. Bars of sunlight broke through the clouds, lighting the mesa.

She was about to question him more about the reason for his visit when he patted his back pocket and pulled out a pager that was vibrating.

"A problem?"

"Just a friend. I'll take it in the other room," he said casually.

A woman friend, Kit thought.

She glared at Wolfe's retreating back. Not that it mattered to *her.* He was a free agent and so was she. Sex with this man was not on her agenda, no matter how amazing his body looked, or how provocative that little half smile he made was.

Kit sighed. Breakfast was over and she had work to do. She had to stop thinking about Wolfe. She could hear his quiet murmurs from the living room, but made no effort to listen in.

Get over him.

When she finished her coffee, the dogs were gathered at her feet. "Anybody feel like a walk?"

Instantly Baby picked up her water dish and shook it from side to side. Butch chased Sundance in a dizzy circle.

Kit smiled at the dogs' response. For a moment she couldn't speak, struck by the force of her sudden pride. A voice whispered that this was the very best work she would ever do, and these were the finest dogs she would ever train.

She had spent two years at college in Tucson, studying hard and dating dutifully, trying to fit in. But she'd missed her family, missed the ranch and the blue expanse of the high desert sky, so when her scholarship was cut back during her third year, she'd come home. Lost Mesa was where she belonged. She didn't mind isolation or hard work. How could she mind when the rewards were so great?

As she crossed the room, Diesel dive-bombed her leg. Butch and Sundance jumped into the air and barked wildly. She grabbed the dogs' leashes and went back to the living room. Wolfe was still talking on the phone, so she held up the leashes and pointed to the door.

Although he nodded, she wasn't sure he was paying attention. Just like Trace, he could stand right beside you, but his attention would be on the other side of the world.

One more reason the man was trouble. As soon as she got back, she would tell him that to his face.

Then she'd thank him politely for breakfast and kick him out on his gorgeous butt before he managed to worm his way back into her life.

She had enough problems.

Wolfe heard the door to the courtyard close. "That's right, sir. No, there's been no sign of Cruz." He watched the four Labs circle Kit, barking insistently. "The dogs are in excellent health and their speed is exceptional." He felt a momentary twinge at reporting on Kit to Ryker, but orders were orders. If he was going to

123

guard the dogs and Kit, he had to understand their strengths intimately.

He shielded his eyes and stretched, relaxing the tension that had been building in his neck since his first sight of Kit. It didn't help that she was drop-dead gorgeous, even with wet hair and no hint of makeup. Her old jeans molded her long legs like a man's perfect sexual fantasy. Not that he was fantasizing about sex with Kit.

As he focused on the distant horizon, the pain in his head faded, and he picked up the thread of Ryker's conversation — an update on the questioning of facility personnel regarding Cruz's escape.

"I'd better get outside, sir. She's taking the dogs for a walk. Yes, I'll check in as arranged." Wolfe's eyes narrowed as he scanned the distant ridge, picking up motion, something that bore no resemblance to a coyote or cougar.

He rang off and headed for the rear of the house.

The man was crouched beneath the shade of a cottonwood tree. After watching him for ten minutes, Wolfe was certain he was a pro. He was quiet and observant and never remained long in one spot, always wiping his tracks clean with a juniper branch.

Even if he was good, Wolfe was a whole lot better.

The man barely had time to gasp before Wolfe's fingers clamped over his windpipe. After a short, fierce struggle, he sagged and Wolfe jerked his wrists behind him, sliding on plastic tactical restraints.

The heavy lifting was done. Now it was time to ask some questions.

Quickly, Wolfe took stock. His unconscious captive wore desert camouflage pants, a tan camo shirt and military issue combat boots. A tan canteen rested in a shaded crack between two boulders.

Wolfe squatted down in the wash, but despite a thorough search, he found no wallet, no keys, and no credit cards. All the man carried was a compass, chewing tobacco, and a big high-carbon steel knife that looked a lot like the one Wolfe wore hidden in his own boot. A black hydration pack and a small LifePack with rations were stowed beneath the nearby sagebrush, along with a first-aid kit and some water purification tablets. Wolfe studied the hard features streaked with dark face paint, certain that he'd never seen this man before.

Mercenary? Common criminal?

A simple voyeur?

He looked back up the hill. After a quick inspection, he found a pair of expensive tactical-grade binoculars hidden between two boulders.

This was no garden-variety peeping Tom.

At his feet the man gave a little lurch as he regained consciousness. Wolfe leveled the carbon steel blade at his face.

Neither said a word, each silently assessing tactical scenarios and possible outcomes. In Wolfe's experience, the only soldiers who blustered and threatened were the ones in movies. In real life, nothing happened for hours. Then things moved in a blur, fast and silent, with no time for posturing or ego. Death often came on a whisper.

The wind shook the branches of a small piñon pine. Green needles scattered in the restless sunlight as Wolfe covered his captive's mouth with duct tape before things got noisy.

The man showed no hint of emotion when Wolfe moved the knife to his neck, just above the carotid artery. The narrowed eyes turned defiant as his jaw worked back and forth.

Too late Wolfe recognized the odd sawing movement of his mouth. Dropping fast with one knee on the man's chest, he slit the duct tape and pried open the locked jaw.

White bubbles trailed over Wolfe's fingers. His captive's face contorted in a grimace and his body jerked twice.

He didn't move again.

The poison capsule must have been hidden inside a false tooth, where it could be accessed and crushed easily.

Wolfe checked the man's pulse and scanned the nearby slope in case there was backup waiting among the trees, but only shadows raced over the ridge. A dying wind shook the branches of a nearby sage bush.

After dragging the body beneath a stark granite outcropping, Wolfe returned for the man's equipment. When that was moved, he swept the slope clean of footprints and drag lines with the same branch the dead man had used earlier. With every trace of their presence wiped clean, Wolfe settled back in the shadows and fingered his encrypted cell phone.

He knew that Ryker was going to want every detail.

The phone rang once. "Ryker here. What have you got, Bravo?"

"First contact, sir."

"Cruz?"

"Negative. No ID or personal information on the man and he died before interrogation. He had a poison capsule hidden in his mouth."

Ryker snapped a low curse. "What have you got that we can use?"

"His pack, his rations and his binoculars. Nothing else."

"Bag them and sit tight. I'll send in a removal team, but not until nightfall. Were you hit?"

"Negative, sir."

"Hold on, Bravo."

As he waited, Wolfe studied the nearby ridge, then checked the courtyard where Kit was doing some kind of throw and retrieve game with the dogs.

Ryker came back on the line. "I've authorized pickup priority for the body tonight, Bravo. Moonrise won't be until 0224 hours, so I'll get a team to you between 0100 and 0200 hours. Meet them at the insertion point."

"Copy."

"Now get the body out of sight. There's an old BLM service shack three hundred meters west of your present location."

Wolfe didn't have to wonder how Ryker knew his position. The chip imbedded in his shoulder provided a constant GPS locator reference — and that was only part of its tactical use. "Copy, sir."

"Be sure you bag a sample of that poison. It may help us pull an ID on your dead friend."

"Understood."

There was a sudden burst of activity below Wolfe. He saw Kit race along the wall of the kennel. "Sir, looks like something's wrong down at the O'Halloran ranch."

"Get on it, soldier. Whatever happens, remember that Cruz is out there. You won't see him, you won't hear him, but he'll be there. And I want that bastard *alive*."

The line cut to static. Wolfe could see Kit talking on a phone, moving down the hill. He switched on a small headset, listening in on her call. There was no mistaking the urgency in her voice as she talked to her vet. Diesel appeared to be having some kind of respiratory attack and Kit was heading to the vet's clinic in Santa Fe.

When her old Jeep fishtailed down the gravel driveway, Wolfe was out of sight behind her in a nondescript pickup truck with Arizona plates.

CHAPTER NINE

Kit paced back and forth beside the big metal examining table where Diesel lay listlessly. Liz Merrigold, her vet, gently tested the dog's neck and abdomen, a frown between her eyes.

"How is he, Liz? Is it a virus or a digestive problem? Don't tell me it's distemper, because I know I gave Diesel the medicine you —"

"Would you please shut up?" The petite veterinarian shone a penlight into Diesel's eyes, watching his response.

"Sorry." Kit took a deep breath and stared at the nearby wall, where a big poster announced summer internships for exceptional college students.

"Los Alamos," she read, trying to distract herself. "Doesn't your brother work there? Something classified, right?"

Liz didn't answer.

"You told me that the two of you used to work together on projects in college." Kit stared at the bright yellow poster, afraid to look at Diesel's motionless body.

"My brother has far too big an ego to allow a mere female into his perfectly ordered lab for long. Now can I work here, please?"

Kit turned away and ran a hand through her hair as she studied a public health poster. "Do you think it's Valley Fever?" She leaned down, scanning the chart. "I thought that was limited to Arizona and California." She turned back quickly. "Liz, you don't think that Diesel has —"

"Kit, let me *work.*"

"Right. Sorry. Very sorry." Kit took another deep breath and shut up. If anyone could help Diesel, it was Liz. Despite their relative isolation in Santa Fe, the trim, forty-something veterinarian still published academic papers, traveled to medical conferences twice a year, and was obsessive about staying current with the advances in her field.

After what felt like hours — but was probably no more than five minutes — Liz gave Diesel a gentle scratch behind the ears and stood up. Her fingers tapped on her stethoscope. "Why don't you stay here and keep Diesel company until I get back?"

"What's wrong?"

"Give me a minute. I need to go check a reference on my computer."

She was gone before Kit could argue or demand answers. Anxious and impatient, Kit sat down next to Diesel, who licked her hand weakly. "You're going to be fine. Don't worry, big guy." She kept her voice firm and comforting. "Tonight we'll take you back home. You'll be digging in the dirt and chasing Frisbees before midnight. I promise," she said fiercely.

Diesel stared up at her and his tail thumped once.

"You're going to be fine. You *have* to be fine. If you're not, I —"

The door opened. Liz came in with a thick medical book under her arm. "If he's not what?"

"Nothing."

"It wasn't nothing, Kit. Worrying about Diesel is normal, nothing to hide."

"It's not only Diesel. They've all been acting odd."

The veterinarian stared at Kit, surprised. "You mean the other dogs have been experiencing respiratory problems, too?"

"No, they just act strange — that's the only way to put it, Liz. They stare up at the mesa and make a funny little whimper, almost like they're in pain."

Liz put down the stethoscope she had

used on Diesel. "When did this start happening?"

"Four or five days ago. It was so subtle I didn't notice at first."

"And they do it at the same time?"

Kit reviewed the events of the last few days and nodded. "Baby seems to be the most restless. It's almost like she's watching for something. She loves the rain, but I don't think it's that."

Liz walked around the examining table. "Maybe a family of coyotes have moved in or the weather is about to change. Or they could be on edge, sensing the cougar you told me about." She smiled as Diesel nuzzled her fingers. "I wouldn't worry about it."

"Can you tell me what's wrong with Diesel?"

Liz put her medical book on the examining table. "I need to run more tests, take some blood work. Maybe by midday tomorrow I'll have something definite."

"He's not staying here overnight," Kit said tightly.

"You don't trust me?" Liz stiffened. "After all these years, if you can't trust me . . ."

"It's not you, Liz. I want the dogs with me. It's my job to take care of them. I won't have them forever, you know."

"And that bothers you?"

"Of course. But that's part of the job I'm hired to do."

Diesel roused, licking Kit's hand.

"It would be irresponsible to pull Diesel out of here before he's strong enough." Liz shook her head. "For you to drive him back to the ranch would be plain stupid, and you're not a stupid person."

"If there are any negative developments —"

Liz snapped the medical textbook open and pointed to a bookmarked page. "Open your eyes, Kit. Diesel is very sick. He could have any one of a dozen illnesses in here. Come to think of it, you don't look so good either."

"I don't know what —"

"You keep rubbing your hip and wincing whenever you bend down to pet Diesel. What's going on?"

"I haven't been feeling well, that's all."

Liz studied her face. "I'm worried about you. You're working too hard with no help."

"I'm insulted." Kit kept her tone light. "You're telling me that I've gone to seed. Is that your professional opinion?"

Liz slid her stethoscope around her neck. "I'm worried about you as a friend as well as a doctor, Kit. I've known your family since I first moved here."

"Watch out. Diesel is going to —" Kit nudged her friend out of the way a second before the big puppy struggled to his feet. With a wrenching spasm, he spilled his last meal over the examining table. Oblivious to the mess, Kit spoke soothingly to Diesel as another round of spasms began. She didn't pull away when her sleeve came within striking range of the sick animal.

The vet moved beside Diesel, checking his pulse. "This is the best place for him, Kit. If you're really worried, you can sleep here tonight. I'll put a foldout cot in here, and the other dogs can stay, too."

Kit hesitated and then shook her head. "I'll be back later. Then we can see how he's doing."

"You aren't driving all the way back to the ranch, are you?"

"No, I'll stay with Miki here in town. She has a sofa bed."

"Blood tests aren't instant, you know. I may not have answers until tomorrow." Liz dropped her stethoscope into a drawer and rubbed her neck as if it hurt. "Go over to Miki's, get some rest and leave Diesel to me. That's what you're paying me for, re-member?" Her cell phone rang and she sighed. "If anything changes here, I'll call you immediately, I promise. Now I really do have to take this."

Golden light shimmered over restless water.

Kit closed her eyes, trying to relax. She was floating in Miki's heated saltwater pool while her dogs amused themselves nearby. Liz had called to report that Diesel was finally sleeping and he looked much better. Until he woke up, Liz advised her against coming back and agitating him.

Kit watched Butch and Sundance gnaw on rubber chew toys, while Baby methodically demolished a dog bone. Closing her eyes, she ran a hand through her hair, feeling the sun's heat on her upturned face. She had never realized just how *hard* it was to relax and do nothing.

Her old friend, Miki Fortune, drifted on an orange float nearby, rattling off details of her recently failed romance.

"Do I have wrinkles on my stomach?" Miki glared down at her stomach. She twisted to one side, staring at the tiny fold of fat that appeared when she moved. "Like it or not, our bodies define us. Susan Sontag says that . . . oh, I can't remember. It's too gorgeous out here to think."

"You're in great shape, Miki."

"No thanks to exercise. It never works. Besides, who has energy after ten hours hunched over photographic paper and chemical baths?"

"Why don't you get a digital camera like the rest of the civilized world?" Kit hid a smile, knowing full well that this would trigger a frenzy.

"*Digital?* Digital is for people with no sense of history or technique. Film may be a lot like gambling, but you see the moment the paper changes in the chemical bath, and it takes your breath away. That's what the cavemen must have felt like when they saw lightning hit a tree and make fire." Miki closed her eyes and sighed. "You did that on purpose — got me ranting again."

"It was a good rant. I bet you feel better now."

"I do. But it's you I'm worried about."

First Liz and now Miki. Why was everyone worrying about her? Was her life that depressing?

Miki lifted her foot and watched water trickle down her toes. "Let's talk about something really important, like when you're going to come down out of that cloud and let a man into your life."

Kit squinted into the sun. "I don't need a man in my life." She hesitated, then took the plunge. "Besides, Wolfe is back."

"*What?*" Miki shot up so fast the float nearly overturned. "Wolfe Houston, your brother's gorgeous friend?"

That about described him. Kit cleared her throat, trying to sound casual. "He showed up last night. Someone tried to break in, too." She frowned at the coincidence of the two events on the same night.

"You shouldn't be out there alone." Miki's face tightened. "Your dogs are great but it's still not safe. And even though you have rifles, I doubt you'd use them on a burglar."

"Everything turned out fine."

Except that Kit could feel Wolfe like a virus, threatening to invade her bloodstream again. "He was still at the ranch talking on the phone when I left this morning." She made a sound of disgust. "When Diesel got sick, I forgot everything else. I'm not even sure where Wolfe went, but he can take care of himself and he knows where I keep a spare key. Meanwhile, I'm going to be fine. You are looking at a woman who is in remission from the Wolfe virus." It was a slight lie, but Kit was more determined than ever to drive him out of her mind.

"Are you sure about that?"

Kit stretched broadly. "I am completely over the man, Miki. There's no cause for worry."

"How can you be over him? You've been obsessed about Wolfe Houston for years and nothing has ever happened. To be over him, something has to happen so you can get him out of your system once and for all."

"Something as in . . . ?"

"Something as in sex. Take control for once. Grab the man by his excellent butt, strip off his tight jeans, push him up against the nearest wall and have no-holds-barred monkey sex with him."

Kit swallowed, attacked by a sudden case of lust that felt terminal. The images were tormenting. "He was wearing camo pants, not jeans," she muttered.

"Better and better. A man in uniform." Miki's lips curved in a speculative smile. "Very hot."

"That's a crazy idea," Kit snapped.

"Why? This is your lucky day. Do something about it," Miki urged.

It didn't feel like Kit's lucky day. It felt like a recipe for disaster. She wasn't cool and confident like Miki. She was big on obsessing about things, too. "Forget about it because it's not going to happen. He won't be here long enough. The man is the ultimate drifter."

"All the more reason to act *now.*" Miki leaned forward. "One night. Great lust. Fabulous sex. Then he's gone and you've got him out of your system. Boom, insanity over."

"I'm perfectly happy the way I am." It was almost true. Kit ran the ranch by herself. She was considered one of the top ten dog trainers in the United States, and her personal credit rating was almost back in the stable zone. Her only real concern was her health, but having a wild night of lust wasn't going to change that.

"What you need is great sex," Miki repeated. "With Wolfe."

"What I *need* is a month's vacation in Tahiti."

"Sex is better than Tahiti any day. Plus, it doesn't take twenty hours in a stuffy plane eating nothing but salted peanuts to get there."

"I don't want a man cluttering up my life," Kit said crossly. The words brought a sudden sharp image of Wolfe stripped to a towel as he stepped out of the shower. Kit had seen him that way once when she was thirteen, and she'd never been able to forget his rock-hard stomach and sculpted arms.

Miki rolled her eyes. "Who said anything about life? I'm talking about one night here. Limited, conditional insanity, then everything goes back to normal."

"Can we just forget about this?"

"You can't turn your back on a chance like this." Miki stretched on her inflatable orange raft. "I'm not suggesting you get married, or even involved. You just need to go with the flow. Pick out a man you like, a man who makes you laugh. Then go have some great sex."

The problem was, Kit couldn't remember the last time a man had made her laugh. For that matter, she didn't have a clue about initiating no-holds-barred monkey sex. Her few experiences had been forgettable as opposed to mind-blowing.

"That is a ridiculous idea."

Miki made a disgusted sound. "Listen closely, because I'm only saying this once. You wear white cotton underwear from Kmart. This morning when you got here, you had dog barf all over your jacket. I don't think I'm going out on a limb when I tell you this is not the best way to get a man interested."

Kit watched sunlight glint across the water. "I can't change who I am, Miki."

"I'm not suggesting that you *change.* I'm telling you to loosen up and go beyond your comfort zone for once."

Kit smiled just a little. "So you think the dog barf tends to put a man off his game?"

Miki drew lazy circles in the water with her finger. "I've known some Neanderthals who wouldn't have slowed down if the dog bit them. You know the type."

Kit shifted uncomfortably. She didn't want to discuss her knowledge of men, mainly because there was so little of it. "Let's talk about you instead."

"No way." Miki wriggled again and loosened her swimsuit top. "Today we focus on you. This is your life, Kit O'Halloran." She stared narrowly at Kit. "What's going on with your leg? Why do you wince when you crouch down to pet the dogs?"

"You're imagining things."

"Like hell I am."

"How about we change the subject?"

Her friend paddled closer and splashed water in Kit's face. "Fine, we can move on. We can talk about why Wolfe is here. Maybe he's always been more interested than you thought."

Not likely. Kit was invisible where Wolfe

was concerned. They were in two different universes. And that was probably just as well, because a man like Wolfe was trouble with a neon *T*. "He said Trace told him to check in on me. There's nothing deep or mysterious about it."

Miki's eyes narrowed. "Do you want there to be?"

"Makes no difference to me," Kit snapped. Miki saw too darned much, she decided. That was the problem with best friends. "Can we change the subject now?"

"Why? This is just getting good. So Wolfe strolls back into your life with a lame story that my eight-year-old nephew could top and you *believe* him? I'd say there's a lot more to this whole thing." Miki stared off at the horizon. "Funny how Wolfe always seemed to show up when you were trying to be adventurous."

Kit paddled slowly around the pool. "What do you mean?"

"I mean that Wolfe may consider himself some kind of guardian. After all, he caught Calvin Henderson trying to take off your bra in the ninth grade. He broke up your little party with Jeff Morrison in the back seat of his father's '82 Mustang the day after Christmas."

Kit squirmed uncomfortably at the

memories. She wondered why Wolfe seemed to figure in all the most awkward and embarrassing moments of her life. Thank God he was usually off in some foreign country, doing spooky, dangerous things like her brother did.

"You're reading too much into this, Miki."

"Like hell I am. I am right on the nail about this. It's time you cut through this whole protector routine of Wolfe's." There was a glint in Miki's eyes. "We're going to need good tools, of course."

Kit groaned mentally. Sometimes best friends were a real pain in the butt.

"I'd say some chocolate body paint and a bikini wax should get things started nicely. And tomorrow I'm taking you shopping so you can get some *real* lingerie, and it won't come in basic white cotton either."

"What's wrong with Kmart? I like their stuff just fine. And I *don't* want a bikini wax. I don't even want to think about a *razor* going . . . there."

Miki gave a long-suffering sigh. "Will you please get with the program? It's time you channeled your inner *Cosmo* woman. Tomorrow we're starting from scratch at Victoria's Secret. Push-up bras and crocheted thongs, here we come."

"I've got a bad feeling about this," Kit muttered. On the other hand, playing safe had gotten her exactly nowhere in the relationship department.

Not that she was looking for a long-term relationship, or any other kind of emotional involvement. All she wanted was to find out what she'd missed all these years, and in the process to wipe Wolfe out of her system for good.

Maybe Miki was onto something here.

"There's a Victoria's Secret in Santa Fe?"

"You bet. And you're looking at one of their charter shoppers. I happen to have their credit card in three different colors."

Kit sighed. She still had her doubts about this plan of Miki's. But since her life was tanking pretty fast on its own, she decided some hot lingerie therapy couldn't make matters any worse.

But she was drawing the line at a bikini wax.

CHAPTER TEN

He didn't want to be hearing any of this.

He didn't even want to be *thinking* about it.

Hidden on the other side of the adobe wall, wedged between a cholla cactus and a cottonwood tree, Wolfe could hear every word Kit and Miki said. The wind had died down and the sky bled from pink to purple as day faded gracefully into twilight. Stretched out on the ground, he adjusted the microphone at his ear and frowned. He'd meant to check on Kit's plans for the day to map out appropriate surveillance. But he hadn't expected to hear his own name come up. Especially not in connection with sex.

What the hell was Miki getting at, telling Kit to buy chocolate body paint? And telling her to get a bikini wax — whatever *that* was. Wolfe scowled. He'd been out of the mainstream for a while, but a man still had his imagination. And how had *his* name gotten tossed into the middle of the damn conversation?

He was pretty sure Miki was the problem. Her outrageous suggestions were definitely not helping matters.

Irritated, he watched the dogs run in the back yard, while the past pressed down on him like cold stones. He'd spent three years of high school growing up at the O'Hallorans' house after his mother had left. During those years he'd become pretty close with Kit's family. She was practically a sister after that, and you just didn't think about your sister naked. As for the rest — the thing about her and that dork in the back of his father's Mustang — Wolfe had simply been doing what any brother would do. When he'd read the vibes, he'd snuck up on the car and found the jerk trying to push past Kit's defenses and get into her pants.

Wolfe had seen red. In a haze of fury, he'd yanked open the car door and tossed Bozo-brains out onto the driveway. Kit had been shocked and trembling when she stumbled out of the car, her blouse torn and her face pale. If Wolfe had had his way, he would have wiped Lover Boy across the hood of the Mustang a few times, just to be sure he got the message.

Only the abject embarrassment on Kit's face had stopped him.

Didn't she know she was worth a lot more than a kid who had only one thing on his mind?

He had never mentioned the episode to Trace. He figured he would spare Kit the added embarrassment of her brother's questions. Because Trace was absorbed in repairing a beat-up Chevy at the time, Wolfe had made it his business to keep an eye on Kit and who she was hanging around with during that long, hot summer.

His concern was purely that of a surrogate brother, of course.

Crouching in the tall grass, he surveyed the wash behind Miki's sprawling back yard. He didn't know why in hell he was suddenly dredging up the past. For years he had managed to push the memories out of his mind.

On the other side of the fence, Kit and her friend were arguing — not angrily, but in a comfortable way. They were also speaking some kind of strange female shorthand he didn't understand.

Not surprising. Wolfe didn't spend a lot of time around women these days. It had been months since he'd spent a quiet afternoon with a woman just talking or laughing or arguing about movies, baseball and the state of the world economy.

He heard Miki laugh. Water splashed and then he heard Kit roll off her float. Water rained over the wall above him.

What the heck were they doing in there?

He heard a breathless shout. As he sat up, going for his gun, something flew over his head. Whatever it was hit a cottonwood tree, rolled twice, and drifted down onto the spiny arms of the cholla.

Blue and white stripes. Nylon.

A bikini top. A *tiny* bikini top that curved suggestively around a cactus arm.

He glowered at the cloth dripping water a few feet away and tried not to imagine smooth, wet skin revealed without the bikini top. It had been too long since he'd laughed with a woman, then undressed her slowly and —

Never let it get personal.

Ryker's first training rule burned through Wolfe's mind as he stared at the fabric fluttering in the wind. The bright blue stripes seemed to mock him.

Across the wall, one of the dogs barked sharply. *Baby.* Already Wolfe had begun to distinguish their barks — Diesel's excited and fast, Butch and Sundance sounding very similar, both lower-pitched. Baby's tone was always short and insistent as if she knew she ruled the pack, but her barks usually ended in a vulnerable little sneeze.

He shook his head. If his Foxfire team-mates saw him bonding with a bunch of puppies, his reputation would be shot to hell. Everyone knew that being soft got you killed. The only question was how long it took.

Wolfe clenched his jaw, remembering Ryker's Rule #2.

Never forget that you're different.

He rubbed the small lump on his right shoulder, a personal memento of a pre-dawn ambush in Malaysia. The fracture had been serious, knocking him off duty for six months. Even now it kicked up occasionally when the weather was about to change.

But the pain had a purpose. It reminded him that being careful was the only way to stay alive.

He remembered the sudden shouts that night, followed by curses as the targets realized they were being hunted. Trace had been hit by a grenade fragment and Wolfe had carried him out on his back, despite the fractured shoulder and pain that left him staggering.

A supercilious government observer had overridden the team's usual requirement of secondary surveillance. After satellite intel and local informants had confirmed a safe L.Z., Wolfe had okayed the jump. But they had been attacked at the landing strip, four of their local village support team dying in the crossfire. Two of Wolfe's team had been wounded, including Trace.

Now he knew there were only three things you could trust in life. Yourself, your team, and the probability of fungus where you least wanted it.

From his elevated vantage point, he was able to study every corner of Miki's back yard. Judging by the noise, the dogs were chasing butterflies and Kit and Miki were swimming laps, arguing between every stroke. Wolfe heard something about belly dancing classes — or it might have been belly button piercing. How the hell was he supposed to maintain a secure perimeter and optimum response time when the two crazy females remained highly visible and noisy targets?

So he did what he did best. Staring at the adobe wall, he let the noise slide away, concentrating on Kit and Miki. Breathing deeply, he locked on their energy drift exactly as he had been trained to do, holding the contact, letting the fragile threads become a steel cord, growing tighter and tighter while he built a rich 3D image in his mind and then shot it out into his target area.

Sweat raced down his face.

Burning hot. Terrible, blazing thirst. Going inside . . .

He pulled at the steel cord, molding the tangible heat in his mind. Then he drove it out into their direction.

Thirty seconds.

Ninety. He had to watch the time. Had to remember contact boundaries. Too long and he'd tap out, maybe to unconsciousness. Even now the process still had variables that Ryker and his experts hadn't been able to pin down.

On the other side of the fence, water splashed loudly. "Damn, it's hot out here all of a sudden." It was Miki, sounding irritable.

"No kidding. I could swear it's gotten ten degrees warmer."

"Why don't we go inside and watch a movie? Maybe Jet Li in *Hero.*" Water sloshed and footsteps slapped along the lawn behind the wall.

"Okay, but I've got to go see Diesel soon." Kit sounded breathless. Wolfe saw her climb out of the water and pull on her bikini top, red flowers on top of smooth tanned skin. Even though he instinctively looked away, the memory of her skin burned his eyes and twisted his gut.

Miki trotted across the courtyard toward the house. "You take the shower first, Kit. I'm cranking up Jet Li. That man can manipulate *my* energy zones anytime he wants." Miki stopped suddenly. "I guess I should go get my top."

Out of the corner of his eye, Wolfe saw the blue-and-white cloth fluttering on the cactus. He held an image in his mind, shaping it to one clear word.

Later.

Miki stared at the back fence and then shrugged. "No, I'll get it later."

Wolfe reinforced the thought. The focus was becoming harder to maintain, pulling on his reserves. Working multiple subjects was always harder.

"Do it later," Kit said, sounding tired. "Baby, what's wrong? Where are you going, Butch?"

Wolfe heard a rustle on the other side of the wall, followed by a soft growl. The dogs had detected him and his maneuver.

He didn't move, pulling in his energy until he was invisible.

Wind raced down the mountain. The cottonwood leaves above his head danced like golden coins. Baby sneezed twice, and

Wolfe heard her race back across the lawn.

"Do you think she heard something out there? Baby, what's wrong?" Kit said sharply.

The dog kept right on running, up the stairs and across the back porch.

"Forget about the dogs, will you? Let's go in. It's too damned hot out here to think." Miki shrugged a towel around her shoulders, motioning to Kit.

The other two dogs raced along the grass beyond the fence. "Let's go," Kit called. "Everybody inside." The door closed with a snap.

Wolfe looked down and forced his body to relax, surprised that it never got easier. There was always disorientation when you finished, always a price that you paid for messing with Mother Nature.

He ignored the tension at his neck and the sweat streaking his body. Even now, after five years, the mental process still felt strange, powerful and very unnatural.

He left the philosophy and science of it to the tech team at Foxfire. Otherwise there were too many questions that only led to more questions. Right now he had a perimeter survey to complete. Then he needed to check Diesel's medical status with the operative in place outside the clinic in Santa Fe.

★ ★ ★

Miki looked the way she always did — vibrant and striking in three shades of red and orange. Her current fashion statement was an old pair of cropped jeans and a neon Hawaiian print shirt unbuttoned over a lace camisole.

Somehow on her six-foot frame the look worked perfectly.

She crumpled an empty cardboard milk carton and tossed it in a perfect arc, hitting a garbage can shaped like a coyote. "So we're at the movies. Jackie Chan is into perfect southern kung fu moves. Then the jerk I'm with goes for his zipper. And I'm supposed to be thrilled. What was he thinking?"

"About getting you into bed," Kit murmured. "Men do that a lot."

Miki went on as if she hadn't heard, trying to demonstrate a kung fu kick and nearly hitting Baby in the head. "Sorry, honey." Crouching, she smoothed Baby's fur. "Bad Miki."

The puppy closed her eyes and rolled over, luxuriating in the attention. Seconds later Butch and Sundance crowded in, determined to get their share. Laughing, Miki stretched out on the floor and played dead, while all three dogs huddled around her, licking her face.

155

"What's the word on Diesel?"

"So far Liz hasn't found anything concrete. She's still waiting for blood test results."

Miki stood up. "Don't worry. It's going to work out fine. You've got great dogs here." She sniffed the air. "I think the lasagna's ready."

A pink teapot threatened to topple as Miki swung past, and Kit caught it quickly. She had always assumed that Miki would outgrow the occasional clumsiness that struck the summer she grew four inches, but it hadn't happened. As a result, Kit had grown adept at rescuing ceramics and stemware from sudden death in her friend's wake.

Miki bent low, digging in the back of her refrigerator. "Don't think I haven't noticed that thing you do — following me around and rescuing stuff when you think I'm not looking. It's annoying." Miki made an irritated sound. "I have nightmares that I'm going to break something really important one day. Where was I when they were handing out the coordination genes?" She shook her head, pushing a wayward strand of hair out of her eyes. "Don't answer that question."

As she walked to the sink, Miki glanced across the back wall.

"Why do you keep looking out there?" Kit followed her friend's gaze, but saw nothing.

"I could swear something moved in those piñon trees beyond the wash. Probably my imagination." She wrapped a set of silverware in a napkin and tossed it to Kit. "Let's eat. Then I think you should try calling the ranch. Wolfe will be wondering what happened to you."

Kit rolled her eyes. "I doubt the man has paid me a second thought."

As Wolfe made his third surveillance trip around Miki's house, he couldn't shake the feeling that he was being watched.

Keeping to a row of scrubby mesquite trees, he trained his binoculars on the nearby foothills, then turned to study the down-slope recess where he'd stashed his knapsack.

Something moved in a bank of wild grass. Silently, he circled back up the slope, coming around the spot from behind.

When he was in position, he inched forward, parting the tall grass.

A man was squatting in the dirt, going through his field rations.

CHAPTER ELEVEN

Silently, Wolfe pulled out a length of nylon cord, watching the man search his pack. In one sharp move he wrapped the line around the man's throat, feeling the immediate defensive recoil and the search for any points of weakness.

Wolfe left no chance for a counterattack. The nylon cord tightened; the man slumped. Neither one said a word.

Before he could straighten, something hit Wolfe's chest. He grunted, the world flashing into a corona of white light as fifty thousand volts from a Taser exploded against his ribs.

He managed to stagger back, grabbing a boulder for support, then dropped out of sight down a steeply eroded wash.

Boots crunched on gravel behind him. "Don't fire, damn it. Ryker sent me."

Wolfe had his Sig Sauer in his hand with the safety off when he heard the man's sharp warning. When he didn't answer, the man moved a little closer.

"Don't shoot. My hands are up, and the

Taser is on the ground. Ryker sent me with new information." He stopped, coughing a little. "Call him to verify. The code word is Eskimo."

Hearing the code word, Wolfe lowered the gun slightly. So far half of his story was right, but half wasn't good enough.

Wolfe took a shooting stance, arms extended, his focus locked on the spot where the man's head would appear as he rounded the boulder.

"I came in by chopper to the ranch. When I saw you tailing Kit O'Halloran into town, I followed you."

Wolfe didn't move. He felt a sharp pain at his eyes and he blocked the attacking energy. What the hell was going on?

"Ryker told me you were stubborn. He said if you weren't inclined to believe me, I should remind you that 'two plus two equals seven.' "

Wolfe dropped his Sig to port arms position. Ryker had specified a secondary code phrase in case of last-minute mission changes. Even though this new arrival didn't appear to be a hostile, Wolfe still had doubts. "Stay where you are and tell me why Ryker didn't notify me that you were inbound."

"He's tied up. The rest of the Foxfire team has been deployed."

"Keep coming, hands up. Stop beside the wash."

A tall man with a striking resemblance to Denzel Washington appeared above the steep wash, his hands raised high. "Call Ryker. Tell him Ishmael Teague needs clearance."

Wolfe's eyes didn't leave the man's face. "Why was Foxfire deployed?"

"An embassy attack in Indonesia. Two U.S. senators were visiting at the time, and things are heating up fast. Ryker needs you here or you would have been on the plane with them."

It made sense. And the pain behind Wolfe's eyes was fading. "Why the energy loop just now?"

The man turned, one eyebrow raised. "Beg your pardon?"

"Energy. I felt it a minute ago."

"Afraid I don't have a clue what you're talking about. I'm strictly on the tech end."

Wolfe watched him search his vest and pull out a small ID. The likeness was good and the stamps seemed authentic.

"So you're Teague?"

The man nodded.

Wolfe knew the name. Ishmael Teague was a legend in espionage circles, with a reputation for getting nasty jobs done and leaving no trace.

"Mind if I put my hands down?"

"Go ahead. Sorry about that. I wasn't expecting a contact until somewhere between 0100 and 0200."

Teague put his hands down and rubbed his throat. "Last-minute changes can be a bitch." He looked down the hill toward the swimming pool. "Kit O'Halloran and the dogs are down there, I take it."

Wolfe rolled his shoulders and stood up. "Only three of the dogs are with her. The biggest one, Diesel, is still in town with the vet."

"I heard about that. Any diagnosis yet?"

"The blood work hasn't come back. I'm monitoring Kit's cell phone, and as soon as she knows, I'll know."

"Sorry about the Taser, not that it seemed to stop you for long. Ryker slipped up. He should have notified you."

"I'll be sure to mention it to him." Wolfe gestured at the black case beneath Teague's arm. "I don't suppose you've got a six-pack of Dos Equis on ice in there."

"No such luck, Commander. This is a laptop with a DVD player. Ryker wants you to watch some surveillance tapes from the lab."

"Listen, Teague, I don't have time for —"

"Call me Izzy." He pulled out a sleek, high-tech computer. "There have been some new developments, and Ryker wants you fully briefed."

Wolfe checked the surrounding terrain. Nothing moved, and the earlier energy hit was gone, leaving no trace. If Ryker was sending in a man for a new briefing, the news had to be bad.

"What did you mean by that reference to an energy — what did you call it — energy loop?" Izzy asked.

"Forget I asked." Wolfe fought his impatience. "Kit is supposed to be back at the vet's at six, which doesn't give us a lot of time."

Teague powered up a titanium laptop and studied Wolfe for a moment. "You're not going to like some of what you see here, Commander." He tapped a button on the laptop, and the screen filled with motion.

Wolfe saw the well-equipped lab with dozens of caged animals. His body tightened when he saw Cruz in the middle of the room — gaunt, determined, his eyes blazing with arrogance. "What the hell is wrong with him?"

"Finish watching. Then we'll talk."

Cruz looked half dead. What was he doing in a government lab, naked and looking more animal than human?

As the tape progressed, the animals grew increasingly agitated. Wolfe wasn't sure he believed what he was seeing. He wasn't sure that he *wanted* to believe it.

When it was over, Wolfe didn't move. "Why didn't Ryker tell me this sooner?"

"The man is a law unto himself. You've worked with him long enough to know how he thinks — need-to-know and all that shit." Izzy closed the laptop and pulled a file of papers out of his backpack. "Ryker had that surveillance tape thoroughly analyzed. There's no doubt that Cruz used the animals to escape from that room."

"Impossible." Wolfe's face was a mask as he squatted on the ground, staring at the opposite ridge. "If he had the ability to control animals, one of us would have known." Wolfe had been led to believe that he was the first and only member of the team to be able to influence animals, and even his skills on that front were still rudimentary. A thought came to him, one he didn't like. "Unless the government was working on something secret in that lab, using Cruz as a guinea pig."

"If they were, they didn't tell me." Izzy met Wolfe's gaze squarely. "And if his new skills came out of that facility, it still doesn't matter. What you saw on the video matters. Now that he's free, you can count on him to do it again. Meanwhile, six security officers were killed there."

"Ryker told me." Wolfe was still struggling to understand why Cruz had been hidden away, his existence kept top secret for all these months. The next question was why Cruz had gone right to the computer. "He was getting information from the lab computer. What files did he tap?"

"The dogs," Izzy said quietly. "Kit O'Halloran's puppies among them."

"We all knew that the government was testing a variety of animals for military use. To control their unusual abilities, there would be a need for humans trained to work with . . . unconventional skills." Wolfe turned, staring down the hill at the house below them. "Like Cruz, apparently."

"He pulled up your service records and your recent assignments before he vanished. Any idea why?"

Wolfe picked up a pile of pebbles and tossed them from hand to hand. "Cruz and I worked together from my first day in Foxfire, and we got very close. If he's looking for me now, it's because he believes I'll help him."

"Will you?"

Wolfe stood up slowly. "If you ask that question again, you're going to be spitting up blood from a broken jaw."

"The question has to be asked and answered, Commander. Cruz can be a persuasive man, and your history together won't make it easy to say no. Ryker wants to be certain you're aware of his interest in you."

"Cruz has no hold over me." Wolfe tossed away the pebbles and checked his watch. "Kit should be leaving shortly, so let's wrap this up." He passed a plastic evidence bag to Izzy. "The operative I caught earlier provided this evidence. I swabbed the man's mouth and put a sample of his saliva in the bag. The poison was very fast acting."

Izzy folded the bag carefully and slid it inside his backpack. "I'll handle the analysis myself. Any distinguishing facial features that might be useful?"

Wolfe shook his head. "The man was no amateur. No ID, no notes, no wallet, no maps. What's the connection between him and Cruz?"

"Speculation is a waste of time." Izzy

stowed his laptop inside the backpack. "I'll update you when we have this analyzed. Ryker's got a forensic team waiting to examine the body tonight."

"Still no sign where was Cruz headed?"

"None that can be verified." Izzy shrugged. "Ryker doesn't tell me everything."

But Wolfe didn't expect Cruz to leave tracks. The man had top-flight survival skills, and regular trackers wouldn't find him.

It would take another member of Foxfire to do that.

"Did Cruz have friends or family in this area?" Wolfe knew Cruz well, but team members seldom discussed their families.

Izzy shook his head. "Only a brother. He used to work at a small airport, but he died doing volunteer work in a forest fire last year."

"Was his body ever recovered?"

"Not that I know of."

Wolfe didn't move. "Did his brother have any surviving relatives?"

"His ex-wife lives south of Albuquerque. They had three kids."

"Put a surveillance team on their house. Training or not, Cruz is going to need support to stay hidden."

"Already done."

"Did Cruz's brother have a military background?"

"Marine sniper training and demolitions work. According to his discharge records, he had better backwoods skill than his instructors."

Suddenly Wolfe flinched beneath a wave of pain hammering inside his head, this attack focused and definitely hostile. Defensive tactics kicked in as he blocked at all levels.

Cruz.

Nearby?

He was aware of Izzy studying him curiously, but he shook his head when Izzy started to ask a question. Ignoring the pain, Wolfe scanned the hills above the house, putting out a net in search of Cruz's energy signature.

Long minutes later he gave up. The terrain was clean.

Had Cruz tracked Wolfe — or followed Izzy? The rules kept changing, Wolfe thought, partly because he still didn't know exactly what skills Cruz had acquired since his supposed death.

His cell phone vibrated. He scanned the caller ID, noting the Los Angeles area code. He showed the phone number to Izzy, who shook his head.

Wolfe couldn't pick up any details about the caller, despite a quick probe. He blanked his mind, releasing all emotion, then answered the call. "Yeah."

Static crackled.

"Hello?" Wolfe repeated.

"Welcome to hell, Houston." There was no mistaking Cruz's voice, with the long, flat tones of his native Montana.

"Who is this?"

"Cut the crap. You know exactly who this is. What you don't know yet is where and why. But you will."

"Cruz?" The name was cold on Wolfe's lips. "You're dead."

"That's what they wanted you to think."

"I went to your funeral, damn it. I carried your casket and saluted while the rifles snapped off the volleys. You're *dead.*"

"Ryker set it up. You've seen one face of Foxfire, but I've seen another." Cruz's voice hardened. "Pray to God that you never have to see that side."

"This is bullshit."

"You want it to be bullshit." Cruz's voice was low, persuasive. "But you know that I wouldn't lie to you. Not after Bogotá. Not after Kabul."

Wolfe's fingers tightened on the phone. Only half a dozen people knew about the secret operations Foxfire had carried out in those cities. Only Cruz and Wolfe knew how Cruz had saved Wolfe's life in Bogotá following bad intel and malfunctioning equipment. Wolfe had repaid the favor three months later in Kabul.

"Words," he said harshly. "Why should I believe you?"

"Because we shared the dark nights, my friend. Especially in Kabul when that forward skirmish team nearly got me."

Wolfe said nothing. The identification was unshakable. Only Cruz knew those particular details.

He saw Izzy pull a small box out of his backpack and gave a warning wave with his hand. He didn't want Cruz to get a hint that he was being tracked or monitored.

"Even so, why contact me?" Wolfe demanded.

"I'm sure you've heard the story by now, at least Ryker's version. You've probably even seen the surveillance tapes. I doubt they'll tell you about the tests they began after my body began to deteriorate. The cage they kept me in won't appear on any front page either."

"What cage?"

"The one I lived inside," Cruz said tightly. "My home for the last two years."

"You're full of shit, and you're wasting my time. I'm hanging up now."

"Wait."

Wolfe heard the desperation in that single word. Was part of the old Cruz still alive, hungry for contact with the people he'd known best? Or was this simply another way to mess with his mind?

"You want to kill me, don't you? Their pet project slipped the leash and they sent you out to clean up the mess. You'd like to reach through the phone and strangle me right now." Cruz laughed coldly. "If you were the new man, you probably could."

The new man. Wolfe tensed. How had Cruz learned about the newest recruit to Foxfire? The man had talents in manipulating electrical equipment unlike anything Wolfe had ever seen. "I don't know what the hell you're talking about."

"Bravo. Ryker would applaud your performance."

"You're boring me with this story of yours. Tell me what you want."

"Time. That's what they stole from me while I was locked in that filthy cage. What is two years of a man's life worth?" Cruz's voice dropped. "I'll let you know when I have the answer. Until then, tell Ryker he's wasting *his* time. He'll never find me."

The phone went dead.

Izzy stopped pacing. "Cruz?"

Wolfe gave an angry nod.

"What was that about a cage?"

Wolfe didn't answer. He wanted to consider everything Cruz had told him first. "What's important is that he's on the move. He said to tell Ryker he'd never track him."

"Why did you stop me from tracing the call?"

"He might have picked something up. The last thing I want to do is scare him off. Better to let him think he's in control."

They both turned at the sound of sudden barking.

Kit came out of the house, followed by the dogs. After watching a few minutes of playful racing around the backyard, she gave a "down" order, and all three dogs immediately went flat.

Izzy looked fascinated. "How does she get them to obey without raising her voice?"

"They trust her," Wolfe said quietly. "I saw her face down a cougar to protect those dogs, and she did it without a weapon."

"Fascinating." Izzy finished zipping up his backpack and swung it over his shoulders. "Ryker's counting on you to keep them safe."

"I plan to." Wolfe looked down the hill, scanning the area around the house. "While you're looking at that poison, get me a report on this." He held up the map that had fallen out of Emmett's pocket. "Pull any prints and locate the paper source. I doubt this has anything to do with Cruz, but I'm taking no chances."

Izzy looked down the hill as the door opened a second time. Miki appeared, holding a Frisbee. "What about Kit's friend? Is she reliable?"

"If you mean would she be involved with Cruz, I doubt it."

Izzy's eyes were cold. "Are you certain?"

Wolfe rubbed his neck. "Right now, Teague, I'm not certain about anything. It's a hunch, but a strong one."

"So noted. Now I have one last question for you. What happened right before he called? You looked like you'd gotten another Taser hit."

"Cruz was probing me," Wolfe said curtly. "If you want to know anything more, ask Ryker. All I can say is it's classified."

Kit bent down in the shade of a big cottonwood tree and scratched Baby's head, while Miki tossed a Frisbee to Butch and Sundance. Suddenly Baby shot across the shaded courtyard. Raising her head, she stared at the tall grass above the house.

Miki shaded her eyes, watching. "What's gotten into her?"

"She smells something up on that hill. I saw something up there, too." Kit felt an odd prickling at the back of her neck. "No, don't turn around." She picked up a sun hat from a chair, turning slowly until she had a better view. "I don't see anything now."

"Funny, I thought I saw something up there earlier." Miki strode toward the house. "You have a gun locked in your Jeep?"

Kit nodded. You didn't go anywhere in the backcountry unarmed. Not if you were a woman traveling alone.

Baby was still at the far side of the yard, her head raised to the wind. She whined softly, then looked back at Kit.

"I've got a bad feeling about this," Kit muttered.

"You and me both." Miki dropped the Frisbee at the back door. "But if someone's up there watching us, they're going to get a big surprise. Let's go."

CHAPTER TWELVE

Cicadas droned from a cottonwood tree.

Kit felt the weight of her father's handgun tug at her front pocket. She didn't relish the thought of exploring the nearby slope, but Miki showed no sign of backing down, and Kit couldn't desert her friend.

They stopped at a curve in the wash. A family of quail flowed across the ground, a restless brown wave that disappeared beneath tall desert mule grass. At the top of the wash, Miki crouched behind a boulder. Kit sank down beside her. From there, someone could see the whole slope, along with all of Miki's courtyard and back property.

Kit looked around but saw no sign of footprints.

Her watch alarm chimed softly, and she stabbed a button to halt the alert. Silently, she dug into her pocket for her pills and swallowed two dry, grimacing.

"What was that?" Miki whispered.

"Headache. I think I may be coming

down with some kind of bug." The truth was, her right hip was aching again.

"You never get sick."

Kit ignored her friend's questioning look. A shadow crossed the high ridge, cast by a red-tailed hawk drifting smoothly on the thermals. A second shadow followed a moment later.

Hunting in pairs, Kit thought. What one missed, the other would catch. She wondered what it would be like to glide that way, with no resistance and no pain.

Miki squeezed her shoulder. "We're going to talk later," she whispered. "Let's get this finished."

Below them, the wash circled around a mesquite tree. A jackrabbit crossed the shadows, then stopped in the afternoon sun, showing no trace of wariness.

"Doesn't look like anyone's here." Miki stood uncertainly, hands on her hips.

"We'd better be sure."

Kit led the way, climbing quietly. At the top of the wash, she crouched low and peered past the rocky bank. The only thing moving was a gray antelope squirrel, its tail hiked over its head and its cheeks filled with food.

"See anything?" Miki whispered behind Kit.

"Quiet as a tomb. Wild goose chase."

"But what about the movements we saw? What about Baby's weird behavior?"

"Could have been a coyote." Kit rubbed her neck, working on a knot of tension. "Maybe it was the wind shaking some deer grass. If there was something else here, it's gone now. I don't see any prints."

"Nearly scared the bejeezus out of me, I don't mind telling you." Miki snorted, scraping the ground with the toe of her boot.

"Stop."

"Stop what? I was just —"

Kit knelt carefully and brushed aside a piece of gravel near Miki's toe, then held up a stringy piece of brown fiber. They stared in uneasy silence at the dry piece of beef jerky, stirred up by Miki's restless digging. Teeth marks were clearly visible at one corner.

"Somebody *was* here. Looks like his snack got interrupted, too."

"Not many cougars or coyote carry jerky," Kit said grimly. "On the other hand, this could have been here for weeks."

Clouds raced overhead. The wash felt cool. Here and there dry leaves danced on the wind.

The skin at Kit's neck prickled yet again.

"Don't you want to check the other side of the ridge?" Miki leaned closer. "What if —"

"Forget it." Kit was already on the move, her feet crunching over the sand and gravel. "I'm not going any farther, and neither are you. You can be brave, but that doesn't mean being stupid."

"You win." Miki sounded relieved.

As they moved down the wash, Kit could have sworn she felt hidden eyes trained on her back.

Sand skittered down the wash.

"Are they gone?"

"Finally." Wolfe rose slowly from behind a lip of black granite near the top of the ridge. "Idiots, the pair of them. If someone had actually been up here . . ." The words trailed off.

"Maybe you should consider using one of your Foxfire techniques." Izzy's voice was thoughtful as he emerged from a prone position a few feet away. "Keep them inside for now."

"I've considered it." Wolfe didn't mention that he'd already carried out one effort successfully. Secrecy was a habit, and Teague was still on a need-to-know basis.

"What about those lab photos I left you?"

"Next item on the agenda."

"Good. If anything comes to mind, call me. I don't care how odd or insignificant it seems."

Wolfe laughed dryly. "The only wrong question is the one you don't ask."

"Damned right. You knew Cruz better than anyone. Ryker's hoping you'll pick up a clue the rest of us have missed."

Wolfe flipped through the photos slowly. In the first one Cruz was staring at a caged gorilla, his smile very cold.

The use of internal surveillance didn't particularly bother Wolfe. He knew cameras were frequently — and secretly — mounted throughout Foxfire facilities. He had accepted that his life would become military property the day he signed on the dotted line to join Foxfire.

Searching in his vest, he pulled out a small jeweler's loupe, which came in handy for track and footprint identification. "Give me another hour to get back to you on these."

Izzy started up the wash. "I'll be in the area." He pulled out a cell phone and gave Wolfe a two-finger wave.

The sound of Miki's door opening

brought Wolfe upright as he stowed the photos in his pocket. "There's movement downstairs. Gotta go."

"Watch your back."

CHAPTER THIRTEEN

Kit raced out to her Jeep, checking her watch. Liz had just called to say that Diesel was waking up, and if she wanted to see him, she should come as soon as possible. Liz also suggested that she bring the other dogs.

She threw open the back door to her Jeep. "Everyone in," she called. One by one the dogs jumped up and settled inside the back compartment, their noses over the front seat.

Miki shook her head as she watched the happy chaos. "You spoil them rotten, not that I wouldn't do the same. Promise me you'll call when you're ready to leave. I'll warm up the Bruce Lee boxed set. How long do you think you'll stay at the clinic?"

"Depends on how Diesel's feeling." Kit closed the back door of the Jeep and locked it. "Funny, it's not half as hot as it was an hour ago."

"I noticed that, too. Go figure." Miki reached through Kit's window, petting Baby's head. "Be sure to tell Diesel that

Aunt Miki has his favorite food all ready for him."

"Steak rare?"

"Are you kidding? Cheese spread and deviled ham. Junk food all the way."

"What the hell do you mean, there have been more developments?" With a secure cell phone braced against his ear, Wolfe watched Kit barrel past him in her Jeep.

Izzy went on, undisturbed. "Colorado police found the body of a waitress outside an isolated diner near Durango. She'd just gone off shift and according to the short order cook, she'd been acting strange."

"Strange how?" Wolfe pulled into traffic four cars behind Kit.

"She was wandering around the parking lot, completely disoriented."

"So what?" Wolfe slowed for an ice cream truck with children crowded around the side door. "Maybe she was sick. Maybe she'd had a few drinks."

"There's a security camera at the front of the diner where she worked. We have clear shots of her speaking to someone at the counter before the camera stopped working."

"Was it Cruz?"

"Can't see. Whoever it was stayed just

out of range. But we had one piece of luck. About five minutes before the camera stopped, there's a decent shot of a man's hands taking something out of a knapsack." Izzy's voice hardened. "It's a government issue knapsack. According to Ryker, one just like it was stolen two days before Cruz left the lab."

Wolfe frowned at the line of traffic, keeping an eye on Kit's Jeep. He was driving the dusty pickup, staying back where she wouldn't see him. Up ahead her Jeep sailed through a yellow light, and he cursed softly.

"Something wrong?"

"She got past me at a red light. Hold on, I need to make a quick detour."

"I can punch up visuals and an alternate route via my GPS," Izzy said. "Give me a second and —"

"No need. I remember my way around Santa Fe." Wolfe took a quick left, shot down one block, and made a sharp right. A few seconds later, Kit drove past. "Got her." Leaving a safe distance, he pulled back into traffic. "What about the waitress?"

"The woman's body shows massive trauma from the impact of a truck that ran into her, but she had contusions on the face, neck and shoulders. There were also deep punctures consistent with talon strikes by a large predatory bird, along with feather traces at the wound sites."

"You believe Cruz caused this attack?"

"That's the assumption."

"Animal attacks?"

"It's no harder to believe than a man who can see infrared light signatures," Izzy pointed out. "No more bizarre than a man who can distort and replace memories at will."

Wolfe's fingers tapped on the steering wheel. The Foxfire team was trained to work with energy patterns. Some did simple assessment and others carried out disruption and disorientation. Beyond that, each team member had additional, special-ized skills. For Wolfe, that meant image dis-tortion and memory manipulation.

But to Wolfe's knowledge, only he had any ability to control animals. When — and how — had Cruz mastered the skill? "What did Ryker tell you?"

"Not a lot. The man eats, breathes and sleeps secrecy. Sometimes he makes me wonder whether we're on the same side. Which brings me to the next point." Izzy cleared his throat. "There are parts of the facility surveillance tapes you weren't shown. It was Ryker's decision."

Typical, Wolfe thought. "Why bring it up now?"

"In the uncut tapes the animals in the lab clearly go berserk. According to what we can piece together, Cruz managed to make two Rottweilers open their cages. After that, they brought him an electronic access card."

"Is that what Ryker was working on with Cruz? If so, why did Ryker keep it a secret from us?" Wolfe couldn't keep the anger from his voice.

"I can't tell you that," Izzy said.

"What the hell *can* you tell me, Teague?"

"That Cruz was put there for his own protection. He had begun to exhibit medical and psychological problems, and the deterioration was getting worse."

"Cruz set the benchmark for all of us. He was in perfect physical shape the last time I saw him."

Papers rustled at Izzy's end. "There might have been a medication problem. Cruz's immune system could also have been fighting some of his implants."

"So now you've got a renegade Foxfire operative whose system may or may not be degenerating along with his mental state."

"That's an affirmative."

Wolfe considered his next words carefully, shocked by what Izzy had just told him. "That means my whole team may be facing similar problems."

"So far there's nothing to suggest that. The problems appear to be limited to Cruz."

Wolfe slowed to let a mother with two children cross the street, bothered by everything he'd just heard. First the covert research, and now the possibility of unpredictable medical problems. What else could go wrong?

"Ryker could pull Kit right now. He could hide her and the dogs someplace safe where Cruz couldn't track her. But he's not . . ." Wolfe's fingers clenched around the steering wheel. "Ryker is counting on Cruz to go after the dogs. He's using Kit as bait."

Izzy didn't answer.

"Cruz taught me most of what I know about image distortion. Now he's got new skills. But Ryker wants to dangle a civilian in front of him?"

"I don't like it either, Houston. But the fact is, she's caught in the middle of this, no matter what you do. Taking her to a safe house could prolong the wait, but Cruz will find the dogs and her with them.

If it happens now, at least you'll be there to protect her."

"What does Cruz gain?" Wolfe muttered.

"Ryker didn't authorize me to tell you about this, but screw protocol. One of the former Soviet states has offered a ten-million-dollar bounty on any of the dogs in the U.S. program. Two other dog trainers connected loosely to Foxfire were attacked yesterday. One is dead and the other is missing. They weren't with their animals at the time, so the thieves didn't get the dogs."

Worse and worse, Wolfe thought. "The bounty must include a trainer as part of the deal."

"That's what I'd figure."

"If they kidnapped one trainer, Kit's now expendable. They don't need her — all they need is her dogs."

"Affirmative. There's no reason for Cruz to keep her alive, especially if she comes between him and the Labs, which you and I both know is *exactly* what Kit would do."

"Then tell Ryker to get her off the board. Ship them all to Alaska or anywhere else that's secure."

"That's no longer an option. Ryker is firm."

"I won't go along with this."

"You've got your orders. I've got mine." Izzy didn't sound happy, but he wasn't backing down either. "Kit is every inch the professional in her line of work, and her dogs are service animals, bred to face danger. This is exactly the sort of mission they'll encounter once they leave Kit."

"When they're trained," Wolfe snapped. "Once they're fully grown. Not now, and not against a man like Cruz."

He watched Kit nose through the downtown Santa Fe traffic and turn into the driveway of a rambling white Victorian house. Three cars and a van were parked in the side parking lot.

"I've got to go, Teague," he said flatly. "Tell Ryker I need one of my team here for backup."

"No can do. They're all in Indonesia."

Wolfe pulled into a shaded spot and parked, watching Kit herd the dogs up to the clinic door. "We don't have a clue what we're dealing with here. Cruz isn't playing by the rules anymore."

"Then you need to change, too. Going rogue may be the best way to keep Kit alive."

Wolfe had already come to the same conclusion. "Whatever you do, don't let

187

Trace know that Ryker has put his sister in harm's way. Trace will kill him."

If I don't do it first.

Diesel was awake but listless when Liz Merrigold brought him into the examining room. His eyes looked glassy, but as soon as Kit scratched behind his ears, he rolled over on the examining table, one leg raised in the air.

The vet shook her head. "He may be weak, but he's never too sick to be scratched."

When Diesel raised his head and licked her hand, Kit tried to be optimistic. "Did you get the blood work back yet?"

"Still too soon. Probably first thing tomorrow." The vet took Diesel's pulse, then slid her stethoscope back around her neck. "He looks better. His breathing isn't as labored, and his pulse has settled down nicely. I'll give him another shot in an hour." She pulled a vial out of her medical case. "Let me keep an eye on him here and you can —"

"I don't want him here alone tonight."

Liz stared at her. "It's a clinic, Kit. Keeping animals is what we do." The vet tossed her stethoscope onto the examining table. "What if Diesel has another allergy attack in the night? What if his throat swells shut or he has a reaction to the medicine? Are you going to give him a shot of adrenaline? Don't you want him in a place where he can receive immediate treatment?"

Kit ran a hand through her hair. "I've got adrenaline in the Jeep if it's needed. You know I have emergency training."

"If you give this dog an injection without consulting me first, I'm washing my hands of you. Is that clear?"

Kit knew the anger in Liz's voice came from concern. She tried to ignore her own emotions and concentrate on being logical. "So Diesel's definitely not out of the woods yet? Do you expect —"

The vet made an exasperated sound. "I'm a doctor, not a mind reader. If you want mumbo-jumbo, go find the Amazing Kres-kin."

Diesel pushed closer, resting his head on Kit's leg. Clustered around the table, the other three dogs were restless. Kit asked herself if she was being selfish instead of concerned.

She looked out the window and sighed. "I'll come back one more time tonight. Diesel can stay, but I'll be here at 7:00 a.m. to pick him up."

Liz's expression softened. "I can live with that as long as he doesn't get worse."

Baby raised her paws, peering over the edge of the examining table. Diesel woofed gently, brushing his nose against Baby's.

"I'm not trying to make this harder for you, Kit."

"I guess I'm being stupid."

"I hate to say it but you look beat. Maybe you need to stop worrying about these dogs and start taking better care of yourself." Liz looked from Kit to the dogs. "One day they'll be gone. You know that."

Of course Kit knew. She just didn't like thinking about it.

Letting go was always the hardest part of her job, but it couldn't be avoided. The dogs were smart, destined for service work. Kit knew that and accepted it with the cool, logical part of her mind.

The primal part of her turned weepy at the mere thought.

You took a dog, gave it your heart, your time and every bit of your patience. And then your reward was to see the bond you created cut in two.

Life sucked, all right.

She gave Liz a weak smile. "I can live with it. You are looking at a well-adjusted adult and a consummate professional," she said wryly.

Some days, anyway.

Kit's stomach growled loudly as she said goodbye to Diesel and herded the dogs into her Jeep. "Time to go, guys. We'll come see Diesel again later." Baby's tail thumped on the seat as she jumped neatly into the back of the Jeep, followed closely by Butch and Sundance.

When Kit revved up the engine, she realized she was almost out of gas. She also needed to eat. Her experimental medications were hell on her stomach if she didn't manage small, frequent meals. A burger and fries would have to do, since she didn't want to drive back to Miki's on an empty stomach. But first she had to get gas.

The sun was low and red when she pulled into a self-service gas station about a mile from Liz's office. She turned off the motor, then looked back at the three dogs. "Stay." She made the command clear and very firm.

Baby's tail twitched once, and Kit quickly calculated when the dogs would need to eat again. As a precaution, she had packed enough vitamins and food for two days. With luck, the extra driving wouldn't make Baby and Butch carsick the way it usually did.

Distracted, she started the pump and watched traffic race past. After the tank was full, she replaced her gas cap and slid behind the wheel.

Behind her in the line a car horn honked. Irritated, she reached for the ignition.

Her car keys were gone.

Fuming, Kit dug in all her pockets, checked the floor, then searched the compartment between the seats. Again, she came up empty-handed.

She had only been outside for a few minutes, and no one had come near the car. Besides, the dogs hadn't made a single warning bark. She tried her pockets one more time and checked the back compartment.

Nada.

Another car horn blared. Kit ignored it, searching all the way back beneath her seat and finding an old chew toy and a glow-in-the-dark Frisbee, but no keys.

Metal tinkled near her ear. Looking up, she saw a set of keys — *her* keys — swinging in the air at the open window. Someone was leaning against the car, just out of sight.

"Looking for these?" a familiar voice asked.

CHAPTER FOURTEEN

The words died in Kit's throat.

He looked even tougher than she remembered from that morning, and she couldn't read his face any better than she ever could.

"Why are you here?"

"You left your keys in the car. Not a good idea."

"It's a *gas* station."

"And criminals don't need gas — or cars?"

"Whatever." Kit held out her hand. The keys dropped, landing in her lap.

But they were forgotten when Wolfe leaned through the window. His dark eyes tracked her with an intensity that left her mouth dry. She suddenly remembered that nobody did *intense* the way Wolfe Houston did. She also remembered why she'd had a mind-wrecking crush on this man for almost a decade. He was *hot*. But even more, he was a man who got whatever he went after, and while he did it, he would be dangerous and unstoppable.

The keys slid down between her legs and onto the seat of the Jeep. Kit took a deep breath, trying to ignore Wolfe and the keys. She didn't *want* to feel anything. She wasn't going to get dragged back into pointless emotion because of him.

He was a virtual stranger now, and that's how it was going to stay — as soon as she got her surging hormones under control. "Are you going to tell me why you're really here?"

"R and R." Sunlight fell over his shoulder, casting half his face into shadow. The effect was unsettling, as if his features struggled to move against a carved mask.

Someone honked a horn again. Straightening, Wolfe glared at the source of the noise.

The honking stopped abruptly. Even the dogs were still.

"Why did you come back home? Why now?" She whispered the words, not buying his flimsy story. In the sunlight's glare, she noticed a scar on his neck that hadn't been there when he'd left. Lines cut into his forehead as if he had seen too much, in too many places.

His jaw clenched.

"Home." He found the keys on the seat and slid them into the ignition. "Do me a favor and don't say home is where the heart is."

She heard the flatness in his voice. She'd heard enough stories — and seen an occasional bruise — to know why home would never mean anything good to him.

"I want an answer."

"Maybe, just this once, you could skip the questions. Your dogs like me, so why can't you?"

Liking him wasn't the problem. Kit had *liked* him when she was eleven. By the time she was thirteen she was hyperventilating at the mere sound of his voice. At fifteen her stomach twisted in knots whenever he was close enough to touch.

And if that wasn't pathetic, she didn't know what was.

Baby stretched forward, resting her head on Kit's shoulder as if she wanted into the conversation.

"Gorgeous, aren't you? Got a kiss for me?"

Kit's pulse kicked hard. Then she realized he was talking to the dog. She scowled at him. "Actually, that's not a good idea. Pet-borne parasites can be transferred via saliva. There are also viruses and allergies —"

She shook her head and stopped, aware that she sounded ridiculous. He was turning her brain into mush again.

Ignoring her, Baby pushed between the seats and sniffed Wolfe's hands. When she was done, her tail wagged, banging into Kit's face.

"Down, Baby."

Kit realized she was looking at Wolfe's strong, broad hands. She couldn't stop imaging how they'd feel on her skin. Maybe Miki was right.

Maybe one long, sweaty night in Wolfe's bed would stop all her obsessing, and then she could forget about him.

But when she looked up, Wolfe was gone. She leaned out the window, but saw no sign of him.

Typical.

Furious, she peered through the windshield. The man was a natural disaster in the making. There ought to be some kind of national siren alert when he was in the area. Or maybe just an announcement. *Elvis is in the building.*

"Jerk." She started the Jeep. "Irritating, unreliable, stupid —"

Wolfe opened the other door and slid into the seat beside her. "I take it that was me you were ripping to shreds." He calmly handed Baby the rubber chew toy that had fallen between the seats.

"Well? Are you leaving or staying?"

"Staying. For now at least." He buckled his seat belt calmly. "Why did you race off from the ranch so fast? I was lucky I saw you here getting gas."

There were holes the size of Indiana in his casual explanation, but Kit didn't point them out. If he wanted to lie to her, that was his problem. It wasn't as if *she* had any hold over him.

"Diesel was sick. I took him in to the vet."

"How's he doing?"

"Better, but he'll probably have to stay overnight. Meanwhile, I've got errands to do. I can't drive you —"

"I'll tag along. Not a problem." He made no sign of moving and she couldn't exactly push him bodily out of the car so she pulled out into traffic. He was up to something, but she didn't know what.

Of course, there was Miki's outrageous plan to consider. What if she actually leaned across the seat and went for his belt?

No way. She'd never be able to carry it off. He'd laugh at her, and she'd be crushed.

Kit decided that this obsession with Wolfe was unhealthy. She needed an intervention. The problem was, she didn't have a clue how to go about changing things.

Her cell phone rang and she answered with one hand. "What?"

"Gee, I was calling Kit O'Halloran. How did I get the Wicked Witch of the West?"

"There's traffic, Miki. Sorry, but I'm driving."

"How's Diesel?"

"Better. Still not out of the woods."

"Are you headed back now?"

"I need to stop at the pet store. Baby needs a leash, so I thought we'd take care of that now."

"Hold on. Replay for me, please. *We?*"

"Wolfe's with me," Kit said carefully.

"*Yes!* The time is right. Make your move. Go to a hotel. No, come here to my place. I'll tidy things up and clear out. You can use the couch, then give the bed a workout."

Frowning, Kit cupped her hand around the phone. "I — uh — don't think that's possible."

"*Why not?* Do you like this limbo you've been stuck in for years?"

"No, meat loaf would be fine." Kit avoided Wolfe's face, aware of his focused attention.

"He's listening, isn't he? Put him on the phone, Kit."

"Yes, thanks for calling. I'll talk to you then."

"Put him on," Miki said quickly. "I'll invite him over here. Then I'll leave and you two can be as wild as you want. I'll even chill a bottle of champagne. It's domestic but decent."

How had she even *considered* any of this? Kit wondered. She couldn't pull off a pre-planned orgy with Wolfe. She was tongue-tied at the very thought.

"Something wrong?" Wolfe asked. "I can hear yelling."

She realized her hand had slipped and he could pick up Miki's loud questions. "That's right, I'll call you then," she said into the phone. "Bye." She hung up when Miki was still in midsentence. "That was my friend, Miki. She asked what I wanted for dinner."

Except Kit suddenly had no appetite. The thought of seeing Wolfe naked affected her that way, hard and dirty. Below the belt with a capital *B.*

She chanced a quick look.

Uh-oh. He was looking dangerous again. The kind of dangerous that left her fascinated and more than a little flushed.

"You can't go with me. I've got errands," she said.

"What kind of errands?" His long fingers curved over Baby's head.

Kit thought about them wrapped around her leg. Maybe climbing up her thigh. Definitely her breasts.

Enough. Sheesh.

There were probably moral concerns here. Definitely there were cellulite issues involved. "Errand errands. You know — deodorant, flea powder. . . ."

Her cell phone warbled again. She scanned the LED and rolled her eyes. "Miki, what now?"

"Check your handbag."

"Why?"

"Just do it. I added a few new things today after lunch."

"What kind of new things?"

"Pink thong underwear. Very slinky. They should crank up his motor in record time."

"Miki, I don't want —"

"And a scented candle. I use ylang-ylang, but there's also tuberose. Very sensual."

"Will you stop trying to —"

"And some edible chocolate body paint. Food and foreplay at the same time. How good is that?"

Kit stared grimly out at the highway.

"I'm going now, I may call you again in about thirty years. Then again, maybe not."

Miki ignored her. "There's a red velvet bag there, too. No wires, so you can take it anywhere. The batteries are fresh. Your hair is going to stand on edge when you try it out. This is one hot mama that will take you straight to o-land."

Kit felt blood streaming up into her face. She was going to *kill* Miki. Maybe slow-acting poison. Or maybe she'd cut her up into tiny little pieces with a dull paring knife. "I'm going now. I do not know you. In fact, I have never even *wanted* to know you." She made a crackling sound against her cell phone. "We're going into a tunnel now. My phone is breaking up. Can't hear you. Bye —"

"There are no tunnels in Santa Fe." Miki was laughing. "And you are such a liar. Fate's giving you a lottery ticket here, so stop being a chicken-heart."

Kit figured there were some things you couldn't change about yourself, no matter how you tried.

Thing like the shape of your ears. Your DNA.

An aversion to sex toys.

She hung up. She *was* a chicken-heart. Miki was right.

"More meat-loaf questions?"

201

There was something smoky in his voice that made her wonder just how much he'd heard. "No, everything's fine. Excellent, in fact." She had thong underwear and a vibrator in her purse, along with a nearly empty bottle of flea powder.

Something was very wrong with this picture.

Her watch alarm chimed, coming from somewhere in her purse. Kit realized she'd put it there before leaving Miki's.

Time for her medicine.

"Your alarm's going off." Wolfe picked up her purse. "You want me to —"

"No!" She grabbed for the strap without looking away from the road. No way was he going to find the X-rated equipment Miki had stashed. The embarrassment factor alone would leave her crippled for life. "I'll get it myself, thanks." Blindly she searched the outer flap pocket and dug out her watch along with two individually wrapped pills. She chewed them up with a grimace and swallowed them.

"What were those?"

"Vitamins."

Her eyes dared him to ask any more questions.

He asked anyway. "You take them dry?"

"I'm tough."

Baby and Sundance pushed up next to Wolfe's face, panting happily. As the wind raced through the windows, Baby dropped her chew toy in his lap, and it landed at his feet. He searched the floor with one hand, but instead of the chew toy he pulled out a white paper bag with pills. "These yours?"

The question sounded deceptively casual.

Kit pulled the paper bag away. "Gee, I've been looking everywhere for those vitamins," she lied. These were her extra stash, always kept somewhere in the car, just in case she couldn't get back home. "What do you know?"

Her purse began shaking on her lap. She felt it creep across her thighs, making a dull *brrr* as it rocked up and down. Miki's damned gift.

She swatted blindly at the unseen velvet bag, trying to shut the motor off before Wolfe noticed.

"Anything I can do to help?"

"*No*. Just ignore it."

His brow rose. "You sure you don't want me to check?"

Over her dead body. Kit shoved the bag down at the opposite side of her seat. "It's my cell phone — on vibrate mode." Miki was definitely dying for this. "So," she went on brightly, "what about those Lakers?"

"What about them?"

So much for that line of distraction. Her purse was still vibrating, and she wondered how this particular scenario would look in that little automated bunny commercial.

Be cool, she told herself. *Don't let him get under your skin.*

A moving van pulled out in front of her, passing on the left. But the driver misjudged the speed of the oncoming cars, and he wasn't going to make it back into the lane without causing a three-car pileup.

Kit hit the brakes and pulled onto the shoulder, her sharp maneuver making the dogs topple in a row. "Stupid driver." She shoved the car into neutral, then swung around to look at the dogs. "Are you okay back there?"

Baby's tail thumped. Butch yawned. Sundance made a quick lunge for Baby's chew toy, but was rebuffed.

Apparently all was normal.

Wolfe leaned over to brush a strand of hair out of her eyes as wind gusted through her window. "You can't drive with this in your face."

With her emotions still jangled from the

near accident, Kit shoved his hand away. "Are you saying that I messed up?"

"No, that's not what I'm saying. You did exactly what needed to be done. That was excellent driving."

She wished he'd said something awful. Anger would have bolstered her resistance. Instead, it required a huge dose of willpower to keep her hands from sliding up around his neck, the way she'd wanted to do since she was thirteen.

Very bad idea.

Wolfe had had women chasing him since before he was old enough to drive. By the time he'd left, he'd become very, very good at sex, if even half the stories she'd heard were true. He was strictly out of *her* league. There would be nothing casual about sex with Wolfe Houston, and Kit was going to make *casual* her new mantra.

Just as soon as her stomach stopped churning.

Baby made a little sound in the back seat and sneezed.

"Let's go." Kit checked the rearview mirror, ready to turn back onto the road. "I've got two stops to make before the stores close. After that I'll drive you back to your car."

Then he was on his own.

Out of the corner of her eye, she saw Baby drop an old blue towel onto Wolfe's lap. "Baby?" She lunged sideways. "Baby, *wait.*"

Too late.

The puppy whimpered and threw up all over Wolfe.

CHAPTER FIFTEEN

He'd sure as hell had better days.

Wryly Wolfe surveyed the mess in his lap. He'd barely caught up with Kit at the gas station in time to grab her keys. Then the moron in the truck had nearly run them off the road. As a precaution he'd memorized the plate number, but his instinct told him it was a coincidence. He doubted Cruz could have tracked them down so fast and without Wolfe picking up any trace of his energy.

He felt something warm on his leg and looked down at Baby's limp body. The spunky little Lab wasn't having such a good day either.

Dog vomit wasn't high on Wolfe's list of favorite things. On the other hand, he'd had to wade through a whole lot worse, including several sewers that he didn't like remembering.

Kit was pulling tissues from a carton under her seat. "Poor Baby. She gets carsick. All the dogs do, but Baby is the worst."

"Anything I can do for her?"

"She'll be fine." With one hand soothing Baby, Kit picked up the towel from Wolfe's lap and shoved it into a plastic bag. Then she leaned down and dabbed at the wet spots on his legs. Her smooth movements told him that she had done this before.

But when she bent closer, blotting a stain just below his belt, Wolfe stopped thinking about dogs.

And started to think about Kit.

Naked in his bed. With her hands all over him, her full mouth sliding across his chest, and then down —

"What's wrong?"

"Wrong?" His voice was rough.

"You look weird." She was biting her lip, working it between her teeth, and the sight made heat tunnel straight to his groin.

"Sorry about the dog vomit. I know it's disgusting. Well, not to me, because after a while you actually get used to dogs throwing up. But to you it must be disgusting." She attacked another spot, in the process smoothing her palm over his thigh.

Wolfe's eyes closed. Agony set in.

"Don't worry, I'm almost done. Everything will be fine."

Abruptly her hands opened on his zipper, and Wolfe was a hundred percent certain that nothing would ever be fine again. Ryker's tattooed blond threat was nothing compared to Kit's provocative innocence.

He gripped her wrists and held them still. "You can stop now."

She stared at him, wide-eyed. "Why?"

She truly didn't have a clue, he realized. "I'll take care of the mess myself." He shifted, trying to get comfortable. "I've got clean clothes in my bag. Is there someplace I can change?"

She finished wiping her hands on a paper towel. "My next stop is the grocery, and they have a bathroom. After that, we hit Pet Land."

"Fine with me."

As she checked traffic, Kit frowned. "Baby usually gives more warning, but she's been jumpy about something for the last few days. All the dogs are acting odd."

"Odd how?" Wolfe gave up trying to dry his pants. He was far more interested in what Kit had just said.

"Anxious, mostly. Or restless, as if they were waiting for something. Sometimes they stop eating and stare up into the mountains like they know something's out there."

They could have been sensing *him,*

Wolfe thought. Or was it Cruz? If anyone could find the rogue agent, it would be these special dogs. Was that the next task on Ryker's agenda?

Kit pulled into a crowded parking lot and found the first available space. "I'll stay here with the dogs while you go in."

"Here." Wolfe stared at the football-field-size store and rubbed his jaw slowly. "You mean inside?"

"You said you wanted to change your clothes. After you're finished, maybe you'll watch the dogs while I go pick up some things for Miki."

He hadn't been to a shopping mall in six years. He wasn't used to crowds unless they were trying to escape a war zone. Ironically, that seemed to be fairly close to the case here.

A man with two screaming children stalked past, his cart filled to overflowing with cereals that Wolfe had never heard of. A few lanes over half a dozen teenage boys with pierced noses and purple hair were arguing with half a dozen teenage girls with pierced noses and blue hair. Cars circled and crept down one row and up another, jockeying for any available parking spaces.

Wolfe rubbed his neck, aware of how

alien the normal working world had become for him. "I can change out here and keep an eye on the dogs at the same time. You go ahead and run your errands."

"Are you sure? Baby should be fine. She usually recovers fast." Kit shook her head when she saw the puppy in question perched behind the front seat, her nose nearly touching Wolfe's shoulder.

"Don't worry," he said calmly. "I'm pretty good with animals, trust me."

"I don't know. They may whine when I leave." Kit opened her door slowly.

None of the dogs paid the slightest attention. Butch nudged past Baby, then raised his head to lick Wolfe's chin.

Shaking her head, she grabbed her purse. "Or not."

The Jeep was empty when Kit returned fifteen minutes later.

At least it looked empty. When she turned the corner, she saw that the rear door was open and the dogs were lined up in a row, all panting, their heads hanging out the back.

Wolfe was squeezed in between them, looking completely content as he scratched Baby's head with one hand and Butch's stomach with the other. He also appeared to be scanning the parking lot.

She held up a shopping bag. "All done. Next stop, Pet Land." She noticed that Wolfe was wearing a clean shirt and pants. "You managed to change, I see. I'm impressed. But I still can't believe how quickly the dogs have taken to you. No barking, not even a growl or two. They've *never* done that before."

Wolfe reached down and scratched Sundance under the chin. Not wanting to be left out, Baby squeezed in closer for her share of the petting. "We got along just fine, didn't we, guys?"

No kidding. He *was* good with animals, Kit thought. In a minute she'd have to remind them she was here.

"What's this other store like?"

"Pet Land is the best place in the world to buy anything for your pet. Even though it's thirty minutes away, it's worth the drive." She frowned at the oncoming traffic. "Unfortunately, it's Friday night."

"What's wrong with Friday?"

"Everyone's out. Brace yourself. It's going to be a war zone in there."

Wolfe thought she was using a figure of speech.

War as noisy, gleaming spectacle.

War as smoke and adrenaline. Civilians did it all the time, he thought grimly. Their assumptions about combat usually came from the latest hit movie or eight-minute CNN interview. But the fact was, you couldn't understand combat unless you'd been there, cordite burning acrid in your throat, every nerve juiced by fear while you went deaf from shoulder-fired antitank grenade launchers blazing all around you.

What could Kit know about war zones?

Then she took a corner and he counted about two hundred dusty pickup trucks and gleaming new Volvos jammed side-by-side in the crowded parking lot, with more cars overflowing onto the nearby side streets. There were kids crying and parents shouting and dogs barking.

Maybe there was something to this analogy of hers.

At first he'd tried to talk her out of the errand, but Baby needed a new training leash and Kit wanted a special chew toy to cheer Diesel up when he came home from the clinic.

More trucks pulled up, music blaring. A car drove along the row, bouncing up and down in time to the music.

Houston, you've been out of things here at home for way too long.

"I need to take Baby inside with me to make sure her leash fits properly. Dogs on leashes are allowed in the store, so you could bring the other dogs in, too."

He rubbed his neck. "I think we'll sit this dance out."

"Are you sure?" She snapped a leash on Baby and opened the door. "You look a little pale."

Wolfe watched a poodle in white booties and a rhinestone jacket that spelled out *Elvis*. His owner was dressed in matching attire.

If the sensory overload hadn't been so noticeable, the whole scene would have been amusing. As things were, it was going to be a long night.

Twenty minutes later Butch and Sundance were walking restless circles in the back of the Jeep, and at every pass they stopped to nudge Wolfe's arm. Dogs of all shapes and colors had come and gone, but there was still no sign of Kit and Baby.

As Wolfe sat warily, trying to decide whether to take the other dogs inside, Butch barked once and dug beneath a pile of blankets in the back of the Jeep. He emerged with a leash, which he dropped on Wolfe's lap. Seconds later Sundance dropped a matching leash beside the first one.

"Two to one, guys. No fair doubling up on me."

Butch looked out the back window of the Jeep, then barked sharply. He picked up the leash and shook it hard, his eyes like laser sights. On instinct, Wolfe focused, trying to read the source of the dog's anxiety.

The minutes stretched out. He didn't move, staring at Butch, waiting.

Nothing came across. Not one speck.

Which was a little odd. Wolfe could usually pick up at least a few stray images here and there when he scanned the people around him. On the other hand, none of the team had ever worked specifically with animals, so the result didn't entirely surprise him.

After another quick scan of the parking lot, he gave in. "Okay, you two win. Let's roll. Tight formation." He snapped on the leashes and checked to see if anyone paid undue attention to him or to the dogs. Satisfied that everything was normal, he locked the car and looked down at his excited companions. "Brace for contact, troops. This could get nasty."

Especially if there were any other Elvis impersonators in the area.

Shopping carts were backed up by the dozens as irritated pet owners argued over flea powder and kibble. *Zoo* was definitely an understatement.

Where the heck were Kit and Baby?

Wolfe looked around at the flashing lights while music blasted from the big front doors. Shrill announcements spit like gunfire from a tinny loudspeaker. He couldn't remember the last time he'd seen a store so big. Even standing outside the entrance and looking in put his senses on overdrive. He could face Stinger missiles and AK-47s, but the chaos of Pet Land figured nowhere in his field training.

Ignoring a beagle wearing a red baseball cap, he wiped a bead of sweat off his neck. "I can do this. What's so frightening about a bunch of crazy pet owners and a whole lot of noise?"

Butch barked once, staring out into the parking lot. When Wolfe followed the direction of the dog's gaze, he saw nothing but a sea of cars. Then Sundance moved closer, pressed against his opposite leg and growled.

Wolfe pulled out his secure cell phone and punched in two numbers.

Izzy Teague answered on the first ring. "Joe's Flower Shop. Roses to go."

"Very funny, Teague. I'm at Pet Land with the dogs."

"Say again?"

"Pet Land, you heard me. Kit's inside with Baby, and I've got the other dogs leashed here at the door. But they're acting odd, very restless about something. I need you to check out the parking lot without calling any attention to yourself."

"No problem. I can do low profile or high profile."

"Definitely low."

"On my way."

A motion caught Wolfe's eye. "Take some pictures, too. We may turn up that missing car belonging to the waitress."

"Afraid not. It was found abandoned off the freeway outside Albuquerque."

Wolfe ran a hand slowly along Sundance's back. The puppy was motionless, staring down a row crowded with cars. "I'm taking the dogs inside. I can guarantee you that someone's out here. Focus on the fifth row with the green Subaru."

"I'm on it. Watch your six."

As he walked inside the crowded store, Wolfe fought an odd compulsion to turn and stare back into the parking lot. The urge came from nowhere, sudden and brutal in its intensity. He was instantly certain it was Cruz, probing his defenses and preparing for an attack.

Either his ex-team leader's original skills had grown exponentially or the government had been developing some new techniques with Cruz. Either way, the situation spelled danger.

Inside the front door, a man cut Wolfe off with a cart, and a German Shepherd nearly peed on his foot while his owner laughed.

Not good for the first twenty seconds.

He hadn't gone two feet more when a small dog with trailing white hair and a red satin bow blocked his way, barking incessantly in short, shrill bursts that Butch answered with stunning disdain.

"Good dog," Wolfe muttered. "This is just ground fire. Ignore it, buddy." But the white dog kept barking.

Wolfe guided the Labs away, turning down the nearest aisle. Trying to ignore the chaos of noise, color and motion around him, he scanned the shelves, stocked high with rhinestone dog collars and puppy diapers.

Puppy diapers?

The world had definitely changed since he'd been recruited for Foxfire. Looking around, he felt like Rip Van Winkle starting to wake up, and the experience wasn't pleasant.

Butch and Sundance didn't move, taking in the chaos with calm interest. Their behavior made Wolfe smile. "She did a damn good job on you two guys, didn't she?"

Sundance's tail gave three quick wags.

"Okay, let's move before we suffer another hostile response." He headed toward the center of the store in search of Kit, wondering how there could be so many different colors of leashes. And who in the hell needed sixty varieties of dog food?

At the next corner, he nearly tripped over a tiny Pekinese who had pulled away from its owner and raced under his feet. When he turned around, a blonde with a tight T-shirt cut to showcase about five inches of naked stomach was looking his way. Her eyes narrowed. Smiling, she wiggled a little so that her jeans slipped lower and the T-shirt slid higher.

It had been months since he'd had a normal social interaction in a civilian situation, and the standard protocols were a little dim. As the blonde waved at him and crossed the aisle, he gave a wary smile. Before he could take evasive maneuvers, she'd blocked his path.

"Wow, what cute puppies. And they're so

well behaved." She wiggled again, making the jeans slip even lower. "I can't reach the dog treats. I hate it when they put them so high." She looked down, showing some cleavage and making kissing noises at Butch and Sundance. "I'll be glad to hold these gorgeous puppies if you wouldn't mind. It will only take you a second."

"I wish I could help, ma'am." Wolfe glanced around, but there was still no sign of Kit. He tightened his hold on the leashes. "I'm afraid my puppies aren't very good with strangers. Sorry." He gave a little shrug to soften the refusal, but the blonde flounced off in search of new prey.

"What's wrong with her?" Kit came around the corner with Baby. Under one arm she had two boxes of puppy vitamins and a new leash.

"She wanted help to reach something. I didn't want to give her the leashes and it got her steamed." Wolfe stared at a display with two plastic dogs that ran back and forth in a line, promoting a new brand of dog shampoo. He wasn't sure if he was amused or revolted.

"Is something wrong?" Kit frowned at him. "The other dogs didn't throw up on you, I hope."

"No, they were great. Their training is excellent."

"Then what? It's like you've never been in a pet store before."

Wolfe tried to shut out the barrage of distracting stimuli. He ignored two men arguing over choke chains. He even managed to ignore a display of talking dog diapers. The truth was, he'd never been in a store that was remotely like this. Kit had no way of knowing that, of course, and he wasn't about to discuss his Foxfire training and private life with her.

He waved a hand. "It's . . . big," he said.

She was still looking at him, eyes narrowed. "That's why everyone comes here to shop. One stop does it all." She walked over to a huge pyramid display built with cat food cans. "The prices are also twenty percent cheaper than the neighborhood store. How can you beat that?"

A boy ran past her, pushing a child-size cart and racing as only an out-of-control six-year-old can run. His mother followed grimly, holding the hand of a younger boy. "Benjamin, *stop.* Come back here right now."

The boy speeded up, his cart whipping past boxes and shelves. He was watching the talking diaper display, mesmerized, when his cart hit the pyramid of canned goods full force. The structure shook and then the top can fell sideways.

A dozen more cans shook free and plummeted, only inches away from the oblivious child.

Wolfe sprinted along the aisle. As the whole structure began to shake, he swept the boy under one arm and turned, catching the wave of falling cans against his shoulders. He also managed to grab a piece of defective metal shelving that appeared to be the cause of the problem.

All around him men were shouting and dogs were barking, but he barely noticed. He was still holding the boy against his chest when the explosion of cans hitting the floor finally stopped.

Silence fell. Then came a few muted questions. Seconds later he was surrounded by people pounding his back, asking if he was okay and was the boy hurt and how had he reacted so fast? Wolfe didn't understand why they were so concerned. He held out the boy to his mother, then tried to move away but he was caught fast as the harried woman cried and laughed at the same time, hugging her son and trying to hug Wolfe, who was at least a foot taller than she was.

Solemn and a little unsteady, the boy held out a smashed piece of candy bar. Wolfe eyed the bar, eyed the little boy, and then took a bite of the chocolate. "That's good stuff you've got there, pal. But maybe you should go back to your mommy now. I think she's worried." He winked at the boy. "You know how women can be."

The boy nodded gravely, his eyes huge.

When Wolfe turned to walk away, the crowd of curious onlookers parted in respectful silence. Then a man with a store uniform called out to him. "Man, you were greased lightning when you grabbed that kid. You play football or something?"

Or something.

Wolfe shrugged, uncomfortable at the attention. When he reached Kit's side, he took Butch's leash and walked toward the front of the store without looking back.

"What's wrong?"

"Nothing," he said calmly. "Can we go?"

Kit hurried to keep up with him. "How *did* you move so fast?"

He strode down the row of cars toward her Jeep, studying the area for any unusual activity. "I don't know what you're talking about."

"You know exactly what I'm talking

about. But if you want to play games about it, fine," she said flatly.

"Kit, I —"

"Never mind. You don't owe me an explanation." Her voice tightened. "In fact, you don't owe me anything at all." Her shoulders were straight, her body stiff as she walked past him, holding the dogs' leashes tightly.

Baby turned once, gave a quick wag of her tail and blinked her big eyes.

Almost like she was sympathizing.

Wolfe was *almost* sure that was impossible.

CHAPTER SIXTEEN

"What's the problem?" Wolfe frowned as Kit pulled out of the parking lot in a hail of gravel. She was staring straight ahead, her mouth a tight line.

He couldn't figure her out. Why would she expect him to talk about what he'd done? It was simple training and reflexes, nothing that made him a hero.

Besides, he'd messed up by getting himself noticed.

"You're modest about saving that little boy, and I can understand that. But when I ask you what's wrong — *bam,* you bite my head off. Of course, I'm upset." She took a deep breath. "Who are you, Wolfe? I look at you and I see a complete stranger."

"You're making a big deal out of something small. Let it go, Kit."

"The way I should have let it go years ago. Good idea." She stared at the road and shook her head. "Where do I drop you?"

He was fascinated by the cool sheen of her skin and the emotion that filled her eyes. It was like watching the det-cord burn on an explosive fuse. You knew that you should get away fast, but some morbid fascination made you want to stay, waiting for the moment when everything blew.

He remembered now that she had always had a temper, and her brother's nonstop practical jokes hadn't helped much over the years. "You're not dropping me anywhere."

"Think again." She accelerated into traffic, then cut left to pass a slow-moving dairy truck. "You can get off at the next corner. There's a hotel where you can find a taxi and they're open until nine."

The dogs were pressed up against Kit's seat. They almost seemed to be following the details of the conversation, Wolfe thought.

"Kit, look —"

"No, you look. I'm tired of whatever game you're playing. You appear in my house with a string of flimsy excuses and my dogs don't bark once, which, trust me, never happens. Then you watch the road like you're expecting something bad from any direction. Inside that store you react — well, faster than I've ever seen a person move, and when I say something about it, you glare at me. You insult me with your stories, Wolfe. No, you insult us *both.*"

He didn't speak. He couldn't say anything that she hadn't already said and he didn't want to lie to her, but he had no choice.

"And for the record, I know why you're here." Her expression was stony. "And the answer is no."

"You know?"

"Of course I do. The last time Trace called, he made it very clear that he wanted me to sell the ranch. He said it was too much responsibility for me, and I should move into Santa Fe."

Trace had said that? If so, he was a fool. Anyone could see that the ranch was where Kit belonged.

On the other hand, Trace might not have looked too hard. People usually saw what they wanted to see.

She didn't wait for him to answer, plunging on. "He told me he wasn't coming back soon and I couldn't count on him for help." She reached around to Baby, who was hovering between the seats again. "As if I didn't already know that. Of course Trace isn't coming back. His heart was never out there at the ranch." Her voice fell. "But that doesn't mean he has the right to order me to sell. So I *know* why you're here. Trace sent you to convince me to put the ranch up for sale. But you can go right back and tell him it's *not* happening."

"Trace hasn't said a word to me about what you should or shouldn't do. If he had, I'd have told him he was crazy. Any idiot can see this is what you're meant to do and the ranch is where you're meant to do it."

She shot him a stricken look. "We don't owe you money, do we? I mean — has Trace borrowed from you?"

Wolfe shook his head.

"That's a relief. A few times before . . ." Her fingers opened and closed on the wheel, and he sensed how it hurt her to bring up the whole issue of her finances. She and Trace were similar in that way, both stubborn and proud to a fault.

The silence was broken by the shrill ring of her cell phone. She grabbed it quickly. "Hello?"

Wolfe turned slightly so he could listen in. The caller appeared to be her friend Miki again.

"We just left the pet store. No, forget it." Kit's voice tightened. "We'll discuss that later." She turned her head away from him, frowning. "I need to go, Miki. I'm driving." There was another pause. "What kind of car? Where?" The frown between her eyes grew. "How long has it been there?" She darted a quick glance in Wolfe's direction. "You'd better lock your doors, then call the police."

"What's wrong?"

"Hold on, Miki." She stared at the dark line of distant mountains, their ridges veiled by clouds. "There's some kind of van parked two houses away from her. It's been there all day, according to her neighbor, but no one on the street's having any work done."

"Tell her to get the license plate," Wolfe said. "Is there anyone inside?" He pulled out his cell phone, dialing Izzy while Kit shot his question back to her friend.

"There's no one in the front that you can see. Okay, Miki, give me the plate number." She rattled the numbers back to Wolfe, then pressed the phone against her chest. "Have you gotten us in some kind of trouble?"

"Pull in at the next turn. There's a res-taurant on the right."

Her face was tense as she drove into the expansive entrance of a French restaurant with a marble driveway and about fifty valet parking attendants.

"Give me a minute." Wolfe opened his

door, dialing Izzy. As he got out, he waved off an eager attendant. "Izzy? Yeah, we've got problems. There's a van parked over at the friend's house." He repeated the plate number quietly. "No sign of a driver and the neighbors say no work is being done there."

He heard the click of a keyboard.

"Not to worry. He's one of ours. I put him there this morning, just in case."

"Move him and shift cars. He's been made. It seems to be a tight-knit community and people notice stuff like this. Miki certainly did."

"I'm on it."

The line went dead.

Wolfe realized Kit was staring at him. She wasn't going to buy anything but the truth, which he was under orders not to tell her. But Cruz was somewhere close, already in pursuit. Wolfe's instincts told him that they hadn't been all that smart, only lucky so far. One more reason he wasn't going to stay too long in one place.

Thanks to his glare, the valet staff was keeping a safe distance. He rubbed his neck, then walked around to Kit's side.

"What's going on?" she demanded.

"Look, I'll tell you what I can. Things are a little complicated right now."

"Complicated how?" She looked down as his pager began to vibrate in his front pocket. "What's that?"

Wolfe checked the LED and looked north, studying the road. Izzy had signaled him to get moving. They would meet as soon as Kit reached Miki's house. "We need to go, Kit."

"Go *where?* Aren't you going to answer any of my questions?"

"I'd prefer if you let me drive."

"You don't think I can handle this car? I've been driving Jeeps on the ranch since I was ten."

"It's not a question of competence, but training. I've been trained in close pursuit and evasion."

She didn't move, staring at him in the blue twilight. "Are you telling me that we may be pursued?"

He swept a glance across the parking lot and checked the busy highway nearby. "I'm telling you that I'd prefer to drive."

She sat stiffly, her eyes wary. "What was in that page you just got?"

"Later."

"You're on some kind of mission, aren't you? Tell me the truth, Wolfe."

"Later. We need to go now, Kit."

After a deep breath she slid out of the

car reluctantly and went around to the passenger side. Within three minutes they were back in the heavy flow of Santa Fe's weekend traffic.

Neither one spoke.

He headed north, away from the commercial strip. As the traffic thinned, he took a sharp left, watching to see if any cars followed.

None did.

Trees lined the road above steep irrigation canals to right and left. Waist-high reeds rose like spikes against the fading light.

Wolfe heard the drone of a big motor, coming fast. When he looked back, headlights cut through the darkness. It was possible that the lights behind them belonged to a rancher coming back from Albuquerque with a month's feed supply, nothing more.

Like hell it was. How many ranchers drove a late-model Hummer?

Without drawing his eyes from the rearview mirror, he dug the cell phone out of his front pocket and punched a button. "We're on Highway 180, and we just got company. Black Hummer with Missouri plates, number Bravo Foxtrot 6214." He lowered his voice. "I saw it back at the pet store, and I'm pretty sure it was parked one block over at the vet's clinic today, too."

Kit started to ask a question, then stopped, her mouth thinning to a tight line.

Wolfe rang off, calculating their options as he glanced into the rearview mirror. "Do these irrigation canals continue on both sides of us?"

"For another two miles, at least." Her voice was stiff and angry. "After that it's pretty deserted."

"Get the dogs into the front seat." He put one hand on her knee and squeezed briefly. "After I pull around that next hill, I'm going to stop. You and the dogs need to drop down beside the canal and stay out of sight." He shrugged off his dark jacket. "Put this on. No noise until I come back — no matter what you hear or see."

The lights were closer. She pulled on Wolfe's jacket quickly and called the dogs one by one into the front, squeezed against her feet and lap.

"Give me your sweater," he ordered quietly. When she handed it over, Wolfe pulled it around his shoulders, so that the red wool would be visible from the side window. "Do you have some kind of sun hat in here?"

He took the battered circle of straw that she found behind her seat and tugged the hat down over his eyes. "You can't let them see you, Kit. Not you, not the dogs."

"We can manage." She gave him a tight smile. "What about you?"

"Don't worry about me. Just keep yourself and the dogs out of sight. No noise. No movement." He took the curve fast, the Jeep fishtailing over gravel. As they climbed, the road lay behind them, a narrow ribbon against the gathering darkness. The Hummer was steadily closing the distance.

"Ready?"

She nodded.

"Now." He slammed on the brakes as soon as they cleared the hill, out of sight of the Hummer. Kit wrenched open her door and jumped out with the dogs right behind her, tails wagging as if it was another training game.

"Heel," Kit ordered, skidding down the muddy bank toward the dark reeds and the faint silver gleam of water.

As soon as Wolfe saw that she was safe, he floored the Jeep and roared off.

All she could see was a black screen of reeds.

Shivering in the sudden cold, Kit pulled

the dogs around her. They huddled close, sinking down into the muddy water.

Abruptly, car lights cut through the darkness. A black Hummer raced past, and she had a blurred glimpse of two figures inside.

Cold and wet, Baby's nose nudged her neck. Sundance pressed against her knees, while Butch lay against her lap. She had a sudden impression of stars blazing fiercely against the sapphire sky as her eyes adapted to the dark. Even in her fear, she felt the rugged beauty of the night in this place of isolation.

A rifle cracked. Kit realized the distant shattering sound meant someone had just blown out her Jeep's back window.

CHAPTER SEVENTEEN

Wolfe hit the accelerator as he came out of the turn. After a last look to be certain that Kit and the dogs were out of sight, he put his full attention on the approaching Hummer. The Jeep was more maneuverable, but the Hummer had size and indestructibility in its favor.

He had to buy time until Izzy showed up. He considered his options as headlights cut through the back windshield. A Hummer was good. He'd driven a whole lot of them over the years, so he also happened to know they were worthless in narrow spaces like a twisting wash. Or a narrow irrigation ditch.

Up to the right he saw a broad adobe gate that marked the entrance to a ranch.

He jerked the wheel sharply. As he headed under the gate, rifle fire cracked behind him, and the rear windshield exploded, chips of glass shooting through the inside of the Jeep like popcorn.

But flying glass chips were a minor problem. The Hummer was gaining on him.

As the road turned, he cut the Jeep's lights altogether. Instantly the gravel road in front of him was swallowed up by darkness.

He heard the Hummer swerve, then keep right on coming.

Wolfe had more or less expected that.

The thin silver ribbon of the canal glittered to his left. He judged his speed, compensated for the slope, jerked open his door and jumped. The Jeep kept moving along the narrow ditch, with one tire resting on the bank. He figured acceleration would carry it another sixty feet before it slowed.

Prone in the wet grass, he slid his firearm out of his holster under his arm and waited. As the Hummer thundered past, he had a quick glimpse of a man in the driver's seat and the shadow of another man inside. Taking both of them out would have been easy, but he needed at least one alive to interrogate.

The Jeep bumped over a pile of broken bricks and came to a halt, with the Hummer's lights blazing through the shattered back window. The passenger's door opened slowly, and Wolfe saw one of the men raise a rifle with a scope.

It wouldn't take them long to realize the

Jeep was empty. Then they'd backtrack and come hunting.

But Wolfe had other plans.

He considered a quick, focused image disruption, but if Cruz was nearby, the energy pattern would pull him right to Wolfe. You couldn't fool another Foxfire team member — especially one as powerful as Cruz had become.

Crawling silently through the reeds and down into the water, he crossed the ditch, emerging on the far side of the Hummer. The dark metal body was outfitted for field operations, and the back window was removed, allowing him a good view of the driver, who appeared to be talking quietly on a cell phone. Still hidden, Wolfe worked his way toward the second man, who carried his rifle level as he approached the empty Jeep.

The reeds shook in the canal, and the closest attacker spun fast, tracking the sound. Three high-power cartridges slammed into the water in a tight line. As the man scanned for a response, Wolfe came up behind him from out of the grass. Because he wanted the man alive, he didn't risk close-quarters gunfire. One kick drove the man to his knees. Within seconds the target was facedown in the mud, his hands locked in plastic tactical restraints, a gag in his mouth. When he began to struggle, Wolfe knocked him out with a single blow to the head.

A powerful flashlight beam cut through the darkness. "Alpha, report."

Wolfe went prone in the mud.

Light cut past the spot where he had been standing.

"Alpha, are you there?"

Up the bank big boots squished along the mud. Wolfe heard the same whispered question as the man from the Hummer circled to the side of the Jeep, his weapon pointed through the muddy window while static burst from his walkie-talkie.

"Alpha, do you copy? Do you have the woman and the dogs?" The man flashed a light into the Jeep. The powerful beam struck broken glass and muddy water.

The man turned, laying down a pattern of fire from his automatic as he ran back toward the Hummer, and Wolfe followed on the other side of the canal, low and silent. Certain that Cruz was nowhere nearby, he changed tactics.

Now he hit his target with an image of a dozen snarling wolves, leaping straight across the top of the canal.

Gunfire chattered sharply. Wolfe cut his

way around the back of the Hummer, grabbed his cursing, confused target, and tossed him against the side of the black vehicle.

Grunting, the two fought, slipping in the mud. Wolfe knocked a handgun out of the man's grip, then felt his attacker's weight shift.

The man toppled sideways, and Wolfe realized he was too late. One quick self-inflicted knife stroke had brought blood pumping in dark waves from the man's ravaged neck.

Who in the hell *were* these guys? Wolfe didn't bother searching for a pulse. It was too late for that. At least he still had one assailant unconscious but alive and fit for interrogating. He also had the dead man's cell phone for Izzy to examine.

Grimly, he checked inside the Hummer, but the vehicle was empty. No maps, no computers, no documents of any sort. No sign of who had sent them or what they'd come for.

FUBAR.

Staring into the darkness, he pulled out his cell phone and dialed Izzy.

Huddled on the muddy bank with her dogs, Kit shivered in the darkness. Everything had happened too fast. She couldn't process, caught in a blur of fear and shock.

She was soaked from slipping into the canal twice. Her feet slid through the mud and her hip ground against a rough concrete girder at the edge of the ditch, pain lancing down into her joint.

She closed her eyes, certain she was going to black out.

Her hands tightened around Butch's body, and the big puppy wiggled closer, licking her face. When she finally struggled back onto dry ground, she saw that the Hummer had stopped near her Jeep.

A man left the car. Then the driver emerged, a silent, lethal silhouette with an automatic weapon.

A heartbeat later, something moved in the reeds. The dogs tensed at the muffled thud of men fighting. But it was harder and harder for her to concentrate on the sounds around her with her right hip burning as if someone was twisting the socket. Staring up at the night sky, soaked and frozen, she tried to ignore the pain and focus.

The stars jumped back and forth in jerky lines above her. Dimly she heard the sigh of the wind along the tall reeds beside the canal.

The fighting suddenly stopped. Baby's head nudged her neck as a wave of dizziness hit her.

There was no sign of Wolfe in the darkness. She listened for sounds of fighting or footsteps while her fingers tightened in Baby's warm fur, but the cold settled around her. She was having trouble keeping her eyes open.

Pain left her light-headed, her thoughts jumbled.

Why had a car followed them into the darkness? Why had a van been parked near Miki's house all day, and how was Wolfe involved?

But the cold was worse. Shivering, she closed her eyes and laid her head down on Baby's neck, slipping into the darkness.

"Nothing here." Izzy glared at the inside of the Hummer. "Who are these guys?"

"Just what I'd like to know." Wolfe shone his flashlight into the back of the Hummer. "They knew what they were looking for. I heard the driver ask his buddy if he'd found the woman and the dogs yet."

"Well briefed and well financed, just the way Ryker suspected." Izzy studied the body of the man who had slit his own throat moments before. "What the hell are these people so afraid of?"

"Maybe it's not fear," Wolfe said quietly.

"Then what?"

"Loyalty." Wolfe studied the motionless body. "Or the belief that they are following a higher code." He pushed to his feet. "I need to find Kit and the dogs. We're going to require transport, since they shot the hell out of her Jeep."

"Get my truck. I'll clean up here and take our other friend along for questioning." Izzy tossed the key to Wolfe. "Across the canal, then make a sharp left."

By the time Wolfe drove Izzy's truck back toward the spot where Kit had jumped, the night was absolutely silent. Even though no other cars had followed them, he had to force down images of Kit, bound and gagged, taken captive.

But if there had been an attempt to take her, he would have known. Even Cruz, skilled as he was, would have left some subtle energy trail for Wolfe to follow.

Somewhere to his left a low growl erupted near a clump of reeds.

"Baby, is that you?"

The long stems shook. A dark figure raced up the bank and slammed into his leg. Wolfe bent down and patted Baby, scanning the darkness for any sign of Kit.

"Good dog. Where's Kit? Go find her, honey."

The reeds shook again. Two more bodies raced toward Wolfe. Butch and Sundance plowed into his chest, rocking him back from the impact. "Where's Kit, you two?"

Baby shot off over the mud, with Wolfe following closely. A narrow track looped up the bank, then back down toward the silver line of the canal.

A dark shape was stretched out beside the water. With a sickening jolt Wolfe realized it was Kit.

He stabbed at his cell phone as he ran toward her, snapping orders the moment Izzy answered. "Teague, Kit's down. Can you hotwire the Hummer?"

"Not a problem. Where are you?"

"Back at the canal. Get moving."

Wolfe cut the connection as he dropped to his knees beside Kit, sliding wet hair off her face. "Kit, can you hear me?"

When she didn't answer, he searched her wet body, checking for signs of blood or trauma, but finding none.

She still didn't move. Cursing softly, he pulled a penlight out of his pocket and flashed it on her face. A nasty cut ran along her right eyebrow. A line of bruises rose starkly at her upper cheek. At least she was breathing.

He cupped her jaw gently. "Wake up, sleeping beauty. We gotta move."

She didn't budge.

He heard the low growl of the Hummer behind him and waved one hand to guide Izzy closer. Even then his gaze didn't leave Kit's face. She was pale and fragile in the beam of his pocket light, and Wolfe felt something squeeze hard in his chest. He didn't have a name for the emotion. Maybe he didn't *want* to have a name for it.

Grimly, he pulled off his sweater and draped it over her wet body. "Come on, honey. Rise and shine, damn it. Wake up and curse me some more. Kick me or kiss me, I don't care which." His voice turned hoarse. "Damn it, Kit, can you hear me?"

He was afraid to move her for fear of broken bones. Izzy, trained as a medic, would make that decision. Baby was quiet, huddled on the ground, pressed against her shoulder. None of the dogs moved, watching him intently.

Looking back into the darkness, he shouted at the Hummer crawling along the bank. "What the hell is taking so long, Teague? We're over here."

The gleaming metal body seemed to take

forever to reach him, and all the while Kit hadn't moved.

Wolfe gave up trying to believe that this was just another mission. Kit was more than a civilian target he'd been assigned to protect. She was part of his past — and possibly part of his future, even if he couldn't face all the implications yet. He'd wondered how the situation could get any worse. Now he knew.

She was trapped in a place of fog and nightmares, a place where the wind burned, cutting her skin and weighing down her too-fragile bones. In the distance sounds came and went, disjointed and low.

After a while none of it mattered.

At least the pain was familiar. In some way it was even comforting. She knew she should wake up, feed the dogs, check the kennels — work, always work.

But today was different. Something important had happened to her today. She frowned, unable to remember what had happened or why it was so important. Then she was too tired to care.

After a while she drifted back down into the fog while pale stars glittered like false promises high above her head.

CHAPTER EIGHTEEN

Foxfire headquarters
Somewhere north of Los Alamos

"Did you see that?" The civilian inspector sent as liaison from D.C. hunched forward, peering at his split-screen monitor.

Lloyd Ryker didn't bother to answer. Of course he'd seen. He'd seen the damned video feed a dozen times by now, and it never got any better. It was a walking, talking PR nightmare in the making.

But Ryker made sure that none of that showed on his face.

Control.

Confuse.

Conceal.

"See what?" he said calmly.

His newest visitor was ex-NSA and inclined to be a little excitable. *"That."* The liaison officer stabbed a finger toward the flickering screen of his computer. "One minute the man was there, the next minute he's gone."

Ryker eased back in his chair and

studied the monitor as the images flowed past, ghostlike. He'd tried to block the facility inspection. He'd pulled strings and tried every kind of back-alley bargaining.

No dice. Now he had a civilian breathing down his neck, and it couldn't have come at a worse time. But you didn't argue with the liaison from the head of military appropriations.

So Ryker sat tight and figured how to run damage control. For starters he had edited the tape with Cruz, blurring his face and cutting details wherever the changes wouldn't be too obvious. The next thing to go had been the shots of the lab animals under Cruz's control. All his visitor knew was that the facility was doing animal tests in connection with a new nanotechnology protocol.

The liaison from D.C. sat forward, frowning at the screen. "Can't you get your techs to clean up this tape? I can barely see what's going on in there."

That was the whole idea, Ryker thought grimly.

"I've got three of them working on it as we speak," he lied smoothly. "But I didn't want you to wait. I know how important your time is, Mr. Garvey."

More images flickered past. Twenty

seconds later the animals in the lab were free and there was no evidence of Cruz's ability to manipulate them.

As Ryker watched the tape, he felt sweat trickle down his neck. It was hell having an outsider dissect his security tapes. He knew that his political future — and maybe even his life — depended on tracking Cruz down before the inspection went any deeper.

On the screen Cruz hunched over the computer terminal, typing quickly, seen only from the back.

"He doesn't know you added a third camera inside the fire extinguisher," Garvey said smugly. "Not so smart after all."

The man's IQ is higher than yours and mine put together, Ryker thought.

On the screen, a password prompt appeared, followed by a string of dots as Cruz entered the security code.

Garvey swung around in his chair, frowning. "How did he get active passwords?"

Hell if Ryker knew. That scared him more than anything.

Garvey was studying the screen, and he didn't look so smug now.

"Maybe we should take a break." Ryker

stood up and stretched. "Get a cup of coffee and clear the cobwebs."

"Later." Garvey frowned as addresses, contact names, secret government operations and specs for high-tech equipment scrolled past on the screen. "I don't understand any of this. What are these coded files?"

Garvey sounded irritated, as well he should. Foxfire was a highest-clearance, restricted operation, and Ryker had made sure to doctor as much of the tape as he could, effectively concealing the program's true purpose.

"What the hell's going on here, Ryker?" Garvey snapped. "What kind of work are you doing in this facility — and why wasn't the committee informed about any changes?"

Because it's way above their security level, son. Definitely above yours.

But Ryker said nothing. He had known one day Washington would send one of their glib experts to ask questions like this.

His voice was calm as he reached for his cup of cold coffee. "We've been trying out some new surveillance equipment here, but we retired the program six months ago. Sounded good on paper, but no strategic value." His fingers eased to his pocket, closed around the angular body of his Sig 9 mm. "We pulled the plug before the accounting drones could trash us in their facility review. Stop looking so paranoid." The explanation sounded logical, completely unrehearsed.

Sounding honest had always been Ryker's greatest skill.

The liaison officer was quiet, staring at the computer, where the details of a fourteen-year military record scrolled past. Ryker had itched to destroy the last part of the feed, but he didn't dare. The change in timestamp and length would be too obvious.

Instead he'd blurred the file and chopped out several of the final crucial seconds.

Garvey stopped the frame. "Wolfe Houston?" He frowned at Ryker. "I know that name. Wasn't he the sniper we sent to Ecuador last year during the oil crisis? I didn't know he'd left the SEALs."

Ryker didn't answer. He cradled the Sig in his jacket pocket lovingly. All it would take was one bullet. Then no more review and no more questions.

The bureaucrats would take over the world, if you let them.

There were no cameras running inside this room. Ryker had always made that a requirement in his command areas. When accidents happened, the last thing you wanted was video feed your enemies could use against you.

After twenty-four years in secure operations, Ryker had a whole pack of people waiting to rip out his throat in the most painful way possible.

He'd have to get rid of Garvey with more concocted stories, buying time until Houston snagged Cruz. It had been a colossal mistake to turn any of the experimental canines over to a civilian, that much was clear. Ryker had argued against the plan from the start, but he'd been outnumbered.

It was time the dogs were brought back into the lab where they belonged, inside cages, under constant surveillance, undergoing the strict training that produced guaranteed results. No more of this feel-good coddling that wasted taxpayer dollars.

But first Foxfire needed their prize guinea pig captured alive. Cruz had begun to show impressive new skills in the last few months and Ryker desperately needed to isolate exactly which protocols had triggered those skills. After that, Cruz would be as expendable as any other rat in this well-hidden lab. Ryker might even enjoy killing Cruz himself.

But first Wolfe Houston had to find Cruz. Then he had to bring him in. Neither task would be easy, even for a Navy SEAL with Houston's impressive record and enhanced skills.

Ryker realized Garvey was staring at him. "What?"

"You've got a call on your line, sir." Garvey stood up, closing his laptop with a snap. "I'm packing it in." His face was thoughtful as he locked his laptop in a secure drawer for the night. "I'll call you later if I have any more questions."

There would be thousands of questions, Ryker knew, but he hid his irritation. "That will be fine. I've got a long night of reading in front of me. You know how important it is to stay up-to-date with the new research."

"I appreciate that you're so accommodating. Cooperation is always looked on favorably by the committee."

After Garvey left, Ryker stared at the drawer containing his secure laptop. He thought about overriding the lock to see what data Garvey had acquired, but he decided against it.

The situation was bad, but not that bad.

His phone light continued to blink. He cleared his mind and lifted the receiver.

"Ryker here." As he listened, his eyes narrowed. "Tell me what you've got, Teague. And your news had better be fantastic."

CHAPTER NINETEEN

"Can't you *do* something?" Wolfe's voice was raw as he tried to see what Izzy was doing.

"Stop crowding me." Izzy nudged him away with his elbow. "Go get the Betadine from the shelf near the window."

"Where?"

"Small brown bottle. Blue label," Izzy said calmly. "And settle the hell down. She's going to be fine. Some cuts, a few bruises, but she'll be good to go soon." With deft fingers Izzy wrapped a piece of gauze around Kit's wrist, where he'd just finished cleaning bits of gravel out of a jagged, shallow wound.

"Then why isn't she waking up?" Wolfe snapped. "It's been twenty minutes."

"Sixteen minutes, thirty-two seconds." Izzy rolled his shoulders. "Stop worrying, Navy. Her pulse is strong and her color is coming back." Gently, he lifted Kit's eyelid, checking for a response. Then he made notes in the little notebook that went everywhere with him.

Bright halogen lights blanketed the small examining table where Kit lay motionless. The Hummer was gone, on the way to the government lab for analysis. Wolfe still wasn't certain how Izzy had managed to procure the snug, self-contained van filled with medical equipment, and he didn't bother to ask. There was a reason that Ishmael Teague was known as a miracle worker.

"You're sure you've got medical experience, Teague? I mean *real* medical experience, not stitching up dogs or overseeing mental cases."

"I've got more field training than most senior surgeons at the Mayo Clinic, pal. And these cuts are largely superficial. She'll have a knot on her forehead for a while, along with the mother of all headaches when she wakes up. Watch her for dizziness, double vision — I'll give you the list." He snapped a glance at Wolfe. "Where's that Betadine?"

"Right here, Doctor Frankenstein."

Izzy snorted as he opened the bottle, poured dark liquid on a clean piece of gauze, and brushed Kit's wound. "Sugar would work just as well, but knowing your suspicious nature, you'd probably go evil on me, Houston."

"Sugar? What kind of jive is that?"

Izzy's brow rose. "That's no kind of jive. Sugar and honey have been used to treat battlefield wounds for centuries. The Greeks did it, the Egyptians did it, and it works. We used it over in Bosnia on occasion. Not many people realize that topical sugar is a universal antimicrobial agent. You don't have to worry about dosage or allergic reactions either. But I'll spare your sensibilities and go hi-tech here instead." He smiled as Wolfe glared at him. "True story, I swear it. The sugar melts in a few hours, mixes with fluid from the wound and actually helps inhibit bacteria."

"What kind of sugar?" Wolfe definitely wasn't buying this.

"Regular grocery store granulated white stuff. Hell, in tests they had a 99.2% cure rate," he added smugly.

"I never can tell when you're dead honest or full of shit, Teague."

"Just the way I like it. But I happen to be telling the truth on this one. Tuck the fact away, too, because you may need it in the field sometime." Wolfe did just that.

Teague's people had already cleaned up the scene of the attack and were transporting the captive to Ryker for questioning. Now Wolfe focused on Kit. He thought he saw her eyelid twitch. "Did you see that?"

"I saw it." Izzy washed his hands, checked his watch and made a note in the pad beside him.

Kit's other eye twitched.

"What happens now?"

"Be sure that she keeps those cuts clean. I've left antibiotic cream for you, not sugar," Izzy said wryly.

The dogs sat up suddenly, then trotted to the bed and licked Kit's motionless hand.

"These animals are pretty amazing." Izzy packed tools and plastic bags back into his medicine case. "Think you can get one for me?"

"Dream on, Teague. Our pals here are way above *our* pay grade." Bending down, Wolfe scratched Baby's head and noticed fluffy white flakes drifting down outside the van. "Can you believe that? It's starting to snow."

Izzy glanced up and shook his head. "Weird weather. But I guess when you're at eight thousand feet, anything can happen."

Wolfe remembered a few storms that had rolled in as late as June and as early as September when he was growing up. Snow probably wasn't all that strange after all.

He moved around the world so often now that he wasn't sure what normal was.

Butch wedged his head between Baby and the examining table. The puppy's tail banged hard against Wolfe's leg. "Like the snow, do you?"

Butch barked once.

"We're almost done. You can go out soon, buddy. I promise."

Izzy shook his head. "I guess you're right about the dogs. And who wants a pet that's smarter than you are?"

Kit's fingers twitched. Her eyes opened and she took a deep breath.

"There you go, Houston. Just like I said. She's looking good."

Wolfe muttered a few choice phrases, then bent over the table, taking Kit's hand gently in his. When he looked up, the lacy white flakes were everywhere, filling the night sky. If he hadn't been so damn worried, he might have found the scene magical.

But Wolfe didn't believe in magic, and all he could think about was Kit.

She opened her eyes blankly.

She was on some kind of cot and two men with blurry faces were looking down at her. She could have sworn that one of them was Denzel Washington. Was she dead or just hallucinating?

Kit cleared her throat. "I loved you in *Manchurian Candidate*."

The man with Denzel Washington's face patted her arm, then took her pulse without speaking.

"You're —"

"He's not." Wolfe was staring down at her. His voice sounded strained. "Trust me, he's not even close. What happened to you?"

Kit realized that her head was throbbing. She also realized that Wolfe was standing right beside her and his hands were wrapped tightly around her wrists. "Hurts," she croaked.

"What?" he said harshly. "Your leg? The cuts?"

"My wrist — where you're squeezing it."

The man with the face like Denzel Washington's gave a muffled laugh. Kit frowned at him. "You're not Denzel Washington?"

"Afraid not. But I'm better in bed and I do an excellent suture. Ole Denzel isn't going to be doing field debridement any time soon, that's for damn sure." He finished putting away his tools and closed his medical case with a snap.

Kit stared at him suspiciously. "Where am I?" She shot up abruptly. "Where are the dogs? Diesel — I have to see Diesel."

"Diesel is at the clinic sleeping. We've got surveillance in place."

Wolfe's eyes were very dark. They reminded Kit of a seasonal stream above the ranch, fed by snow melt every spring. There was something fascinating about his intensity, about the hard set to his jaw.

Forget it, O'Halloran. He's mega-trouble. Look at the chaos he's created in your life already.

"I have to go." She tried to raise her head and winced at the sudden stabbing pain behind her eyes.

"Take it easy," Wolfe snapped. "The other dogs are right beside you. Izzy could barely get past them to clean you up."

She looked at the other man with the cocky smile. "You're Izzy?"

"Just call me Ishmael," he muttered. "Sorry to spoil your daydream."

Kit smiled as Baby licked her hand. Butch and Sundance barked and lifted their paws onto the edge of the examining table. "Story of my life," she said sleepily. Though she fought to focus, her eyes drifted shut. "Wolfe?"

"Right here. And lie still," Wolfe ordered

quietly. "Tell me what happened back there."

Kit stared up at the bright light wavering above her head. It was hard to think with her head throbbing madly. "It had something to do with lots of mud. I'm pretty sure that there was a piece of cement involved, too." Vaguely Kit felt his callused hand wrapped around hers. "The man who was chasing us . . . you took care of him?"

"I took care of him," Wolfe said grimly.

"Knew you would. You're good at that . . . taking care of things." She felt pain gnaw into her hip. How long had it been since she'd had her last dose of medicine?

After a moment, she gave up trying to remember.

For some reason she felt herself drifting back in time . . . far back. Like the majority of her teenage memories, this one involved Wolfe. "I saw you taking care of Marijo Felton once. You were in the back seat of her father's white Cadillac. I was thirteen and she was seventeen. Do you remember?" Even now dark fingers of heat swirled up at the memory. "She was making a lot of noise. So were you." Kit wasn't sure, but she thought she heard Izzy chuckle and Wolfe curse.

A door closed nearby.

"Wolfe?"

"Right here, honey."

"Do you remember Marijo?"

"It's been a long time since Marijo Felton." His fingers brushed her cheek. "You were watching us?"

"From the cottonwood tree. I figured I had to learn about sex somehow. The school hygiene classes just weren't cutting it."

"You could have asked me." His voice sounded a little hoarse. "I would have told you whatever you wanted to know."

"Words. Didn't want words. Wanted to see for myself." She smiled a little, in spite of the pain. "Marijo left her underwear in our driveway that night."

Wolfe made a strangled sound. "Your mother and father . . ."

"Don't worry, I found them first." Kit frowned. "Marijo told all the girls at school that you were a great f— er, lay."

For some reason everything seemed abstract, so that she wasn't in the least embarrassed to discuss what she'd seen that hot summer night. "Marijo told Trace that you had the mouth of a true artist. I asked Trace what that meant, and he was furious. Told me to shut up and stop asking questions. I think he had a crush on Marijo. A lot of boys did." She squinted up at Wolfe. "Do you have the mouth of a true artist?"

He cleared his throat. "Marijo Felton liked to hear herself talk. Forget about it. You'd better rest now."

"Didn't answer my question. Nobody ever answers my questions. What's the big deal about sex anyway? You get sweaty and pant a lot. So what?" She cupped her hip, shivering a little.

Wolfe leaned over her. "Are you in pain? Should I get Izzy, and have him give you something?"

"Hurts. Big deal. *Always* hurts." She heard the words echo as if they were coming through a long tunnel. "Going to sleep now. You can tell me about what you did to Marijo Felton when I wake up."

She thought she heard him curse. "Like hell I will."

She didn't hear anything after that.

Izzy was studying a detailed topographic map of New Mexico when Wolfe slid into the front seat of the van. The snow had stopped as abruptly as it had come, though the night sky was still hidden by clouds.

Izzy tapped the upper corner of the map. "A small truck was stolen up near Many

Farms on the Navajo Reservation about an hour ago." Izzy frowned. "According to police witness reports, two coyotes jumped on the hood and then attacked the driver."

More animals.

Wolfe filed this new fact away for serious consideration. If Ryker had a new experiment in place, Wolfe wanted every possible detail.

"You think Cruz was behind it?"

Izzy's face was unreadable. "We can't rule it out. Ryker admits that Cruz was receiving specialized new training at the time of his escape."

Wolfe stared out into the darkness. This confirmed his suspicions. "But what the hell was he doing up in that area?"

"We've had rumors of a militia group operating in the Four Corners region near the Navajo reservation. Some of them are washed-out marines and SEALs. A few of them are ex-law enforcement."

"And Cruz could be involved with these people?"

"That's speculation at this point, though they would make a natural power base for a man like Cruz. We're monitoring credit card usage in case anyone uses the plastic stolen from the waitress's purse. So far there's been nothing."

"There wouldn't be." Wolfe stared at the map. "Cruz is too smart for that."

"That's what I figure, too." Izzy folded up the map neatly and slid it into the glove compartment. No marks had been made, and Wolfe noticed that Izzy locked the glove compartment when he was done.

No one was taking any chances on leaks.

"She's pretty tough, your friend."

Wolfe started to say that Kit wasn't his anything. Instead he stared out into the night and wondered when his disposition had started to turn surly. "She's handled the ranch by herself since her parents died. She can take care of herself." He shook his head. "She always was stubborn."

Izzy held up a Thermos bottle. "Coffee?"

Wolfe shook his head. He already had enough adrenaline churning through his system.

"Smart. Stubborn. Good sense of humor." Izzy's voice was slow and casual. "Great legs. A killer body in those muddy jeans." He tapped quietly on the steering wheel. "*Especially* in those muddy jeans."

"You have a point hidden in all this?"

"Yeah, there's a point. She's got a thing for you. From where I'm sitting, I'd say you've got a thing for her, too."

"Even if it were true, I could still handle

this mission." Wolfe glared into the darkness. "And it's not."

Izzy blew at his coffee. "You'd better make damn sure of that. Cruz is dangerous and unstable. He'll use whoever or whatever is available to accomplish his objective. That means Kit and the dogs."

"Make your point."

"If you can't handle this assignment for personal reasons, I'll have someone else from Foxfire pulled in to replace you."

"Like hell." Wolfe shot the answer back. "I know the terrain. I know Cruz. I'm the best man you're going to find."

"Under normal circumstances, I'd agree with you on that." Izzy nodded his head toward the back of the van. "The woman lying back there — she changes everything."

"Not for me, she doesn't." Wolfe's voice was cool and sharp, like one of Izzy's precision scalpels.

For a long time Izzy didn't move. Then he released the emergency brake and headed toward the truck Wolfe had been given to replace Kit's now derelict Jeep. "Make damn sure you're right about that, Houston. A whole lot more than your sex life depends on it."

"The day I can't handle myself is the

same day I pull out of Foxfire." And it wouldn't be happening for at least a decade, Wolfe swore silently.

"There's one other thing you should know. Those pills Kit takes —"

"She said they were vitamins."

"I found the bottle halfway up the hill, above the spot where she fell into the canal. And they aren't vitamins. They weren't anything I'd heard of. So I made some calls, checked with NIH."

Wolfe sensed something coming that he didn't want to hear. "Go on."

"She's sick, Wolfe. It's in the rheumatoid arthritis family. Early stages, according to the files of the doctor who's treating her in Albuquerque."

"How the hell did you get into his files?"

Izzy gave a small, dismissive shrug. "No security in these places."

"How bad?"

"Deterioration of the major joints. Substantial pain, currently moderated by experimental medications. But eventually they'll stop working. Then she'll have to try a new drug."

Wolfe was barely aware of his fists clenched at his thighs. "How long will that go on?"

"I'm not a mind reader." Izzy sounded

angry. "There are no crystal balls in science." He glared into the darkness. "She'll probably get worse. The pain will probably increase. She probably won't be able to take her current meds, because they'll eat out the lining of her stomach. They may already be doing that. It's a known side effect."

Wolfe ran a hand across his eyes. "What else?"

"No kids. That's absolutely out now that she's taking this current medication."

"Does she know about that?"

Izzy shrugged. "Experimental meds can't be dispensed to test subjects without full disclosure of known side effects so I'd say yes, she knows. But having children is the least of her concerns." He took a hard breath. "Unless there are some unexpected breakthroughs, the deterioration is going to increase."

"Define increase."

"She won't be able to walk," Izzy said quietly. "Then she'll be looking at surgery."

CHAPTER TWENTY

Wolfe stared at Izzy. There were a hell of a lot of things he thought about saying, but where did you start?

No children. Decreased mobility. Constant pain.

He closed his eyes and leaned his head back against the seat. "You're certain about this, Teague?"

"Only one thing's ever certain. Life's a bitch, and then you die."

"Great bedside manner you've got."

Izzy glanced across at Wolfe. "I'm sorry if I sound blunt. Over time I've learned there's only one way to deliver bad news — fast and ruthless. Otherwise you hurt people more in the end."

Wolfe looked out the window at the stars flickering between racing clouds. "Kit doesn't know any of this?"

"She would know about the side effects. I saw some consent forms for meds in her file. I doubt she knows the full picture yet."

They passed expensive homes dotting the foothills on either side of the road.

"You'll be staying up near the top of the hill," Izzy said. "We have our people set up in all the nearest houses."

None of whom would stop Cruz for a second, Wolfe thought. Only another Foxfire member had any hope of doing that. And with Cruz's enhanced abilities, the mission's difficulty had taken a serious spike.

"You'll find encrypted cell phones in the back seat, but the land line in the house is clean. Use it if necessary. There's a safe room with food, medical supplies, and weapons in the basement."

"All the comforts of home, in other words. Nice prep."

Wolfe felt bone-tired as he climbed out of the van. He was superbly trained, calm and resourceful in the face of ambush, amphibious assault and automatic weapon fire. But facing Kit's future was something else. He had no weapons in his arsenal against a silent, progressive disease.

"What about the dogs? That's the first thing she'll ask me."

"We've set up a short-term kennel in the den. Give me a list of anything we didn't think of. Since it's not my area of expertise, it could be a long list."

Wolfe glanced back at Kit, who hadn't

moved since they'd begun their drive. "What am I authorized to tell her about the dogs?"

Izzy didn't answer.

"Give me an answer, Teague." Wolfe's voice was biting. "They're what she loves most, and she's poured twenty-six hours out of every day into training them. Isn't she entitled to know what they are and who she's really working for?"

Izzy stared back at him without expression. "She is not authorized to have that information at this time. She got the dogs from a breeder with military and police connections. That is all she's approved to know."

"What about the fact that they're in danger?"

"You get the same answer."

"That's bullshit and you know it."

There was a thump on the road behind them. Izzy glanced into his rearview mirror and cursed. "Damn back door. We lost the spare tires again. I've had to fix that cargo rack outside twice already. Whoever requisitioned this piece-of-junk van should be shot."

"I'll get them." Wolfe sprinted after the two heavy-duty tires vanishing into the darkness. He blocked their roll, then slid one under his arm and balanced the other on his shoulder. When he walked back to the van, Izzy was outside staring at him in the glow of the lights. "What's wrong?"

Izzy shook his head. "Those tires you're tossing around weigh close to a hundred pounds each."

Wolfe shrugged. Given his peculiar skills and the genetic expertise that had fine-tuned his body, this kind of lifting was child's play. He could probably carry four of the tires without raising a sweat.

Izzy's brow rose. "Can everyone in Foxfire do that?"

Wolfe took vicious delight in his curt answer. "Sorry, Teague. You aren't authorized to have that information at this time." He slid the tires back into the rack and closed the doors quietly, so he wouldn't wake Kit. When he looked back, the dogs were curled on the floor with their ears up. As usual, they didn't miss a single movement around them.

"They must be giving you some kind of meds to keep you in shape like that. Aminos. Maybe steroids, too." Izzy stared at him. "Or worse."

"Not authorized to answer, Teague."

Izzy looked back at the road, frowning,

"Keep an eye on the mix. You saw what happened to Cruz."

Wolfe had seen all too clearly. He couldn't get the image out of his mind. If the experts at the Foxfire lab were pushing their biology too far too fast, the whole team could end up imploding — pumped up and strung out like Cruz.

Hell if he'd let that happen.

"Duly noted, Teague."

"If you need outside medical advice, I'm available."

Not a small thing, Wolfe thought. Izzy would have access to a variety of resources closed to most. "I'll remember that."

"Good. In the meantime, stay alert. Cruz knows where Kit is now. Our friends in the Hummer leave no doubt about that. Cruz is probably on his way here now."

"Neither she nor the dogs will be out of my sight from now on," Wolfe countered tightly.

Izzy pointed to a dramatic timber and adobe house at the top of the hill. It was more home than Wolfe had ever seen, much less spent the night in. "You'll be staying up there."

"A little rich for my blood."

"You'll survive." After passing a dozen custom homes, they pulled into a narrow driveway. Izzy made a thumbs-up gesture to the man in a black uniform who appeared at the side of the van. "Take her inside and keep her safe. I'll contact her friend in Santa Fe so she doesn't start making anxious phone calls to the police."

Wolfe had forgotten about Miki. But he knew making anxious phone calls would have been only the start of her response, if she thought Kit was in danger. "Kit's going to need dry clothes."

"Already on it. My people will pick up some clothes and keep tabs on the black Lab at the clinic too. As far as her medical condition, let me see what I can find out." Izzy's tone didn't hold much hope. "There are always discoveries and new research. Tomorrow everything could change."

Like hell it could.

Neither said it, but the words hung in the air.

Kit deserved something better than a bleak prognosis of pain. Given all the geniuses connected with Foxfire, Wolfe vowed to find it for her.

She was as light as the weight of dreams in his arms as he carried her up the steps to the brightly lit house. Her hair drifted over his hands and her skin was cool with a scent of cinnamon. She was no longer a girl, not even close, and what he felt for her was turning dangerous, leaving them both vulnerable.

In spite of that, he savored the moment and all the unfamiliar emotions of close contact with someone other than a stranger on hire to the Foxfire medical staff.

The three dogs tagged close behind, restless and panting as Wolfe strode through the living room. He wanted Kit cleaned up and wearing dry clothes by the time she woke. He wanted . . . hell, he wanted her, period. In his arms and naked in his bed.

Fool.

Baby brushed against his leg.

"Fog." Kit moved restlessly. "Men coming."

Wolfe didn't understand, but he nodded anyway. "There's no fog here, and no men but me. In a few minutes you're going to be in bed, and then you can really sleep."

"Sleep?" Kit opened her eyes, blinking. "Is this where you live?"

"No, not here." He pushed open the carved pine door with his foot. "We're just going to use it for a little while."

"Too bad. I'd really like to see your bed."

She smiled sleepily. "Can I?"

"Sometime." Wolfe's stomach clenched. He felt a new tension that had nothing to do with lust. How was he going to keep her from getting hurt? Cruz wanted her dogs, and Ryker wanted her as bait. Somehow he would have to protect her from both men.

Maybe even from himself. Lately she seemed to strip right through his defenses.

"We need to get you cleaned up."

She fought his hands. "*Stop.* Where are my dogs?"

"They're here beside us. Right, Baby? And Diesel is doing fine, too. I checked a few minutes ago."

Kit relaxed when she heard Baby bark. "Probably they're ravenous. Their food —"

"I'll take care of it."

She curled closer against his chest. "They need a special diet, and I only use the food I make for them." She yawned. "Out in the Jeep." Her eyes flashed wide open. "Do I still have a car?"

"Got that covered, too." Izzy had already arranged for the Jeep to be towed and repaired. He'd also sent someone to Kit's ranch to pick up a week's worth of food for the dogs, along with Kit's training equipment.

"Why weren't you always this nice to me?"

277

Wolfe's smile faded. *Nice* wasn't his specialty. *Nice* didn't get the job done. For practical reasons, he was weak on niceness skills.

When he looked down, Kit had drifted back to sleep. Relieved, he carried her upstairs to a bedroom filled with Navajo pottery. Leaving her in the middle of the huge bed, he grabbed a wet washcloth and a clean towel from the bathroom, ready to tackle the job of cleaning her up. For some reason, the prospect left him uneasy.

Grimly, he focused on her damp jeans and the mud caked up to her knees from the fall in the canal.

At least he *tried* to focus. Her shirt had a hole in one arm and ground-in mud across her chest. He wasn't about to strip her unless it was absolutely necessary. Touching her any more than he had to seemed like a bad idea.

So she was wet and dirty. He'd start out easy and work from there.

She gave a soft sigh and reached toward him sleepily as he pulled off her wet shoes.

Toward, not away, he realized. The weight of her trust made him feel even more uncomfortable.

He focused on the hole in her shirt instead of the way her nipples rose to soft points against the damp cotton. He didn't want to see the details revealed by the wet fabric, and he *definitely* wasn't going to think about having sex with her.

Quickly he dried her hair, dropped the towel on the bed and unzipped her jeans. Her skin was cool and smooth as the zipper whispered and denim parted. His mouth went dry when he saw the curve of her stomach with a small half moon tattooed just below her navel.

Suddenly her arms flailed out, swinging at his shoulder. "Hmmh."

Wolfe realized she was still asleep, but she might not be for long. Moving fast, he lifted her hips and tugged the jeans lower, his eyes narrowing at the sight of slim legs and the wedge of cinnamon hair beneath plain white bikini panties.

Not that he was looking. He wasn't even *thinking* about looking. But a man was a man, damn it. With her underwear soaked, he could see one hell of a lot.

Wolfe forced all images of hot, panting sex out of his mind. He would label this as one of Ryker's training scenarios, nothing more. He'd had women climbing all over him and his control had never slipped before.

Grimly, he finished pulling off Kit's

jeans. The contact would not be personal or pleasurable. Her body was irrelevant to him.

Even if his hand slipped twice as he tried to open her bra and it took him three tries to get her shirt unbuttoned.

He muttered a curse. The woman was reducing him to tactical incompetence.

It was time to be tough. He stripped her shirt and tossed it onto the floor. Wielding a towel, he mopped the mud off her arms and bruised legs. He did it all in record time, like a desperate man crossing thin ice. He kept his eyes on her face as he worked off her wet bra and panties, ignoring the brush of her tight nipples against his hands.

Instead of her pale skin, he focused on the newest requisition order he had placed for 15x image stabilizing night vision goggles. He recited the specs and the serial number to keep his mind off the sight of her smooth hips and the dark tangle of hair that goaded his senses.

Kit muttered softly when he pulled the thick duvet around her, but she didn't wake, which was a small mercy. He turned off the light and walked to the door, then slanted one look back into the deeply shadowed room.

Her face was pale, her hands tense on

the covers. She murmured something he couldn't make out. Was she dreaming about a vacation? A new car?

A man?

It hit him suddenly that he knew miserably little about the woman Kit had become. He knew about the articles she'd written for two professional search-and-rescue organizations and her growing reputation in canine behaviorist circles. He knew that she'd saved her ranch from tax foreclosure after her parents' sudden death, fighting her way out of debt with back-to-back training assignments. He knew she'd taken high-paying jobs with dogs written off as untrainable. In the process she had replaced choke chains with simple clarity, cages with six-hour exercise sessions outdoors. Her animals ate better, slept better, looked better — and they adored her within days.

She didn't yell, she didn't scold, and she definitely didn't hit, yet her success rate was unmatched. All of this was in the government file Wolfe had read.

But nowhere had he seen a single word about Kit's personal life or any intimate relationships. In spite of the conversation he'd overheard between Kit and her friend, he figured that a woman with Kit's spirit and beauty had to have a man in her life. If not currently, then in the recent past.

His fists clenched at the thought of Kit with another man. He pictured her smiling, saw her opening a belt, her clothes dropping. After that he forced all feeling away. She wasn't his to claim and he didn't have time for fantasies. The sooner he drove that fact home to both of them, the safer they would be.

Ten minutes later, Wolfe was talking on his cell phone when he heard Baby skid across the plank pine floor. She tried to stop, scrambled hard, and slid to a halt in front of the couch where he was getting an update from Izzy.

He leaned down, scratching behind Baby's ears. "Something wrong, honey?"

"Honey?" Izzy repeated dryly.

Wolfe muttered a pithy phrase that made Izzy chuckle.

"I doubt that's anatomically possible. So Kit's there with you?"

"No, it's Baby, and she's looking very restless." Wolfe's eyes narrowed as Butch and Sundance charged across the room. "Update that. Here come Butch and Sundance. You can't keep this team apart."

Baby gripped Wolfe's sleeve in her teeth

and tugged sharply while Sundance mouthed his other sleeve. What the heck was going on?

Abruptly he realized why the dogs looked so urgent. "Gotta go, Teague. The dogs need to go out for a pit stop, and they're not being subtle about it."

"Watch where you step," Izzy said dryly. Then the phone went dead.

Wolfe looked at the puppies lined up in front of him and found himself grinning. "All right troops, move out. Field formation, eyes forward."

But no one moved. Baby looked at him, then barked insistently. Instantly the three dogs shot across the room toward French doors that opened onto a wraparound patio of travertine marble.

Wolfe shook his head. Clearly, Baby was the team leader in this group.

After checking out the back yard, he opened the doors and stood back while Baby rocketed past him, paws skidding. Butch and Sundance shot down the steps right behind Baby. The trio raced around the back yard half a dozen times, sniffed at a big mesquite tree, then stopped in a neat row near the side wall.

Legs rose in a line. Baby squatted.

Pit stop.

Wolfe watched them, smiling wryly. Mission accomplished. They even seemed to do *this* as a team. With their pressing business complete, the dogs looked back at him, then tore around the big yard in dizzy canine delirium. Just watching them made him feel twenty years younger.

He tossed a big stick across the grass, laughing as the dogs jumped up, changed direction in midair, then tore out after their target. Butch reached the stick first, grabbed it and waved it madly between his teeth.

Instantly, Baby bumped him with her head, growling playfully. Though Butch was probably twenty pounds heavier and two inches taller, the big dog dropped the stick and stood back while Baby picked it up.

She trotted back with the stick and waited.

"Nice moves, Slim. What do I get for an encore?"

Baby waved the stick close enough to brush his hand.

Wolfe lunged — but somehow the stick was gone and Baby was six feet across the yard, spinning in happy circles.

He studied the dog uneasily. "How the hell did you do that?"

Baby trotted back briskly and bumped his leg with her head. When he was looking directly at her, she tossed the stick up in the air near his hand and caught it neatly.

Challenging him. The absolute nerve.

Wolfe lunged.

In a blur the stick shot through his fingers and vanished, gripped in Baby's mouth as the three dogs tore across the yard in a tight cluster.

Incredible, Wolfe thought. Was he exaggerating their speed? He sprinted after Baby, only to find his way blocked by Butch and Sundance, who feinted left as a unit, then raced back toward him, blocking his way until Baby was out of reach.

The damned dogs had football moves. Maybe they could sign on to coach the Chicago Bears.

When Baby trotted back across the grass, Wolfe could have sworn that the three dogs were grinning at him, tongues lolling. This time he charged straight for Baby, feinted right, then jumped over Butch and Sundance when they came to Baby's aid.

But the dogs turned a split second before he did, and his knees struck fur and muscle. Instantly he twisted sideways to avoid hurting them, in the process hitting the ground on one elbow. He plowed into a planter, struck one knee, and lay still, seeing stars.

The stars blurred into the form of a looming shape above his head. Wet and rough, a tongue lapped his face.

Wolfe winced as puppy drool dripped onto his cheek. "Hell, Baby, give a fellow operative a break. No more slobber in the face."

When he pushed to one elbow, Butch and Sundance immediately nosed in beside Baby, all three licking his face in excitement. Then Baby dropped the stick neatly in Wolfe's lap, sat down and barked once — as if rewarding Wolfe for his satisfactory performance.

Who the hell was ordering around *who*?

Wiping off more dog drool, he stood up. "Nice tactical advance, guys, but it won't work a third time." He grabbed the stick and sprinted toward the gnarled oak tree in the center of the yard. In a flying jump he caught an overhanging branch, knifed his legs up, did a tight pull-up and circled the branch. Yeah, it was cheating because dogs couldn't climb, but whoever said life was fair?

Sitting on the branch in the moonlight with his legs dangling down, Wolfe grinned at the Labs ranged below him. "Show me some moves, guys. Unless you're a bunch of wimps." As the wind brushed his face, Wolfe realized he was sitting in a tree talking to a row of panting dogs, and he was having more fun than he'd had in years.

There hadn't been any games or laughter in his house. Growing up, he'd known only curses and pain, both quickly suppressed for fear of more beatings.

As he shoved away the thought, he could have sworn that Baby's head tilted as if in concentration. She looked up at the tree, then turned around in a tight circle and looked at him some more, growling low in her throat.

Butch trotted closer and Sundance drew up on the opposite flank, the scene looking for all the world like a NFL huddle. Wolfe watched Baby trot to an open chaise lounge and jump up with Butch right behind her. Sundance jumped up next, shot onto Butch's back and then stood stock still.

What the hell were the three Einsteins planning now?

He had his answer a second later. Baby jumped down and raced back to the far end of the yard. Then she lowered her head and shot over the grass, hit the lounge chair, rocketed up onto Sundance's back and sailed higher. Grabbing a higher limb in her teeth, she dangled for a moment, and then dropped onto the same branch where Wolfe sat, stunned and speechless. With her tail high, she crossed the branch carefully, slid onto her stomach and laid her head on Wolfe's lap.

And then she took the prized stick gently in her teeth and tugged it out of his unresisting fingers, while her tail wagged at high speed.

"Holy shit, who *are* you guys? Forget the Bears — you're ready for SEAL training."

Baby bumped him happily with her head and licked his face. Before he could react she dropped the stick down to Sundance, who caught it in one flying leap and tossed it back to Butch.

Wolfe couldn't move. Okay, maybe this was all a trick of the moonlight. Something to do with clouds and shadows and his exhaustion.

Except his eyesight was way beyond normal limits and shadows didn't bother him for a second. Exhaustion wasn't a problem either, because he could go for three days without sleep. What he'd seen was no illusion. This kind of organized planning and teamwork was exactly what the government had hoped for, and despite being kept in the dark, Kit had nurtured those qualities perfectly.

Wolfe was looking at three dogs that were smarter than most people, that could carry out advanced problem solving and work together as a tight, enthusiastic team.

He shook his head. "Think what Lloyd Ryker could do with you guys."

The image caught him up cold. These dogs had exactly the abilities Ryker needed, put to use in hostile environments. Out in the field, they wouldn't understand the danger or the risks they took. Thanks to Kit's dedication, they would spill their hearts, performing to the full extent of body and spirit.

Right up until one of them took a bullet in the throat or razor wire through the chest.

He closed his eyes, one hand slipping protectively to Baby's head. Tactical work under deadly fire was what they were designed for. Like him and his Foxfire teammates, they were trained to obey and succeed, at any cost.

But unlike the dogs, his team had been given a choice. They'd volunteered, fully aware of the dangers and the consequences.

The dogs hadn't. They would be at the mercy of Ryker and others like him.

Baby nuzzled closer, her tail banging against the branch. She licked his hand as if she had known him all her life. As if he was a littermate.

And in a way, he was, thanks to their shared genetic technology.

There in the moonlight, with Baby's head on his knee, he grappled with what he had just seen and how it would change the future. He was looking at a new world and possibilities that seemed almost unbelievable.

A snowflake danced in front of his face.

Then another.

Wind sighed through the mesquite leaves as the sky paled, filled with drifting flakes.

The sudden moisture jolted Wolfe from his odd reverie. What he thought or wanted was unimportant. Science marched forward inexorably. Once the technology existed, it was only a matter of time until someone shaped it and used it for practical ends. Better that it be *his* government than anyone else's.

"Time to get moving, team." He looked down at the ground and shook his head, not about to let Baby jump. "Come on, honey. Let's do this thing together." With

Baby tucked safely against his chest, he pushed free and dropped, landing hard but staying upright.

Baby wriggled free and jumped down, sniffed the ground, then turned and went still. Instantly Butch and Sundance moved in beside her.

"What's going on, you three?"

Baby moved warily toward the back wall. When she was twenty feet away, she stopped. Her head rose, pointed directly at the darkest part of the high, shadowed adobe. Wolfe felt the hairs rise at the back of his neck. He realized that the wind had died, and the night had gone silent. Only a few flakes drifted past his face now.

He focused, listening carefully, scanning the darkness for any sign of movement or abnormal energy signatures. Before he had felt nothing, but now . . . there was *something.* He crossed the yard to Baby.

The dog ignored him.

Whatever he felt was behind the eight-foot wall. Wolfe started toward the shadows and was shocked to hear Baby growl, her teeth clamping down on his boot. A moment later Butch caught his pants leg and held him in place while Sundance gripped his hand hard enough to keep him still.

Someone — or something — was out there waiting. The dogs knew it, and they weren't going to let him get any closer.

Wolfe was not a man who frightened easily, but he knew the touch of fear now, like a cold knife brushing his skin. If this was Cruz, he had changed his energy signature beyond recognition. Or else he had somehow learned to hide all his traces, even from one of his former teammates.

Wolfe took a step backward, away from the wall, feeling Butch strain to make him hurry. He leveled his Sig at the wall, releasing the knot of tension in his shoulders, keeping his fingers loose for a clean shot.

He still felt no trace of Cruz. Nothing moved.

Somewhere a bird circled in the darkness.

Wolfe sensed danger like an acrid taste in his mouth. The three dogs tugged him back hard and he followed reluctantly, daring the darkness to move. Daring Cruz to reveal himself.

It could be no one else.

The little hairs rose at the back of his neck. Baby tugged harder. There was no sound in the chill night, but the silence felt charged and oppressive.

His cell phone vibrated inside his pocket

and he flipped it open with one hand. "What?" he whispered.

"Checking in." Izzy's voice held a question. "Everything okay there?"

"No," Wolfe muttered. "Meet me inside."

He hung up.

They were almost at the porch now, man and dogs bound in a tense awareness of danger, the mutual ties of protection as old as primitive cave fires and hunting with spears. Somewhere beyond the trees the bird called again, and Wolfe heard the soft whoosh of wings, the noise unearthly.

Was this an image distortion pattern directed at him, another new skill Cruz had acquired since his "death"? For a moment the darkness blurred. Instantly Wolfe targeted the pattern's source, shielding his and the dogs' presence with an image of running water over high boulders.

The darkness shifted again, moving along the wall like a greasy film.

Baby made a throaty sound and pressed against Wolfe's leg as they came to the first step of the porch. With the patio light falling in a warm pool around him, Wolfe opened the door for the dogs, which shot inside and then turned back. Motionless in a row, they waited for him to follow.

Despite the threat, they stayed in defensive array, alert and fearless.

Wolfe turned to stare into the darkness, alert for any movement, any threat, even a blurred sense of Cruz's distinctive energy signature.

None came.

Could his old partner vanish completely now? Was that another skill he'd acquired under Ryker's secret training?

A hawk swooped low and then vanished, swallowed by the night. Frowning, Wolfe closed and locked the patio doors, but the tension did not leave his neck.

Outside the darkness seemed to move forward and wrap itself around the house, mocking him.

CHAPTER TWENTY-ONE

"Say this again. You saw *what?*" Izzy paced in a tight circle. "You're telling me that Baby managed to jump up onto a branch beside you? No way, Navy. Dogs don't climb trees, not even superdogs like these."

"It happened, Teague. I *saw* it happen. The dog was a foot away from me."

"In the dark you could have —"

"But I didn't. I have perfect vision up to 500 yards at night. We all have photo receptor enhancements, and those dogs did *exactly* what I told you." For a second time Wolfe described the scene in the back yard.

"Incredible." Izzy stopped pacing and sank into a big leather wing chair. "Hard to believe. Why hasn't Kit noticed any of this?"

Wolfe jammed his hand through his hair. "My guess is it's new behavior, possibly triggered by my presence. Our chips and nanotech are similar. Maybe our bio-enhancements are creating some kind of feedback between us." He stared out at the back yard, frowning. "I'm no biologist, so don't ask me for details. But I can tell you they definitely felt someone outside near that wall. They knew before I did."

Baby trotted into the room, carrying her water dish. "At least that's easy to understand." Wolfe followed the dog into the kitchen and refilled all three bowls while Izzy stood up to pace again.

"Okay, so they're geniuses. From what you saw, they work as a team. We knew it was likely, and now it's been demonstrated."

"Whatever I felt left no physical traces. There was no sound or movement and none of Cruz's old energy pattern." Wolfe moved to the window, unable to forget the sudden oppressive weight and the brush of fear. "Baby and Butch nearly bit me, trying to pull me back from the wall."

"I'll check it out." Izzy started for the door, but Wolfe blocked him.

"Take someone out there with you. Be sure you verify his identity before and after, too. If it's Cruz, you won't see anything — not until he wants you to. And what you *see* won't necessarily be what's really there."

"Image displacement?"

"Count on it." Wolfe laughed grimly. "Cruz was better than any of us. He learned it first and set the gold standard. Now, with his enhancements *and* paranoia, he'll be tough and nearly invisible. Finding him won't be easy."

"Especially now that we've lost our interrogation subject. The guy snapped and he's gone totally psycho. Cruz must have gotten to him at a distance. Ryker knows more than he's saying about it, and he's mad as hell." Izzy shook his head. "I'm not sure I want to know what you and your team are capable of."

Izzy flipped open his cell phone. His voice was cool and controlled as he strode to the front door, ordering a complete perimeter scan carried out via paired units with reports every two minutes.

Wolfe wanted to head outside with him, but that would mean leaving Kit and the dogs unprotected, and he sensed that that was exactly what Cruz wanted.

If the situations were reversed, it's exactly what he would have done.

After checking to make sure Kit was still asleep, Wolfe stood at the picture window overlooking the yard. As he watched Izzy's team comb the darkness, he made a mental check for any disruptions or signs of Cruz's field signature, but the night seemed calm, even welcoming now, the moon a silver chip adrift on racing clouds.

He told himself the strange feeling he'd had in the back yard was irrelevant, a function of stress, darkness and too much adrenaline. But he couldn't ignore the dogs' behavior near the wall, and he was too experienced a soldier to discount an adversary just because he couldn't see it or touch it.

Unable to relax, he triggered his cell phone.

"Yeah." Izzy's voice was a whisper.

"What have you got?"

"Jack shit. No people, no animals, no nothing. There's no hint of anything unusual out here."

"You checked IDs for every man on your team?"

"Twice. Everyone is *exactly* who they say they are. But I'm upping our alert level. We'll do overlapping rotations for safety. New pass codes every hour, too."

"Keep me updated."

"Will do. Meanwhile, you should get some shut-eye, and leave the heavy lifting to us." There was a pause. "You do *sleep*, don't you?"

Wolfe laughed dryly. "Need to know, Teague. And you *don't.*"

He flipped the cell phone shut and sank down on the big leather couch, trying to relax, the way Izzy had suggested. One of the benefits of his enhancements was a shortened sleep cycle. Even a twenty-minute nap would leave him reenergized.

Something brushed his arm, and he realized Baby was on the couch, watching every move he made. Kit's white cotton bra was dangling from the puppy's teeth.

"What? Is something wrong with Kit?"

Baby's tail banged on the couch. She dropped the bra in Wolfe's lap and gave a whine that sounded like distress.

Wolfe took the stairs two at a time, then raced down the hall, but Kit was exactly the way he'd left her, asleep on the big bed, one leg dangling from beneath satin covers with a pillow wedged against her chest.

No broken windows.

No intruders.

What was going on? When Wolfe turned around, Baby was right behind him, and Kit's bra was still caught between her teeth.

"Troublemaker." If the dog had a message, it was beyond him. Or maybe it was some new search and retrieve game. He'd noticed that the dogs seemed to love playing games of any sort.

He headed back to the couch and flipped off the light.

Feet padded softly. The three dogs stopped in a row in front of the stairs.

Wolfe watched them stretch one by one, then lie down. He'd been on all kinds of missions in all kinds of hellholes, but none had been half as strange as this assignment.

He shifted to one side, moving his shoulder holster to get comfortable. What would the dogs say if they could talk? What threat had they sensed out in the night?

Too bad they couldn't tell him.

As he closed his eyes, he let his thoughts wander. With a controlled breathing pattern, he drifted down into the edge of theta, enjoying a pleasant encounter with three women wearing orchids, hot smiles and nothing else.

Then he realized that every one of the women looked like Kit.

You're losing it, Houston. She's getting under your skin.

Something hit the floor upstairs. As he shot to his feet, Wolfe heard Kit scream his name.

CHAPTER TWENTY-TWO

He hit the floor running and was up the stairs to Kit's bedroom in three seconds. Kicking open the door, his Sig level, he sighted through the doorway, side first to minimize his target area while he watched for shadows.

Nothing moved.

A crack of light outlined the bathroom door. Wolfe heard the shower running. Why would she be taking a damned shower *now?*

He strode across the room and waited, hearing nothing but the sound of water. In one fluid motion he threw open the door and tracked his Sig across the room.

There was no sign of Kit anywhere as he saw the shower curtain fluttering beneath the pounding spray. He moved closer, peering around the curtain.

He was stunned to see Kit on the floor of the shower, her legs drawn up against her chest.

"Honey, are you okay?"

With her eyes closed and the shower at

full force, she didn't seem to know he was there. After checking the windows and closets to make sure both rooms were clear, he walked back to the door.

Her face was tight with pain, her body shaking. He didn't want to frighten her, so he moved out of sight and twitched the shower curtain a few times. "Are you there, Kit? Everything okay?"

He heard her muffled gasp. "F-fine. Go away."

"Sure I will, honey." *Like hell he would.* "First tell me what's going on. I heard a bang and then you screamed."

"I tripped, that's all. There's no need to stay."

Wolfe frowned. Did she really expect him to buy that? "Can I do anything? Bring you a towel or —"

"*No.* I'm going to finish in here, then go back to sleep." Her voice was tight. "I'll be fine."

Water raced between them in a steaming trail. Wolfe didn't answer her, hidden behind the curtain. She must have tripped, fallen sideways and hit the floor. There was no mistaking the bruises he'd seen darkening her hip and leg. He could imagine the pain she must be in now.

And she thought he wouldn't notice?

"I'll help you back to bed." His voice was cool and impersonal. By fierce effort he drove down his anger at the sight of her white face. Shivering, she huddled against the wet wall in the grip of an illness that would slowly whittle away her freedom and her confidence.

She made a small, broken sound. "Just g-go, Wolfe. I don't want you to —"

He pulled back the shower curtain and stepped through the steaming water. Ignoring her angry questions, he scooped her up, flipped off the shower, and grabbed a towel on his way out to the bedroom, where he wrapped the towel around her shivering body and laid her gently on the bed.

Kit's eyes squeezed shut. "Go away," she said hoarsely. "Please, Wolfe."

"You called my name because you needed me."

She didn't answer, turning her face away to avoid his eyes.

With quick, gentle motions he dried her hair and body. "I'll be done shortly. Then you can relax."

"Relax?" She gave a choked laugh. "Not in this lifetime. Not after you saw me in there — like *that*."

Wolfe kept his voice impersonal. "What happened?"

After a long time she opened her eyes. "I fell." Her face was tense, daring him to show pity.

"Sorry to hear it." He tried to ignore her soft hips, her long legs. When had she gotten so damned gorgeous? It seemed only yesterday he'd caught her trying to fly by jumping off an old, broken-down pickup truck on the ranch.

Times change.

There were spots of color in her cheeks, and he knew that she was mortified. He wasn't too happy with the situation either. "Tell me what happened in there. Was there something at the window? Did you see someone in the room?" He had to be sure there were no signs of threat that he had missed.

Her eyes narrowed. "You think someone followed us? Are those men from the Hummer coming *here?*"

Wolfe finished drying her shoulders, forcing his eyes away from the curve of her breasts. "I don't expect them to," he said gruffly. "On the other hand I've got a lot of enemies." He finished fast, drew the covers up over her, then let out a slow breath. "Go to sleep. You can handle the rest yourself."

She ignored him, gripping the covers. "I

was sleepy before, but I'm wide awake now. I want answers, Wolfe. Who are these people following you?"

He decided to let her go on thinking that *he* was the target. There would be fewer questions that way. "I told you, I'm not exactly popular in certain quarters. My guess is that someone tracked me to Santa Fe."

"But why did you bring me along with you? I'm not part of this."

"Until I'm certain we weren't followed, this is the only way to keep you safe." *More lies.* "Now let's talk about you," he snapped. "How long have you been falling like that?"

She closed her eyes. "None of your business."

"It doesn't take a genius to see you're in pain, Kit. You've got new bruises mixed with five or six older ones on your legs. What's going on?"

Her chin rose. "I was tired and I got clumsy. End of story."

"Back in the canal tonight, was that clumsiness too?"

"It was dark. I slipped. So sue me."

He didn't want to sue her. He wanted to shake her and kiss her until she wrapped her legs around him, took him inside her and moaned his name, out of control with lust. The force of that need left him shaken, and he had to look away. His control was slipping and it made him furious. *Nothing* shook him. Nothing ever frightened him, either.

Until now. First the scene in the back yard with the dogs. Now Kit's pain and the knowledge that there wasn't a damn thing he could do to help her medically.

Her fingers savaged a seam on the white quilt. "Two men in a Humvee tried to drive us off the road tonight. Then they shot at you and basically destroyed my Jeep. That's bad enough, but all you'll tell me is some of your old enemies are up to no good." Her voice rose on an edge of hysteria. "Not good enough. I want more or I'm going to the police."

"Okay, calm down. I'll tell you what I can. I was doing covert surveillance in the area, arranged by your local authorities. There's been a security leak at a nearby research facility and I'm tracking someone involved."

"What kind of security leak?"

"I can't discuss that, Kit. You know how this works."

"So that's all you're going to tell me?"

"Sorry if you were expecting more details, but that's not the way the government works."

"Something else is going on, Wolfe. I need to know what." She didn't move, her whole body tense. "Look at me."

"That's all you're getting." He sat on the edge of the bed and forced all emotion from his face. "Take it or leave it."

"I know the rules. Whatever you're doing here is probably dangerous and classified to the nth degree. I can accept that part. What I can't accept is the thought that my dogs are at risk."

"It's fine to endanger *you,* but not your dogs?"

"That's right." She shook her head as if the question made no sense.

Stubborn and impossible, Wolfe thought. Generous and amazing.

"Well?" she said flatly.

"Well what?"

She swung out her arm, gesturing at the fine carpets and precious old pottery. "This house where you've brought me — that's part of your simple surveillance, too?"

"Damn it, Kit. I can't talk about —"

She cut him off, her eyes dark against the pallor of her face. "Am I involved? Are my *dogs* in danger? That's all I need to know. No details. You owe me that much, Wolfe. Just yes or no."

"There's no danger to your dogs." He lied coolly, aware that his orders gave him no other choice. "I'm sorry this happened — and that you were involved. I'll see that your car is repaired, I promise."

She nodded slowly. "And Diesel?"

"Resting safely at your friend Liz's clinic." At least this much was true. He'd checked with Izzy.

"Thank you for the truth." Somewhere downstairs a clock chimed, the sound echoing through the silent house. "I could still break both your legs for not telling me sooner." Yawning, she pulled the covers up to her neck. "I think maybe I can sleep now. You can leave."

"So we're not going to discuss what happened in the shower?"

"No."

"Damn it, Kit —"

She rubbed her eyes. "It's been a long day, Wolfe." She shot him a glazed look. "Drat. Dogs — have to go out. They need to be walked."

"Already taken care of."

"Water, too." She frowned, trying to sit up.

"Ditto."

"No kidding." Her eyes closed. "That makes you *almost* human in my book. Not enough for Miki's ridiculous plan."

"What plan?"

"Preemptive sex. Perfect thing to nix an obsession, she tells me." Kit yawned again. "Crazy idea."

Preemptive sex? Leave it to Miki to come up with a mush-brained idea like that. Wolfe had something better in mind to cure what appeared to be a rapidly growing case of mutual, unpredictable lust.

The answer was simple. They'd have a calm, frank talk with all their cards on the table. That would clear the air just fine.

In the silent house he stared at Kit's hands, motionless on the white quilt. He could almost feel the warmth of her skin, the faint skip of her pulse while she slept.

She had welcomed him home. Didn't she know that home was a cold memory he'd worked hard to erase? Didn't she understand that one of the reasons he was so good at his work was the very lack of protection and kindness he had growing up? His past had made him strong and ruthless. Now he had a skill for destruction without emotion or regret.

His mouth twisted in a bitter smile.
Welcome home.

They were inches apart, their bodies almost touching. They might as well have been on opposite sides of the ocean.

Lying on the rug, Baby sneezed. Her tail banged once.

"You three troublemakers had better get some sleep," he said quietly.

Butch rolled over, his legs in the air, while Sundance scratched at one paw.

A log hissed in the fireplace, setting off a rain of orange embers.

Maybe *this* was home, Wolfe thought dimly. Not a place, not a building, but a state of mind.

Or maybe it was a state of grace.

The sand was white, crunching beneath his feet. The drinks were cold and the woman walking toward him, removing a skimpy red bikini bottom, was *very* hot. He felt his body respond, saw her inviting glance.

Suddenly her face changed. Not a stranger now, she smiled with Kit's smile and laughed with Kit's laugh.

She had a sprinkling of freckles across her breasts when he pulled off her bikini top. She was full and lush beneath his hands, whispering his name while her body flowed against him like silk.

He felt the sand, hot on his back, his body on fire as he slid one finger along her tight cleft, dragging a moan from her soft mouth. Sure and expert, he made her moan again, until she clawed his back and shuddered to a fierce climax with her legs wrapped around his waist.

Even then he focused on her response, goading her to pleasure with expert skill. He had been trained to know a woman's body, trained to use her arousal against her when a mission required it. The training was completely impersonal, and he'd never felt a hint of guilt at using it.

Until he looked into Kit's dark eyes in the middle of a hot, reckless dream.

Wood creaked.

Cool air brushed his face.

Wolfe shot to his feet as the dream fled. One hand on his holstered Sig, he clawed back to wakefulness, checking for intruders in the same instant.

She was up on the stairs silhouetted against the light from the hall, a pillow and blanket bunched under her arm. The dogs were right beside her.

"What's wrong?" he demanded, his voice hoarse.

"I couldn't sleep. I thought maybe we could talk."

CHAPTER TWENTY-THREE

The perfume hit him first, light and subtle. As Kit's body moved, Wolfe saw firelight glow in her hair.

Sometimes life conspired to destroy all your best plans.

She tossed her pillow down beyond the end of the couch and wrapped her blanket close, sliding onto the floor. Light touched the rug and the priceless old Pueblo pottery, brushing her face with restless color.

Her beauty unnerved him. Her strength inspired him.

But this wasn't anything like he'd foreseen. Their talk was *supposed* to be impersonal.

Oblivious to his discomfort, she wriggled until she got comfortable and then leaned over to scratch Baby's head. "Wolfe, about tonight in the shower . . ."

"You can't talk down there."

"I'm fine. I've got my pillow and —"

Muttering, he scooped her into his arms and lifted her onto the couch, tucking the blanket around her. "Go to sleep."

"But we need to talk."

Hell.

Suddenly talking seemed like a lousy idea. He was pretty sure that talking would be a prelude to touching and taking her about a dozen different ways.

Grimly he moved to a chair, praying that distance and a little discomfort would help clear his mind. Pulling up a leather ottoman, he stretched out his long legs. "Okay, we'll talk. Shoot."

Kit cleared her throat.

Wolfe scratched his neck.

Neither said a word.

Branches tapped at one of the windows and the fire hissed, strangely intimate in the silence of the night.

Kit sighed. "It's been . . . a long time. I don't know where to start."

Didn't that just make two of them?

She tugged the blanket up to her neck. "I'd talk about you, but I'm not sure that you're the same *you* I used to know. The things you've done and places you've been have changed you, I think. You must be very good at what you do. . . ." She seemed to hesitate.

"So I've been told. What's the *but?*"

"But you left and I stayed. Sometimes I feel as if my life is rushing past me like a river, and I'm stranded on a boulder in the middle watching the boats go back and forth, bound for Rio and Hong Kong. Everyone's happy and having fun but me."

"You want to travel? I never knew that."

"On bad days, I feel trapped. There's always the ranch, always the responsibilities. I'm an O'Halloran in a town where almost everyone knew my parents, and most of them expect me to fail and lose the ranch."

"Are there a lot of bad days?" he asked quietly.

"Not so many." She grimaced. "But when everyone knows you, it's hard to stretch your wings. Harder still to break a few rules."

She wanted to break rules? This was more news to Wolfe. "Do you get many of these rule-breaking urges?" He felt Baby brush his leg and curl up next to the ottoman, her head across his feet. As moonlight streamed through a high window, he had a sharp sense of belonging, so fierce that the weight of it constricted his throat.

Foxfire meant no ties and no family. You couldn't talk about your training or any mission, past or future. After a while, the team was all the family you could afford. No one else would ever understand the danger and the pressure that became your daily fare.

Wolfe had never minded the isolation before.

Now he did. Here in the firelight he wanted more.

Quickly he shut down his emotions, trying to pull back from a world he couldn't afford — and a belonging that could never be real.

He realized Kit was studying him, her face shimmering in the firelight. "What about you? How does coming back home make you feel?"

Home. That word again.

He started to dismiss the question with a shrug. How could he explain that feelings, all feelings, had become foreign to his life? He could calculate wind resistance and bullet trajectory without a second thought, but emotions scared the hell out of him. Even now it was a struggle to dig down and find the sensations he had become adept at burying.

Leaning back, he stared into the fire. "Like crap. You weren't dumb growing up. You knew that my parents —" He stabbed his fingers through his hair. "No lies. I promised myself that when I left home. No euphemisms and no rosy pictures later. Only the truth."

"Which is?"

There was calm interest in her voice, not pity or revulsion. Growing up, Wolfe had known only the latter two from friends and acquaintances. As a result, he'd learned never to discuss his childhood with anyone. At first he'd been too frightened of his father's retribution. Later he'd been too resigned, certain that no one, friend or professional, could help him. So he'd helped himself. In the process he had reclaimed his life and his pride by stripping away all feelings of family from his memory. Going back through it now felt like crossing a minefield in bare feet.

"My mother — well, she didn't want me, not that it was personal. She didn't want ties of any sort, and a kid was just that. I heard her tell my father often enough that I was a mistake."

"She didn't deserve to have a child," Kit said fiercely.

"Probably not. But she got one. And I wasn't the easiest person to live with." Wolfe laced his fingers behind his neck, surprised by a sudden flood of memories.

Waking up to a silent and empty house

on Christmas morning. Pleading for a dog one summer and being hit for the request. Coming home after school with a note from the football coach, anxious because Wolfe had played half a game with a sprained ankle that he hadn't reported to anyone.

And wasn't that funny because he'd lived most of his childhood with some kind of bruise, cut or sprain incurred during his father's binges or his mother's forgetfulness.

But the worse had been when his father was stony and sober, cornering him in the kitchen or somewhere in the cramped garage where Wolfe generally went to escape the unbearable tension of a loveless house.

When his father was sober, he knew exactly what he was doing. He took his time planning the best way to inflict pain.

One summer he'd burned the half dozen books a teacher had given Wolfe — and then he'd burned Wolfe's neck with the same lighter. Another time he'd grabbed his son's arm and broken it carefully, precisely in three places without a flicker of emotion. When Wolfe had cried out, just once, he'd gotten his other arm broken as an object lesson while his mother looked on blankly.

He'd never cried again after that, never shown any emotions to the two people he'd come to hate with white-hot ferocity.

He knew, rationally, that he was not to blame for any of the things that had happened to him as a boy. As a man he'd sorted through the layered pain of old memories and concluded that his only mistake had been being born to such imperfect, unhappy people.

He'd put the pain and self-analysis behind him at sixteen and swore that he would never leave himself open to betrayal by another person again.

Now Cruz had betrayed him and the country he'd vowed to protect. But even worse was the betrayal of his own control. He of all people should know better. Trust was an illusion, safety a prize won only through the force of constant vigilance.

But looking at Kit, feeling Baby's warm head nestled on his foot, he felt safe in a way he never had before. Worse yet, he wanted to hold that precious sensation wrapped around him forever. But there was no safety in life. When violence came, as it surely would, he had to respond instantly. If he relaxed or knew a moment's weakness, someone could end up dead.

So he'd tell Kit what he could and hope

it drove her away, filled with revulsion for the misfit parents whose blood and genes he shared. With distance and detachment restored, he and Kit would be safe from this dangerous distraction.

"I hate them, whether you do or not." Her voice was rough.

"I never took it personally. I was just a kid — some kind of stranger who wandered in front of the train wreck that was their lives. They're both dead now, and I'm not going to wallow in bad memories."

"You don't hate them? You don't even care that they were complete monsters?" She sounded outraged, furious on his behalf.

"Hate makes you just as weak as love. I can't afford to feel either one."

Kit stared as if he'd spoken Martian to her. He tried again. "Look, I was lucky. I got away and lots of kids don't." He scratched Baby's head slowly. "If it hadn't been for your parents, I might have stolen a car or picked a fight and ended up in jail — but I didn't. I owe your parents for that, and even more I owe you and Trace for making me see that families don't always deal in pain."

She nodded slowly, staring into the fire. "I remember thinking how skinny you were that week you came to live with us. My mom said we weren't supposed to ask you any questions about what happened. Trace kept bragging that he was going to find out even if he got punished."

"No one asked me anything, as I recall." And he recalled that first week perfectly.

Kit rested her chin on her knees. "Mom said to give it time. If we still had questions, we could ask you later. But after a week you weren't a stranger anymore and we forgot all about it. Kids don't worry about things the way adults do, I guess." She straightened, hands locked. "But I'm not a child now and I'm asking you straight. They hurt you, didn't they? They left scars and bruises — inside and out."

Wolfe felt pressure build in his throat. Odd how hard it could be to say one little word, even years later. "Yes."

Baby moved her head, draping her body over his other foot. Butch snored noisily.

"I hate them for it. If they were here, I'd hurt them back." Her voice was harsh with emotion. "I'd hit them the way someone should have hit them all those years ago."

"Forget about it." Wolfe wanted to smooth the tension from her face and feel her mouth soften under his. Suddenly the future was far more important than dry details of a barren past. "I have, believe me. You want me to hate them? I can't." His voice fell. "You want me to forgive them? I can't do that either. All I can do is keep going — and make damned sure that I never turn into what *they* became."

"I always knew you were different. What you just said proves it." Her voice was soft and sleepy.

Wolfe stared at the fire. "Don't put me on a pedestal, Kit. My feet are every inch clay."

And they have polymer-based joint enhancements.

Not that he could tell her that.

When she didn't answer, he looked up and saw that she'd fallen asleep. He was spilling his guts out here and she was sleeping right through it.

He eased her back against the couch and smoothed the blanket over her, with the dogs watching every move. But when he tried to leave, she rolled onto her side and anchored his arm beneath his body.

"Umhm."

Her scent reached him, faint as a memory. She moved again, in the opposite direction this time, her head against his thigh as he stood beside her. With one tug of her hand, she pulled him onto the couch, and before he knew it she was wedged against him, curled across his chest.

He closed his eyes, wanting miles of distance between their bodies.

Wanting never to move again.

"Are you asleep?" he whispered.

"Nhm."

Yeah, that was asleep.

She murmured and twisted, kicking off the blanket while her pink nightshirt climbed up long glorious legs, giving Wolfe a glimpse of white panties. Lust hit him like the blast from a Harrier jet engine, but he didn't move, afraid he would wake her, afraid he might *plan* to wake her in the most intimate, demanding of ways.

So this was hell, he thought. Being close to so much pleasure — forbidden to do anything but look.

And look he did. With her restless twisting, he had more to see every second, until he finally had to close his eyes to guard his sanity. Life wasn't remotely fair.

But he'd learned that long ago.

She muttered hoarsely. Wolfe realized it was a command for the dogs. "Down," she repeated sleepily.

Which was damned good advice for him, too.

Unfortunately, his body wasn't close to listening. The zipper of his jeans strained tighter, and he shifted, trying to get comfortable.

After five more minutes he gave up the effort. Due to the ongoing variety of medications to support Foxfire's bio-enhancements, his system responded with hair-trigger speed and prolonged endurance.

Not that his sexual skills would even be an issue with Kit. He *wasn't* going down that road. Not now, not ever. She deserved more than a trained killer beefed up with medication and secret technology. She needed a regular life and a nice, normal husband, the kind of man with an optimistic outlook and sensible career plans.

Wolfe hated the jerk already.

Without warning she twisted again. Her head slid onto his thigh, her breath warm and damp through his worn jeans. Closing his eyes, he tried to forget that her lips were inches from his straining zipper.

He opened the top snap of his jeans and forced himself to relax, drawing upon all the control he possessed. Bush firefights and predawn raids hadn't gotten to him. Neither would this. By sheer force of will he put himself in a different place, cut off from both pain and pleasure, running over a black sand beach beneath a quarter moon.

Better.

His breathing slowed. Once his control returned, he felt a wave of relief. He wasn't losing his edge after all.

Kit muttered sleepily. Her nails dug into his thighs.

"Easy, honey." He moved her searching fingers away from his legs and out of the danger zone, but she pulled free, caught in bad dreams.

Her fist hit his jaw. Then her elbow slammed into his thigh. Wolfe had no choice but to lift her against his chest to calm her struggles. As he held her still, he tried not to notice the way her nightshirt climbed up to her waist.

Her eyes snapped open, dazed with sleep. *"What?"* she snapped.

"Not a thing. You were dreaming."

Her body froze. "It's really you, not a dream?"

He smiled tightly. "I guess that depends on what kind of dream you were having."

She closed her eyes, and he saw her sudden flush. She turned her face into his bare chest and stretched sleepily. "You're sure the dogs have enough water?"

"All systems go."

She smiled against his chest. "Want an energetic but *very* low-paying job?"

"Already got one. Uncle Sam would probably take a dim view of me moonlighting."

"Yeah, but what does the government know?"

Everything, he thought wryly. Through his imbedded chips he was tracked constantly. Even his heart rate and blood chemistry were monitored 24/7.

And knowing Ryker, there might be more bio-sensors implanted that Wolfe hadn't been told about yet.

He had a sudden, arresting image of three scientists in white coats monitoring his conversations, maybe even using some kind of remote technology to view his life in real time via a tiny camera.

No, that can't be possible.

There was a muffled chime between their bodies, and Kit grimaced. "Gotta take my pills. In my purse —"

He reached deftly to the end table. "Right here. Give me a minute and I'll get you some water."

He was gone for what seemed like forever.

Still groggy, Kit pushed to one elbow,

peering into the shadows beyond the firelight.

Feeling jumpy. Just on the edge of frightened.

"Wolfe?"

There was no answer.

She was wide awake now, her hip
starting to ache. She didn't want to think
about her clumsiness or the bruises from
her fall in the shower. She *really* hated the
idea that Wolfe had found her there on the
floor like a klutz. A stark naked klutz, no
less.

She dragged a hand through her hair.
She probably looked like hell. Her nightshirt kept climbing up, too. She wondered
how much he'd seen before he left.

She tried to finger comb her hair and
gave up. How she looked didn't matter because *nothing* was going to happen. She
wasn't going to discuss her medical problems with him either. This was her situation, not his. He had his own worries to
deal with right now.

She sat up slowly, rubbing her face.
Hadn't she offered to sleep on the floor?
How in heaven had she ended up draped
across his naked chest?

"Here's your water."

Wolfe returned, standing right in front of

her. She didn't see the glass of water he was holding out. She didn't see her pills or anything else in his hands.

Her gaze arrowed straight toward his chest and the sculpted muscles of his abs. Gorgeous.

She looked lower.

His top button was open, well-worn jeans riding low at his trim hips. Right now they were pulled tight over an unmistakable erection.

Wow, Kit thought. How had she slept through a sight like that? She forced her gaze back to his face and met his cool, unblinking stare.

"See something interesting?"

"No. That is — I wasn't paying attention." She looked away, desperate to hide the flush she could feel crossing her cheeks. "I was thinking about something else."

"Is that a fact?" His tone was very dry. "Like what?"

"Um — I was thinking about Diesel," she said quickly. "And then I remembered it's my birthday tomorrow."

The glint in Wolfe's eyes told her that he wasn't buying her hasty explanation for a second, but he didn't say anything else, shaking two pills onto his hand.

"Thanks." She avoided his eyes. "For talking. For letting me sleep on the couch." *Draped all over your warm chest.* "For taking care of the dogs, too."

"My pleasure. They're quite a handful." After Kit took her pills, he leaned down to scratch Baby's head. "Damned smart, all of them."

"You noticed that, did you?" She stifled a yawn. "I know I'm biased, but they seem to get smarter every day." She saw a muscle tighten at Wolfe's jaw. "You think that's weird?"

"Not really. So how come you forgot your own birthday?"

Kit pulled the blanket over her legs. "It's no big deal. I never do much anyway."

He took her face gently between his big hands. "It should be a big deal. You should get dressed up in something tight and black, then go dancing all night long."

She swallowed hard. The pressure of his hands made her stomach turn flip-flops. "Are you offering to take me?"

Something moved in his eyes. She felt his hands tighten.

Then he stood up, his face a mask. "I wish I could. But neither of us has any dance time in our immediate future. Whoever came after the Jeep on that deserted road could decide to come back."

Kit stared at him, trying to take in his sharp change of mood. "So I'm stuck here with you? Like some kind of prisoner?" Her voice tightened.

"For the moment, yes. It will be safer. I'm sorry, Kit."

She settled back on the sofa, studying his body. The muscles in his arms bunched as he leaned down to put her pills on the side table. Light brushed the hair scattered over his amazing chest.

She had to work not to drool.

The captive part was A-okay with her. Maybe she should reconsider Miki's plan, too. When would she ever have another shot at her top birthday gift, namely a night of wild sex in Wolfe's bed?

She took a slow breath. "So we're stuck here together? All night? That's very cool."

His brow rose. "You don't mind?"

Mind being held hostage by the man she'd lusted after secretly ever since she was thirteen? Mind seeing that hard body at seriously close range?

What part was she supposed to *mind*?

She managed to make her voice light. "I'll survive."

"So what *do* you want for your birthday?"

Kit stared into his dark eyes. Hot, sweaty sex in front of the fire came to mind. She cleared her throat. "Miki says I need La Perla and Manolo Blahnik."

"Ma-no-*what?*"

"Just stuff, Houston. Expensive but gorgeous. Never mind, you wouldn't follow." She blinked as he held out a foil-wrapped bar. "What's this?"

"Field rations. You should always have something in your stomach when you take medicine."

"How did you know that?" Kit was hit by the paralyzing thought that somehow he'd tracked down her medical history and details about the powerful pills she was taking.

"Common sense. That's what doctors tell everyone." He opened the bar and broke it in half. "Go on, eat it."

She took a bite and was pleasantly surprised. "Cinnamon brownie. Not half bad, either." She watched him take a bite. "So what's in these things, steroids or amphetamines? Some kind of secret growth hormone and tissue regenerator?"

He coughed sharply. "What do you mean by —"

"Just a joke. You're so — buff. I mean, your chest." Probably all the rest of him, too. Kit looked away, frowning. "You should take the couch. It's no problem, because I won't be able to fall asleep again. I never can."

Drat. Why had she let that last part slip?

She felt the couch shift. His thigh brushed her hip.

Her breath piled up in her chest as he slid an arm around her shoulders.

His eyes narrowed, focused entirely on her. He looked irritated and very restless. "What are you thinking about?" she whispered.

"You. About your long legs and soft skin. God help the man who tries to have any willpower around you."

She heard the edge to his voice. His hand was cradling her neck and his body had gone absolutely still. His eyes moved, fixed on her mouth.

I'm going to do this, she thought wildly. *I'm going to kiss him and then I'm going to pull off his jeans and see all the rest of him.*

It was crazy, but she'd waited long enough.

Her heart hammered as he leaned closer, whispered her name. He traced her mouth slowly with his thumb and her body felt liquid, boneless. She wet her dry lips, wanting to feel his mouth.

A shrill ring cut through the silence.

She sighed in irritation when she realized the sound was coming from her cell phone, shoved inside the pocket of her nightshirt.

Maybe she could ignore it. When the ringing stopped, he would kiss her. With luck he might make love to her for the next forty-eight hours.

Even one hour would be good. She wouldn't be choosy where he was concerned.

"Aren't you going to answer that?"

He didn't sound at all disturbed. In fact, he was smiling faintly as he reached across her and pulled out the cell phone.

Life was simply not fair, she thought angrily. For the first time in her life she had a shot at reckless, sweaty sex with the man of her dreams and her damned cell phone had to go off and ruin everything.

Diesel. The thought brought her down to earth with a crash and she grabbed the phone. It was three o'clock in the morning. Who else but Liz would call her at *this* hour?

She scanned the incoming caller ID and answered. "Liz, is that you? Is something wrong?"

"I'm glad I got you, Kit. I tried Miki earlier but she said you weren't there.

Then I tried the ranch. Where *are* you?"

"I'm not at Miki's. Tonight I —" She stopped as Wolfe shook his head sharply. "I'm staying with a friend," she finished. "Is something wrong with Diesel?"

The silence stretched out. Through the pounding of her heart, Kit heard papers rustle and a chair creak.

"Diesel's just the same," Liz said. "He's no worse. I was actually calling because —" A desk chair squeaked again. "I got some unusual blood work back a few minutes ago. Diesel's granulocytes are out of sight and the rest of his white count — well, let's just say I've never seen abnormals like this before."

Kit stared into the air above Wolfe's shoulder, confused. "There's something wrong with his blood tests? You think he might have some deeper condition causing the asthma?"

She felt Wolfe lean closer. She could have sworn that his hand smoothed her hair. Focused on Liz's call, she couldn't be sure.

"At the moment, I don't know what's going on. I'll have to do more tests, maybe check with some people in Albuquerque. But I wanted to speak with you first."

"I don't know what to say, Liz. He's had

asthma attacks before, but otherwise he's always been strong as a horse. The only blood work he's ever had was with you."

"I see. If you think of anything, give me a call. I'll talk to you in the morning." Liz laughed dryly. "Except it already *is* morning."

"Maybe you should get some rest." Kit watched sparks pop in the fireplace. "You sound exhausted, Liz."

"Occupational hazard, I'm afraid. I'll call you as soon as Diesel's up and around."

The line went dead, but Kit didn't move, cradling the phone.

"Something wrong with Diesel?"

"We're not sure. His vet says the blood work is weird."

"Was that the technical term?"

"Actually, she said she'd never seen anything like it." She sat stiffly, barely aware that she was gripping her cell phone. "You don't think that Diesel could have hanta virus, do you? Maybe that new form of equine flu? What if —"

She felt Wolfe's fingers lift her hair. Then his mouth touched her skin, tracing a warm path across the most amazingly sensitive spot on her neck.

No one had ever touched her there before.

No man had ever kissed her so gently, until her blood raced and her heart seemed to melt.

His lips did more of that same amazing thing, and heat hit her like a summer dust storm.

"Uh — what are you doing?"

"Distracting you." His voice was husky. "So you'll quit playing what if. It's always an exercise in futility."

"But Diesel —"

"Shhh."

Casual was her new mantra, she kept telling herself. She was *not* getting emotionally involved. *Casual.*

Something beeped nearby, and she realized it was her cell phone again. Not now. Not when she was on the verge of perfect fantasy.

She glanced at the LED screen and sighed. "Who is it?"

"Miki."

Wolfe pulled the phone from her hand. "Forget it. We've got more important things to do."

Kit blinked as he tossed her phone onto the couch and slid his hands into her hair. "Like what?"

His eyes darkened. "Let's break a few rules."

CHAPTER TWENTY-FOUR

Kit cleared her throat. "So you want —"

"Yeah." He bit her upper lip gently. "I want it bad. Call it an early birthday present. For both of us." He pulled away, a frown between his eyes. "Unless you've got different ideas?"

Not want sex with Wolfe?

She'd have to be dead and decomposing not to want sex with him. "N-no. I mean, yes. I've always wanted you, ever since I was thirteen and you stopped me from trying to jump off the back of my father's pickup truck."

"You were so damned determined. You halfway had me believing you could hold out that big plastic sheet and coast a little," he said hoarsely.

Kit felt desire arrow through her body. Her arms slid around his neck as he drew her against him. "I'm flying right now. Who needs a truck?"

"We haven't even started flying. Trust me on this."

She did trust him. She always had.

She rocked against his chest as he carried her over the tiled floor. "Where are we going?"

"You'll see."

But when he set her down, it was on a polished tabletop rather than smooth sheets. They were in the kitchen and he was pulling things out of drawers. "Don't tell me you're going to cook?"

"Not cook, but you're definitely eating more than a protein bar. Medicine can hurt your stomach," he said gruffly. "Take this."

A warm mouthful of chocolate chip cookies filled Kit's mouth. She sighed in earthy pleasure, licking his fingers to savor every rich speck. "More," she said, struck by greed.

He fed her another mouthful, as warm and freshly cooked as the last.

"These are amazing. Where did you find cookies?"

"Izzy's team doesn't miss a beat. They were in the oven, still warm."

Kit bit his fingers lightly as she finished, leaving his hand damp from her mouth.

"You like to play dangerous, I see."

Caught between his open thighs, Kit felt his erection nudge the fragile barrier of her bikini panties. The man was definitely prime. If this was another dream, she was going to kill someone.

She tilted her head up and kissed his chest. His hands slid around her and he cursed.

Pleased with his response, Kit tried it again. This time his fingers dug into her hair and his mouth crushed hers. He was hungry and angry and giving, all at the same time. The mix left her blood pounding.

She wriggled over the table, her thighs opening around him until they fit together tight, exactly the way she had always imagined they would.

Wolfe muttered hoarsely against her mouth.

"What did you say?"

"I said, find a gun and shoot me now." He twisted a finger in the edge of her panties. "This could get rough."

"Promises, promises."

He pulled the panties free, dropping them on the floor.

Kit's face filled with heat as he looked at her, his eyes hot. "Wolfe, I —"

"*Shhh.* Don't disturb me while I'm living the best fantasy of my life." A muscle moved at his jaw. "You're gorgeous. Strong. You've got me on my knees, honey."

She felt the cool brush of air as her nightshirt opened, button by button. Her breasts hardened beneath his callused hands. Then she felt the warm slide of his tongue, the wet friction of his mouth, and both of them were dragging her straight to delirium.

A clicking noise echoed through the kitchen and she realized the dogs were right behind Wolfe, watching every move.

He gave a hoarse laugh. "No voyeurs allowed, guys. Out of here, all of you." Baby whined, staring up at him. "You too, Baby." The puppy barked once, then trotted back into the living room, with the others right behind her.

Wolfe kicked the kitchen door closed with his foot.

The movement gave Kit ample opportunity to savor the sculpted lines of his body. "I need to touch you." She reached for his jeans. "Right now."

He parried her hand neatly and in one smooth movement slid her nightshirt from her shoulders. "I've got other plans."

Kit ran her tongue over dry lips. Her body was flushed and aching where their thighs met, and his jeans rode against her naked skin in a subtle friction that was fast driving her to a frenzy. "Wolfe, please. You don't know —"

"Like hell I don't." His voice was razor-sharp with tension. "You've got me twisted inside out. I'll be damned if I'm going to hurry now."

She made a broken sound as his hand slid over her stomach and combed the nest of curls at her thighs. His finger slid inside her, stroked her in a slow, hot caress that made her push blindly against him.

She closed her eyes, lost in pleasure. This was Wolfe, and she was finally here, with his hands touching her, goading her, making her body wet and lush in the grip of the best sex she'd ever had or even thought of having.

Then the heat took her and she came against him, stunned past words by pleasure. She shuddered as his fingers teased deeper and drove her up again, across a shining rope of trust and memories and maybe even love.

But she refused to think about love or even tomorrow. She dug her nails into his back, panting, as her body tightened again and she fell back to earth, shuddering.

When she opened her eyes, he was watching her. The sight of the old scars on his chest and shoulders made her suck in a breath. "What did they do to you?" she whispered.

"What had to be done. What I let them do."

But Kit saw a boy betrayed. She saw a man hardened by combat.

And she grieved for his pain just as she grieved for a world that required his sacrifice of blood.

She kissed him slowly, starting at his shoulder and lapping his skin, nipping gently. Then she bit down harder, summoning the violence she sensed he always kept hidden, very well leashed. She didn't want him controlled. She wanted him stripped to the core the same way she was, both captive and captor. She sensed that would free him as few other things could, and if he hurt her inadvertently, she would bear it without regret, her gift for a man who had given so much and never asked for anything in return.

When he leaned down, she tried to wriggle free, but his thighs closed, locked around her. His hands opened and his hot, skillful mouth moved, tasting her in ways no man ever had, until she was lost and panting against him. Slow and gentle, his tongue stirred unbearable waves of pleasure, and then she was *there,* caught in pleasure. Twice she cried out his name, but he didn't stop. She shuddered, raked her nails across his back, every nerve aflame.

Then she collapsed, breathless, all her strength gone.

When the shudders finally stopped and her sanity returned, she pulled free and glared at him.

"Did I hurt you?"

"Yes," she whispered.

His body tensed. "I'm sorry. It was the last thing I wanted."

"Not with your touch, Wolfe. With the touch you didn't give me." She turned, sliding against his chest. "I won't break, damn it. I'm not afraid of what you are or what you've done."

"Maybe you should be."

"Maybe you should stop moving away when I touch you. There are things that I've been waiting for, too."

He circled her wrists, his eyes like a winter's twilight. "What about the things I can do, the pain I might cause? I'm stronger than you realize. Aren't you afraid of that?"

Her hands slid to the waist of his jeans. "I'll never be afraid of you." She felt his zipper stretched taut.

"You should be. Everyone else is." His voice fell. "Even my bastard of a father was in the end."

"Because he knew you were better and

stronger than he'd ever be, so he hated you for it. As for everyone else — they haven't seen your soul the way I have."

Wolfe stood very still. "I don't have a soul. Not anymore."

She smiled faintly, saddened by his lie. Saddened that he thought she couldn't see deep enough to know it *was* a lie. "Then I'll take whatever you have to give me." She opened his zipper and took him between her hands, stroking him slowly, ignoring his low curse.

Even then his control didn't waver, despite the smooth squeeze of her hands.

Or her mouth.

She honored him with that hot touch, telling him what he refused to believe about his own worth. She wondered briefly what he'd had to do to become so distant, so controlled, but the thought faded beneath the rough pleasure of his body's powerful response against her lips and hands.

His fingers tightened in her hair. "Damn it, Kit, you don't understand. There are things I can't tell you —" His breath caught as her tongue feathered across him lovingly. "That won't change. Not ever."

"Do you want me?" she asked gravely.

He nodded.

"That's all that matters. I'll love you enough for both of us, since you can't seem to love yourself."

Something seemed to snap inside him. When she drew him back, stroking him with her mouth, he muttered her name and forced her to stop, his breath harsh and labored.

"You're turning me inside out, honey." He lifted her to her feet as if she weighed nothing, guiding her legs around his waist. A muscle flashed at his jaw. "I want *us*. Even if you regret it tomorrow."

"Never."

"Never is a long time." Then he pinned her against the shadowed wall, against the moonlight slanting down in a pale bar. His body was a line of shadow when he kicked his clothes away and took her there, the first time slow and fierce, every stroke robbing her of breath. He drank her ragged cries with his mouth, driving her up again, giving her no pause, no quarter.

Kit knew she was lost, knew she'd never be able to take another man like this again, with her heart given completely and time standing still. He might be gone in an hour or in a day, but this would be enough, his body driving her against the cool wall in deep, pounding strokes while his hands dug at her hips and his breath came harsh at her forehead. This she would never regret.

His body hardened. With a curse he lifted her.

She felt cool honed granite at her back as he set her against the counter. She watched his face change, watched his jaw clench and his control finally begin to slip.

This is real, she thought. *This is sweat and lust and the dark slap of his skin on mine. This is Wolfe naked, deep inside me.*

Filling me to breaking.

Loving me. Whether he knows it or not.

He rasped her name as if the sound was torn against his will. Then her body betrayed her, wet and shuddering, gripping him in her climax even as she struggled to wait.

Their bodies locked, straining. Then she fell, boneless and blind, stunned to feel him follow, his thighs rigid as he drove his hot seed inside her.

Moonlight shivered around them.

Light against shadow. Hope against despair.

"We should go upstairs." Wolfe's voice was husky. "A bed would be good."

"Ummm." Kit's mouth nuzzled his chin.

He was still leaning against the counter, one arm supporting her. She wondered vaguely how he managed to do that even now, after the most mind-blowing, heart-stopping sex she had ever known.

His fingers eased behind her back. "You're pressing against the outlet," he said gruffly. "That's got to hurt. What about those bruises on your leg? Damn, I forgot all about —"

"Can't feel a thing." It was true. She was sated and insensible, beyond anything but bliss and smug in the aftermath of her last stunning climax. "Since I can't move a muscle, I guess we'll have to stay this way for a few centuries."

She heard his low chuckle. "I know the feeling." But he didn't seem to have any problem lifting her.

"No," she muttered. "I want to stay here, exactly like this, with you inside me."

"I will be again, believe me." His voice was ragged, smoky with hunger.

"Again?" Kit's eyes slitted open. "You can still —"

His kiss cut her off. When he pulled away, his eyes glittered. "You're damn right I can. Only this time will be in a bed."

"In that case, I'll have three more of the same." As he crossed the floor, moonlight brushed his shoulders, and Kit couldn't seem to tear her gaze away.

"There's something I need to tell you first."

"Let me guess." Her lips curved. "You're married?"

"Not a chance. Something else."

She feigned shock. "You're using me for irresponsible, impersonal sex, but you're trying hard not to show it."

Wolfe bit the soft finger that was trailing across his mouth. "Honey, if this is impersonal, then I never want to see *personal.*" His mouth flattened to a line. "It's about protection — or the lack of it. In case you didn't notice."

"I noticed." Kit slid her arms slowly around his neck.

Wolfe took a deep breath. He was trying to be practical, to be honest with her, but her body was robbing him of all thought. "There's no reason for you to worry, because it won't be a problem."

She studied him uncertainly. "What does that mean?"

"It means no babies. No chance of it on my end."

Her finger traced his cheek. "Are you going to tell me why not?"

"It's a long and not very interesting

story, believe me. Bottom line — I can't."

"I'm sorry," she whispered. "What a terrible shame to waste such good genes."

She was painfully serious, he realized. She didn't have a clue about the black humor in what she'd just said. "The world will survive."

"Maybe there's something that can be done. Have you seen a doctor?"

"It's final, Kit." He shoved open the bedroom door with his foot. "I just wanted to tell you so that you wouldn't worry."

He put her down in the middle of soft white sheets, but when he tried to stand up, her hands tightened, pulling him closer. There was more than need in her eyes, more than desire.

There was something that felt like belonging.

He closed his eyes, rocked by the image of Kit pregnant, round and radiant with a child they'd made together in love.

Never going to happen, you fool. You're Foxfire property, stamped and processed. Children are neither in the technology nor the job description.

He dropped the jeans he'd carried upstairs. Her hand slid down his stomach, making him curse. Foxfire protocol proscribed ongoing personal relationships. Sex was fine as long as it was arranged through well-screened government sources. But it was never the same woman twice and the contact was never cluttered by emotions or discussion afterward.

Ryker's rules, and they were never broken.

Wolfe frowned. He'd just broken that rule in spades.

He'd have to end his contact with Kit soon. God knows, he shouldn't have started this. But his resolve wavered as her smile warmed him in the moonlight, and her eyes darkened with welcome and acceptance.

He had never known either. The combination was a sucker punch.

He could withstand torture and gunfire, but not Kit's smile.

So he forgot Ryker's rules, knowing it was stupid and maybe even dangerous, but unable to turn away from all she offered. For once he needed to feel exactly what it meant to *belong*.

One last time, he vowed, pulling her atop him.

"You're scowling at me."

He ran his hands across her stomach. Smiling, he cupped the silken weight of her breasts. "Because I'm trying to go easy with you." He bent closer, kissing the dark, aroused nipples that left his body hard again. "You're not helping too damned much either."

"When I want easy, I'll tell you. Right now I'm thinking along the lines of hot and fast and bone-jarring. Got a problem with that?"

Hot and fast was right up his alley.

Something buzzed noisily on the floor by the bed, and he cursed. "My beeper. I have to get it."

Kit sighed. She started to roll onto her side, but he caught her hips and held her against him. "Wrap your legs around me," he ordered. With one hand at her waist, he slid to the edge of the bed and leaned over, searching the pocket of the jeans he'd dropped. He found his pager, checked the ID and frowned.

"Look, I'll go," she said quietly. "I mean, if this is important . . ."

He dug his cell phone out of another pocket. "Don't even think about moving. I'm not close to being done with you, honey."

Her face filled with color. She laughed shakily. "You're going to talk on the phone while we — while I'm —" She stared at him, her legs riding against his growing erection.

"Multitasking is the motto of the new Navy."

"No way." She bit her top lip. "Not even *you* can do . . . well, that."

Good thing she didn't know about some of Ryker's kinkier training exercises, Wolfe thought darkly.

His eyes narrowed. "I can't?" He nudged her legs apart and slid inside her, grimacing at the wet silk feel of her. His long, probing strokes made her gasp, her nails raking his back.

He realized that watching her come all over again was going to be high on the list of his best life memories. "Don't let me stop you from letting go."

He held his slow, powerful rhythm, watching her rise to meet each stroke. With the slightest wince, he flipped open his cell phone. "Yeah."

Kit's eyes flashed open, her face filled with color. She tensed as he drove harder, deep inside her. She whispered his name, staring at him blindly.

And then to his fierce delight, her back arched and she came again.

When she would have cried out, he muffled her mouth with his palm. Her eyes were dazed, her body flushed, and he had never seen anything more beautiful than her passion.

"Houston, it's Teague. Everything quiet in there?"

Wolfe felt his pulse kick as she moved beneath him. "As quiet as it needs to be," he said hoarsely.

"Nothing moving out here." Silence. "I saw the living room light go out."

"Nothing to worry about."

"How's Kit?"

Wolfe's eyes narrowed. The subject of the question was currently panting hard, ready to crest in another wave of pleasure. "Asleep." His jaw clenched as her velvet muscles squeezed him.

His control was unraveling fast. All he could think about was her body, stroking him in hot, shivering tremors, scrambling his focus.

"Grab some shut-eye. Even you Foxfire hard bodies need quality time in theta."

"I'm trying." His voice hardened as Kit went boneless against him. "If there's nothing important . . ."

"Not out here. The coast is clear."

"Later."

Wolfe cut the connection and dropped the phone. Something glinting and wicked filled Kit's eyes, and she gripped him hard, drawing him deeper inside her. "Hurry up," she whispered, biting his hand.

Squeezing him intimately, she pulled him deeper until he felt his control snap.

He pinned her beneath him. "You live dangerously, honey."

"Because a certain man leaves me no choice." Her voice was husky. "I want you wrapped around me. I want the imprint of your body so I'll never forget tonight. Fill me up. Turn me inside out. Let me feel you lose control."

It was the easiest thing he'd ever done to let her smoky voice pull him deep until he did what she wanted, locking their fingers and rising to his elbows, driving her across the bed with hard straining stokes until she came beneath him again.

As he drank in her broken cries with his lips, Wolfe let his control shatter and found his way home inside her, dimly aware of her mouth sliding into a smile before pleasure swallowed them both completely.

CHAPTER TWENTY-FIVE

"You took forever. Get back under the covers *now*."

Wolfe frowned into the darkness. He'd talked to Izzy and then checked the downstairs perimeter. Nothing seemed irregular or felt out of place when he did an energy scan.

But he was restless, just the way Kit's dogs were restless. "I took seven minutes, honey."

"Forever," she said sleepily, curling up against him.

He couldn't stay here. Touching her was becoming an addiction.

He took slow breaths, focusing on the dark house. The branches of a big cottonwood tree scraped the nearby window, and he shifted his concentration, running it through the house as he checked for noises that were out of place or subtle energy trails that felt wrong.

But nothing hinted at Cruz's presence. And that awareness only left Wolfe more edgy.

He heard Kit's steady breathing beside him. She was asleep again, her leg across his thigh, her fingers curled around his shoulder. Desire was a pleasant torture as she twisted in her sleep, her warm body open to his.

Wolfe knew he shouldn't be cluttering his mission with emotions.

But something bothered him more than that. Ryker could have ordered that Kit and the dogs be taken to a safe house unrecorded in any government database, guarded 24/7 until Cruz was back in custody.

But he hadn't put her into isolation, and Wolfe knew why. She and her dogs were the best bait Ryker had, and he meant to use them any way possible. He would do whatever it took to avoid having Cruz's face splashed across the six o'clock news while reporters shouted messy, unpleasant questions about a military program that didn't officially exist.

Ryker knew that Cruz would come after them, and Wolfe would be her only real defense when the bullets started flying.

Until then, he had to stay close — and stay ready.

Curled up beside him, she murmured softly, her hand opening on his chest. She said something about chew toys in her sleep and sat up quickly. "Why did you let me fall asleep?"

"No reason not to."

"You're still awake and you don't even look tired." She shoved the hair out of her face and glared at him. "How come you aren't exhausted?"

"Training," he said smoothly. "I'll catch a nap later." He changed the subject, staring at her neck. "You're going to have a mark there in the morning. Maybe more than one."

Kit stretched beneath the quilt, smiling smugly. *"Excellent.* I've always wanted to be debauched and seductive, like Ingrid Bergman in *Notorious."*

"That's an old movie, right?"

"One of the best. Don't tell me you've never seen it."

Wolfe shrugged. The only kind of movies he saw regularly involved demolition techniques and round trajectories.

"Where have you been living, the eighteenth century?"

"Not quite that far away." He toyed with the hair at the back of her neck, letting it spill over his fingers.

He didn't want to ask personal questions, but he had to. "If any of the men in your life have hurt you, I'll find them." *Actually, he'd kill them.*

"That sounds very plural." Kit traced his stomach. "You must think I've been busy."

He pulled her up and kissed her with grim possessiveness. "I think you're unforgettable. How could you not have men lined up wanting you?"

She stared out the window for a long time. "There was only one. At the time he seemed important." She sighed. "You don't really want to hear this."

"Try me."

"He was an archaeologist working up on the mesa for a summer. That tent of his looked so damned hot that I felt sorry for him. He used to come down for showers and air conditioning on the weekend. One thing led to another. . . ."

Wolfe's muscles tightened. He hated the man already. "Things usually do."

"We agreed on everything at first." She laughed bitterly. "Except on marriage. I wanted to and he didn't. And about kids. I wanted six and he wanted zero. He also wanted me to give up my canine work, leave the ranch and follow him to North Dakota." She closed her eyes and Wolfe watched moonlight play over her face. "How could I leave? How could I ever give up my dogs?"

"He was a fool to ask," Wolfe said harshly. "Worse than a fool."

"Maybe. Or maybe he was used to getting exactly what he wanted." She rolled over, drawing her fingers down his chest. "It doesn't matter."

Branches scraped against the window. "Did you love him?"

"I loved thinking that I did. As for the rest — no, I didn't."

"How can you be so sure?"

Kit smiled crookedly. "Because I know how the real thing feels. I've probably always known." Leaning down, she kissed him with slow abandon.

Wolfe's chest tightened. Honor made him slant her face up to his. "I can't stay, Kit. It's — what I am and what I do. I won't lie to you or make promises I can't keep."

Something shimmered in her eyes and then vanished. "I've always been a sucker for a man who tells the truth. Even when it's not what I want to hear."

He didn't try to answer her.

"Stop looking so angry. I don't want promises from you." She slid her leg across him, bringing their warm bodies together in a slow, erotic friction.

"Kit, you can't —"

She traced his cheek, then bit his ear.

He closed his eyes at her touch. "When I'm gone —"

"Shut up." She pressed against his erection. "Where's that multitasking you're so proud of?"

The moon struggled through dark branches outside the window. Looking outside, he realized the wind had picked up. Soon would come the worst part of night and the last chill hours before dawn.

But he turned his back on the night, watching her face as he moved inside her with desperate care. He knew she would be hurt, no matter what he did, because she held back nothing and asked nothing in return.

She broke his heart with her honesty. How in the hell was he going to walk away from her when the order came down?

She slid her hand between their bodies, and his world tilted. Wolfe pulled her astride him, thigh to thigh, buried in her heat.

Desire burned white, consuming all thoughts of tomorrow.

CHAPTER TWENTY-SIX

4:46 a.m.

Wolfe moved through the house, checking doors and windows. He felt the welts of Kit's nails on his back and chest and wondered how many marks he'd left on her.

She had welts of beard burn on her face.

On her breasts.

Especially on her thighs, where he'd enjoyed a slow, thorough exploration until she'd writhed in hot pleasure. One more image he'd never forget.

Crossing the living room, he checked his watch. He was about to call Izzy for an update when his cell phone rang. By habit he checked the caller ID before answering.

Private.

Izzy's prior calls had listed a 202 area code in the D.C. area, no doubt bounced back and forth through multiple relays for security.

Wolfe's finger froze over the power button. He sensed a sudden trail of energy that he hadn't felt in days.

Cold, he thought. Sticky.

Swiftly, he pulled out a second phone and hit a prearranged number. "Izzy, I've got a call coming in. It's showing as private and I've got a bad feeling about it. Can you lock in with a trace?"

"Does it snow in Fargo?" The line went dead.

Wolfe raised his defenses, jacking up his focus. His finger hit the button. "Yeah."

For long moments he heard only the snarl of the wind over the hiss of moving leaves. "Hello?"

"Am I interrupting anything important?"

There was no mistaking that voice.

"Cruz." The word was cold on Wolfe's lips. "Stop wasting my time."

"Open your eyes, Houston." Cruz's voice hardened. "Have you checked your meds lately? Do you know what they're giving you?"

"This is bullshit."

"You want it to be bullshit." The voice was low, persuasive. "You can't trust Ryker."

"Why aren't you back at the facility?" Wolfe said flatly.

"They didn't tell you how my body started to screw up? It's happening to me right now. The rest of you will be next."

361

"You're full of it, Cruz. Nothing's happening to me or my team."

"It was my team once."

"I'm hanging up now."

"Wait."

Wolfe heard the desperation in Cruz's voice. Or was this another trick? "You want to tell me sad tales? You were a lot of things, but you were never a whiner."

"I'm your worst nightmare now." Cruz laughed acidly.

"Get to the point. Make your demand if you're going to."

"Oh, I will in time. Count on it. Right now you're sweating. I can read you, remember? I can *feel* when you're telling a lie."

Then you must be close, Wolfe thought.

Standard mental wave forms, the kind the Foxfire team was trained to pick up, had a narrow dispersal pattern. Wolfe prayed that Izzy was tightening his fix on the call at that very moment.

"Forget it. They won't find me unless I want to be found."

"So what do you want?"

"A small Tahitian island? A handful of perfect pink diamonds? No, that's too easy. I'm thinking of time. What would you give for two years of your life?" Cruz's voice dropped. "Two years with *her?*"

Wolfe kept his voice steady. "Who?"

"I saw her in the car. I heard her laugh. The pet store was crowded, but I watched you together. The little dog is better than I imagined."

So Wolfe's instincts had been right. Cruz had been out in the parking lot. Since Cruz had already seen Ryker's canine profiles, Wolfe didn't bother to deny any details. "All of them are smart. But they're nothing without training." Wolfe glanced at his watch, determined to stretch out the call. "You should know that. I was no good until you got your hands on me."

"You had raw talent driven by old emotion. Emotion was both your strength and your biggest weakness." Silence stretched out.

As the seconds passed, Wolfe heard a droning sound carried by the wind.

A train whistle? Some kind of heavy equipment?

"Have you had her yet?"

Wolfe spit out a low curse.

"You're angry, so I'd say that means yes. Enjoy her while you can, because I'm coming." Again the droning tones drifted on the wind.

Wolfe wanted to punch hard, throwing

his enemy off balance. "How did you kill the waitress?"

The silence turned menacing. "Did they tell you about the wounds on her face and neck? Did they tell you what I can do now?"

"You destroy. That's all you can do."

"We all destroy. Death is our greatest creation. Ryker saw to that." Cruz's voice shifted. "I'm coming for the woman and the dogs. Stand in my way, and I'll destroy you, too."

The line went dead.

Wolfe was still holding the phone when his other unit chimed. He answered with hands that seemed stiff.

"Sound pattern screening verifies that was Cruz. I tracked the call, too."

"Where was he?"

"Paris. Buffalo. Mexico City. The bastard is good, I'll say that. His relays shifted every twenty seconds, which leaves us no-where."

"Not exactly." Wolfe climbed the stairs swiftly. "He wants contact, Teague. Some part of him remembers what it was like to be part of a unit. He wants that sense of belonging, and I can use that. It could be the only weakness he has left." Wolfe didn't mention the odd whine he'd heard.

He was operating on a hunch.

"What did he mean about Kabul when he called last time?"

"Long story. Some day when we're eighty, I'll tell you." Wolfe opened the door to the bedroom. Kit was still draped over his pillow, fast asleep. Her three dogs were stretched out around the bed in full protection mode.

He walked quietly to the bathroom, checking the windows and scanning the roof. "You got the rest of what Cruz said, the part about the medicines?"

"I heard. You want me to look into it?"

"Don't bother. He was just rattling my cage."

Wolfe finished checking the windows and walked through the dark bedroom. "Have your people at the clinic monitor Diesel constantly. As soon as the dog can travel, I want him brought back here. Cruz is close, never doubt it for a second."

"How can you be so sure?"

Because I squatted beside him in the freezing mud. Because we've been to hell and back together.

What did the Chinese call it?

"Because we've eaten bitterness from the same bowl, Izzy. Because I know how he thinks. Sometimes I wish to hell that I didn't." He glanced at his watch. "I've got to call Ryker."

It was raining now, heavy drops that beat against the windows.

He felt a moment of weariness, staring out at the rain-swept roof. "I have to tell Kit something, Izzy. She's not stupid. She and her dogs are Cruz's primary target, and she needs to know what she's up against. Otherwise she'll be flying blind."

A sound in the darkness brought Wolfe around in a lightning crouch, his Sig drawn and level, his finger hovering at the trigger. He tracked the shadows, looking for threats, but saw only Kit.

Her face was pale, her eyes glittering with anger. There might have been a hint of tears, too. "You cold bastard. How *could* you lie to me that way? Everything's been a lie. They train you to do anything and say anything to get the job done. You're just like Trace — nothing matters to you but the mission."

"You're wrong, Kit."

"No, I'm just waking up." She bit back a broken sound. "You're using us as bait, aren't you?"

"Kit, listen to me —"

"I don't want to listen anymore." She

watched him holster his gun. Her voice broke. "This is for my dogs. It's also for me."

Then she slammed her fist into his face.

CHAPTER TWENTY-SEVEN

Wolfe didn't rub his cheek, though it throbbed from her full-force punch. He figured Kit had earned a good shot at him. "You want to say that again?"

"You *told* me we were safe."

"You are," he said flatly. "No one is getting past me or Izzy."

"That's not what you just said. 'She and her dogs are Cruz's primary target.' I heard you, Wolfe. What have you gotten us into?"

"Sit down and I'll tell you."

"Another lie?" She cradled her hand as though it hurt. "I'm leaving now, and I'm taking the dogs. I don't trust you anymore."

"You can't leave, Kit."

"No? You'd have to use that gun to make me stay here now."

"If it will keep you alive, I'll do just that."

"It's over." Her voice was empty and tired.

It was better this way, he thought.

Colder, faster. Like Izzy said, the quick way was always best. "Your call," he said finally.

She stared at him, her face hidden in shadows. "It was over the second you lied to me and endangered my dogs." When he moved closer, Kit raised her hands between them.

His eyes narrowed. "Don't fight me, Kit. Believe me, it's the worst thing you could do right now." He walked through the bedroom and stared out at the rain sheeting across the roof. "Ask your questions," he said without turning. "I'll answer what I can."

She sat on the edge of the bed, her hands clenched. "Who is Cruz?"

"Someone I used to work with." Wolfe frowned at the rain. "He's gone rogue."

"Why does he want me and my dogs?"

Wolfe considered his words carefully. He couldn't cancel out years of training, years of secrecy. "He's been looking for dogs to use in training programs. Somehow he found out about your background and credentials. We think he may be headed here."

"Damn you," she whispered. She looked at the floor, where the dogs sat expectantly. They ringed the bed, absolute trust in their eyes. "When?"

"Impossible to say." He wanted to touch her, but he knew that *this* Kit — the one who was angry and determined — would stand a better chance against Cruz. "Could be an hour, could be a week."

"What does he look like?"

Wolfe pulled out a picture, cropped to show only Cruz's gaunt face. "Have a look."

Kit studied the photo carefully. "He doesn't look dangerous. He looks more like a POW in the WWII pictures I've seen."

"He's dangerous." Wolfe looked at the picture before sliding it back into his pocket. "There's something else you need to know." He knew he was skirting the edge of insubordination to hint at a program and skills that had to remain top-secret. "You may not recognize him. He's trained in . . . disguise. He could even pass for me or you."

"I don't believe that."

"Just accept it — and don't ask for explanations. From now on, if anyone calls you or tries to enter the house, I want you to ask them how the weather is in St. Louis." His eyes darkened. "Even if it's me. Do you have that?"

"I just ask that question?"

Wolfe nodded. "If they say anything except 'mostly cloudy, a hint of snow,' then get the hell out of here." His voice hardened. "And be sure the dogs go with you."

Kit took a deep breath. "This all sounds ridiculous."

He filtered out more of the truth to give her. "I'm sure you've noticed your dogs are special. Don't ask why. Just accept that they are gifted in ways you can't imagine. If you want to stay alive and protect them, you need to do what I say." He bent down and scratched Baby's head. "I've programmed your cell phone. If anything happens, hit *0. Izzy will take the call immediately."

She looked at him for a long time. "What about you?"

"I may be . . . unavailable." It occurred to him that she hadn't questioned him about Izzy or the men outside the house. She'd accepted their presence as necessary. She might be angry with him, but she still trusted him to make choices to protect her.

She started to say something, then looked away. The branch was scraping the window again. The hours they'd spent together in bed seemed a century in the past.

"Fine. I'll remember."

The tension grew. The dogs stirred rest-

lessly, staring from Kit to Wolfe and back
again.

He glanced at the clock. There was
nothing more to say. "I have to go make
some calls." He rubbed his neck, frowning.
"Try to sleep."

She made a sound that was too hard for
a laugh but too soft for a curse. "Right."
Rain gusted against the window. "Go make
your calls."

Nothing more to say, Wolfe thought bitterly.

"Damn it, Houston. You're eight minutes late. You were to check in at 0500
hours."

Wolfe stood motionless, cell phone to his
ear. "Sorry, sir. We had a call from Cruz."

Ryker's breath hissed out. "Teague
tracked the source?"

"Affirmative. But Cruz used relays to
half a dozen cities, changing every twenty
seconds."

"So you got nothing. What did he
want?"

"To taunt me. To let me know he was
alive. To tell me he's coming after the
dogs."

"He's gone over the edge. What about
using an energy net to track him?"

"He was always the best at energy surveillance. If you want a net, I need Trace O'Halloran here with me."

"I don't *have* O'Halloran. I have you, damn it, and you'd better start earning your pay."

Pay? It was enough for himself since his expenses were nil, with food and lodging at Foxfire's various facilities, but not enough to support a wife and family.

Wolfe took a deep breath. Why was he thinking about a family? The program medications had destroyed any shot at that months ago.

As rain drummed on the roof, he worked back through every second of Cruz's call, replaying the distant drone that continued to bother him.

Something teased at the back of his mind.

Summertime.

Darkness.

There'd been crickets then, but they hadn't obscured that odd mechanical cadence. Some kind of heavy equipment . . .

"Houston, what are you doing to track Cruz? That's your primary objective."

Not saving Kit.

Not protecting the dogs.

"Don't worry, he'll come for us. He said

that clearly." Wolfe stopped. His hands clenched. "I've got to go, sir."

"Commander, what did you mean by —"

"I'll have Teague finish the briefing, sir." Wolfe strode toward the door, ending the call. He swung his pack up from the floor, his eyes on the rain, thinking about a summer thirteen years before.

He found her in a chair in the kitchen, the dogs around her. She had a glass of milk that hadn't been touched and a book that hadn't been read.

"I have to go out. Stay here. Izzy will be with you."

"I'm sorry it had to be . . ." Kit shrugged. "Like this."

"Forget it. This would have happened sooner or later. The military makes a damned jealous wife."

"I wish . . ." She swallowed. "I wish that things were different."

"But they aren't." Wolfe checked his Sig and shoved it into his waistband underneath a black ballistic nylon slicker. "You deserve champagne and roses. Don't ever forget that."

"You're not coming back?"

He needed to get Cruz before Cruz could get to her. If he succeeded, he wouldn't be coming back anytime soon.

That was the best thing for all of them.

He bent down, scratched Butch under the chin. "Hard to say. Keep an eye on stuff here, you guys. You're one hell of a team."

Baby licked his chin, and Wolfe chuckled. But when he stood up, his smile was gone.

Rain gusted through the door as he headed out into the first gray light of dawn.

The shed was up the northern slope of a rocky ridge. The railroad tracks were barely visible from the road and completely out of sight of the house.

Wolfe circled up the far side of the slope and came in from the back, squinting against the rain. The outside lock, a simple aluminum square, was sheared through. But the lock had been rehung so anyone not looking closely would see nothing amiss.

Wolfe hadn't come within twenty yards of the door before he knew this was the place. Cruz's energy hung in the air, thick and smoky, physical enough to mock him. But Wolfe felt only remnants, nothing that seemed *alive.*

Touching the door, he waited. When he sensed no threat, he flipped on his xenon penlight and went in.

Empty plastic water bottles littered the floor. They were all the same brand and he wondered if Cruz had robbed a machine nearby. Food wrappers covered a single rickety table, along with a huge stack of old magazines, everything from *Scientific American* to *Cosmo.*

Cruz was catching up on news and culture, it appeared. But how the hell had he gotten here so fast? Judging by the trash, he must have arrived about the same time Izzy had brought them in. No one had followed them after the attack on the road, Wolfe had made certain of that, and Izzy's team had noted no surveillance.

Cruz was too damned good.

Wolfe picked up one of the water bottles and rolled it between his fingers, slipping into altered theta to enhance his impressions. He had a sense of Cruz near the window, absorbing a science article and tossing the empty bottle over his shoulder.

He picked up a food wrapper, reading the energy thread it carried. This time he sensed gnawing hunger.

Motionless, he studied the rest of the small room.

A mouse flashed across the rough plank floor. Wind hissed through the only window, held together with duct tape.

The place was dead. Cruz had left, and some subtle cue told Wolfe he wouldn't be back.

Lifting a dirty scrap of curtain, he checked the view from the window.

Sonofabitch.

The second story of the safe house was just visible over the line of the ridge. Sitting here with binoculars, Cruz could have kept a record of activity inside the house without moving a foot.

Grimly, Wolfe pulled out his secure cell and hit a button.

Izzy answered immediately. "Is he there?"

"Gone. But he's been way too close, watching almost as long as we've been in place. How the hell did he know where we were?"

"My people are all handpicked." Izzy's voice could have scored granite. "There's no way Cruz could turn any of them."

"That's not what I'm saying. I'm thinking that sometime, somewhere, one of the people who reported in or took your call *wasn't* who you thought he was."

"He's really that good?"

"Believe it. You have passwords in place? And your people know what to do if someone has a completely logical story for why he missed being briefed on the codes?"

"Already taken care of."

Suddenly Wolfe heard the din of Kit's dogs through the cell. "What's going on, Izzy?" He turned and hit the door, already on the run.

"Something on the back porch." Izzy's voice was cold and calm. "The dogs are in the kitchen and they're going nuts."

"Where's Kit?"

"Right here with me and my Glock."

"Keep her there," Wolfe snapped. "Get the dogs in the room with you. And don't let anyone in, not even *me.*"

CHAPTER TWENTY-EIGHT

Wolfe sprinted along the service road and cut through a park that looked right out of a Disney movie. Squinting through the rain, he vaulted a stone fence.

He was close enough to hear the dogs barking now. They were in a frenzy by the time he stopped near the high brick wall at the back of the house. He stripped off his pack and slicker and pulled himself up quietly, hand over hand, jamming his fingertips into random spaces between the bricks.

He didn't need much. A skilled and conditioned climber could hang from one finger for ten minutes, and Wolfe had clocked in at twenty. Cruz had the same ability.

At the top of the wall, he stayed motionless, scanning the back yard. Through the rain he picked up a faint movement on the porch outside the living room.

A second later, pain bored into his forehead, the violence of the attack nearly making him lose his grip. Closing his eyes, he locked his fingers, hanging motionless as the wall of pain rolled over him.

Learning to set a protective energy framework was part of the basic program in Foxfire, but Cruz's skill had always been to attack before the enemy suspected his presence. He attacked now with a focused energy net that shot out of the rain.

Wolfe countered pain with pain. He knew Cruz, knew how to get to him. As he clung to the bricks, he threw full focus into an image of the wall collapsing onto the patio, fully aware that being buried alive was Cruz's deepest fear.

Sweating, he held the image, driving it forward through the rain to target the shadows on the patio. The door rattled. The patch of shadow crossed the porch and suddenly the back yard was blasted with light from the second floor roof and both back walls. For an instant he had a clear glimpse of Cruz.

Wolfe pulled onto one elbow and squeezed off six fast shots. Cruz stumbled against a low planter, lurched upright, then sprinted across the side yard, holding his shoulder.

Wolfe dropped to the grass and followed, jumping a lawn chair and a hibiscus bush.

He managed to grab Cruz's elbow at the side of the house, and they fell in a blur of stabbing movement. A knife dug through Wolfe's right hand.

Ignoring the pain, he lunged for Cruz again, and the two grappled in deadly silence, arm to arm in the beating rain.

Suddenly Cruz seemed to vanish.

Wolfe grabbed at the air with his hands and reached out for the familiar energy trail with his mind.

He saw a shadow move at the corner of his eye. Shooting to his feet, he vaulted over a heavy garbage can and caught a shimmering image of Cruz whipping hand over hand up the far wall.

By the time Wolfe topped the wall and looked over, Cruz was gone. Taillights were disappearing down the end of the long drive.

His bird had flown.

Wolfe sprinted toward the front porch, snapping orders into his cell phone. "Get a car to the gate. Watch for a black sedan, probably a Camry. No plate visible. He's headed your way."

Izzy opened the front door. Behind him Wolfe saw Kit holding a book, the dogs in a huddle beside her. He gave the code phrase quickly. "The car just left. We'll get him at the gate."

"You're hurt." Kit was looking over Izzy's shoulder, frowning.

Wolfe barely glanced at his bleeding hand. "Not important." He scanned the room. "Everything quiet in here?"

"A-okay."

Both men stopped, turning to stare impatiently at Kit, their faces shuttered.

"You want me to leave?" She dropped her book on the sofa. "One of you had better tell me something. I don't want state secrets, just a reasonable idea of what the hell is going on."

She didn't wait for an answer, lifting Wolfe's hand and wincing at the bleeding cut. "Get him cleaned up, Izzy. The man is too stubborn to do it himself."

After she left, Wolfe wrapped a torn piece of gauze around his hand as he headed for the garage. "It was definitely Cruz. I'm going after him."

"You had a visual ID?"

"Visual and every other sort. He's wounded now, but that will only make him more focused." He headed toward the garage. "Don't leave her."

"Count on it." Izzy nodded curtly. "Stay in touch. Code word only."

When Wolfe reached the gate, half a dozen men in black uniforms covered the road, checking debris scattered over the cement.

A man with a walkie-talkie sprinted up to Wolfe's window and the code words were given. "He knocked the damned guard building into pieces. We've got two men down here."

Wolfe didn't stop for explanations, staring out into the cold gray dawn. "Which way?"

"Left. At least I think so. There was some kind of fog and I can't be absolutely sure."

Wolfe studied the road. *Not fog. Cruz.*

But was this just another feint to throw him off?

He put away his irritation and anger, letting every element of the chaotic scene sharpen and eat down into his awareness.

Car lights.

Shouting.

The screech of walkie-talkies and angry questions.

There — the shifting trail of energy. . . .

Wolfe closed the window and pulled away from the chaos, dialing Izzy.

"Izzy, he's here, somewhere near the

gate. He could be any one of your people."
Wolfe paused. "Yes, it's mostly cloudy in
St. Louis. A hint of snow." The code
phrases asked and given, he continued.
"Don't let *anyone* in." He turned the
corner and pulled onto the gravel as soon
as he was out of sight. "I'm going back for
a closer look."

How do you catch a shadow?

Wolfe frowned, faced with the challenge
of tracking down a brother officer, one
whose skills appeared to have grown exponentially.

This was his real purpose, he knew.
Foxfire's prime directive would soon expand to prevent hostile operatives with
similarly enhanced abilities from infiltrating
the U.S. government, military and civilian
facilities.

Learning new skills was the reason they
had all volunteered for the program, and
Foxfire would be the first line of defense
against twenty-first-century attack.

But they had never imagined they
would have to operate against one of their
own.

Wolfe pulled the gray cold of dawn
around him like a cloak, building the
image inch by inch. Once the gray illusion was firmly in place, he trotted back

into the chaos, waiting for the slightest hint of recognition on any face.

As he moved through the crowd, two men passed him without stopping.

A tech officer carrying a silver case would have run into him if Wolfe hadn't stepped aside. A man built like a defensive lineman picked up a broken plank from the entrance gate and swung it away onto the grass.

Wolfe was invisible amid the activity.

At the same time, he felt Cruz's energy becoming more and more faint, like a light flickering. After sweeping the scene again, he stopped in the middle of the road. A pinkish stain trailed along the concrete, dimmed by the rain.

The blood looked fresh.

Crouched in the rain, he touched the fading blot and picked up anger and pain. Cruz would be slower now, but far from incapacitated. He was also in full combat mode.

Cars passed. Windows opened as passersby gaped at the gate wreckage. Any one of them could be a construct to hide Cruz.

Wolfe watched the line for ten minutes, oblivious to the cold and his own wound. By the time he finally gave up, the sun had climbed above the mountains to the east.

A chill rain had swept away the last of Cruz's blood.

"I lost him."

"How the hell did you manage that, Houston?"

"He's faster than I am." Wolfe would have given a fortune to know exactly what kind of training Cruz had received since his fake funeral — and what had been done *to* him. But Ryker never gave details unless he had to.

"He found a surveillance post nearby. He's been watching the house for most of the time we've been here, and he seems to know what we're doing as soon as we make a decision."

"Damn the man," Ryker snapped. "What does he want?"

"He wants the dogs. He told me that on the phone." Wolfe flexed his bleeding hand carefully. "He also wants back two years of his life."

"Find him, Houston. Otherwise we'll have reporters and congressional aides crawling all over us. If *one* of them gets a whiff of this situation, Foxfire will be history. Do I make myself clear?"

"Absolutely, sir."

★ ★ ★

Up in the bedroom, Kit stood at the window watching a dozen men in black uniforms clean up what looked like debris and broken wood from the road near the security gate.

Probably they were part of the security team organized by Izzy Teague.

More men, more violence. What had happened to her hectic but largely uneventful life? First the attack on her car, now this — in a place where they were *supposed* to be safe and completely anonymous.

Who could she really trust?

Wolfe?

Hardly. He had lied to her with no compunction. He was carrying out his mission exactly, and using her, as ordered.

Her joints ached and she hadn't slept more than an hour the night before. She still didn't understand the conversation she'd overheard.

She and her dogs are Cruz's primary target.

Why? Her dogs were valuable, and would be even more so once they were fully trained, but they were hardly worth the full-fledged paramilitary operation exploding around her.

She needs to know what she's up against.

Kit rubbed her arms, shivering. It was true. She didn't have a clue what she was up against and she wanted answers.

The truly pathetic thing was that she'd come looking for Wolfe to tell him about her medical situation. She wanted him to know the truth in case he had second thoughts about her or a long-term relationship.

Stupid, she thought wearily. Instead of the truth, she'd stumbled across lies.

Against the rain, she heard the low chime of her cell phone. She checked her watch, frowning.

6:10 a.m. Even the cell phone solicitors didn't start *this* early.

The number was blocked. She answered tentatively, surprised to hear Liz. "Is Diesel okay? Did he —"

"Diesel is stable." The vet yawned. "You answered so fast. Weren't you asleep?"

"I've been up for awhile." *Watching my dreams go up in smoke. No big deal.* "Why aren't you asleep?"

"Some nights I can and some nights I can't." Papers rustled. "I was up watching the rain and feeling glum, wondering where the last ten years went." Liz laughed

388

mirthlessly. "Feeling like shit, not to put too fine a point on it. You want to cheer me up?"

Kit watched rain blur the window. "You may be asking the wrong person."

"You too? Someone said it was a Mercury retrograde or a Saturn trine — something bad. I've always thought we make our own fate, but maybe I've been wrong all this time."

Kit stared off to the east, where the sun was struggling above a cold wall of clouds. "How about I pick up two artery-clogging caramel macchiatos with whipped cream when I come?" Something crackled against the phone. "Are you still there, Liz?"

"I dropped my necklace, that's all. One of these days an animal will eat it if I'm not careful." Silence fell. "Come by whenever. Diesel and I will be here. And bring the other dogs. They'll be good for Diesel."

"Sure thing."

As Kit hung up, she remembered her security concerns. Wolfe would insist that he or his friend Izzy accompany her, if they allowed her to go at all.

On the other hand, having several big men around as backup seemed like a *very* good idea right now.

"It's done." Liz turned slowly, her necklace gripped in her hand. "She'll be here with the dogs. Any other old friends you want me to betray?" she asked bitterly.

The gaunt man sitting at her desk looked supremely pleased. "When there are, I'll be sure to tell you."

CHAPTER TWENTY-NINE

"Give him the shot."

Liz glared across the room, one hand on Diesel's head. "No."

"I need the dog out cold and ready to travel. Give him the shot *now.*"

"I can't. His blood work is still way off."

"Of course it's off." The man across the room studied the lab reports on Liz's desk. "White count high. Red count low. Just what you'd expect, given our shared background." He smiled thinly. "You thought I didn't know?"

Liz turned away, frowning. "I don't know what you're talking about."

"Of course you do. You and your brother helped set up the animal side of this whole program. Hank used to come and visit the lab every few weeks to keep an eye on the animals' white count."

Liz jammed her hands in the pockets of her white coat. "I'm not involved in Hank's work over at Los Alamos."

"The hell you aren't. You've been watching these dogs since the day you and your brother finished their genetic profiles."

"Hank shouldn't have discussed that with you."

"He didn't. I had file access."

"Why? You aren't involved in the research."

"There are things you don't know, honey. Things about me . . . and others."

"Like what?"

Cruz took her hand in his. "You have to trust me. I know all about Project Home Run, even though the dogs' trainer is unaware. That was a nice performance you gave for her on the phone."

Liz's hands tensed. "It wasn't a performance. I was worried about Diesel's health. Kit also happens to be one of my best friends."

"But you set her up."

"I don't know what you mean."

"You stirred up all the old stories about the Apache treasure hidden on her ranch. To cap the plan off, you had some fake maps distributed. It didn't take much to pull Emmett and his friends to her ranch."

"How did you know —"

"I've been watching you, honey. I've had someone in place since Mexico."

Liz flushed. "That was a mistake. I told you, we can't be involved."

Cruz's strong hands tightened. "And I said you were wrong. We *are* involved. I need you."

"When you called you said you were worried about the dogs." Liz tried to stay cold and unemotional. She had loved Cruz once, but the man with her now seemed volatile and cold, almost a stranger.

She had met him during one of her brother's visits. Hank was deeply involved with the government's animal bio-enhancement research, and Enrique Cruz had been his driver. Liz suspected he had been Hank's bodyguard too, but she hadn't asked for details.

"She's got the dogs. They know her, and not you. That bothers you, doesn't it?"

She shoved her hands into the pockets of her lab coat. "The research people wanted an outsider, and Kit has an excellent record for training success." But he was right. Liz had helped Hank conceive the program. It made her angry that she couldn't have a bigger role in the dogs' training, but her brother had ordered her to keep out of the way and say nothing to Kit, only to watch.

"I'm worried about Diesel."

"You don't need to worry. He'll be fine. It's a temporary inflammation. All the animals experience that."

"How do *you* know?"

Cruz shrugged. "I've had some first-hand involvement. Let's leave it at that."

Liz stared at his hands. Once he had been ruggedly handsome. Now his hands shook and his eyes were hollows of madness.

"Why are you here, Enrique? It's been months since we . . ." She flushed and looked away. "Since Mexico."

"You want more time with the dogs?"

She nodded.

"I can help you have that. I have found someone interested in private research. He will pay well for the dogs. You can go with me and oversee the work. There will be all the money you want for a facility and workers."

"Take them from Kit, you mean?"

"They're not hers. They belong to the government. But I can change that — and you can be part of the plan." His voice fell. "Time is running out. My buyer isn't a patient man."

"I don't understand. Who is this person? Where —"

"There will be time for all your questions later. For now you need to trust me, Liz."

"How *can* I trust you? I hardly know you now. You're different, Enrique."

She had been checking on Diesel, almost ready to curl up on the sofa she kept in her office when her inside door opened and he had appeared. She still didn't understand how he had gotten inside with all the doors locked.

On the examining table Diesel whined weakly, his breathing labored. She wondered if it was a simple problem, the way Cruz had explained. Frowning, she checked the IV line.

"He'll be fine. I already told you that."

She turned sharply, anger overcoming her confusion. "How do you know so much about these dogs?"

"I got a detailed look at what they can do. I saw your brother at work in the lab, remember?" He glanced at the cabinets nearby. "Are there any vitamins here?"

"A few." She pointed to the far wall. "But they're for animal use only."

He strode to her cabinets. "That will be fine. I need your amino acids, too."

Shaking her head, she scanned a nearby drawer. "In there."

Cruz grabbed three bottles and checked their contents. "What about kelp or iodine?"

"I don't think so." She started to ask why he wanted them, but the look in his eyes kept her quiet.

"Get me all the other pills you have. Do it now."

His sharp order surprised her. She took a step back, frightened but trying not to show it.

The tremor in his hands was growing worse. What if she shoved a lab chair at him and made a run for the back door?

"Forget it. You aren't fast enough or strong enough." His smile was cold as he dumped a bottle onto its side, scattering pills over the counter.

"What are you looking for? If it's tranquilizers or amphetamines —"

"They don't sell the mix that I need." He tipped six pills into his hand and swallowed them dry. "High potency aminos — mainly L-glutamine. My system runs hot now. One more side effect of —"

"Of what?" Liz was almost afraid to ask.

"The program they pulled me into. High tech and very secret." He studied the pills scattered on the nearby counter. "These will do for today, but I'll need kelp for the iodine. Thyroid changes are routine and I'll have to adapt to new intake requirements."

Did that explain all the differences she saw in this man she had once loved and admired?

"What's wrong? What are you worrying about?"

Liz forced a smile. "You've learned a lot, that's all. I'm surprised." *Could he read her mind now?*

"I had time on my hands. I turned myself into something of a chemist living inside my cage."

"Cage? What do you mean, Enrique?"

"Forget it." He scanned the room. "I need a scalpel."

She swallowed, rigid with fear. He'd become delusional. His comment about the cage proved that. What if he turned on her?

"I need your help, Liz. Sedate the dog and I'll transport him tonight to my buyer. After I have the other dogs, we'll vanish like smoke in rain. Ten million dollars will buy you a lab and time to complete the research you started with your brother, and in a few years you'll have dozens of dogs — with no one giving you orders or cutting you out of the research."

God help her, she was tempted. With that kind of money she could develop her theories about cortical stimulation without interference or distraction.

But to do that she'd have to leave the country she loved. She could never stay here after doing what he suggested. She would become a fugitive and a traitor.

She looked out the window into the darkness and realized that success — the kind he promised — carried too high a price tag. "I can't do this."

"I want you, Liz. But you're going to have to pick a side. It's the government or me."

She hesitated a moment longer, seduced by all he promised. But she no longer trusted this man to keep to their agreement that no one — and no animals — were to be hurt. She shrugged. "I can't leave this country, Enrique. The government has been good to me. They've supported my research all this time. There's too much at stake for me to leave now."

And she was afraid. Deathly afraid.

Afraid of the glitter in his eyes and the tremor in his hands. What had *happened* to him in that secret program he'd mentioned?

"You're telling me no?"

She took a deep breath and nodded.

"I've thought about you every day for weeks. That kept me fighting when I would have given up." He caught her chin in his hand, forcing her to look at him. "Tell me it's over."

"Enrique, don't do this."

"Tell me."

"Fine. It's over." She struggled to make her voice calm. "I can't leave my clinic and my work. I can't betray my government."

"But you can betray *me?*"

"If you force me to choose, yes. That's my answer."

"I won't let you go," he said harshly. "It's too late for you to back out. Now where are your scalpels?"

Reluctantly, she pointed to a locked drawer in the side of an examining table.

"Open it."

"I don't have anything —"

"Do it now."

With trembling hands, she unlocked the drawer. Cruz studied the array of blades lined up inside. He pulled out the biggest one and held it up to the light. He seemed to have forgotten her as he picked up two more scalpels and pulled off his shirt. He stretched his left arm across the examining table and jammed the scalpel into the fleshy part of his forearm four inches above his wrist, then blotted the wound with a piece of gauze.

"You're not the *only* one who can do surgery. Your brother taught me how to do this."

"Hank? When?"

"Eight months ago. He was testing one of these." Cruz held up a small silicon chip flecked with blood and laughed harshly. "That leaves five of them left inside me." He lifted the chip with a pair of tweezers and carefully broke off one edge. His face was grim as he carried the fragment to the bathroom and flushed it down the toilet. He came back with a glass of hydrogen peroxide, which he used to clean the chip thoroughly.

Liz watched every move, fascinated despite her fear and revulsion. "What is it?"

"A government tracking device — new design with internal power. Don't worry. I used a magnet in the lab to throw off the readings." He stretched out his opposite arm and dug into the same spot, showing no reaction to the blood staining the table. "I'm a very valuable commodity, you see."

Liz swallowed. "Who put those chips inside you?"

"Your brother's team at Los Alamos. He designed them."

Liz paled. "That's impossible."

"Hank didn't tell you his team was testing on human subjects?"

"He told me they were five years out, at the very soonest. He said there would be primate tests first, then monitored short-term trials on larger mammals before —"

"He lied." Cruz's whole body seemed to vibrate with barely contained energy as he dug out another chip. "Clinical trials and safety protocols aren't on your brother's agenda." Carefully, he cleaned the second chip and set it on a piece of clean surgical gauze.

"What does that one do?"

Cruz carefully broke off another fragment. This one, too, was flushed down the toilet. "Monitors my heart and all bio-systems. The lab rat has to stay healthy enough to run through all the mazes." After wrapping both chips in more sterile cotton, Cruz sealed them inside a plastic specimen bag. "To the right people these are worth a villa in Florence. Maybe even a private island in the Pacific."

When he touched her jaw, Liz felt old scars on his fingers. She couldn't hide a shudder.

His eyes narrowed. "Stop running away from me."

She took a step back and crossed her arms at her chest, forcing herself not to pull away. There was no way to predict what would set him off. "Clean your arm. There's alcohol in the drawer."

He held the scalpel in front of him,

studying the blood that darkened the blade. "You think I can't feel that I scare you?" When she didn't answer, he slid the flat side of the scalpel down her cheek, marking her with his blood.

"No." She prayed he wouldn't see it was a lie.

Turning away, he sat on a nearby chair and stretched out his leg. Without a word he held his thigh and dug the scalpel in deep until blood welled up over his jeans. His face showed no emotion as he pulled out a third chip and studied it in tense silence. Then he smiled. "This one is the best," he said. "Second generation nano-technology. It should net us another million on top of the ten." He wrapped this chip up like the others, but sealed it inside a separate bag.

"Why, Enrique? What did they do to you?" she whispered.

"They made me into a god," he said gravely. "Or maybe a monster. Lately, I get the two mixed up." He studied the blood on his hands intently.

She couldn't watch him any more. She was checking Diesel's IV when the dog barked weakly and sat up on wobbly legs, then toppled back in a heap on the table, eyes glazed. Quickly she pulled a syringe out of a locked cabinet.

"What the hell do you think you're doing?"

"I'm giving him the epinephrine I should have given him fifteen minutes ago. Unless you want him to die on that table."

Scowling, Cruz moved out of her way. "Give him what he needs. He's worth more to me alive than dead." He glanced at his watch. "The trainer should be here soon." He leaned closer, his finger tracing her mouth. "Not a word about me, remember?"

She kept her face blank, nodding.

"When does your cleanup boy show up?"

"Not for an hour. Tommy has early soccer practice this morning."

Cruz's eyes narrowed. "When he gets here, send him home." His hand lowered, cupping her breast. When Liz turned, she saw their joint reflection in the mirror.

She shoved him away, repelled by his alien behavior. "I already told you. I won't betray my friend or my country."

She saw a muscle twitch at his forehead, then he pushed her back against a row of cages. "It seemed easy when you first told me what you wanted to do. It didn't seem real then."

"This is all very real, believe it."

A dog barked in a nearby cage. With one fixed glance, Cruz sent the animal whimpering back into a corner.

What kind of man had powers like this?

"Frightened now?"

She met his gaze angrily, her pulse pounding in her ears. "Terrified. Does that please you?"

He shook his head slowly. "I don't want your fear. I want you to *understand*. I need *someone* to understand."

Liz tensed as footsteps crossed the front porch. "That's Tommy. They must have cancelled his practice today."

"Get rid of him." His fingers tightened on her arm. "Not one word about me, understand?"

She jerked free. With shaking hands she smoothed her lab coat. Forcing a smile, she opened the door to the waiting area.

Tommy Woo was sixteen years old and skinny enough to be twelve. He was putting away his key and trying not to yawn as he pulled off his jacket. "Morning, Doctor Liz. No soccer today." He glanced around the waiting room. "You want me to run the vacuum in here before I start cleaning out the cages in back?"

Liz tried not to think about Cruz, deadly and watchful behind her. "Actually, I'm not feeling well today, Tommy. I'm going to cancel my office hours and go home."

"You have the flu that's going around?" The teenager shook his head. "Man, I hear that stuff is wicked." He pointed at a pair of full garbage cans and scratched his head. "You sure you don't want me to clean up a little first?" He started for the door behind Liz. "I'll just get the vacuum cleaner and —"

She grabbed his arm. "There's no need. Really." She forced herself to relax. "The garbage can wait, Tommy." She faked a string of noisy coughs. "I'd hate to give you this bug."

The teenager stared uncertainly at the back room. "I think something just fell in there. It sounded like a box of pills or something. Maybe I should —"

"No." Liz forced a smile as she stepped in front of the boy. "I'll pay you anyway. After all, it's my sick day, not yours."

Tommy stared back at the closed door to the examining area. "Well," he said slowly. "If you're sure . . ."

"I'm sure. Really." As Liz tossed him his coat, she blocked his path to the examining area. "Tell your mom thanks for the fried dumplings, by the way. They were wonderful."

"Cool. She'll be really glad to hear that. It's the ginger she uses — or something." Tommy shrugged on his jacket and stifled another yawn. "I can use a few hours off. I've got a Calculus exam today and it's going to be a real bitch." His face went red. "Uh, sorry." He walked to the door, staring out into the gray sky. "Weird weather we've been having. I can't remember this kind of off-and-on-rain. Yesterday it even snowed for about twenty minutes." He paused, one hand on the knob. "Broke some kind of record, I heard."

Leave, please, Liz thought. "I didn't know that. There was no snow here in town."

"Up north in the foothills, they said. Very weird." He turned suddenly. "Hey, I almost forgot. I left my French notebook in the back room yesterday when I was cleaning up. I'd better go —"

Liz gripped his arms, her heart pounding. "It's a mess back there now so why don't I find your notebook and drop it off on my way home? I should be done here in about ten minutes." Liz lowered her voice. "Tell your mom I'll be over shortly, okay? Can you do that? Ten minutes, Tommy. I'll *definitely* be there. Tell her that," she whispered urgently.

"Uh, sure." The boy looked totally confused now. "Ten minutes. Whatever."

Liz watched him shoulder his backpack. For the first time in hours she felt a grain of hope. Tommy's father was a deputy sheriff. If she didn't show up, Brian Woo might come check out the clinic, looking for her.

Maybe she could get away . . .

"See you, Dr. Liz."

The door closed.

Behind her the examining room door opened. "Come here."

She tried to walk away. She put all her focus and will into moving her legs. But they didn't seem to work right. Despite every wish, they carried her back toward the grim man in the doorway.

When she stopped beside him, his hand caught her shoulder. "Ten minutes?" he repeated mockingly. "His dad's a deputy, I understand."

She looked down, trying to hide her despair. "So what?"

"You shouldn't have done that, honey. I told you that I *need* you."

She moaned as he shoved her back against the wall. Summoning all her strength, she jammed her heel into his instep and lunged at him with the scalpel hidden in her pocket. The blade flashed out and sank deep into his side between two ribs.

Furious, he picked her up and threw her against the wall as if she were a rag doll. She felt the bones in her wrist collapse, splintering under her skin, and pain drove her to the edge of unconsciousness.

When the haze cleared, Cruz was gripping her shoulder, jerking her to her feet while she sobbed, her face wet with tears and smeared blood.

He bent down, and she jammed the scalpel into him again, this time at his chest. Cursing, he struck her hard, knocking her against a chair.

She looked up blankly. The room whirled and then she fell back onto the tile floor.

Pain shafted through her neck, and she realized she couldn't move. The agony in her wrist faded. For some reason the floor felt distant and indistinct beneath her.

"Too late," she whispered.

"You're bleeding. Don't move."

Cruz's face swam in front of her. She frowned when she felt her hair catch on her tangled necklace. It was cheap silver, a gift he'd given her on their one clandestine vacation to Mexico.

"I'll call someone," he said thickly. "I'll get help."

She shook her head, the movement using up the last of her strength.

"Why did you change?" he rasped.

"Not me — you. You're different now."

"But our plans — we were going to go away." His voice seemed to fade in and out and she felt blood under her arms. Her legs were numb.

She must have fallen on the scalpel when he hit her. Now all her plans were finished.

She swallowed thickly, trying to see his face. "Couldn't leave," she managed to say. "I loved you once."

Dimly, she felt his hands on her face.

"You still can," he said hoarsely.

She swallowed blood, the numbness climbing to her neck. "Loved you, Enrique." She drew a rattling breath. "But they made you like this. Into a m-monster. Too late now . . ."

Her breathing slowed.

She closed her eyes and felt the cold slip over her.

Cruz fumbled for her cell phone, ready to call 911.

But something stopped him. Instead he gripped Liz's wrist, trying to find a pulse.

It was too late for an ambulance or a doctor.

He didn't move, watching her lifeless eyes. Blood pooled up underneath the scalpel at her spine. Seconds passed and he realized her necklace was digging into his palm. The cross was tarnished and thin, all he could afford at the time, but she'd smiled when he gave it to her in Acapulco. But the man who'd given her that gift no longer existed. He set her down carefully on the floor and her blood darkened on his hands. Gently he touched the scalpel that had lodged in her back when she'd fallen. Then he sat beside her, unable to believe she wouldn't wake up and answer him.

He *needed* her.

Thoughts of her had kept him alive these last months. Now he'd killed her and her blood oozed across his hands like grief, deadening his mind, smothering his energy.

He smoothed her hair and whispered her name, his eyes burning. Then, after a great effort, he stood up.

He put away pain and shock, his only thoughts escape, survival and a final revenge.

One more death to be laid at their door.

One more thing he would see that they paid for.

Outside he heard garbage cans rattle as a truck rumbled up, making its early rounds. People were coming. His brother was waiting for his call. He had to sedate the dog and leave immediately.

He lurched toward the examining table, but now the IV line swung back and forth, yanked free when Liz had fallen. The dog was gone. He focused, spreading a net to locate an energy trail, but the pattern kept shifting. The puppy was blocking him somehow, and time was running out.

He tried to focus, keening with anger and grief like a wounded animal. Car lights flashed against the windows, and he heard tires crunch on gravel, then the sound of voices.

Cornered, he shrank back. Survival instinct kicked in, replacing logic. He grabbed half a dozen bottles of pills and shoved them into his pocket along with Liz's cell phone. His eyes stung as he jerked open the back door. He was careful not to look down at her cold features. He had no time for regret. Wolfe Houston would be tracking him right now and Houston was dogged as well as skillful. Cruz hadn't expected him to find his surveillance point by the railroad tracks so soon. He would be careful not to underestimate his former teammate again.

He pulled the remains of the night around him like a cloak and limped outside, his shoulders stooped. There were men watching the clinic from a van across the street, but they didn't look up when Cruz crossed the small driveway. Wrapped in shadows, he was part of the darkness, visible only to another Foxfire member — and even then with difficulty.

Caught in his grief, he never saw Tommy Woo's terrified face peering through the waiting room door.

CHAPTER THIRTY

Izzy hunched over a laptop in the kitchen with a telephone at his ear. "Yes, sir, I understand that. We've already run the plates and there's a police bulletin out for the vehicle Cruz was driving. Nothing located so far. I suggest immediate removal to a more secure location."

Izzy's second cell phone rang, and he checked the source number. "Ryker, I have a call coming in from my field team. Hold on."

Izzy punched a button on the other phone. "Joe's Pizza. We deliver." As he listened, his mouth flattened into a tight line. He turned and motioned to Wolfe, who was trying to teach Baby how to play dead.

When Wolfe looked up, Izzy shook his head, covering his mouth with one finger as he nodded toward Kit at the stove.

Neither man spoke until they were out on the patio with the French doors closed.

"What's going on?" Wolfe snapped.

"News from the clinic. Bad news."

★ ★ ★

She didn't even like eggs.

Why Kit was cooking, she couldn't say. Her stomach was so knotted up that she couldn't swallow anything.

On the other hand, cooking kept her from thinking about Wolfe and Izzy and the big silent men in black uniforms positioned all around the house. Frowning, she broke another egg in the pan and drew circles in the yolk, her movements slow and mechanical.

Some days sucked. At least she had experienced one of her oldest fantasies. She could definitely agree with the rumors about Wolfe: the man was an unforgettable lover.

A hand touched her arm.

"We need to talk." Wolfe's face was masked, and there was something like regret in his eyes.

He's leaving, she thought. *This is it. Goodbye.*

She turned away, stirring the eggs blindly. "They're almost ready. Then I have to see Diesel at the clinic."

"Honey, we have to talk. I think you should sit down."

"I'm cooking." Her voice was stiff. "I don't want to talk."

Wolfe caught both her shoulders and

turned her gently around to face him. "We need to talk," he repeated.

This time there was no mistaking the regret in his face.

"What's wrong?" Her heart pounding, she glanced at Izzy, who picked up his big titanium case and vanished into the living room.

Bad news. They might as well have worn signs across their chests.

"Is it my brother? Has something happened to Trace?" Her voice shook.

"He's fine." Wolfe pulled a chair beside her and sat down, taking her hands between his. "It's Liz."

Kit checked her watch. "Is she going out on an emergency call? I was just getting ready to leave, but I can wait if . . ." She saw something flicker across Wolfe's face. "Tell me."

Wolfe looked down at her hands, caught in his. "She's dead, honey. We just had a call from the police officer who found her at the clinic. I'm sorry."

She shook her head, watching his mouth, but the words didn't make any sense. "I don't know who told you that, but I have to go now because she's waiting. I said I'd bring coffee." She tried to stand up, but Wolfe held her hands tightly.

"I'm sorry, honey. Liz isn't there. They took her body to the hospital, but she was already dead. Your friend is gone, Kit."

A bubble seemed to expand in her chest, making it impossible to breathe. "No," she whispered, trying to pull away. "You're wrong." Looking at his fixed expression, she felt the bubble grow until she was shaking. She jerked free of his hands. *"No."*

"I'm sorry," he repeated, calm but relentless. "There's no mistake."

Kit sank back into the chair. "I don't — understand. I talked to her and she wanted coffee and I said —" Kit closed her eyes, trembling. "You're wrong."

Wolfe pulled her into his arms. "There's no mistake. She's been identified."

"But why? What happened?"

"The police are still trying to determine that." Wolfe paused. "It might have been a robbery. She had drugs in the office."

Even before he had finished, the tears began to slip down her face. She reached out blindly and felt his arms encircle her.

Panic made her hands tighten. "If Liz is dead, what about Diesel? I have to go get him now."

"Who the hell is Tommy Woo?" Ryker was shouting into the phone, and Izzy raised it away from his ear until the noise stopped. "How did he get past your team?"

"Woo is the high school student who worked at the clinic. He did cleanup work for Liz Merrigold, and he found her body. The boy is shaken up. From what we put together, he went back for a notebook he'd left at the clinic. When he used his key and went inside, he found the vet on the floor, dead from blood loss. She had a scalpel imbedded in her spine. My people got to him as soon as he came out, but it took a few minutes to get his story since he was incoherent."

"Did he get a look at the man?"

"Afraid not. He only heard a few words, and he never saw who was there with her."

"Any reason to doubt his story?"

"None that I can see. He's an honor student and his father's a local deputy."

"What in the hell happened? Cruz knew Liz Merrigold's brother because he was assigned as Hank Merrigold's bodyguard on a number of occasions. Cruz probably met her once or twice. But was she involved with Cruz? Was she helping in his escape?"

"We're still working on that, sir. Liz and her brother did research together when they were fresh out of Duke. Hank had her overseeing the medical records of Kit O'Halloran's dogs, too."

"Did she know about the full scope of Project Home Run?"

"Hard to say."

Ryker was quiet, breathing faintly. "Someone will get his ass fired for this." There was a brief silence. "We'll have to question Hank Merrigold. There's a chance that he might be in this with Cruz. Wouldn't *that* leave us in deep shit."

"I already checked. Right now Hank Merrigold is away on a two-week vacation." Izzy cleared his throat. "In Bora Bora, as it happens. No phones or faxes. The place is some kind of eco-resort."

"So maybe he's there or maybe he's not. Perfect cover potential." Ryker sounded disgusted. "Send one of your people to track him down."

"He left ten minutes ago, sir."

"Fine. What about the dog that was at her clinic?"

Izzy spoke quietly but with precision, missing no details. When he was done, Ryker chuckled, a thing he rarely did. "So Cruz missed the dog. Looks like his luck just started to head south."

About time, Izzy thought. But he wasn't sure he believed it. Cruz was exceptionally skilled and as tough as they came. With those traits, he didn't need to be lucky.

Ryker continued talking curtly, outlining the next move against Cruz. "A witness was able to identify the chopper leaving the small airport where his brother worked. Tell your team to keep it on the radar, but no pursuit. I repeat, *no pursuit,* because he'll know he's being tracked. And no one gets near him when he lands. Strictly surveillance." Papers rustled. "The White Mountains?"

"So far. Rough country up there."

"Exactly where a rat would go to hide," Ryker mused. "Give Houston the heads-up."

Kit was doing search training through the house with Butch and Sundance when Izzy cornered Wolfe in the kitchen.

Izzy gestured. "How many so far?"

"Three hundred and twelve." Wolfe wiped sweat off his forehead with one hand.

Izzy grimaced as he watched Wolfe pump out twenty more push-ups without a break. "Ryker said to give you a heads-up. You'll be leaving soon. And my team finally found Diesel. He was wedged in the back of a bird cage, hidden behind a fake set of branches. He was drugged, but he still tried to bite the field operative who went in after him."

Wolfe didn't stop his push-ups. "How about his asthma?"

"I've got someone checking him out now. They found Dr. Merrigold's current lab tests, but Diesel's reports were gone."

Wolfe snapped out another dozen smooth push-ups, enjoying the control and the slow burn. "She must have pulled them."

"Or Cruz did, before he left. Although how the hell he got inside past all my men violates a few laws of physics."

"It's what we do. You know that Cruz was good." Wolfe frowned. "Did the boy see anyone at all at the clinic besides the vet?"

"Not that we know. His mother said he couldn't answer any more questions until he rested." Izzy rubbed his neck. "Hell, you ought to be on one of those late-night infomercials. You could probably sell about a million dollars' worth of equipment."

Wolfe just kept moving, up and down, no signs of strain.

Izzy shook his head. "I'm sweating to watch you. Most of *my* battles are fought with pixels and encryption arrays. Different skill set."

"I've asked around, Teague. You've done your share of sweat equity. Don't pretend you're just another IT geek." To Wolfe's amusement, Izzy looked faintly embarrassed. "I also hear you look pretty good in panty hose and an orange wig."

Izzy muttered a short phrase.

"You have a definite flair for eye shadow, too." Finally done, Wolfe collapsed on the floor, sweat rolling off his chest and shoulders.

Izzy's cell phone rang. As he turned away to talk quietly, Wolfe did a few slow stretches. He was emptying a liter bottle of vitamin and electrolyte-enhanced water when Izzy hung up.

"Tommy Woo didn't see anyone inside the clinic — but he said a truck came down the service alley."

"The kid has sharp eyes." Wolfe wiped his face with the towel. "Did he see Cruz leave?"

"Nobody saw *anyone* leave the clinic. Cruz must have been doing some of that weird stuff you do. But we've got something better — the kid got a number for the plates. He thought it was weird to see a truck delivering spring water after the vet had just put in an expensive filtration system."

Wolfe nodded slowly. "But the truck was probably stolen."

"We still tracked it, thanks to Tommy Woo. It was a vanity plate." Izzy's lips twitched. " 'H_2O_2GO.' Easy to remember."

"Never steal a truck with vanity plates." Wolfe pulled his towel off a nearby chair and flipped it around his neck. "Has your surveillance team picked up anything on the family of Cruz's brother? You said you had them all under surveillance."

"Not a peep. But the brother had access to the choppers where he works, and one of them went missing about thirty minutes ago. As a precaution I had them all radio-tagged. We're tracking the outbound chopper now."

Wolfe frowned. "Do not attempt an approach. Cruz will pick it up instantly."

"Ryker said the same thing. The chopper is about two hundred miles west of us."

"Where could he be headed?" Wolfe took the map Izzy held out and reviewed what he knew of eastern Arizona. "This is all forested mountain terrain — not many roads and lots of rough country. You've got a small population and potential boltholes everywhere. An excellent place to hide."

"That's my assessment."

Wolfe knew that if he got close enough,

he could pick up Cruz's energy signature. The man couldn't block 24/7 or his brain would be fried. But first he had to *get* close enough — without triggering Cruz's defenses.

Izzy drummed his fingers on the countertop and shot a glance up the stairs. "Are you going to tell her goodbye?"

Wolfe frowned. Part of him wanted to stay put and watch over Kit. But no other man could track Cruz the way he could, matching him skill for skill, energy sense for energy sense.

But an uneasy twitch had started in the back of his mind. Cruz was clearly unstable now, driven by demons no one else could understand. That made Wolfe more reluctant than ever to leave Kit. Where she was concerned, he wasn't content with speculations. He needed to be absolutely certain that she would be safe.

"She'll be fine, Commander," Izzy said quietly. He took the map from Wolfe and folded it carefully. "I won't leave her, no matter what Ryker says."

"Reading my mind, Teague?"

"Reading your face and that you keep glancing up, as if you're watching for her. If Cruz tries anything, I'll be right beside her. I may not have your . . . talents, but I have a few modest skills of my own."

Wolfe nodded. Under the circumstances, he had no other choice. "What's the ETA on that chopper?"

"Roughly ten minutes. If it's any comfort, ours is a lot faster than the one Cruz's people hijacked."

Wolfe glanced at his black duffel on the kitchen counter. "I want detailed topo maps and weather data. It's always nice to know if you're walking into a blizzard."

"Already ordered, along with full terrain gear. They'll be stowed in the chopper." Izzy glanced at his watch. "Better get moving."

Wolfe didn't waste time on more questions. He zipped his bag, dropped it by the door and headed upstairs to see Kit.

To say the goodbyes that had come far too soon.

She was perched on top of a high-backed sofa, trying to pull a dirty leather glove out of a Chinese vase displayed on a tall bookcase.

Wolfe didn't know much about art, but he knew this piece looked old and valuable. The dogs were watching for him even before he reached the door.

Baby's tail thumped. Sundance whined.

Kit continued to tug at the vase, unaware of his arrival. "No more hiding things up high to fool you three. It never works." Frowning, she clutched the top of the bookshelf for support. "Almost got it. Then we can head outside and —"

Kit's foot slipped and the vase went flying from her hands, along with a heavy encyclopedia from the shelf below. The dogs shot across the room, but before Kit struck anything, Wolfe grabbed the encyclopedia in one hand, parried the vase with his shoulder to send the porcelain flying to a nearby wing chair, and then grabbed Kit.

She stared up at him and took a ragged breath. "How in the heck did you do that? *No one* is that fast."

"Combat reflexes." Wolfe dropped the encyclopedia on a table. "Nothing special."

He cleared his throat, fighting an urge to kiss the soft, generous mouth that was scowling at him.

No more fantasies. He had one to last a lifetime.

"Diesel's on his way. He was hiding in one of the cages."

"*Hiding?* You mean, from whoever killed Liz?" Kit's face paled. "Is he hurt?"

"He appears to be fine." Wolfe couldn't

tell her more than that. Ryker would want to keep the details secret for as long as possible.

"Is the killer the person you told me about — the one who is good at disguises?"

"It's likely." Wolfe felt her warm breath touch his neck. His body responded instantly to the thought of how they'd spent most of the night. But his time was up. "I have to go, Kit."

"Go where?"

No more delays.

Wolfe wiped all emotion from his face, even though he paid a price for the withdrawal. Duty demanded that he go and fight, keeping Cruz busy, far away from Kit.

Leaving was the way it had to play out. He'd always known that. He just hadn't expected it to hurt this much.

"A chopper will be here shortly. I expect Diesel to be on it." His senses flared at the seduction of her scent — a blend of cinnamon and mango. Maybe Ryker was right after all. Emotional attachments were a soldier's worst threat.

He had to remember that.

She stared at him, catching her bottom lip between her teeth. The motion made his body harden, while his mind whispered that he was turning his back on something very rare that he would never find again.

Never forget that you're different. Ryker's rule echoed in his head.

"When will you be back? A week? A month?"

He filled his senses with the warmth of her body, imprinting the memory so he would never forget. "Neither." And then, silently, he stepped away from her, watching shock fill her eyes. "I told you, Kit. It's what I do. It's what I am."

"I remember." Her shoulders straightened. "When you see Trace, tell him to call me. Otherwise I may decide to run his paltry inheritance right into the ground." She managed a crooked smile. "And thanks for being so good to my dogs. They really do like you."

She wasn't happy and she had probably a million questions, but she was gutting it out. Stubborn and proud as always, Wolfe thought.

He wanted to kiss her then. He wanted time to see what they could make of this thing they were both feeling. But he could already hear the faint drone of a chopper coming in fast from the south. There would be no place for farewells outside this room. No place for emotion or regrets.

He touched her hair, just for a second. "I have to go. I wish . . ." His hand dropped. There was no point in voicing wishes that couldn't come true.

The drone of big engines grew louder. "That's my ride. My bag's already downstairs."

Something shimmered in Kit's eyes, and Baby whined, tugging at his leg. Smiling, Wolfe bent down and pulled the three dogs into a wiggling, furry huddle. "You guys remember our offensive plays. And take good care of your boss for me."

For a moment Kit's fingers pressed down, tense against his shoulder, and then they were gone.

Her face was pale but calm when he stood up. "Izzy will stick with you a while longer and his team will be close. We'd like you to stay here another twenty-four hours. Just in case."

She started to ask a question, then stopped, nodding. "Okay."

"Give these three Einsteins hell."

She swallowed. "Sure."

"And talk to Izzy." Wolfe frowned as lights cut across the horizon. "He has some ideas about . . . your medical situation."

Her mouth flattened.

"Look, it's clear you have some kind of medical problem. Izzy happens to be a walking Merck's Manual." Wolfe cupped her chin. "Talk to him. He's a straight shooter."

"I'll . . . consider it."

Wolfe nodded, then turned and walked in a straight line to the door without looking back.

But he would never forget that particular blend of cinnamon and mango, or the pale, strained courage he read on her face.

Gone, Kit thought.

Gone before he had ever really arrived.

No more fantasies.

She rubbed the center of her chest, feeling a hot ache and then the first pangs of emptiness. But she wasn't going to break down or sob, nothing as pointless as that. Her head was high as she followed him downstairs.

The wind howled and branches struck the roof where a black helicopter hovered low, then set down in the middle of the front yard. Walkie-talkies crackled and men in black uniforms poured out. Kit's eyes misted as she saw a man jump down, carrying Diesel in his arms.

The big Lab barked twice, his tail

banging in the man's face while Baby and the other two dogs waited anxiously at the front door.

The dogs looked up at Wolfe.

Not at *her*, Kit thought. How quickly he had won them over.

"You three had better wait here. Your pal will be inside shortly."

Baby barked once, then looked across at Kit as if for confirmation.

Kit nodded her head. "Stay. Good dogs."

Wolfe shouldered his backpack and turned. "I won't say I'm sorry because I'm not. Last night was the best few hours of my life. I'd be glad to know that you felt the same."

Kit swallowed hard, forcing back her tears. "If you're looking for praise, you've got it. You get tens right across the board." She managed a bittersweet smile. "Not that anyone's keeping score."

He fingered the straps of his pack as if he wanted to be touching something else. "I am. And I won't be forgetting a single detail."

Footsteps hammered up the front steps.

A mask fell over his face like a wall of steel locking into place. "I don't like goodbyes, so I'll just say good luck." His lips curved. "Champagne and roses, remember?"

Before Kit could answer, Wolfe's cell phone rang shrilly. She heard Izzy shout. All hell broke loose outside and the door was jerked open by a man she didn't know.

"Sir, we have confirmed apprehension. We need to lift off ASAP."

"He's been taken?" Wolfe's voice was low, but Kit heard the words clearly.

"That's an affirmative, sir. We've got him."

CHAPTER THIRTY-ONE

Eastern Arizona

The windowless van was parked in a barren field of dark red earth surrounded by unmarked service vehicles. As Wolfe's chopper landed, dozens of men in black tactical gear stood at alert, cordoning off the area.

The skids had barely touched down when Wolfe hit the ground at a run. But he hadn't gotten twenty yards when his way was blocked by two men with level M-16s. "Code word, zebra four," he said immediately.

"Stop right *there*. Hands high."

"Going for my pocket."

"Don't move. *Hands high,* where we can see them."

Wolfe raised his hands slowly. "Badge, upper left pocket. Ryker sent me."

"You will hold your position," the bigger man ordered. "Otherwise we *will* fire."

"Damn it, call Ryker. He'll vet me."

Neither of the men moved.

"I need to check that van." Wolfe put out a strong dominance image to back up his words.

The oldest man shook his head, frowning. "Can't do that. My orders are to let no one inside the van — not until the chief arrives."

"I am Commander Houston. Call Ryker to verify my rank and ID, then open that damned van, soldier."

The M-16s stayed level.

Wolfe's cell phone rang. "I need to answer that."

"Negative. You will remain as you are."

Wolfe hit the man with another dominance image again, making him reel.

It wouldn't take much energy to counter with a full-scale image distortion pattern, but that was going to require a few minutes. There was also the question of witnesses. Ryker wouldn't want his team's unique tactical abilities exposed to fifty strangers.

Which left him only one option — to stand down as ordered. "Ryker is going to have your ass in a sling for this, soldier."

The soldier's face was impassive. No one moved as Wolfe's phone continued to ring. Over the hills a line of clouds raced along the horizon, churning up dust and dead leaves like a wall of broken promises.

★ ★ ★

Kit turned off the highway onto the gravel road twenty miles from Santa Fe. The sun had emerged briefly outside the town, but soon vanished behind more clouds, and now rain darkened the distant mountains.

"Crazy weather." She looked back at the four dogs crowded together behind her. Since his return via helicopter, Diesel had been accorded royal treatment. Right now Baby was curled up beside him, her head against his neck.

The smell of rain hung heavy in the air, and the weather befitted Kit's mood, gray and changeable. The dogs seemed restless, too, their eyes on the road that stretched empty and flat back to Santa Fe.

At least her Jeep was repaired. Now she had new tires and a spotless new rear windshield. Kit had been surprised when Izzy told her that plans had changed, and she should pack to leave. His only explanation was that the danger was over and they needed to get moving.

Seeing the hard set to his mouth, Kit gave up probing for more details. Even her questions about Wolfe were flatly countered. Izzy had insisted on hustling her out of the house a few minutes later.

A man in a suit had arrived via helicopter as they were preparing to leave. Ryker, as Izzy called him, appeared to be giving the orders, but Izzy was unbending. When Ryker reboarded the chopper, he threatened Izzy with arrest if he didn't accompany him as ordered.

Izzy gave him a little two-finger salute and respectfully declined, much to the other man's fury. Something about Izzy's cool dismissal made Kit suspect that he was a lot higher on the food chain than Ryker or anyone else knew.

Now Izzy was right behind her, expertly maneuvering a big Ford Explorer with off-road tires and two huge antennae. His moves left no doubt that he'd had evasive and high-speed driving experience.

Kit prayed they wouldn't need those skills anytime soon.

Baby pushed between the seats and barked. Something fell into Kit's lap. When she looked down, she was stunned to see Wolfe's worn sweatshirt draped over her legs. "Where did you get *this?*"

The puppy bumped Kit's shoulder, whining.

"He's gone, honey." Kit took a hard breath. "We've all got to get over him. Dreaming is pointless."

Baby mouthed the sweatshirt, then tossed it up into the air stubbornly, almost as if she was trying to tell Kit something.

But there was nothing left to say. This movie was over, and it was time to get back to reality. Wolfe had probably forgotten her and the dogs the minute he climbed aboard his chopper.

When Baby continued to whine, Kit sighed and reached back to scratch her head. "Hey, what kind of response is that? We should be able to stop soon, and then you guys can run around, raising Cain to your hearts' content. What's the big problem?"

A single snowflake danced across the windshield.

Baby licked Kit's cheek, then twisted around, staring intently out the back of the Jeep.

Toward Santa Fe.

Toward the last spot where they'd seen Wolfe.

Kit gripped the wheel hard and refused to look back.

Done was done. No more dreams for her.

Her cell phone rang. She grabbed her purse and checked the source number.

Miki.

"You're up early."

"Couldn't sleep." Miki stifled a yawn. "Where *are* you? Liz called me early looking for you, so I tried your cell phone but you didn't answer."

"Things have been . . . hectic." Kit decided not to mention Liz's death. It would open too many questions, along with emotions that she didn't want to share via cell phone.

Kit heard voices on Miki's end and the sound of music. Sting was crooning his way through "She Walks This Earth."

"Coffee stop?"

"You bet. Double moccacino latte to fuel preparation for a new assignment I just got. Something tells me I'm going to be mainlining caffeine for the next few weeks so I can be ready to leave."

"What kind of assignment?"

"I'll tell you once the ink's dry. The contract's not signed yet, so I'm feeling a little superstitious. But it's good, Kit. I mean, wow. This could be the break I've been hoping for." Miki's voice trembled. "I just pray I don't blow it the way I always do."

Kit tried to concentrate on driving, but she heard the uncertainty in her friend's voice. "Can't you give me a hint? Have pity here."

Kit heard Miki muffle a curse. Then

there was a thunderous *bang* as her cell phone dropped.

"Miki, are you there?"

Voices echoed from the other end of the line, followed by loud rustling.

"Kit, did I lose you?"

"I'm here. What's going on, Miki?"

"Just some jerk in a hurry. He spilled coffee all over me." Miki sucked in a breath. "Damn, that hurts. Look, I can't go over the details now, but how about lunch tomorrow and make it my treat?"

Kit didn't know where she'd be tomorrow, and she didn't feel comfortable discussing her situation until things settled down. "Can I call you tonight?"

Silence. Then Miki sighed. "It's Wolfe, isn't it? Something happened."

"*Nothing's* happened." Kit suppressed a pang of guilt at lying to her best friend. "But I'm driving now. I should go."

"Wait. Let me switch hands."

Kit heard more rustling sounds.

"Okay, that's better. Jeez, who knew that a moccacino could hurt so bad. My new silk tank top is ruined, too. The jerk." Miki made an irritated sound. "Where was I — oh, right. Lunch. Call me tonight and let me know. I'll drive out to the ranch, if you want. I need to talk about some stuff with you."

"Are you okay, Miki?"

"Fine. Great. I'd just like a cooler head for a second opinion."

Kit didn't feel very cool headed at the moment. Since Wolfe had returned, her life felt like a derailed train on a downhill slope. "Sure. Call me tonight. And go put an ice pack on your arm."

"Will do. Kiss the doggies for Aunt Miki." Miki made loud kissing noises, then hung up, laughing.

Kit frowned, wondering about Miki's mysterious new project and why she needed advice. But with Miki you never knew what mayhem was brewing.

A dry mass of tumbleweeds skipped across the road and wedged firmly against her windshield. Frowning, she switched on her wipers, which only scattered twigs all over the glass.

She flipped on her blinker and pulled over, looking back at the dogs. "Stay."

Baby poked her head over the seat. Yipping, she looked at the road behind them, and Kit knew just how she felt, thinking about the man she'd left behind. She wondered if Wolfe was safe or hurt, maybe lying somewhere in a pool of blood. No matter what Izzy said, her instincts told her that the danger wasn't over yet.

If it was, Izzy wouldn't have insisted on riding shotgun for her like this.

She opened her door and moved around to shove the dry twigs off her windshield. Overhead a shadow darkened the Jeep's window. Something about the rushing blur of movement made her body tense.

Izzy pulled off the road behind her. His eyes narrowed as he watched the owl. "Why'd you stop?"

"Tumbleweed. One of our local driving hazards. If I don't clean these branches off, they'll break up in more pieces and pretty soon I'll be flying blind."

Flying blind.

Kit felt a weight in her chest as she remembered Wolfe's identical choice of words.

"Pretty isolated place here." Izzy studied the encircling mountains, ringed with storm clouds. "Some people might call it desolate."

"The desert has its own beauty, Mr. Teague. It's not soft and green but it's rugged and clean. If you accept that difference, there's beauty everywhere you turn."

Izzy's brow rose. "Reminds me of a place I know in southern Arizona. And call me Izzy." He leaned over to help Kit clean the windshield. "We need to get moving." A faint whine made him look up, frowning. He pulled a pair of binoculars out of his pocket and swept the horizon, then tracked back carefully.

The sound grew louder, but Kit still couldn't see anything except storm clouds backing up over the mountains.

Izzy shoved the binoculars back into his pocket. "Give me your jacket and take mine," he said tensely. "Do you have any other clothes in your car?"

"A 'beauty emergency' bag that my friend gave me. Makeup and nail polish. Stockings, too. Why?"

"Get that too, then call the dogs outside. Do you have a gun?" There was something cool and curt in his voice. It was the same sound Kit heard when her brother took a call that summoned him at short notice from leave. The voice meant *professional mode, danger imminent.*

"I've got my father's rifle." Fear pricked at her neck. "It's in the Jeep."

"Get it and bring it out here." Izzy opened his cell phone, his eyes on the cloud-swept horizon. "Wolfe isn't answering my calls and I've got a bad feeling about that chopper."

"What chopper?" Kit caught a breath as a black speck cut through the clouds, headed straight for them. "Who's that?"

"I'm not sure, and I'm not staying around to find out." As he spoke, Izzy pulled out a nasty-looking submachine gun from his SUV along with a tactical vest, which he slid on. Then he tossed Kit his jacket.

"What's going on?" She tugged his jacket over her shoulders, then took out her rifle with the dogs beside her. "I don't understand."

Izzy drew a pistol from a holster under the vest and shot out two tires on his SUV. He took something from his back seat and ran back to Kit's Jeep, where he grabbed a hat from the floor. "Is there anyplace around here for you to hide?"

Kit frowned. "I think so. I remember there's a —"

"Don't tell me. It isn't safe." He turned around so he couldn't see her leave. "Get moving. Keep to the cover of those cottonwood trees and don't stop. Don't come back either, no matter what you see or hear. Can you do that?"

Kit nodded, her throat too dry to answer.

"Good. Keep the dogs quiet, no matter what. I'll draw the chopper off as long as I can." He opened the door of her Jeep and slid behind the wheel, tugging her jacket up over one arm and pulling on a pair of tan gloves. "Beauty emergency," he muttered, digging two hammered-silver bracelets out of her bag. "You've got a good friend, whoever she is. These just may save your life." He tossed her the water bottle from the front seat. *"Go."*

Kit tried to focus as he reached into the back seat for a big duffel bag, dug inside and pulled out a Benelli combat shotgun with ghost-ring sights.

This was real, she thought.

They could be dead in the next five minutes. But her body seemed to disconnect. She couldn't move, frozen by the sight of the looming helicopter.

"Why are you still here?"

Izzy scowled as he slammed 12-gauge shells into the Benelli. *"Get moving.* And don't come back, no matter what you hear or see. If you think you see Wolfe or me, wait for the code to be given."

She nodded jerkily and suddenly all her mobility came rushing back. The primitive urge for survival sent her flying over the ground, racing for the trees. The Jeep's motor roared behind her as Izzy fishtailed back onto the road, laying rubber as he headed west.

She found cover under the first cottonwood tree, shivering at the sight of the helicopter. She was almost certain there was an abandoned mine up on the ridge. Her father had brought her and her brother into the valley as teenagers, theorizing that it was better to guide them through the danger personally so they wouldn't be tempted to do dangerous exploring on their own. That year they had visited two other mines in the area, both of them carefully chosen and personally inspected by their father to teach them basic safety and orienting skills with a compass.

This particular mine had been Kit's first. She still had flashes of bad dreams about the dripping walls and twisting tunnels below the surface. Now one nightmare was leading her straight into another.

She slid down the rocky bank of a wash, landing in a sprawl with the rifle gripped against her side. Behind her the roar of the Jeep faded, replaced by the throb of a powerful motor.

A rifle shot cracked.

Kit twisted around to look back, but Baby growled, grabbing the leg of her jeans and pulling her forward. With every second the drone of the helicopter grew louder.

Where was the entrance?

She stared around frantically, then scrambled up the other side of the wash, searching the low ridge of rock beyond for any opening through the scrub. Desperate now, she stumbled past waist-high bushes and pressed her hands against the rock wall, working by touch alone.

The drone grew into an ear-splitting roar. More gunfire exploded.

Grimly, Kit crouched behind a sage bush with the dogs at her feet. "Heel," she ordered, her voice shaky.

Baby whined and then broke away. As Kit crawled after her along the face of the ridge, the Lab disappeared. Bushes caught at Kit's legs and branches raked her face as she fought her way higher, guided by Baby's insistent barking. The other three dogs were right at her heels when her left hand hit emptiness.

One minute Kit was in sunlight, and the next she was surrounded by the heavy, fetid air of her nightmares.

"What the hell is going on here?" Red-faced, Lloyd Ryker jumped down from a black helicopter and shoved past three anxious officers. Another helicopter was parked inside a cordon of grim security forces nearby. Ryker pointed a finger at the man with the M-16 aimed at Wolfe's chest. "*You*. What's your name?"

"Sergeant Lentz, sir."

"Get the hell out of my sight, Lentz. Take your friends with you. Houston, report."

"Your men shouldn't have intercepted Cruz's chopper or transferred him to that van."

"My orders got scrambled." Ryker's voice hardened. "Someone will be dealt with for that. What else?"

"Your people had me detained here. I haven't been able to investigate the van, sir."

"Then get to it." Ryker was sweating though the air was chill, damp wind pouring across the mountains.

Wolfe lowered his voice. "Sir, I think you'd better stay back near the chopper. Get the others back, too. For safety I need a clear line of sight all around the van."

Ryker waved a hand at his men and they stepped away from the van. At Ryker's curt nod, one of them tossed Wolfe a key.

Wolfe turned the key in his hand, frowning, then checked his cell phone. He had missed four calls while he was here waiting for Ryker, three of them from Izzy.

Now there was no answer on Izzy's line.

The crackle of walkie-talkies seemed very loud, like meat thrown on hot skillets. Wolfe blocked it all out — the noise, the flashing lights, the keening of the wind. With cold hands he slipped the heavy key into the first of three locks on the heavily fortified van meant to secure Cruz upon his capture.

Metal grated, oiled tumblers falling.

Wolfe moved to the next lock, his body alert, senses revved to almost painful acuity. Did he feel the sticky energy he'd sensed before in the railroad shed? Was Cruz waiting inside to attack him?

As he opened the doors, he saw a man slumped in a fetal position against the far wall. One hand stuck out beneath a thick blue blanket.

Wolfe stood motionless, listening to the shallow breathing, listening to the hiss of the wind outside the secured windowless van and tracking the faint hum of Cruz's mind.

The blanket twitched. The hand opened and closed.

Wolfe felt the drum of his pulse as he jumped into the van and pulled the blanket away. A blond-haired face and pale Nordic eyes glared back at him. Angry bruises covered both temples and most of the jaw.

Not Cruz's face. Not Cruz's eyes. Another trick.

He spun, dialing Izzy quickly. Outside in the wind the walkie-talkies cut in and out, shrill and then muted.

Ryker moved to the door of the van, shoulder to shoulder with a heavy man who scanned the interior of the truck. "See, that's him." The man was loud, confident. "I used the pictures you sent. It was no problem at all."

Ryker's face hardened in fury as he studied the man curled up on the floor. "He slipped through."

Wolfe tried his phone again.

No answer.

He jumped down, staring at the officer beside Ryker. "When you caught him, how many of you were there?"

"What do you mean? Why —"

"How many?"

"Four."

"Did one of your men leave?" Wolfe demanded. "Maybe he was hit or hurt. He'd have a good reason."

"Yeah. Jolson did. He got a bad kick in the scuffle. Probably a fractured —"

"Where?"

"Up that hill. Ryker, why —"

"Show me where. Do it now."

"You heard him," Ryker snapped. "Get us to the spot where it happened."

There was fresh blood beside the road, pooled next to deep tire marks in the fresh mud. Boot prints crisscrossed the wet earth.

Wolfe touched one of the red stains. Instantly the thick, clinging energy wrapped all the way around his hand and up his arm, jerking at his breath with the force of its blind fury.

"Well?" Ryker glared down at him impatiently.

"He had to have switched right at the start, then transferred the images so your men never guessed anything had changed. 'Jolson' was really Cruz." Wolfe stared east, trying Izzy's number again. "He slipped past everyone. He was never in that van at all."

When there was no answer on Izzy's phone, Wolfe stood up. "I'm going back to the safe house, sir. I should have heard from Izzy by now. Something's wrong. My sense is that it involves Cruz."

"Why? Cruz wouldn't be headed there. Besides, Teague left right after I did. He refused a direct order, by God. Said he was taking the woman someplace else for twenty-four hours. 'Sitting it out,' he said. Just in case."

Gone, Wolfe thought. Gone with Cruz in close pursuit, if his instincts were right. Right now every cell warned him that the situation was about to tank fast.

His fingers opened and closed as if they couldn't contain their own energy. "Where did Izzy take her?"

"North, that's all I know. Up toward Chama, I think."

"Get on the phone to him, sir." Wolfe sprinted past Ryker toward the closest Black Hawk. "And then get someone local out there *now.*"

CHAPTER THIRTY-TWO

Kit pitched forward into darkness.

The air was foul with mold and rodent droppings. Somewhere water trickled, echoing inside the broad tunnel. It was a world torn from nightmares, the last place Kit wanted to be. Even Trace had been uncomfortable when they had come here years before as teenagers.

Something scurried past Kit's foot and she bit back a scream. There were more movements in the darkness, along with what sounded like the rustle of wet leaves. Then Baby pressed against her legs and the rustling stopped. "Stay," Kit whispered. "Diesel, come here."

Another head brushed her leg. A tail swished across her knee.

"Butch, Sundance?"

More bodies bumped close.

Trying to ignore the acid smell of mold, Kit felt her way along one wall of the tunnel, listening to a helicopter circle low in the distance.

She dug her fingers into Baby's warm fur.

Automatic weapons spat and the helicopter circled again. This time Kit heard the sharp *whoomp* of tires blowing out, followed by the crack of breaking glass.

She thought of Izzy, somewhere outside drawing her pursuers away. What would happen to him if he was captured?

Uncertain, she looked back toward the cave opening. How could she cower here when Izzy was under attack? Diesel growled low in his throat. His teeth locked on her arm, holding her still.

Shocked, she tried to pull her arm away, but the big Lab growled fiercely. His body rigid, he tugged her back through the darkness.

Dirt rattled down the walls, and Kit heard the distant pop of gunfire. Shivering, she tried to imagine the fight taking place outside while Diesel and the other dogs herded her deeper into the tunnel, their bodies wedged against her legs.

She stumbled as the tunnel sloped downward, crossing pools of brackish water and rusted rails used by old mining cars. Another rat ran across her foot. Wincing, she stumbled sideways and the movement sent her facedown into mud that stank of rust and metal and mold. As she wobbled to her feet, Kit remembered the small carabiner LED clipped on her backpack. With shaky fingers she found the small power button.

Light bloomed.

The tunnel loomed before her like a tortured moonscape, mounded dirt dotting the curved wall where parts of the roof had caved in. Her LED cast eerie shadows of old timber supports, several of which had collapsed in broken sections.

She passed another mound of dirt and the rotted fragments of a fallen piece of timber bracing. Ten feet down the slope she stopped, coughing from the dust and decomposed debris stirred up by her feet.

Baby growled sharply, looking back toward the tunnel mouth. Holding up her light, Kit saw an opening to the left, leading to a smaller tunnel. She caught the glint of standing water and the brief red flash of a dozen glowing eyes.

More rats.

Ugh.

She was picking her way forward when Baby bumped the back of her legs. With a snarl, the dog shoved her to the left, into the smaller tunnel.

"No, Baby. Not there." Kit turned, took a step back, and felt all four dogs around her, blocking her steps. Herding her with their combined strength, they shoved her hard in the one direction she didn't want to go — toward the rats.

As she wavered, pebbles skittered down the slope behind her. Instantly, she switched off her light, her heart drumming in her ears.

No one could have found her so soon. Even Izzy didn't know the location of the old tunnel. But someone was there, tracking her. And judging by the dogs' reaction, it was no friend approaching.

More pebbles rattled down the slope. Distracted, Kit let the dogs nudge her forward while she listened for the sounds coming from the darkness.

Something sloshed through standing water behind her — something big, and coming fast. Fear hit her full force.

Get out of sight and stay there, Izzy had said.

No matter what you see or hear.

Teeth closed on her leg, dragging her forward. On the edge of a sob she lurched through the molding remnants of fortunes made and lost, dreams spun and stolen.

She heard the movements behind her quicken in the splash of water and scrape of boots.

"Kit," the voice whispered, low and re-assuring, completely familiar.

Wolfe.

A whimper of relief squeezed from her throat and she turned back eagerly.

Baby's growl stopped her. Diesel's teeth held her.

Butch and Sundance blocked her.

Ice wrapped around her chest, realization like a mocking chant in her pulse.

You may not recognize him. He and his people are trained in disguise. They could even pass for me or you.

"Kit, where are you?"

It wasn't Wolfe tracking her. Not Izzy either.

Someone else.

And any second he would find her.

"There." Wolfe hunched over the chopper's curved window, scouring the landscape. "That's her Jeep."

But the dark metal was twisted and uneven, two of the tires blown. Glass glittered for twenty feet around the shattered windshield.

Wolfe's mouth stitched into a flat line as he searched for movement anywhere nearby. They dropped low, circled and took another pass, and the pilot gestured at a row of cottonwood trees dotting a small stream.

"Skids, sir. Someone's had a chopper down there. You can just make out where they put down."

Wolfe felt his skin stretch thin, every nerve pulled like a hair trigger, registering Cruz's presence. He tracked his binoculars over the ground and saw footprints leading away from the landing area straight to a tiny stream.

So Cruz had followed the water. He'd waded in and vanished.

"Circle again," he ordered.

Reeds and thick brush lined both banks of the stream. Wolfe searched for more tracks leading out of the water. As they banked again, he felt the tug of awareness, sticky and dark with Cruz's disturbed energy.

"Put me down beside that stream and radio these coordinates to Ryker on a secure channel. Then keep searching until you find Teague."

"Affirmative, sir."

Before the chopper had set down, Wolfe jumped out, tracking the unstable energy patterns he'd come to recognize as Cruz's. He let his mind slip deep into theta and followed the trail.

Along the bank.

Beneath a dying cottonwood, leaves falling like cool green rain.

Sharp turn north, down into a rocky wash.

At the far slope Wolfe froze, touching a long gouge in the dirt. He had a sudden impression of cinnamon and mango. Kit had been here, moving fast. So where the hell was Izzy? Why had the two split up, and why hadn't Izzy answered his cell?

As Wolfe scrambled up the far bank, he felt Kit's energy running north. He sensed the dogs pushing her on, driving her beneath another row of trees, her confusion and panic staining the air.

And if he felt it, Cruz could feel it, too.

Pushing through the heavy brush, Wolfe stayed low, alert for one of Cruz's energy nets. It would be just like his old friend to leave invisible booby traps along his path.

Overhead the chopper banked for another pass. Nothing else moved in the arid landscape.

He was *close* now. His blood hammered with the heavy awareness of Cruz alone and moving fast — unless this was an image distortion. As he stared up the slope, he wondered what abilities Cruz had developed in the last months. They had to be significant, or Ryker wouldn't have been so careful to conceal them.

A red-tail hawk cut through the clouds, its clear two-note cry keening on the wind.

Close.

Wolfe's sleeve caught in the spines of a cholla cactus. He sensed more than felt a dark opening in the rock face as cool air feathered over his face. He gave one quick click on his radio to alert the pilot that their target was sighted and approach initiated.

There was no need for words. Wolfe's implanted chip would guide Ryker's men better than any directions could have. He hoped they were fast. Once he was underground, he would be untraceable.

"You're safe, Kit. Come on out, honey."

She wanted to believe him. Her body strained forward in eagerness and trust, *needing* to believe. Izzy had to be wrong about the danger.

Suddenly she stopped. Her feet tried to move, following the whispered encouragement in the voice she trusted — had trusted since she was twelve — but Baby's body stopped her, wedged against her legs. When Kit tried to walk toward the splashing footsteps and whispered hope,

Diesel's teeth nipped her hand.

Kit's breath caught in shock and pain. In that instant clarity returned, leaving two people inside her head — one frightened, the other a believer, ready to turn back in search of comfort and safety.

Her hip bumped the stone wall of the tunnel, and pain shot through the joint. Relentless, the dogs herded her forward. As she gripped her father's rifle, she heard pebbles skitter behind her in the tunnel.

"You know that your dogs are special. No one else can possibly appreciate them the way you do." Low and seductive, the words lapped at her mind. "Baby is the smartest. You've sensed it since the first day you saw her. She'd follow you to hell and back — but one day you'll have to let her go. Who else cares the way you do? Who else will keep her safe? You know she can't stay with you forever."

Kit closed her eyes, fighting the clever words. If she used the rifle, the force of the shots could bring the rotting timbers down on top of them, along with the rest of the tunnel.

Light flickered across the far wall. More words echoed inside her head. "I'll see that you can keep your dogs as long as you want, honey. We'll train them together. All you have to do is trust me."

Trust me.

Baby gripped her sleeve, pulling her backward so sharply that Kit struck the wall and stumbled. Rocks *pinged,* the sound like small gunshots.

Fur brushed her legs and two of the dogs shot past her up the tunnel. She was about to call out when she saw a man's long shadow swim against bare rock.

Wolfe?

Kit didn't move. Then her heart closed, whispered a warning.

"They'll take them away from you forever. They're planning it already." The voice hardened. "Don't trust any of them."

He rounded the curve of the tunnel. Kit stared at his broad shoulders, his dark eyes, all of it familiar — and all a flawless deception.

She took another step back, meeting cold stone. The tunnel stopped abruptly, abandoned decades ago. It was a dead end. *Nowhere to go.*

She swallowed a knot of fear and worked the lever action of her father's old Winchester, loading a round into the chamber. "You're not Wolfe."

The light in his hand cast weird shadows

across the ceiling. His face seemed to change in the shifting light.

Wolfe, then not Wolfe.

He didn't move. "You'd risk killing the dogs?"

Diesel began to bark, blocking the man's way. Kit racked another shell into the second barrel. "Leave now and I won't hurt you."

Something flashed in the unsteady light. Kit gasped as pain burned along her shoulder from the dart he had shot at her. Another dart hissed past, sinking into Diesel's back.

Baby's frenzied barking filled the tunnel, then seemed to waver as if distorted by a wall.

Blurry, Kit thought. *Drugged. Have to stay awake to fight him.*

Something brushed her eyes, soft like a flake of snow. She wobbled, leaning against the tunnel wall. There was no snow here. There was nothing here except fear and lies.

She moved the rifle and tried to focus. Suddenly Diesel yelped in pain and his shadow launched against the line of black where her attacker stalked closer.

She gripped the worn wooden stock of the Winchester, aimed and fired. There was nothing human in the angry shout that followed, piercing the tunnel's silence. Without pausing Kit levered up another round and fired again.

The tall shadow leaped back and dirt rained down on Kit's face. Over her head a beam cracked loudly. Drugged, she fought to keep her eyes open, her body sinking against the wall.

"Kit." The same voice, but this one came from a different place, sounding clear but far away.

Pounding feet. Another splash of water. *Wolfe.*

She tried to stay upright, one hand gripping Baby's back.

The rifle slipped from her fingers, clattering over stone, and then the tunnel blurred. She watched one shadow become two.

Someone grunted in pain.

A rock fell from the tunnel ceiling, hitting her arm. Whining, Baby licked her face, the only thing that kept her from sleep. *So tired.*

A fist smashed against bone. Shadows drove back and forth, long and grotesque to Kit's drugged eyes. Dimly, she heard Diesel bark.

One shadow wavered. The other one

loomed toward her while the floor of the tunnel vibrated.

"You should have joined me when I asked. We could do things no man has ever done. But you've let them shape you, control you."

Voices drifted in and out. Kit looked up to see Wolfe's face above her, the eyes fierce. But was it really Wolfe she was seeing?

He picked her up and tossed her over one shoulder, kicking at the three dogs that tried to bite his feet and arms.

"Put her down, Cruz."

The world tilted. She struck blindly at the hands gripping her. He kept moving, dodging the dogs that snapped at his hands.

"With her, I have her dogs. We both know that. You won't fire in here, not with this rotten wood everywhere. She's already knocked out one of the beams."

Dizzily, Kit saw Baby back up, head erect. In a blur of motion, the Lab raced forward and jumped, landing in a sprawl across her attacker's shoulders.

Kit twisted hard. Gasping, she shook free, landing on the tunnel floor, while Baby's growls mingled with her captor's muffled curses. Diesel crawled next to her and through her pain she saw the dark shapes of two men struggling. Suddenly white flakes dotted the air, melting on her cheeks. *Snow?* But how?

"You see what they can do, Houston? They're worth more than anyone knows. But I'll kill them if I have to. And you along with them."

Kit struggled to her feet, swaying drunkenly, something wet and cold on her face even though it couldn't really be snow, just some kind of hallucination.

One of the shadows leaped forward. Both men fell in a sprawl, tumbling through mud and water while the dogs closed in warily. Baby grabbed one of the shadows, growling in a frenzy.

Voices boomed from the mouth of the cave. "Houston, are you down there?"

With a muffled sound of fury one of the shadows pulled free and kicked Baby away, charging toward the bigger tunnel with Wolfe in close pursuit. Their racing steps echoed between the narrow rock walls.

Then they were gone.

Shadows closed around Kit. Someone lifted her carefully off the ground while the dogs watched suspiciously.

"Ms. O'Halloran, Izzy Teague sent me for you."

She tried to point down the slope where Wolfe had vanished, but her arms wouldn't move.

"Just rest. Everything will be fine."

"Wolfe," she mumbled, coughing as dust swirled up. "Down there. T-two of them."

"Take it easy, ma'am. You're going to be fine."

"Dogs . . ."

"Your dogs are good to go. The big one's out cold, but his pulse is steady."

"Izzy?" She worked to keep her eyes open. "Hurt?"

The voice tightened. "We got to him in time. He's being treated now. We need to get out of here."

Someone lifted her into the air. She tried to look back into the darkness. "Can't leave . . . him."

But she was already being carried up the tunnel.

Just before Wolfe reached the turn in the mine corridor, Cruz jumped him. His old colleague was stronger than he'd ever been and the first assault came without warning. Driven against the tunnel wall, Wolfe grappled with Cruz, tossing out razor-sharp images of a mine collapse. Being buried alive was Cruz's worst fear, and Wolfe played on that fear now with image after image.

But Cruz's grip didn't waver. He shoved a knife against Wolfe's neck. "Don't make me do this, Houston. You could be useful to me — it doesn't have to end here. I need assets like you."

Wolfe didn't answer. It would have been a waste of breath. Instead he put all his will into deflecting the knife at his neck. How had Cruz become so damned strong?

"You're not convinced? Too bad." The knife twisted and Cruz lunged sideways, driving his arm forward.

Wolfe felt a bone snap in his wrist. Pain roiled up his arm, but he stepped out of the sensation, turning his awareness into something cold and hard.

Cruz had done the same long ago.

"They threw me away like garbage." He slashed Wolfe's arm with his knife. "They'll do the same to you one day. Your chips will degrade, the medicines will fail, and you'll be tagged, hunted, listed as dead. Then they'll come for you the way they did for me."

Wolfe tried not to listen. Cruz was a head case, gripped by full-blown psychosis. None of his predictions had basis in reality. Ryker had a team of medical experts watching for just this kind of problem in the new technology.

"Are you listening to me, Houston? Don't you —"

Wolfe lunged low, pulling out of Cruz's reach, ignoring a savage wave of pain as he snapped a roundhouse kick high and right toward Cruz's head. His foot slammed into Cruz's neck and sent him flying back. He recovered in seconds, dropping to the tunnel floor with a low, horizontal kick that drove Wolfe onto one knee.

Cruz had always been good at taekwondo, and his strength was explosive, but now his focus was unstable, shifting as he glanced back up the tunnel.

Using the momentary advantage, Wolfe kicked at Cruz's knee. He followed up with the syringe he'd wedged into a pocket of his tactical vest. One dose of the neurotoxin was enough to fell a horse, according to Ryker. All Wolfe had to do was deliver it.

The effect would be nearly instantaneous. Ryker had made it very clear that he wanted Cruz immobile but alive.

With a hiss, Cruz slashed his knife down, the blade drawing blood the whole length of Wolfe's arm. "It's a good day to die, my friend."

After that no more was said, neither questions nor threats. Whatever followed would be played out in silence and to the death.

Blood oozed down Wolfe's hand. He pretended to stumble and hit the tunnel wall. When Cruz came after him Wolfe jammed the syringe up to the hilt in his attacker's neck. A muffled roar of shock and fury exploded through the darkness, and Cruz staggered backward, digging blindly at the air.

A high-velocity round cracked, raking Wolfe's cheek. Cruz aimed wildly with one hand and fired again. Something struck Wolfe's leg and he heard Baby bark, shooting past him.

Butch and Sundance were only steps behind, blurs in the darkness.

Cruz snarled and fell back. As the dogs circled him, he hesitated, then turned and was swallowed up in the dark maw of the main tunnel. Wolfe staggered in pursuit, cold air brushing his face. Dust swirled up and a section of the roof collapsed.

Baby whimpered and stood stock still, ears raised. Another timber support collapsed, filling the air with acrid dust.

The three dogs inched away from the deeper part of the mineshaft. Then Baby gripped Wolfe's arm and pulled him up the slope while the other dogs followed, keeping their bodies between Baby and the tunnel depths. Some part of Wolfe's mind found time to marvel at this new example of the dogs' teamwork.

The floor shook. Another section of the roof fell. Wolfe saw something glint near his foot. He flashed his penlight on the ground and saw a small silver cross dangling from a tarnished chain caught between two rocks. He shoved the necklace in his pocket as a chunk of stone tore from the roof, plunging past his shoulder.

"Get moving," he shouted hoarsely. Herding the dogs in front of him, he sprinted up the slope, jumping to avoid fallen debris, rocks and roof beams.

Behind him musty air surged up and dust raged in angry brown clouds as the ground heaved and a section of the wall collapsed. With rocks slamming against his face and shoulders he raced toward the sunlight already obscured by swirling dirt. Wolfe saw the dogs jump and he ran after them through the dust, leaping through the tunnel opening in front of a wall of dirt and debris. He hit hard, rolling down into a rocky wash. Wreathed in dust, he watched the mineshaft cough and heave, then disappear, its mouth covered by rocks and earth.

Wolfe pushed to his knees. He staggered up the slope but now there was only a wall of stones in front of him, no entrance to be seen anywhere.

No one could have escaped alive. Cruz had been drugged, disoriented. Now he was dying in the rubble or already dead.

Wolfe felt Baby near his hand as he sank onto one knee, thinking about a man who had once been a hero, close enough to be his brother. They had shared danger, tasted fear together. Now Cruz was buried, his wild delusions and awful hate buried with him.

Wolfe coughed and felt two furry bodies press against his other leg.

It was a good day to die, he thought. But it was a far better day to live.

CHAPTER THIRTY-THREE

A medical officer was peering at Kit over the rim of an oxygen mask. He stared into her eyes, frowning.

Her voice sounded weak and thready when she demanded to know where Wolfe was and what was happening in the tunnel.

"Right here, honey. Don't talk. Everything's fine."

She closed her eyes, tears burning. She felt the hands tremble, locked in her hair.

"What about my dogs?"

"All present and accounted for. Diesel's been six inches away from you, snapping at everyone." Wolfe gave a dry laugh. "He nearly bit the med tech trying to take your pulse."

Kit was too worried to smile. "What about Izzy?"

"Airlifted to the hospital in Albuquerque. Broken ribs and . . . a few other things." Wolfe's voice was tight. "He will get excellent care, don't worry about that."

"What happened in there? I feel completely weird."

"Tranquilizers. You'll be groggy for a while."

The medic leaned down and wrapped something around Wolfe's arm, pulling it into a sling.

"Get some rest," Wolfe said quietly, smoothing her hair. "It's over."

The ground rumbled and Kit smelled dust on the air. "But Wolfe, it snowed," she rasped. "Inside the tunnel, I saw snow. I know that's impossible." She took a hard breath. "And that man — he looked just like you."

Wolfe stared toward the collapsed tunnel, his expression unreadable. "It was dust, not snow. That was just an illusion, honey. There were a lot of things that weren't what they seemed in there." His body tensed against her back, and Kit sensed that there were things that he couldn't or wouldn't ever tell her.

But that was fine. She trusted him to tell her what was necessary.

She felt Baby wriggle in underneath Wolfe's arm, and then they were surrounded by all the puppies. Diesel actually crawled into Wolfe's lap and bit his chin.

The sight was so comical that Kit laughed until the world went blurry again.

EPILOGUE

Two weeks later

"Don't tell me that you've got soy burgers and low-fat cereal in that bag or I may have a serious relapse."

"Have you eaten anything today?" Kit glared at Izzy, outstretched in the hospital bed with a broken arm, broken rib and a broken leg.

"Sure I have."

But when Kit glanced covertly at the nurse nearby, she shook her head.

Sitting in a nearby chair, Wolfe sniffed the air expectantly. His eyes never left Kit's face though his expression was controlled. "Smells great. What is it?"

"Health food for two. Whether you like it or not."

Izzy sighed. "Whoever invented tofu should be shot."

"Not that kind of health food. I'm talking green chile quesadillas and tortilla soup. Chicken mole poblano. All home-made." As Kit spoke, she laid out steaming

473

plates of food. She had the men's attention now. "And for dessert, steak rare with mashed potatoes."

Izzy closed his eyes on a reverent sigh. Wolfe sat forward in his chair, trying not to wince.

"Houston, did you hear that? We're in clover now."

Wolfe gave Kit a long, lingering glance. "We sure are."

The nurse hid a smile as she took Wolfe's pulse. "I'll pretend that I didn't hear that talk about food. Both of you need broth, fruit and more rest, according to your medical team."

The two men grimaced in unison.

"No way. Just don't get him started on the whole push-up thing," Izzy muttered.

"Me?" Wolfe studied Izzy's bandaged arms and leg with a critical eye. "When will you stop trying to reach things yourself and start asking for help?"

"At exactly the same time you do." Izzy gestured at Wolfe's arm. "Where's that sling the doctor told you to wear?"

"I don't need it."

"Tell that to the X-ray tech who showed me where your wrist and most of your arm got shattered."

"I'm doing fine." He cleared his throat

as he met Izzy's eye. "I happen to heal very fast, I'm told."

Kit put down the last of her bags with a loud bang. "If you two would stop arguing, you could eat some of this food before it gets cold."

"Sounds good to me." Izzy glanced toward the door. "Just don't let that other night nurse see what you've brought. The woman's a dragon."

The day nurse shook her head and left.

"I think she has a crush on you," Wolfe said smoothly. "She was in here four times this morning, and I swear she didn't glance at me once."

"Quiet."

The men looked at Kit. Then they stopped arguing and meekly watched her fill up plates with hot food.

She knew that their nerves were on edge. Both of them were highly trained and in full mission focus, even now. It was clear that they were not about to submit to extended rest with a good temper.

Kit had had her hands full keeping them distracted. Of course, the dogs had helped. Wolfe and Baby had spent hours doing search games up and down the floor. Diesel had crawled onto Izzy's bed and gone to sleep beside him. Baby had stayed inches from Wolfe whenever Kit had brought them to visit.

None of the military hospital staff or administrators had complained. Since this end of the floor was sectioned off and restricted for their use, there was no problem with privacy either. If Kit hadn't already guessed how important the two men were, their treatment would have spelled it out clearly.

A special set of doctors had been flown in for their care, along with other staff. Not that it made either man less irritable.

"If you two VIPs will stop criticizing each other, you can tell me what you want to eat first."

"Steak," the two said in the same breath.

Kit grinned. "Figured that. I would have brought margaritas, but the doctor said no alcohol for either of you." Izzy made a low sound of pain and Kit hid a smile. "I still don't understand what happened or why I don't remember any of the details about that cave in. The doctor here told me it was stress, but I've never forgotten things before."

"It was more than stress," Wolfe said gravely. "There are all kinds of gases in old mines. Carbon monoxide can collect and you never know it's there. But you'll have some strange reactions."

Kit slanted a glance at Izzy's arm, still hidden beneath white gauze bandages. He had been found unconscious under a creosote bush, where he'd crawled after the attack. Wolfe had given her the general outline, and she hadn't asked for more details. She was starting to understand just how strict military security could be.

Kit straightened the bright green sweater and capri pants she had chosen so carefully with Miki this morning. She knew she looked decent because two orderlies had whistled at her on the way up. But Wolfe hadn't seemed to notice anything she wore since the day at the mine. He was considerate, friendly but politely distant.

And it was driving her *crazy*.

"So it was a gas that affected me? That could make sense." She smiled as a weight was lifted from her shoulders. Thanks to a new medicine that Izzy had suggested, Kit's pain had decreased significantly. But she had been afraid that the mix was causing side effects, disrupting her memory. It was a relief to know that the real source lay elsewhere.

She was slicing huge slabs of chocolate cake when Baby rummaged beneath the chair beside the bed. Holding something in her teeth, the Lab trotted to Wolfe's side and dropped the bright length in his lap.

Kit realized Baby had given him her sheerest camisole. Hot pink silk and ecru lace, it was a recent gift from the ever-meddling Miki.

"Nice taste, Baby. The pink's a nice touch with your fur. But I think it may be a little loose around your front paws," Wolfe murmured.

"Give me that." Kit grabbed at the piece of lingerie. "I've been looking for that all morning."

"No way." Wolfe parried her hands smoothly. "Baby wanted me to have this."

Kit's cheeks were flushed. "We can discuss this later." She glared at Baby. "And *you* are a troublemaker."

There was a noise at the door.

Lloyd Ryker strode in with two aides in tow. He was wearing an understated but perfectly cut gray suit, and he looked extremely pleased with himself. "How are they doing, Ms. O'Halloran? Giving you more trouble?"

"Nothing I can't handle."

"It looks that way." Ryker studied Baby thoughtfully. "Your dogs look better every day. But I expect everyone tells you that."

"I have a lot to be thankful for." Kit glanced at Wolfe and Izzy. "If these two could manage to recuperate as fast as my dogs, I'd be very happy."

Ryker cleared his throat. "I want to discuss something with you, Ms. O'Halloran. It concerns your dogs."

"No. You can't have them." Kit's voice was polite but firm. "They need more time. They have to work on corner training and learn more chained commands, along with hazardous zone searches. They're nowhere near ready for service placement yet, sir."

"Our police and military units desperately need dogs like this," Ryker said thoughtfully. "But I have to agree, they aren't ready yet. I've been going through your reports since they were referred to me. They would be an excellent asset for me."

Kit thought she saw Wolfe and Izzy share a look. She didn't know what kind of unit Ryker oversaw, but she did know it was important. "I'm not sure what kind of service work your unit carries out, sir."

"We do this and that," Ryker said vaguely. "Here and there." He looked at Baby for a long time. "I'm proposing, Ms. O'Halloran, that they stay with you for another twelve months. At the end of that time we'll evaluate their progress. And assess their . . . strengths. I'm assigning Commander Houston to be my personal liaison in this matter. Will that be acceptable to you both?"

"Yes." Wolfe cleared his throat. "Sir."

"Perfectly," Kit murmured.

"So that's settled." Ryker gestured at the box on the nearby table. "Now how about a slice of that chocolate cake? I hope this is another recipe of your mother's, Ms. O'Halloran."

"Yes, it is." Things were always uncomfortable when this man appeared with his silent entourage. Kit sensed tense undercurrents among the three men and references to things she didn't — and never would — understand. But she wouldn't dwell on Lloyd Ryker. He seemed like he could be a difficult man, but his offer was reasonable. She decided to accept. Working with Wolfe would give her the chance to figure out the next stage in this odd relationship they seemed to be having, even though he hadn't said a personal word to her since the attack in the mine. If Kit had her way, it would be straight into bed. She'd enjoy seeing how inventive he could be with just one arm.

And now that they had business together, he couldn't keep avoiding her.

She handed Ryker the slice of cake he'd requested. "I haven't had a chance to thank you for putting in the new security system at my ranch, sir. That was very thoughtful."

"I consider it a business investment. We've all got hard work ahead of us, young lady. I don't want you distracted with problems." Ryker glanced at his watch. "I've got to be on a plane in forty minutes. I'll draw up a contract about the dogs and we can talk after I get back. By the way, I thought you'd want to have this. One of my men found it while he was burying the lines for your new security system." Ryker held out a handmade leather pouch with red beadwork and long suede fringe. The bag was worn but intricate and clearly valuable.

Kit took the small leather bag, her touch reverent. "You found this at my ranch?"

"Near the well. Do you know what it is?"

"It's a medicine pouch, probably Apache. My father had one just like this." Her fingers closed gently around the stiff beaded leather. She had a sudden suspicion that she was looking at the Apache treasure Emmett and all the others had searched for over the years. The leather was pristine, the beadwork exquisite. A fine object like this, well preserved and with a personal provenance, would be worth thousands to a serious collector.

And Kit didn't consider selling it for a second.

"Thank you," she said quietly, slipping the bag into her pocket. She'd take the time to study it later, sorting through the bittersweet memories of her father that the bag inspired. But first she had to see that Izzy ate more and that Wolfe did his rehab exercises.

Training high-strung, energetic service dogs had taught her a thing or two about managing men like this. After they finished, she was going to herd everyone out of the room so that Izzy could rest. Not the dogs, of course. They seemed to make him relax when nothing else could.

After that, Kit had her own offer to make to Wolfe.

"You'll be hearing from me soon," Ryker said curtly. Then he strode out, followed by his aides.

The mood lightened immediately.

Kit stared at Izzy. "Have a second piece of cake." She cut a slice and put it on the rolling table in front of him. Ignoring his scowl, she helped him eat all of it.

"Damned bound hands," he muttered.

Wolfe was very quiet, and Kit swung around to face him next. "Out in the hall. We need to talk."

But as soon as the door closed behind them, Wolfe turned and pulled her against him, using his good arm. "Don't suppose you'd be interested in spending the night with me tonight."

Kit's pulse spiked. "To talk about canine training regimens?"

"To make love until we both drop," he said harshly.

"Your bed or mine?"

"Both," he muttered. "Then the floor. Then any tables that happen to be handy."

"That can probably be arranged." Kit smiled uncertainly. "As long as you don't hurt your arm."

"To hell with my arm." Wolfe pinned her against the wall as his mouth skimmed and savored. "I've got a few hours' leave and I'm going to enjoy it to the full extent of my tactical capabilities."

The possibilities made Kit's heart lurch. But she sighed and pulled away as Miki and Trace approached down the hall. They were arguing, as usual.

"Wolfe, they're *coming*."

"So what? I've waited two weeks to talk about our future, honey. I figure that you needed a little time to get your breath. But I'm not stopping now."

Kit gave up being discreet. Sighing, she flowed into the heat of his body, feeling as giddy and vulnerable as she had at thirteen when she'd watched him fumble with Marijo Shelton's bra in the back seat of her car.

The flood of hot fantasies left her flushed and she took a deep breath.

"What's wrong?"

"You. I lose my train of thought whenever you're in the same county."

"That's about the nicest thing anyone's ever said to me, honey."

Kit stared up at Wolfe, loving his hard face and his dark eyes and the lines around his forehead that came from staring into the sun in places that didn't appear on any map. "Just assuming that I decide to have sex with you —"

"Make love," Wolfe said firmly. "It was always more than sex, Kit. You know that. We need to talk about making this relationship permanent." He cleared his throat. "As in contracts. Blood tests. Marriage."

Her eyes cut to his. "You're asking me to marry you?"

"I sure as hell am." He took a breath. "But I may have to cut some red tape first.

Meanwhile, I thought you could consider the possibility."

"Yes." There was no doubt in Kit's mind. Not a second's hesitation. Suddenly she was struck by his odd choice of phrase. "What kind of red tape?"

Trace and Miki were coming closer. "Later."

Kit didn't argue, touching the faint scar that had already healed at Wolfe's jaw. Her smile was teasing and sultry. "So what about the dogs while we're hitting the sheets and having noisy, out-of-control sex?"

"Those four troublemakers?" Wolfe linked their fingers and pulled her hand up to his mouth, kissing her palm slowly. "They're going to have to find their own entertainment tonight. Now shut up and kiss me, O'Halloran. I think it's time for us to break some more rules."

ABOUT THE AUTHOR

New York Times bestselling author **Christina Skye** loves a good adventure. As evidence, she has climbed the Great Wall in a snowstorm, eaten snake meat in Shanghai and bicycled in search of folk art in mountainous Fujian. Christina has penned historical romances, contemporary romantic-suspense novels and paranormal romances. Her award-winning Code Name series showcases her signature blend of action, humor, navy SEALs and white-hot passion. Her recent title in the series, CODE NAME: PRINCESS, was selected as a *Cosmopolitan* magazine Book Club selection for December 2004, Borders Best Romance of 2004 and *Readersread.com* Best Book of 2004. She is also a 2004 RITA® Award finalist and *Romantic Times* Career Achievement winner for contemporary romantic suspense. Christina enjoys hiking in the nearby Arizona mountains, but most often you'll find her hard at work on her next hot Code Name navy SEAL adventure for HQN books.

The employees of Thorndike Press hope you have enjoyed this Large Print book. All our Thorndike and Wheeler Large Print titles are designed for easy reading, and all our books are made to last. Other Thorndike Press Large Print books are available at your library, through selected bookstores, or directly from us.

For information about titles, please call:

(800) 223-1244

or visit our Web site at:

www.gale.com/thorndike
www.gale.com/wheeler

To share your comments, please write:

Publisher
Thorndike Press
295 Kennedy Memorial Drive
Waterville, ME   04901